WHAT MAKES A WIZA.

Just taking the Wizard's Oath isn't enough.

First you have to pass through your Ordeal.

Every wizard's Ordeal is intensely personal, and sometimes intensely dangerous. Each Ordeal is tailored to the would-be wizard who may pass it... or fail to. Each one reveals the nature of the candidate who accepts the challenge offered by the undying Powers that Be: a chance to face off against the Lone Power who invented entropy and death.

And if you do pass the Ordeal, then you're a wizard—and your life (and the world around you) will never be quite the same again.

In these four untold Ordeal-tales, alien prince Roshaun ke Nelaid, Irish schoolboy Ronan Nolan Junior, new-hatched saurian Mamvish fsh Wimsih, and one unusual Owl, match the Lone One's deadly threats with skills and smarts and heart... hoping their new wizardry will be enough for them to best the dangers they encounter—

ON ORDEAL

IN THE INTERIM ERRANTRY SERIES

Young Wizards: Interim Errantry

Interim Errantry 2: On Ordeal

Coming in 2022: *Interim Errantry 3: A Day at the Crossings*

INTERIM ERRANTRY 2:
ON ORDEAL

DIANE DUANE

ERRANTRY
PRESS

Interim Errantry 2:

On Ordeal

Diane Duane

Published by Errantry Press

County Wicklow, Republic of Ireland

A division of the Owl Springs Partnership

Requests for permission to make copies of any part of the work should be mailed to the following address:

Donald Maass Literary Agency
1000 Dean Street, Suite 252
Brooklyn, NY 11238
USA

This Errantry Press paperback edition is v4.02 of the work, dated December 30, 2021. See the rear matter for the work's full version history.

𝔖 Created with Vellum

for @neilhimself

with a h/t for the RT
and quite a lot more

THE WIZARD'S OATH (A COMMON TERRAN RECENSION)

In Life's name and for Life's sake,

I assert that I will employ the Art which is its gift in Life's service alone, rejecting all other usages.

I will guard growth and ease pain. I will fight to preserve what grows and lives well in its own way; and I will change no object or creature unless its growth and life, or that of the system of which it is part, are threatened.

To these ends, in the practice of my Art, I will put aside fear for courage, and death for life, when it is right to do so —

till Universe's end.

INTRODUCTION TO THE "ON ORDEAL" QUARTET

There are some questions for which not even being a wizard will (during one's present lifetime, anyway) ever produce satisfactory answers.

Leaving aside such famous wizardry-specific questions as "What is the meaning of life?", another one that often comes up is exactly *why* the art and burden of wizardry comes to be settled on a given person. The only ones who know for sure, of course, are the Powers that Be. But getting answers out of them can be even more difficult than getting them out of the Transcendent Pig... so wizards who find themselves dealing with the question are pretty much forced to fall back on conjecture.

Any number of aphorisms in the Manual and in casual wizardly discourse deal with the subject. One states that every wizard is the answer to a question (which naturally leaves wizards in general, and each one in particular, trying at some point or another to figure out what that question *is*). Another variation on this theme suggests—as if from a slightly different angle—that each wizard is the solution to a given problem that could not have been solved (or could not have been most *elegantly* solved) without shoving that person into the middle of it and putting wizardry into their hands.

Both these adages leave the thoughtful questioner running up against issues of how (apparent) causality intersects with linear time. After all, the Powers in charge of handing out wizardry aren't limited by the spatial structure and temporal flow of our dimension. They work out of more senior and central domains with far superior numbers of dimensions and much more complex spaces. From these places (not that the word is an adequate descriptor) they can step into our continuum at any desired place or time as easily as a being from our dimension might walk into one room from another.

Past, present, future, they're all rooms in one vast house to the Powers. Meandering from one to the next at their pleasure, they can casually examine from many physical and temporal angles the being on whom they're considering bestowing the Art... assessing how that being seems most likely to behave in short-term crises and over the long haul of a wizardly career. But even the Powers that Be can't make these assessments with absolute certainty. Within the timestream we occupy, no action is even provisionally certain until it's happened (or happened at least once). And even after that, there's a lot of wiggle room for things to *not* happen, unhappen, or happen differently.

From the wizard's own point of view the Ordeal event naturally tends to be seminal. As a result, there's often a tendency to examine other wizards' Ordeals (when that data is available) in search of important information about them. But this view is likely to be based on a skewed level of importance being assigned to a wizard's first contact with wizardry simply because it's the *first*. From the Powers' point of view, mere local-timeline temporal primacy is probably the least significant kind. It's more likely (so the more senior wizardly analysts have suggested) that the Ordeal is just one of numerous rough-and-ready diagnostic techniques that the Powers use to test a being's commitment to the basic principles of wizardry. Thought to be most crucial to these is the answer to the question: Can the new practitioner of the Art rise past or above the limitations of who they have been, into who they're eventually going to have to be to use wizardry to best advantage?

From that issue the Powers' attention (so it's said) most likely turns toward the breadth and depth of the wizard's commitment to the unending battle against the destructive aspects of Entropy—specifically the way these vary during a being's lifetime, and whether the power invested in them has a chance of being wasted due to personal traits gone astray, or influences the wizard is inadequately prepared to manage. A vast number of variables, it's thought, would be weighed against one another to determine whether the Art should be offered to a given being at all. These ruthless mathematics of the most central realms might seem cruel or heartless to those of us without access to enough dimensions to make the sums reveal what result the Powers are ultimately solving for. But wizardry's just one more kind of energy, and beings devoted to making the Universe last as long as it can will rightly do their best not to waste it.

Uncertainty, though, lies in the paths of the Powers that Be just as it does in ours. When all the tests prove inconclusive, and the one Power presently outside their wide society seems to be paying unusual attention to some one being or situation, then the only thing to do is roll the (near-infinite sided) dice and see how they fall.

Here are four rolls of the dice, their details made somewhat public for the first time. The fourth one, newly added to this collection, tells of events occurring in the future of the most recent main-sequence Young Wizards novel, *Games Wizards Play,* and (as of 2021) just in the past of our own.

PART I

ROSHAUN KE NELAID

PROLOGUE: THE TALE OF THAHIT AND THE LOST AETHYR

There once was a sun of ancient sequence and lineage that was golden and kind, and all its worlds prospered. But then into its life and the lives of those who depended upon it came the Aethyr who Went Apart, the one who chose to become the Darkness at the Heart of Things; and in the wake of Its coming, all things went ill.

Here is one way the tale is told.

IN THE TIME just after beginnings but well before any endings, the billion worlds were still so new that for some eons the Lost Aethyr did not have time—even in the timeless time that the Aethyrs use— to get around to them all. And this time lasted a good stretch of years upon years, when the creatures of Wellakh lived together without trouble and in great joy. So glad and peaceful was this long stretch of sunrounds that for months at a time not a spot was to be seen on the face of the Sun, and it was as smooth and untroubled as a mirror of polished bronze.

For all this blessed while so well did matters go that wizards were few, and wars there were none; and among all the worlds that were, almost no one had ever heard of Wellakh. And all its people felt this was just as things should be.

But nothing lasts forever, least of all the inattention of the Lost Aethyr. And when Wellakh eventually came to the attention of the Lost One, and It heard of the unstained Sun, It began to think of how best It might do it a mischief.

Swiftly but secretly the Lost Aethyr came to Wellakh. It went up and down in the world and round about it, and came to know its people and its beasts and all its creeping things and Wellakhit life in all its forms. And dearly It hated the peace and plenty of that world, and how all things went well under that quiet sun. Soon enough the Lost Aethyr thought in Itself, *Here then I see a way in which all things here may be made wretched.*

So It went and spoke to the Sun, and tempted it, saying, "The beings who live in this system do you dishonor and disrespect. For all life on these worlds derives from you. Without you the air would be stone and the water would be ice and the earth of the worlds would be cold as space. Yet the beings here go about their lives as if you were nothing, and honor not you but the Aethyrs, who promiscuously and irresponsibly create, and then abandon to their own devices those things that They have made. You give of your very core's power and shed it in radiance on this world day by day, each day drawing you a little nearer to that day when you will swell and burn the last of your fuel and fade to a warm dark cinder. But who notices you? You ought to put forth your strength and make known to these worlds who rules them, and who truly holds over them the power of life and death."

Now at first the Sun laughed these blandishments to scorn. But the Lost Aethyr had time. Again and again It returned to the system, and each time spoke long in the Sun's secret ear. Long centuries of this passed by one by one, mounting themselves up into millennia. Several of these passed as well, and through them the Sun shone as steadily as it might. But slowly in the wake of the Lost One's attentions spots began to creep across the Sun's surface, and ever so gradually the calm glory of its corona changed and became more ionized and erratic.

Then the Lost Aethyr knew Its murmured policies were well embedded in the roil and tumult of the star's plasma, and sooner or later would rise from the depths to trouble its surface with prominence and spicule and flare. Nor did It rest in Its labors, but continued to return again and again. Steady as clockwork these visits became, so that those on Wellakh whose business it was to watch the Sun saw plainly how at times its breath grew heated and frantic and its surface troubled, and at other times that surface mostly quieted and only a few sunspots cruised across it. Gradually the sunwatchers on Wellakh learned to graph these periods and know when the Sun's mood would be troubled and when it would be less so.

For many centuries so matters went, and the low points of that cycle grew less so, more troubled than ever, as the Lost Aethyr visited that star again and again, whispering doubts and instigations; and the active parts of the Sun's activity curve grew wilder than ever, the depths less quiet. Feeling sure the star was soon about to finally succumb to its dark intimations and destroy its system in nova fire, again and again the Lost Aethyr returned during this upswing of the Sun's angry cycle, each time pressing Its suit. It whispered ever more urgently how the star should nourish ingrates in its neighborhood no longer, but flood its spaces straight out to system's edge with cleansing fire, and let all peopled planets know thereby that they should give proper respect to the primaries that had birthed their worlds and sustained them.

Away the Lost One went again to let the Sun mature its dreadful advice... for though It could feel the star trembling on the edge of some mighty action, It wished to be sure that the Sun thought whatever it was about to do to its worlds was its own idea. Indeed some beings cozened so by the Lost Aethyr went on to be hilariously certain that everything they did to others was the *others'* fault. The Power that Went Astray was never willing to do anything that might derail this delicious result. Ever the Lost Aethyr loves to be able to claim that *It* is quite innocent of any wrongdoing, and that others had unexpectedly become unstable under the stress of events, or had misconstrued it, or (an old favorite) that it had been misquoted.

And so it was that while the Lost One had taken Its attentions elsewhere so as not to (further) prejudice the Sun's behavior, on a time in its cycle of breath—or rather at the bottom of it—came something most peculiar: a time when its surface slowly became unmarred and day by day slid by in utter quiet, without a single stain. The wizards who watched the sky from Wellakh and had learned the Sun's patterns and moods were at first confounded, and then increasingly disturbed by this.

At last the then-Sunlord, oldest and wisest of them, who had seen many cycles since her birth, called the sunwatchers together and told them, "There is nothing wrong. *Nothing at all.*"

Those who knew her best—and this Sunlord, one of the then-new Ruiiliat line, was a cranky and obstreperous being well known for her opinion that there was *always* something wrong, *somewhere* —fell silent in shock.

Afterwards the other wizards went home from this meeting and quietly, casually, but to some extent covertly, observed the Sun, and drew their own conclusions. And then, in haste, but all in secret, they began to make plans. When they spoke to each other, a strange phrase began to emerge: "All things are well, indeed everything is well, and all manner of things are well."

For they knew what the Lost Aethyr had never suspected they might. And so when the Sun flared and burnt half of Wellakh to a scorched and slagged-down cinder, they knew what the Sun knew: that when the Lost One's eye is on you, you must be make sure you have reason to say, "We had no idea," or "Who could ever have known this might happen?" When the whole planet seemed to be in utter crisis, and the atmosphere flashed into fire on the flare side and wizards died sealing the border between it and the rest of the world, when millions of Wellakhit died in grievous pain and panic, neither then nor afterward could there by any means be any revelation of the truth: that plans to save the planet had begun being laid the day after the Sun's surface was seen to be reliably stainless.

Long centuries were spent grieving the many millions who died the day the Sun flared. Yet many fewer died than might have done, for the wizards of Wellakh understood well that resistance takes many forms, and must sometimes (as with an enemy such as the Lost One) be seen to be accidental, lest it take vengeance far worse upon a world than subterfuge makes it possible to escape with.

They knew too that their star dared not do otherwise than it had done. For even as the Lost Aethyr has sometimes snuffed stars out, so it was also in Its power to inflame one past resisting. Whispers had long slid through subspace of how It had goaded stars into novae before their time, punishing them for failing to show It proper respect and fear—for burning as they pleased and not burning cold and faint and small as It would have desired.

So Wellakh suffered, and so very many died, a third of all that planet's lives. It became a byword among worlds, one whole side destroyed, the other one barely surviving—and though it remained the heart of a great civilization, yet it remained also deeply scarred by what it had survived. At the sight of the scar, the Lost One, going Its ways among the times and the worlds, laughed quietly to Itself and passed by.

So it was that the Lost Aethyr's full intention was turned aside not by mighty action—though that was brought to bear as well—but by the subterfuge of apparent inaction and silence, which the Lost Power's bent towards impatient violence and display left It less well-suited to comprehend. Had the sun not gone quiet in covert warning, both sides of Wellakh would have been destroyed and all its life snuffed out. But so it also came to pass that the Sun, which had had no name till then, was afterward given by the wizards a calling-name, *Thahit*, the One who grew Quiet: and so it is still known to this day.

The wizards keep watch and also keep silent, knowing that should the Lost One come to suspect that Its will had been flouted or it had been played, much more evil would follow. But the universe is broad, and the Strayed One bores easily... so all who know the tale take care to say nothing openly but that the name Thahit is a superstitious usage, a propitiation, primitive and full of fear.

This—should the Lost Aethyr hear It—will please it well, just as It would be enraged by the truth: that silence or even the semblance of acquiescence may be as clear as a shout of warning, and those who listen attentively enough to silence may yet be saved, though the Lost One Itself decree their ruin.

1

It was exactly like any other day, right up to and including the assassination attempt. But then things went a bit differently.

THE DAY WAS fair with a warm breeze, even the highest sky settled into that particular shade of blue-green that boded well for the days to come. As he passed out of the sunshine and into the feathertrees' shade, Rho breathed in deep and had to smile, even though until now he hadn't particularly felt like it.

Spring in the southern airt of Wellakh's eastern hemisphere could be very pleasant when the weather patterns were set right, which for a miracle they were right now. The park Rho walked through on the way to his parents' city house was full of the tall crimson feathertrees that came out in blossoms this time of year, spreading that particular spicy aroma of theirs far and wide. Here, under the trees and out of the direct eye of the sun, it was possible to forget things for a little while and just enjoy the day.

It was always good to be coming back from the chilly formal building where his public lessons were held and into this pleasantly natural and neutral space, where Rho had time to relax a little from the way he had to hold himself at lessons, and where no one could easily pick him out for what he was. In the plain dark russet overrobe and loose trousers that everyone at public lessons wore, Rho stood out hardly at all. And since only in the most general way was there a look to being Sunborn—the det Nuiiliat line being well scattered across the planet, so that there were plenty of people as yellow-haired as Rho or as red-haired as his father—he rarely got more than a second glance.

His lady mother, of course, was another story. She had the pale silver hair of the very highest nobility—"its gold comes only from Thahit", as the saying went, "and thus not from flesh but from fire." People stopped in the street to stare at her as she headed home from some meeting, or else they paused in the middle of their shopping to make one of the ceremonial gestures of honor...

Which was when Rho had lately found himself starting to twitch. In fact, the thought of the looks his lady mother got sometimes from others who *didn't* stop, and who didn't mind others seeing what they thought of those who did, was making him feel a little uncomfortable in his skin right this moment. When a passing businessman in dark green provider's robes hesitated just briefly on the path at the sight of Rho, the feeling got more uncomfortable still.

He was tempted to simply pause on the path and feel about in his robe's pockets like someone who'd realized he'd forgotten some vital personal item, until the man lost interest and passed by. Somehow even that seemed too much for him to manage at the moment. However, off to the left of Rho stood a particularly large feathertree, its massive downhanging upper branches spreading close enough over the path to already be snowing downy scarlet pollen onto the pathway's gravel. The branches' long pendant fronds reached nearly down to the park's close-cut ochre turf in a dense curtain of slim downy-furred amber tendrils all hung with small scarlet bells.

On the moment's impulse Rho stepped off the path to slip through the curtain and through it into the heart of the warm-shad-owed space beyond. There he put his back up against the feathertree's broad knobby dark-crimson trunk, and for good measure edged around to the tree's far side, where he couldn't be seen from the path at all.

For just a few moments Rho leaned there against the tree-trunk with his eyes closed, relishing not only not being seen, but not having to be anywhere or do anything or act any particular way. Such moments were too few, too precious.

This is childish, some mutinous voice muttered in the back of his mind, *you are Sunborn, what ails you that you're hiding yourself away like this?*

For the moment Rho ignored it. Waiting for his pulse to slow, he breathed in a few breaths' worth of the metallic-spicy pollen scent that hung heavy all around him... then passed one hand over his face and let the hand fall, a gesture of resignation.

There wasn't any escape from his personal realities for very long. Always within a few minutes the sight of the buildings around the park, or other people on the path, or of the thin pale color of the high sky, would bring the burden back down on him—all those names, hanging around his neck like a weight. *Roshaun ke Nelaid am Seriv am Teliuyve am Meseph am Veliz am Teriaunst* and all the rest of them *am det Nuiiliat, det Wellakhit*—his mother and father and all that crowd of noble ancestors, each name a link in a chain of heritage weighing you down. And the oldest link, the heaviest, the most serious, shackling you to the ground: *am me'stardet Wellakhir.* "Guarantor of Wellakh."

Rho shook his head and opened his eyes, because there was no point in trying not to see the image that went with the concept. It would display itself before his mind no matter what he did: the fire from heaven, the innocent world lying beneath it, and the shadow that fell between—the shadow of those who willingly put themselves between Wellakh's troublesome star and its otherwise defenseless planets. He was one of the ones who cast that shadow—the ancient family that had kept the world from being killed by its star, and was expected to do so until (apparently) that star went out.

Now, as often enough before, Rho said to himself, *One day that's going to be me.* It was a matter of honor to be part of a tiny comity tasked with the challenge of keeping a world alive and well, one that stretched back centuries and would do so, assuming everything went well, for who knew how many centuries more. To be its youngest member—at least for the moment—made him proud.

But it also made him afraid. Reflexively he gulped and tipped his head back against the tree. *The only problem is that some day I'm going to be left alone to meet the challenge unarmed...*

Quite quickly after that thought he started getting angry at himself. *It doesn't matter. It's what we do; what my family does. If some of them are better at it than I am, that's just how our luck's fallen in this generation.*

But it didn't help Rho that this thought had also crossed other people's minds.

At lessons, for example. It wasn't as if any of his schoolfellows said anything to him about it openly; nor were they cruel to him. They didn't dare to be. He was Sunborn.

But that was an entirely different problem. *They're afraid of me, and not for the right reasons... if there* are *any right reasons.* It wasn't anything to do with his physical strength (which wasn't bad for someone his age) or indeed strength of any other kind.

Especially because the kind he *should* have had, he didn't...

Rho shook his head at the thought that always intruded... the truth he could never escape. His family had saved the world. And someday, when he was left alone in his ancestors' wonted place, everybody on the planet would expect him to do the same.

It had taken Rho a long time to understand, when he was littlest, either the danger of this or the pain it would eventually cause him. Everybody knew how the wizards who became the Sunborn had put themselves between Thahit's wrath and Wellakh's people, when the sun flared, and saved millions of lives at the cost of hundreds of their own. The tale was taught as part of every child's earliest lessons about what had made their world the way it was. Rho simply hadn't understood for a surprisingly long time that those lessons—in this generation, anyway—had been about his mother and father. *And maybe, someday, about me...*

Then, when he'd finally made the connection, he hadn't for the longest time been able to grasp why people honored his parents—and apparently, when they realized who he was, him too—but never seemed willing to be their friends.

It had never made sense, when he was small. Since his family *had* saved the world, why did people fear them? He'd lie awake on his couch going around and around with the question, finding no answer that made sense. *Why would you be scared of us?*, he'd say to the night, as if it could hear what he wanted to tell them and pass the word along. *Don't you know we're from the same place, we're who you are, this is just our job?*

But eventually he realized that was the root of the problem. Once or twice in lessons he'd caught the eye of other students during the history modules and seen the expressions on their faces—the unease, the resentment. Saw them, at least, before they turned their faces away. He realized to his shock that people don't *like* to be saved. *People don't like to be beholden. They don't like being unable to save themselves. They don't like their weakness shown, don't like their need to be an obvious thing. When it is... they get angry.*

And then they try to control what they fear.

He let out a breath. Like all Wellakhit students, he had some control over the subjects he studied at lessons. But by the Sunlord's command, the studies he was never allowed to change, in either substance or frequency, were mathematics and history. When he was young he spent a lot of time complaining about this, but the complaints stopped when he started to notice that there were differences between the family's own records of the Disaster—which his father himself reviewed with him—and what was taught in lessons.

Slowly he learned to read between the columns, and saw his life as it really was. He and his parents were kept wealthy by the world government, and lived in a palace, and given whatever they asked for —of merely material things, at least. But the palace was on the other side of the world, away from all the normal people, in the very center of the world's burnt side. The message was never spoken, and always clear: *This is the only thing you're for, and the less we have to think about you, the better. Make sure you do your job. As long as you do that we'll leave you alone.*

It was easy to shrug and take it coldly, sometimes. It was just the way life was. *But being left alone...* Rho thought, and tipped his head back against the tree.

Sometimes when at home after lessons, while spending spare time wandering through the entertainment feeds, Rho came across group-chat presentations in which people talked about how it would be for them if they suddenly became vastly wealthy—from an inheritance, perhaps, or a vast windfall from one of the companies that ran public games of chance. Everyone understood the odds of such a thing happening were well against it; you had a better chance of being hit by a meteorite. Nonetheless all those people were happy to make plans for the eventuality. In the same way, these days, Rho occasionally caught himself wondering what he would do if someone at lessons should ever someday want to keep company with him, laugh with him, joke: if anybody would ever share the walk home with him, regardless of where and what home was.

Then before he was even well started imagining what that would be like he'd scoff at his own ridiculous hopes, for no normal Wellakhit was likely to take the chance of getting close enough to a Sunborn of the ruling family for *that* to happen. If one should possibly fall out with someone so powerful, whose wellbeing could at any moment be vital to the planet—who knew what the government might do to them afterwards? It wouldn't be as if the royal family would *want* anything bad to happen to a non-royal, of course. But in the past reputations had been destroyed, careers shattered, when word got out that there had been problems between a Wellakhit citizen and a Sunborn too highly placed.

So Rho kept his ridiculous and impossible wishes to himself and concentrated on doing his learning-work well, noting (as if from a distance) the wary glances of those who studied with him. If he had to be Sunborn, he would be as good at it as he possibly could be.

Rho sighed, stood away from the tree, straightened himself (pausing to brush off some of the feathertree pollen, which even in that short time had dusted him well with crimson) and moved back through the carmine shade toward the path. He had other business besides worrying about his own troubles. *Our whole and proper occupation,* his father always said, *is worrying about others' wellbeing.*

...And they know it, his mother would add under her breath, nearly in a growl.

The thought made Rho smile for a moment as brushed the feathertree fronds aside and stepped onto the path again. Because of his seniority, the title and position of Sunlord had more or less inevitably been settled on Rho's father. ("A whole twenty-one tendays and a hand of days longer than mine," Rho's mother would murmur any time the subject came up, "you mean *that* seniority?"—while looking side-eyed and accusatory at the Sunlord.) But those who thought that Nelaid ke Seriv had bonded himself to the Lady Miril am Miril simply for the exalted stature of her bloodline and the color of her hair were normally jolted out of the impression within seconds of meeting her. If Rho had her schedule for today sorted out correctly in his head, she would be expecting him back to the city house about now. *And one does not keep the Queen of Wellakh waiting...*

For the moment the path was empty except for him, so for a few tens of paces Rho strolled with his eyes down on the gravel, scuffing at the bright red pollen, here drifted in places a handspan deep. His mother, when she came this way and thought no one would see her, liked to scuff through the stuff and send it flying. Every now and then when Miril would be moving casually around the city house or their rooms on the other side of the world in Sunplace, picking through his father's always-scattered paperwork while tidying her own, Rho would see not the woman offhandedly helping manage the business of a planet, but the woman plopping herself down in their common rooms in some chair carved by one of the planet's great artists, pulling her shoes off and shaking out handfuls of ruby dust.

Rho smiled at the image, which would have completely confused some of the upper-level governmental types who came wandering in and out of the city house between dawn and noon, the Wellakhit business day. Certainly everyone high up in Wellakh's government knew quite well that if you were to convince the Lord Nelaid of anything, you had to first make it through the tangled, razor-edged hedge of questions and proofs that Miril am Miril would erect before you—behind which she would sit at her ease, watching for signs of poor reasoning, weakness or uncertainty. If you won through, she would then direct the interviewee to her royal spouse for the binding decision on whatever matter was at hand, for all the world as if her intervention had been a mere formality.

But everyone who dealt with the ruler (or rulers) of Wellakh knew the truth of the business... and some of them much disliked the arrangement. *One world, one ruler,* they would intone. Rho snorted at the thought. *As if half the Sunlords' spouses haven't wound up running things too. What's a Lord to do? Keep their King or Queen in the cupboard until the Sunwatch passes to their heirs?*

The path was nearing the edge of the park, where the wind had less trouble getting in among the trees and the feathertree pollen had mostly blown away, leaving Rho no more of it to kick through. He sighed and gazed across the broad path that surrounded the park, and the pale-metalled road that surrounded it and separated the park from the block of townhouses across the way, one of them being the Sunlords' city residence.

All these houses were alike, each one a narrow white frontage with classic elective windows faired into the smooth stone, each with its little walled courtyard in front of it, and each with a broad two-leaved door in the wall facing onto the road, and a smaller postern door to one side. And even as Rho looked across to it, up to one of these postern doors from the intersection down the street to the right came a tall woman dressed in a light shortsleeved workaday tunic and loose trousers, with knee-length silver hair tied back in a tail. As she paused in front of the postern she began shifting a carrier bag from one hand to the other so she could touch the sensor plate that would open the door—

And suddenly several people in dull-colored street clothes were coming toward her from behind, from either side of Rho, from other entries to the park. All of them were staring at her, intent, in a hurry—

No, Rho thought, and broke into a run. He gasped in a breath and then caught it, strangling the urge to shout, *because what if it distracts her—!*

One of the men hurrying toward Miril pulled something out of his robes, small and dark and rounded, easy to hide. *Energy weapon,* Rho thought, sprinting toward the rearmost of the men, gasping for breath again, *mepi* no!

The bag fell from Miril's hand. She turned in a whirl of long tunic and hair and made a small swiping gesture with the now-free hand. The three men in motion kept going toward her, and then, as she swiftly sidestepped, kept going past her without volition, like market-show puppets with their strings cut. All together they crashed to the ground, rolled once or twice depending on how fast they'd been going, and were still.

Miril stood looking down at them with an expression Rho couldn't remember having seen before: annoyance, mixed with a very peculiar tenderness, as if she was somehow actually sorry for the ingrates who had just been intent, at the very least, on hurting her, if not killing her. Then her shoulders slumped a bit, and she turned to pick up her bag again by its handles. She looked down into it and tilted her head back in the little gesture that for her meant "This is such a nuisance..."

Rho's momentum meanwhile brought him running nearly straight into his mother before he could stop himself. The main doors to the inside courtyard were already opening and a few of the house staff were coming out in haste to deal with the unconscious men... so that Rho didn't even have the satisfaction of being able to grab her and hug her and call her *mepi*. Instead all he could do was take hold of her upper arms—decorously, formally, in the way one member of the Sunborn greeted another in public—and say in the royal recension of Wellakhit, "Queenly mother, are you unhurt?"

"Unhurt, noble son," Miril said in her soft voice, looking around her as if completely unmoved by what had happened. "But what about you? You're pale. And you're having trouble breathing?"

There was no question of that, because while attacks like this happened to his parents all the time—in casual conversation they just called them "events"—this was the first time Rho had ever had one happen right in front of him. Now he felt as if he'd been punched in the chest. In fact he felt exactly the same way he had all those years back when someone in first-learners' school had truly punched him in the gut... just before the learning-master and a flock of proctors had appeared from nowhere to snatch the other boy away and surround Rho, babbling "Are you all right?" at him as if they were very, very afraid of something.

But their fear then had nothing on Rho's fear now. It had him rooted to the spot, holding his mother's arms tightly enough that he could actually feel the pulse of the big arteries in them. The steady pulse reassured him for the moment. Later, though... later would probably be another story, but he would deal with that when he came to it.

He swallowed and held himself a bit straighter. "It's not— No," he said after a moment, getting enough control over his lungs again to stop that concerned look on Miril's face: a look that hadn't so much as crossed it while armed would-be killers were rushing at her. "I am well enough, my Queen."

She touched his face and then turned away, brushing a strand of that long silver hair out of her eyes as she turned to watch the house staff taking care of business. One steward had come out carrying a few small crushcubes, one of which he now began unfolding into a floater pallet that would hold and restrain one of the attackers.

In the distance Rho could hear a faint echo of the alert tone used by the city's Watch cruisers. "They seem to be running a little later than usual today," Lady Miril said as the staff started loading the first unconscious man onto the pallet. "The traffic was troublesome down around the market earlier. But at least I'd taken care of all my meetings and finished my walk, and I managed to get some of that fruit-cloth your royal father likes, so the trip wasn't wasted."

The noise of the approaching city-Watch cruisers got louder, and much louder, and *very* much louder, all in the space of the few seconds it took for Lady Miril to pick up the bag she'd put down, which had not just the fruitcloth but a couple of long rolls of bark-bread in it. That was a favorite snack of Rho's, but now with sudden intensity he found himself hating the very sight of it, as acquiring it had brought his mother into danger.

At the moment, though, he could do nothing but master himself into calm immobility so as not to embarrass his *mepi* in front of the city-Watch, three of whose cruisers came howling around the corner down the road and settled out of hover in front of the house with an earsplitting whine of signallers and the roar of impellers shutting down. A crowd of white-uniformed proctors spilled out of them and immediately surrounded the Queen and Rho, at a courteous distance of course, all vying to be first to bend themselves double and make the appropriate honorific gestures.

The proctors were already babbling apologies, every other phrase of which seemed to be "noble Sunborn". Rho's temper was threatening to boil over, but this too he tamped down as his queenly mother gracefully accepted all the bowing and scraping and seemed more concerned with alleviating the proctors' anxieties than with berating them for not having had a security presence in front of the house, as they normally did when one of the royal household was out and about on foot.

Let alone two, Rho thought. He cared little about this for his own sake. *Who'd waste their time killing* me, *after all?* But where his mother and father were concerned—and especially his mother—

Rho was going cold and hot by turns with fear and anger, and around him things began going by in something of a blur—the staff passing the still-unconscious attackers over to the Watch and picking up some of their dropped belongings to be sent along with them, his lady mother debriefing them. "No, they won't need special care... the spellweb I threw over them merely damped their neural chemistry down for a bit. It'll be an hour or so before they're conscious, so just make them secure and be certain they're not in a way to injure themselves when they wake. They may be a bit disoriented."

And then the limp bodies were loaded into another of the city-Watch cruisers, and the Queen of Wellakh called after the proctors as they (bowing) got back into their vehicles, "And do make sure these cubes are sent back to us, won't you? We sent *easily* five of them along with the last batch, but someone forgot to return them and it's such a nuisance to configure new ones..."

Rho watched the cruisers lift up and arrow away, knowing perfectly well that at least part of the sense of slight unreality he was experiencing at the moment was shock. With an eye to handling such situations, he had been counselled by professionals in all the possible modes of crisis management practically since he could speak. *But nothing like* this *has ever happened before,* he thought, *and it's not working, it's not—*

"My son," the soft voice said from a little above him. Rho's head snapped up. His mother was tall even for a Wellakhit of royal line, and though the assumption in the family was that his height was coming to him from her, he still had a ways to go to catch up. Now she gazed down at him and said, "Everyone else has gone in, my Prince; we might as well go too."

And indeed there the two of them were, standing outside the city-house all by themselves, with his mother training a most concerned and perceiving look on him. "Of course, royal lady," Rho said, putting his arm through hers and turning her toward the little postern-door, which the house staff had left open for them.

"Your royal father will be home from *his* meetings shortly," she said as they stepped through the door into the gravel and fine-clipped shrubbery of the front courtyard, "and once he hears about the fruit-cloth, there will doubtless be no other subject of conversation for a while. So if there is anything you feel the need to tell me..."

I am useless, Rho thought, *and a waste of space as your son, and as Sunborn; and as future Guarantors of Wellakh go, I am the least useful one ever to be seen by the light of our troublesome sun.*

"Nothing, my Queen," Rho said. "Let us by all means go in."

DESPITE HIS ATTEMPT TO get hold of himself, nothing much registered for Rho as they made their way through the formal front entry and the long cool high-ceilinged hallway leading out of it to the downstairs meeting rooms, and past those to the downstairs common room. The front spaces were broad white-walled rooms purposely underdecorated except with artworks donated by cultural organizations and citystates across the planet, and—like all the furniture in these areas—rather characterless. ("When you choose your furnishings to keep from annoying anyone," he'd heard his father say more than once, "why would it be surprising that it doesn't much *appeal* to anyone, either?")

In the common room that looked out on the back of the property and its little walled garden, at least the furniture was more comfortable. There were scattered couches, a viewing and entertainment wall, and in the arc of the weapons-proof window-doors that let out into the garden sat a trio of deep comfortable chairs, each with its little table beside it. Off to one side was the staircase up to the family's private rooms and the little intimate lounge. Rho glanced at it and realized he suddenly felt as if he didn't even have the energy to get up those stairs.

"Sit down, my son," said Miril, "before you fall down. I'll fetch you something to drink."

She had dropped out of kings'-speak and into the Speech. "Noble mother," Rho said, "the staff—"

"I sent them home early. We're done with the day's business; Lethme the house-steward is locking up even now. Sit!"

Rho sat in his chair, while his mother waved open the wall opposite the entertainment window and revealed the little food suite hidden there. She began rooting about the various shelves and cupboards there, making a couple of small sounds of annoyance on not finding what she wanted immediately. But then she rarely bothered with the cooking suite in town, and only rarely in Sunplace; that was a business she left to Rho's royal father. He made it a point to deal with the family's food, either in terms of ordering it or cooking it, claiming that if he was left no leisure to fulfill most of a Wellakhit husband's traditional roles, he would at least fulfill *that* one.

Rho's lady mother, meantime, finally found the cups, and then came up with a flask from which she poured. Watching her, Rho sighed and leaned his head back against the high back of his chair. This little triangle of space was where the three of them shared their meals, when all their schedules could be made to mesh—not normally an easy task. Between the Queen's business handling the Sunborns' relationship with the Wellakhit world governing body and those of individual polities and citystates, and his royal father's duties supervising the planet's strictly mechanical Sunwatch facilities and archival data, and of course standing the wizardly parts of the Watch himself, and Rho's lesson-schedule, which often involved supervised trips around the world he would someday rule, there were days when all of them left their couches before Thahit showed his face and didn't find them again until he'd been set for many hours.

And my whole life is going to be like this, Rho thought, looking out the projectile-proof glass at the tidy little garden. *Here I'll live and die, bound to the service of a star that's already tried to kill our planet once, and tries the trick again every so often. Chained to a world that's half maimed and a populace that's half convinced it would be better off without the whole lot of us...*

"Roshaun!"

He blinked at the glass beaker that was being held in front of him, full of the clear tangy whiteberry draft he favored. "My thanks, *mepi,*" he said, took it, and drank about half of it in three gulps.

Her free hand dropped to his shoulder. "I used to get quite dry at such times," Miril said.

"And what do you do now?"

The Queen sighed. "Refuse to allow them the luxury of disrupting my routine."

As usual, she'd managed to answer the question he hadn't asked. He opened his mouth to ask her "Would you please tell me *how you do that?"* when a soft chime came from a space under the spiral of the staircase to the upper floor.

It was a place that for the early part of Rho's childhood had been fenced off with a little box of railings (and after that, when he got overly curious, with a day-and-night forcefield) until he was old enough to fully understand that someone might appear there at any time of the night or day without warning. Even then, his *taki* had had to take him out into the barren lands on the scarred side with a portable transit cube and show him what *happened* when a chunk of matter tried to materialize inside another one. Rho's wild applause at the result had made his father cover his eyes... though after that he stayed away from that spot under the stairs unless *mepi* or *taki* actually took him there while holding him by the hand.

"Earlier than I had thought," Miril said, heading back over to the food suite for another flask. And indeed, dissolving into presence in the padspace, there he came in his majesty: Nelaid ke Seriv am Teliuyve am Meseph am Veliz am Teriaunst am Antev det Nuiiliat, Brother of the Sun, Lord of Wellakh, the Guarantor of Thahit—with his long red-golden hair knotted back in a series of more or less effective loops, in trousers that were surprisingly grimy, and wearing a tunic all smudged.

He stood still for a moment, waiting for the final little isosolenoid click that confirmed the transport process had completed itself and made the pad safe, and then stepped off, brushing his robes down and producing a small cloud of haze about himself. "My Queen, my Prince," he said, "you would not *believe* the amount of dust that has appeared in those archives. The new document-environment management system the government has installed is utterly useless. After all this trouble and consultation, it apparently must all be done again."

"Perhaps you should see to it yourself, my King," Miril said, coming over to him and holding out another beaker, this one magenta-red with a distillation of piraunin must.

He took it from her and leaned close to lay his cheek against hers before drinking. "One wonders what the point might be in delegation," Nelaid said, "when the event merely proves that one must do anything oneself that needs to be done rightly." He had a long draft from the beaker, and then another. "The plastic- and metal-based archival materials have already suffered; the humidity in that place is not being properly offset. Another few months of that and the oldest scrolls and codices would have gone to dust, and we'd have to ask the Aethyrs every time we wanted to know what had been in them."

"They have enough to do, I would say," Miril said, turning a dry smile on her royal spouse. "Greet your son, my husband. And sit down with that; this isn't a street stall."

His father came over to Rho and bent over him and stroked his hair. "My Prince—"

"Noble sire," Rho said, looking up into that long, calm face and wishing that some day he could find some of the unshakable dignity it always wore, even when troubled or angry or off-balance, even when dressed more like a cleaning worker than a King, and covered with library dust. The amber eyes looked thoughtfully into his, yet betrayed no response to what they saw there.

"*Nelaid,*" Miril said. Nelaid's eyes flickered toward the Queen of Wellakh and then back to Rho, a small shared joke, private for as long as neither of them let her see what was happening: *see how she rules us as she rules the rest of the planet through us?* But Rho discovered it was harder than usual today to find that funny. And he saw his father's eyes register that, and narrow a little in concern before he composed his face and turned away to sit down in his chair as commanded.

"I should be getting you something to eat," the King of Wellakh said to his queen as he sat down in his chair and took another pull at his drink.

"I'll do that for once," said Miril, turning her attention back to the food suite. "You will shed dust into everyone's food otherwise. I can see it still falling off you. Sit quiet now and drink your must."

He sat quiet and drank, but his eyes were still on Rho, who had to shift his gaze after a moment. "Tell me of your day," Nelaid said to Miril, though his eyes were on his son as he said it.

So she told him, and it was a tale of the normal daily round of meetings and audiences and monstrations—for a Sunborn while in royal office, whether by marriage or by rule, was desired (like the Sun) to be available for viewing by those who depended upon one or the other of them. In the Sunborn's case, it was more a requirement than a request, one that Rho so far had only needed to observe for fairly rare ceremonial occasions. But where others might ride or fly about their business, his royal sire and lady mother very often were required to walk, so that they could be seen. ("And so that our people may take the occasional shot at us without being unduly discommoded by our household security," Rho remembered his father saying some years back.)

"—and got to the market finally," his mother was saying, "and *that* at least proved worth the trip." And without warning she leaned over him in his chair, and on his table put down a little platter with narrow slices of amber and crimson fruitcloth on it, along with some plain pale flat bread and a dollop of bittersweet relish.

Nelaid's expression suddenly lost its gravity and went completely astonished, and at *that* Rho had to smile. Fruitcloth was difficult to make, very seasonal, and could be sourced from only a few artisanal suppliers, so even a Sunlord had to fight to get a share. "My excellent Queen," he said. *"How* did you come by this—"

"There's a secret I'll keep," said Rho's lady mother, looking smug. "I will take my advantages where I find them. And for *you*, noble son —" She put down another plate in front of him, this one with sliced barkbread on it, dark and aromatic and beautifully crisp.

Rho tried to make approving noises and applied himself to the contents of the plate, trying to hide the truth of the situation, which was that chew it though he might and wait for the fierce dark burst of flavor that usually came, the barkbread tasted more like dust in his mouth right now than anything else he could recall. Possibly this was because at the same time he was also chewing over the feeling of utter helplessness that had assailed him in the park even as he ran toward her. *Because there was nothing I could do.* Nothing. *My own* mother. *If she wasn't a wizard, right there she would have died—*

Miril had sat down now in her own chair, between husband and son, and was segmenting a fist-sized, pale-skinned bluedrupe berry to go with some of the barkbread for herself. The conversation between her and Nelaid then veered back toward the meetings she had suffered through that afternoon, and for the first time Rho heard some weariness come back into her voice. His father's eyes went to him again, doubtless putting together something from his expression and his general quietness. "So," he said after a moment, "something more happened than mere shopping."

Miril sighed and shrugged a hand. "Out in the front," she said. "Three objectors ran across from the park, just as Roshaun was coming out."

Nelaid sat up straighter. "But you're quite all right, my Queen?"

"Quite," she said, having another drink of her own must. "None of them got close enough even to touch me."

"Anyone we know? Were you able to—"

"Hear them? Oh quite clearly, Nelaid, they were broadcasting their intentions so. The tallest one you'll see in the remand report when the city-Watch gets it to us, that was one of ke Mebhhan's people—you would have seen him in that last meeting with the Loyal Opposition. Remember the one who ate half the *pikith* at the buffet afterwards?"

"Oh, *that* one." Nelaid scowled. "Raised in an outbuilding, to judge by his manners."

Rho blinked at that. As if anyone's manners, past, present or future, mattered compared to the fact that they had just tried to *kill* someone? —and not just *any* someone, but the Lady of the Lands of Wellakh, the Sister of the Sun, one of those who put her shadow between Wellakh's people and their unruly star. His *mother*—

Yet they went on talking about the attack as if they were discussing some annoying but minor infraction. *How can they be so calm about this! She could have died*—

"His name is eluding me at the moment."

"It's something north-country," Miril said, "from up the Seis Peninsula somewhere. ...Tebemer, that was it." Miril smiled at her plate, sourly amused. "He'd have far preferred to stick a *chey* in me if he could have, but he feared to come so close lest I touch him and curse him."

"I will curse him enough for both of us," Nelaid said very softly.

"Don't jest, my noble love," Miril said. "It ill befits a wizard to wish harm on one in our care. And perhaps his stupidity's curse enough. Either way, leave him to the Aethyrs."

Nelaid didn't look inclined to wait until the Aethyrs cleared time in their schedules. "So they didn't have any real chance to harm you—"

"Indeed not." She sniffed in amusement. "Am I any less a wizard than I was yesterday? And I was busy, but not *that* busy. Have you had a bad day? You should know not to be troubled by this."

"Well, the Aethyrs be thanked then."

"Yes indeed. Meanwhile we should possibly have a word with the city-Watch's security supervisor about our walkabout routines."

Nelaid sighed too. "Yes, they do sometimes seem to believe that we are invulnerable, do they not—"

Rho couldn't bear it, just couldn't stand it another minute. *"Royal father!"*

Nelaid turned to him in surprise and produced an expression of bemusement. "Yes, Roshaun?"

Rho wanted to throw his arms in the air and get up and stamp around the room and yell in frustration, but there were certain things one did not do in front of his father, and they had nothing to do with him being King of Wellakh. "Can we not *do* something?"

"Your mother has," Nelaid said. "You know the way of it, princely son. Your mother is the most senior wizard of her line, as I am of mine, and all Wellakh's people are in our care—"

"They may be, but some of them don't seem to care much about *you.* Just so long as you keep the sun from flaring again and killing the *other* half of the planet!"

His father paused. Rho knew the meaning of such long pauses: his father had scented the trouble in the air and was working out how to deal with it. Eventually he said, "Well, that *is* our job."

The tone was mild, but the gaze that Nelaid was resting on his son was cool and hard as steel.

"Then why don't they appreciate it?"

"Because no one likes to be beholden," his father said, in the voice one uses to repeat a simple lesson for the hundredth time to a child who hasn't been paying attention. "Powerlessness in the face of threat, or the perception of it, routinely provokes fear and anger in the threatened. Though we protect them from the threat, to expect gratitude from everyone is unrealistic. These attacks will unfortunately always be part of our lives. And, in time, yours..."

His kingly father's calmness was driving Rho mad... the resignation, the acceptance. And this was a state *he* was going to be expected to achieve. "It shouldn't be like this!"

"Yet it is."

"It doesn't make sense!"

"Reason is not always everything," his royal father said. "Unfortunately."

"There must be somewhere that it is," Rho muttered. "Somewhere that people are taught better, learn better..." Though where that might be, he had no idea.

"Also unfortunately," his father said, "it's not other worlds we deal with: it's this one." Too well Rho knew it. He had only rarely been off planet, having been told that Wellakh was his business, and he needed to learn it thoroughly before adding other worlds to the mix. "But I cannot blame you for wishing yourself elsewhere, my son. The turf's always browner on the other side..."

"Where there's turf left at all," his lady mother said softly.

He'd heard it a hundred times from them, this saying and its response, as if they were playing some old game with each other. It had never bothered him before. But right now, today, this minute, it was somehow too much to bear.

Rho bowed his head and started picking at his food again, which to his relief Nelaid took as a signal that his son wasn't interested in taking his protests any further in this direction. The King went back to his discussion with Rho's lady mother, and Rho drank his berry-draft and tried to get a grip on himself. But the unbearability of everything just kept grinding in on him: the unfairness of anyone daring to attack his mother, the fact that she and his royal father thought that such occurrences were just the way life was... and that there was no way he could be of help to them.

Because he hadn't been offered wizardry. It was one of those subjects the family had simply stopped discussing, because there was nothing to be gained but pain. No one wanted to return again and again to the uncomfortable theory that there was something wrong with Rho, some weakness, some hidden aspect that made the Powers unwilling to allow him access to the gift that was buried in his spiritual heredity, if not in his physical one.

And with it or without it, he would never be able to be as good a king as his father was. There Nelaid sat, royal to the bone even in tatty work clothes with dust clinging to the folds. Kingship was rooted in his soul, intertwined with the wizardry and with the sense of authority that his communion and relationship with Thahit lent all the rest of his life. Rho looked at him and thought, I *will never have what you have. From now till the day I die, never will I have it...*

Often enough, in the past, his father would've said to him, *You may yet.* But in the look they exchanged right now was the hopelessness of it, because Rho could not believe it... and his father, understanding this, was thinking, *I will not torment you, my son, by insisting on what you are so certain is not true.*

Rho dropped his gaze to his plate again, trying one last time to shove all these inconvenient feelings down inside him and out of the way... but he had no luck. *Can't stand it. Simply can't...*

He pushed his little side-table carefully away, pushed his chair back and stood up. His mother and father looked at him in surprise.

"I beg your pardon," he said, "royal sire, royal mother; I pray you hold me excused."

He knew permission would not be withheld. His father simply looked at him and nodded his head once. But Miril said, "Son, where will you go?"

Rho turned away toward the staircase. "The other side."

HE HEADED to his own rooms down at the far end of the second floor, waved the door open, waved it shut behind him... and then stood there, suddenly breathing hard, gazing around him as if at a place he didn't know.

Even up in their private wing, by his parents' preference the decorating was kept quite sparse and spare. Neither his mother nor his father much liked the idea of leaving personal belongings out where visitors could see them, the whole purpose of the city house being to have a place where people from the government and the various city-states' management organizations could have a place to meet with the Sunborn. "Instead of making them come halfway around the planet," his mother would say, "and making them more unnerved about meeting with us than they already are."

"Instead of making them come to the *other* half of the planet," his father would murmur, almost a growl, "and reminding them exactly what we are good for."

Rho tightened his mouth against the response to *And what are we good for? —Dying for them.* Quickly he made himself busy gathering together into a little satchel some of the clothes and belongings he kept in the city house and didn't care to leave about as clues for the hired help who might possibly sell them, or the knowledge of them, to someone who meant him ill—or more likely, one of his parents. An electronic storyscroll or so, a favorite item of clothing—one of the casual pieces of wardrobe that he preferred when he didn't have to be seen out in the street as one of the Sunborn, always in danger of being held up as a good example to—who, exactly?

Whom, he could just hear his mother saying.

He laughed, a soundless breath of it. *Whom. For* whom *am I possibly a good example?* None of his schoolfellows cared what he did or said or thought (unless of course it turned up on one of the scandal feeds, when it was worth a certain amount of snickering behind his back). *What does it matter? Nothing matters, really. I am useless. Best then to go do it on the other side of the world, by myself.*

He was packed. Rho headed down to the end of the corridor and the little one-step-up dais that held another transport pad with a control plate set in the wall behind it. He stepped up on the pad and reached out to touch the plate. No need to to enter a combination; this pad went to only one place on the planet.

Rho closed his eyes, already sick of looking at the walls of the city house, and relaxed into the warmth of the transport process as all around him the walls of the city house faded away.

IT WAS JUST one tall narrow peak standing up from a landscape that had once been blasted bare when Thahit flared worst—that most deadly of all its ancient flare events that Wellakhit mostly called *amn Mahhev,* the Great Burning. The peak of Sunplace itself was a piece of social and architectural history, the result of centuries of intermittent labor as the institution of the Sunlords had gradually established itself.

As the decades after the Great Burning rolled by and the long slow repair of the planet's atmosphere and biosphere continued, the world's governments had decided that the remaining wizards of Wellakh's two main wizardly lines—now mostly known as the Guardians of Wellakh or the Guarantor Lords—should be given a place of their own to live in perpetuity. It should (it was decided) be spectacular enough to adequately express their world's grati-tude to them, but also isolated enough to give them a place in which to rebuild their depleted numbers in security. If there was purposeful irony in Sunplace's location at almost the exact center of the destruction, no one spoke of that openly. The official explanation was that such a location allowed the Sunlords to be in the best possible position to supervise and evaluate the ongoing work of repairing the weather and land on the maimed side of the planet. Mostly the Sunlords (at least while in office) tended not to mention publicly that the location certainly ensured their absolute attention to quality control, since if anything went wrong with that work, they would be the very first to suffer.

The building itself—insofar as something that started out as an item of terrain could be considered a building—was now the symbol for many things: the disaster of the Burning, the Burning's repair and the repair's ongoing maintenance, the now-royal family that presided over the project, and the institution of Wellakhit royalty itself. Over the centuries that followed the establishment of the Guarantee, Sunplace's original tawny igneous stone had been tunneled and carved into endless halls and chambers, lobbies and vestibules, parlors, galleries and terraces, dwelling-rooms, tiring-rooms, studies and libraries, guest lodgings and storerooms, and particularly the Great Rooms intended for purposes of ceremony, government, and the maintenance of Thahit and its neighboring space.

The city-house's installed transport pad was keyed to a spot directly outside the main doors of what was called "*the* Great Room" to distinguish it from all the lesser ones. Now used as a throne room and formal reception space, it was vast, having initially been the space where much tunnelling and stoneworking equipment had been stored in Sunplace's earliest days. When it was repurposed it was extravagantly redecorated in the most formal design of the day, heavy on bright enamels and ornate geometric stonework and inlay in colored stone, with a vast polished floor featuring a stylized map of the side of Wellakh that had been damaged, with ancient buildings and temples and mighty buildings of old all picked out in inlays of semiprecious stone and bright metal.

The doors to the Great Room proper were open, a sign that the King was not in residence. Otherwise they would have been shut in token of the traditional need to keep him safe. Rho stood there for a few moments just outside the open doors, looking through them into that huge space all hung with banners and tapestries coming apart with age. He thought once more of something he'd said when he was very small, making his father scowl a bit and his mother laugh out loud: *It doesn't matter how much they did to it to make it pretty. It's still an equipment shed.*

Rho sighed, wishing someone had taken some thought about the inconvenience of where this pad dumped incoming royalty. *Then again,* he thought, turning to head down the right-hand branch of the hallway that ended in the Great Room's expansive vestibule, *maybe they did give it some thought. Here, you royals, take a good look and be reminded why we spend so much of the planet's national product on you each year!* Because there was never going to be a time when their work would truly be finished... when the Guarantors could push their personal manifestations of wizardry to one side and say, "Fine, we're done. Now it's *your* problem." Because after the repair was finished, naturally the maintenance phase would follow. *And because what responsible workman refuses to take care of something once it's repaired? It needs to be kept running...*

Running. Even in his unhappy mood Rho had to smile a little ironically, because over the sound of his footsteps echoing against the corridor's high vaulted ceiling, he could hear just that: someone way down at the other end, around the curve of it, running toward him.

Staff. There were always staff here—curators, clerical people and so forth: they had their chambers, meeting spaces and lodging rooms some levels further down in the mountain. Whoever was on watch this shift had been alerted by the activation of the transport pad in the city-House, and was now racing along the corridor toward him to find out which of the Sunborn it was and what they needed.

Rho just kept plodding along with his satchel over his back. Some paces and breaths later he saw the liveried servitor come running around the curve ahead, dressed in the gold and black robes of the Sunborn's support staff, and carrying one of their short golden ceremonial spears. The spear had an energy weapon hidden in it, Rho knew. All the staff were trained in the aggressive arts—the sense being that any of them might have to protect the Sunborn at any moment. *Which makes you wonder: how many of us have been attacked* here, *where we're supposed to be safe, as opposed to in the city, where a certain level of danger is part of the job?* It was worth looking up when he was in a mood like this, rather than wasting on some morning or afternoon when he felt better about his life...

"Lord Prince," said the servitor as he got close enough to Rho that he didn't have to shout to be heard. "Are you alone? Are your royal father or mother coming?"

Which is what they really want to know, Rho thought. *I'm just an extra dinner guest to most of the people here. If the Sun starts to blow up, no need to talk to me...*

"The Sunlord and the Queen have not disclosed their plans to me," Rho said. "You may assume I'll be here alone tonight unless you hear otherwise from the city house."

"Will you be desiring dinner, Prince?"

"Thank you, I ate in town. Are my chambers open?"

"They should be, my Prince. The great door and the terrace doors would have been opened for airing just now, as usual every third morning."

Rho nodded. It was of course early morning here; Thahit would be just rising, as he was just leaning toward his setting in town. "My thanks," Rho said; "that will be all."

The servitor showed signs of lingering to see if Rho would think belatedly of anything else he might need. This was suddenly unbearably grating, and more than anything Rho would have liked to just yell at him "I don't need you, *be off!*" But if he did something like that, sooner or later his father would hear of it and make his life painful. *Royalty has its prerogatives, my princely son, but a man who treats servants badly deserves no respect from anyone, high or low—*

And unfortunately his father was right. "Really," Rho said, "that's all, please go finish breaking your fast—" Because he could see a few crumbs of morning-cake still clinging to the man's undertunic, missed in the fellow's haste to get into livery and get up here.

The servitor bowed. "My thanks, my Prince," he said, and took himself away.

Rho sighed and walked along more or less in the servitor's tracks. His rooms were a bit more than a quarter-hour's walk from here, up stairs, down stairs, along narrow corridors and broad ones. He walked the route more or less automatically, for (faced with surroundings that he knew from his earliest years and could have walked blindfolded) what he kept seeing in his mind's eye was the events of—was it just an hour or two ago now? It seemed impossible. The park, the tree, the road, the frontage of the city-house, the figure of his mother, the three men running toward her— And that little gesture, so small, and the way they fell. *And I could do nothing. Nothing...*

But that was the way it was going to be, and Rho was just going to have to cope with never being able to make the twin of that little gesture himself. As his people reckoned age, it was late for him to be offered the Art. Rho had been passed over, and that too was just the way it was. There was nothing to be gained by pretending otherwise.

Finally he came almost to the end of his route, and the knowledge of that pushed him out of the wearily repeating loop of imagery. Rho took a deep breath and stepped out the last doorway into the sunlight, onto the terrace that fronted on his rooms.

There, outside the glass doors giving on the terrace, Rho dropped his satchel and went to lean on the terrace's balustrade. The wide view spread out beneath him in all directions—the golden and crimson gardens of Sunplace, famous even in other neighboring star systems, laid out like a giant rugged carpet ornamented with endless swirls of abstract design laid out in a thousand vibrant shades. It was all a little shadowed at the moment, the colors muted until the Sun came up: but when it did, all this vista would blaze, vivid, a defiant shout of color fairly vibrating against the blue-green of the sky: *You tried to kill us and you failed. We are not dead yet!*

And the view had more import than was what might seem obvious at first glance. In a way the tended garden was a symbol of the far greater endeavor taking place all across the world's far side, and which still had so far to go. When you came in from space there was no missing that unique and terrible silhouette, one half of the planet shining much brighter than the other, its albedo unnaturally high to the point where from halfway across the system you could see whether the blasted side or the less-damaged one was turned toward you. Even the tiny glint of fire in the sky as seen from one of the inner planets had a different color temperature depending on whether the live side or the dead one was turned toward you.

Well, perhaps not *dead* dead; not any more. The thousands of being-years spent by Wellakh's wizards since the Burning on the slow repair of the flare-scorched side was an ethical pursuit as well as an economical one. Though reclaiming half the world for the planetary population was always an issue, the older and greater one—from the Guarantors' point of view—was that the planet was in its own way a being, one that misadventure had befallen. It had been maimed, and had a right to be made well by those who lived on it and were its care-takers. *A work never really to be finished,* Rho thought. *But one worth doing.*

He leaned there, letting his eyes rest on the view for a while and soaking in the pre-dawn quiet. Above the gardens, which seemed in these conditions to stretch to the edge of the world, the morning twilight was dissolving fast with Thahit's approach. The sky just above the sunward horizon was going fiercely bright with a red-gold much like the shade of his father's hair. Sometimes when their moods and schedules coincided, the two of them or the three of them leaned here together and watched it—the inexorable approach of their family's chief concern, the reason they were royalty and the reason their lives came under such frequent threat.

The light increased, becoming increasingly difficult to look at. Rho leaned there, weary, blinking, and thought of what his father usually did when they were here together. There was a salute one rendered to the Aethyrs, acknowledging what they had made— besides everything else, of course: this dangerous splendor, on which all life depended and which once had almost destroyed all life here.

Rho closed his eyes against the light for a moment, hearing in memory fragments of past years' discussions about the Aethyrs. Rho started out knowing about them what most Wellakhit knew: the Aethyrs worked the will of the Most Central One on the worlds. They were many, and They had many roles. The average Wellakhit in the street honored them in a vaguely affectionate way without paying Them much more attention than that. Some liked to go out to the big temples and acknowledge Them there; some people built little shrines on their property or even inside their houses.

Rho's father laughed softly about that sometimes. "As if one can pen the Powers up like a *thaelth* in the back yard or by the kitchen stove," he'd say under his breath, "to keep the night-thieves out." But then his lady mother would laugh at her royal consort in that *You're-not-fooling-me* way she had, and say, "Oh, the way *you* don't have them in the shrine out back."

"It's not as if they're actually *there*, Miril."

"Except insofar as they're *everywhere*, since as They inevitably interpenetrate lower-dimensional spaces—"

"Yes, well, but I don't go out there and have little chats with Them about politics or the ever-declining state of public discourse!"

"No, you do *that* hanging over the terrace-walls at Sunplace, don't think I haven't heard you!"

And off they would go, fighting—or it could have been mistaken for fighting—but always somehow in good cheer about it. And Rho was always cheered, too, to hear them. *No matter what else bothers them about their lives,* he would think, *no matter what else might go wrong in their lives, at least they're not alone.*

That was a thought that did come back to haunt Rho sometimes. It was a terrible thing to be alone. Sometimes he hated thinking about the future at all, because from early indications—particularly the reactions of his yearsmates at lessons, or even among the younger members of the wizardly det Nuiiliat clans—friendship seemed to be a thing that happened to other people. The thought that Rho would have to do what his parents did, but do it all by himself, without anyone to share the work with and watch his back—that was hard.

He blinked his eyes open again in the face of the growing light. *Still. This is going to be my job. If I have to learn to do it with nothing but the simulator...* This too he hated thinking about. The thing was a crude mechanical aid without any elegance or subtlety, suitable only for teaching the nonwizardly how to manage a star. Thahit deserved something better, a wizard who could talk to it and be *heard*—badly-behaved body though it might be. But what it was going to get as

Sunlord in Rho's time was someone who could communicate with it only through a machine, and only get it to change its behavior by force instead of the persuasion of the Speech enabled by full enacture.

Not the way it will be, though, he thought rather sadly. *Truly I am sorry about that, you bad-tempered ball of plasma.* And it was strange, because he genuinely did feel sorry for once, instead of frustrated or angry. *Probably it's shock,* Rho thought. *Stupid day that it's been.*

He straightened up and regarded the horizon, which was growing more dazzling every second. Strange, in a moment when he seemed to have finally given up some hope he'd been holding onto out of sheer stubbornness, to somehow feel a bit better than he had. *I'm so tired,* he thought. *But no matter.* And as if his father was there with him, he said the words, because it didn't matter if *he* was mostly useless at what he'd been born to do: *they* weren't.

"Here we see the fire at the heart," Rho murmured, "bodying forth Your service and Your art. In such wise You who made it body forth the Fire at the heart of That from which you proceeded. Let our endeavors to tend this star look in fellowship toward Yours, as Yours look toward the One's: workers together we, in the same art, from the lesser to the greater. And so we say, as laborers to one another: Go well, work well, and keep hearts up!"

With that, as if in response, the blinding edge of the Sun came up over the edge of the world, and everything around Rho from here to the horizon made a leap into brilliance and new clarity. Rho's eyes watered and he turned away and stifled a yawn, feeling suddenly exhausted.

All right, ready to collapse for a bit now, he thought, and made his way through one of the glass doors that stood open, into his rooms.

AFTER THE COOL elegance of the city house, Rho was always glad to get back into the fussy coziness of his own space... though it hadn't always looked like it did now.

There had been a time when he'd just started his first public lessons, and overheard some of his agemates whispering about what he must have in his house and how a Sunborn must live: precious metals and costly jewels scattered around like trash, delicate and expensive foods to eat, the spoils of unthinking privilege. He tried to tell them more than once how it really was, but they weren't interested in hearing. Their fantasies were more entertaining to them than any truth he could tell.

So Rho had gone home and gradually began to turn his quarters into something quite different from the relatively sparsely-furnished space it had once been, rather like his parents'. His excuse (when his mother and father asked him what was going on) was that he was interested in the old Demosh architectural and artistic style featured in the Great Room... but he was careful not to answer such queries in the Speech, when one or the other of them would chance to be using it in language-of-discourse mode (as numerous Wellakhit did). Even though such usage didn't bind him to truth, as it did a wizard, it was *so* much easier to hear the lie that there was hardly any point in speaking at all.

Over time Rho's rooms had become furnished in all the kinds of things the public-lessons students accused him of having—richly decorated walls, ornate couches and divans and chairs halfway to being thrones, draperies stiff with embroidery in precious metals, lamps shining through jeweled shades, everything a blaze of clashing colors. It was an exercise in bad taste (so his father had said), and Rho knew it, but refused to admit it. His rooms were a secret poke in the eye to those who'd refused to listen to him. And over time, even though the old anger died away, he got used to the look of the place and refused to change it.

Cost, of course, had never been an issue. Anything the Sunborn asked for was always given them. But Rho's mother would walk in, look around at the place, sigh deeply, and walk out again without offering an opinion. There was, nonetheless, no way to misunderstand her meaning, as his mother *always* had an opinion.

Rho shut the terrace door behind him and waved the glass of all the doors dark; then spoke the names of a few of the lamps, and the room's programming turned them on and dimmed them down. At the back of this high-ceilinged space was a long broad couch that he favored when he was too lazy or weary to go properly to bed. Rho dropped his satchel nearby, pulled off his outer robe, threw it over a convenient chair, and flopped down on the couch.

For a few moments he just stretched and savored the feeling of being off his feet and out of anyone's view, free to do nothing and not be expected to seem any particular way. "Down here," he said to the small reading lamp that hung over the head end of his couch. Obligingly it levitated down on its little impeller and hovered where he wanted it, while Rho felt around under the couch for the adventure-tale codex he had left there half-read last night.

He found it, rolled over on his back, and pulled the codex open. Yawning, he tapped the top of the right-hand scroll handle, instructing the scroll's surface to display again the last portion of text that had displayed. It always took a few moments to do this, and such was Rho's weariness that his arms felt tired from just these few moments of holding it up. He lowered it to his chest and rested it there, waiting for the right section to display.

And as he was about to lift it up and start reading again, someone said in his ear: "Will you serve?"

RHO'S EYES snapped open and his whole body went taut with fear as his head jerked sideways to see who'd managed to get into his rooms without tripping any of the alarms. But the room was empty except for its proper furnishings, and most specifically there was no one standing or crouching by the head of his couch, where they would have had to be to speak so quietly and intimately to him and yet be heard.

Rho stared up at the elaborately decorated ceiling, vague in the dimness and high enough above him that its details ran together in this light. *No voice, then.* Just a trick of the body, one of those snatches of weary-brain babble you caught sometimes when startling awake before falling fully asleep at last.

Sighing, Rho let his head fall back against the couch's head-cushion. *Just fatigue,* he thought. *But then, such a long day...* And as if on cue, back came the image of his mother standing across the road with her shopping, reaching for the handplate of the postern door.

Rho squeezed his eyes shut and pushed the image away. *It's not as if you have not known for years that these things happen to the ruling Sunborn. And that your mother is a wizard, one of the most powerful on the planet. She has walked away safe and sound from far worse attempts in the past. It will take more than a few disaffected types with hand weapons to kill her.*

But this truth was no particular consolation, because it suggested another—one that here in the shadows and the quiet, by himself, there was no avoiding. Even the most careful and powerful wizards could make a mistake, or have an accident. *And even without accidents or errors, all wizards die.*

Rho's throat had gone tight. He swallowed against the lump there, but it didn't help. *One way or another, some day the two of them will be gone. And I'll be left spending the rest of my life handling Thahit with nothing but that machine.*

Rho swallowed again, for this was the truth he hated more than anything to be forced to admit. There was no chance for him ever to be able to do what his parents did—slide into rapport with the star, hear it think, feel his small heart and that great one beat as one. The great joy of his mother's and father's lives, the experience that made all the work and the danger worthwhile, would never be his. There was even a phrase to describe the likes of him, though he'd never heard either parent speak it and felt sure he never would: *ket mawhir,* "under cloud." It was used for one between the Sun and whom there lay a barrier—the impenetrability of uncooperative flesh, or of a spirit that had not been given the tools to do the work that would otherwise have been expected of it.

Rho sighed. *Ket mawhir* Sunlords who held down the position for more than a decade or two were the exception rather than the rule.

Routinely they resigned, or were pushed out of their duties on Sunwatch by vote of the massed det Nuiiliat clans. Or if they were too politically powerful to get rid of, they would cling on to their positions until they died young of overwork, worn out by the stresses of trying to manage so difficult a star with nothing but a mechanism.

And if that happens to me, well, at least it'll be the end of people looking at me as if they're sorry for me. He'd been putting up with that kind of thing for long enough. If you were in the Sunlords' line and you *weren't* a wizard, the assumption was that the Aethyrs felt there was something possibly psychologically or morally wrong with you: some way you fell short, some way you would fail. *Or some way you'll get something catastrophically wrong when you're working with Thahit,* Rho thought, dropping the codex he'd been holding to the floor beside the couch. *And if that was true, who could blame them? Wellakh's had enough of that.*

So just stop resisting what is going to happen. It's time it stopped hurting so much.

...Except that it won't stop. Doesn't stop. "And who do I think I'm fooling?" he muttered.

Whom, said the voice by his ear.

This time he was less taken by surprise. He turned his head and saw nothing, but at the moment Rho found himself untroubled. He'd managed to fall asleep, he assumed, for real this time, and was dreaming. Because why else would someone invisible be correcting his grammar as if they were his mother? "You'll be telling me I should be speaking Kings'-speech next," he said.

And why not? It is how a Sunlord signals to his people that they are dealing with royalty.

"My people are not here, though," Rho said to whatever spoke in his ear. "And since here I lie in the prince's quarters in Sunplace, that's surely a *hint* that I am royalty."

Except in one respect.

Rho tilted his head against the cushion in agreement. "Not holding the world's rule at the moment," he said, "or in charge of the Sunwatch, no."

But some day.

"If the Aethyrs please," Rho said, closing his eyes and not much caring at the moment whether they pleased or not, or ever would. "Don't know why they would, though, because I'm not likely to be as good a king as my father, or even my noble grandsire. It doesn't matter how smart I am, or how good I am with the simulator and the rest of the machinery. I can't *feel* Thahit, learn his moods from the inside... derail them before they get serious."

Yet you're still able to intervene.

"Mechanically, yes. Well, why would I not? What else am I good for? My father's spent so much time on me, I may as well do my best at looking after Thahit until someone better suited to the Watch comes along." Rho yawned.

And you would see that happen without ill will?

"Well, yes! Whether it's me or someone else, Thahit needs watching," Rho said. "For our people's sake. And the world's."

He frowned. "...And its own! Even if there wasn't an inhabited world at stake, who leaves an unstable star to its own devices? Why should it die early? It has its own way of being. Let it have that for as long as it may." That was something his father had said to him only occasionally when he was younger, but it had struck Rho as both deeply important and profoundly sensible—maybe the most important thing about the whole idea of the Sunwatch. Too many Wellakhit talked about the Sun as if it was an enemy out to get them, and that had always struck Rho as unfair. But then he was also used to people assuming things about *him* that weren't so.

Even if that other person is a wizard, as you are not.

Rho opened his eyes enough to gaze up at the intricate designs of the ceiling, near-invisible in the gloom. "If they're better at this than I am, and better for Thahit, why not?" He let out a tired breath. "If that person can be friendly with our star, can keep him company as well as keep him right, then let it be so. And I wish them well of it."

He closed his eyes again. "Company," Rho heard himself saying very softly, "would be quite marvelous. And a friend, beyond any miracle." Which wasn't the kind of thing that Rho would normally say to anyone alive, but all this was unreal enough to absolve him of any concern.

Nor did the unreality appear about to cease. *Companionship,* said that oddly intimate voice, *comes in many forms. And the price demanded for it may be high. Are you prepared to be put in the Lost One's way?*

"What," Rho said, starting to weary of this, "the Lost Aethyr? For the most Central's sake, where am I *now?* Not that every time Thahit rises we're not *all* put in Its way somewhat! But judging by how my life's gone so far, It's been busy with me for twenty sunrounds or so without even paying much attention."

And something occurred to him: *Except, possibly, today—*

For some moments there was silence. Finally Rho realized his odd interlocutor was waiting for an answer. There he lay, seeing in his mind's eye his mother standing on the path across the road from the park, putting her hand on the doorplate—

"But yes," Rho said. "Yes."

Then speak the words.

He could hear his heart starting to pound. "Which words?"

The Avowal.

Rho knew the words. Of *course* he knew them. He had been hearing his parents speak them at regular intervals since he was a tiny child. Often enough when he was too young to know any better, he'd thought, *I will say the words and become a wizard.* But of course nothing happened. As he got older, though he'd found again and again that saying the words made no difference, nonetheless every now and then he would go somewhere quiet, someplace he knew he couldn't be heard, and repeat them one more time... because you never could tell. Perhaps *this* time the Aethyrs would grant his heart's desire. *It never happened, of course. But you never gave up, either.*

Until lately, anyway...

And now here Rho was, lying on his couch—where he'd said the words who knew how many times before without effect—and it all just seemed *funny,* let his heart hammer away as it liked. "Fine," he said. "Why not?"

He meant then to just rattle it all off as if it wasn't important, didn't mean anything. But it *did* mean something. It meant *everything*.

Rho took a long breath and said the words.

"As the Fire that rules our lives lies at the center of our worlds, so the Life that rules all fires lies within them and beyond; and to that Life I this avow, to use the Gift it offers on its behalf alone, in its service and no other's. As the Fire warms life to growth, that burgeoning is my business; what the Fire burns, causing pain, that anguish will I ease. What grows well I will maintain, never changing what's not threatened. Till the last Fire dies in darkness, so long my Art I'll wield in the cause of That which made it and which calls us to the battle, rank on rank among the Aethyrs here and now and ever more!"

Rho stopped and waited...

And felt like an idiot. No thunderclap, no triumphal chorus of otherworldly voices; in fact, none of the results he'd imagined since he was old enough to be let out in public in full-length robes without absorptive undergarments. *Well, what did I expect?*

And *e*ven the invisible source of the voice in his ear seemed to have gone off somewhere else. There was this at least: he wasn't awake, there was no chance anyone could have heard him making a fool of himself.

Fine, Rho thought. *Fine. Still tired. Back to sleep.*

He closed his eyes, again, too tired to even mock himself any further, and let it all go.

2

The next thing he knew, he was lying there still staring at the ceiling—except the lighting had changed, so that the designs and tracery above him were even less visible. The doors onto the terrace were dark though his original setting had shut itself off, and from the color of the sky outside he gathered that Thahit was a couple of hours set by now.

Inside, Rho's room had come up to evening lighting because its management mechanisms knew there was someone in it. Otherwise nothing had changed... though he did have an odd half memory of some kind of dream in which he had been having a conversation with someone.

Rho looked around, seeing no sign that his parents had been there. That was normal: they didn't enter here unless he invited them. He'd simply awakened with a snap as if this was one more ordinary day.

Slowly, the memory of—yesterday? Was it actually yesterday?— slid back into his brain. Rho sighed in slight annoyance at himself. *And I just left them there in town like that,* he thought. *Mother is going to be wondering how I am. If they're here now, which seems likely, I should go let them know I'm all right.*

Rho levered himself up off his couch, stretched, yawned. He hated falling out with his parents—apologizing afterward was always so awkward. *I must think how to do that this time...*

His stomach growled, interrupting his thought. *And that's something else,* he thought. *You didn't have much to eat yesterday. About two slices of barkbread...* Rho let out another breath of annoyance at himself, for the Queen had gone to some trouble to get that for him. *I ought to do her the courtesy of actually* eating *a decent amount of it.* Knowing his mother, she would have brought it here with her. He could always ring for one of the staff and find out where she'd left it, but—

Never mind that, he thought. *Get out of the rooms, find her, tell her you're sorry for being an idiot*— He winced a bit with embarrassment at his own misbehavior, which his mother had done nothing to deserve. *I am enough of a disappointment to them,* Rho thought, resigned, *and here is one more way...*

Well. I can at least make myself presentable before waiting upon them, Rho thought as he headed back for the sanitation suite in his rooms. This at least would be no hardship, for Rho was one of those people who liked getting clean. Though he had had a period during childhood when he was possessed by a burning envy of other Wellakhit children, who were allowed to get dirty and stay that way for more than five minutes at a time, eventually a preference for not smelling bad had supplanted his urges toward grime.

As a result, the sanitation suite in Rho's rooms was something of a showplace. Over time he had caused to be added to it nearly every device that Wellakhit civilization had developed to apply hot water to oneself. After some experimentation Rho had finally settled on a large multifunction refreshment cabin made all of glass, containing a ceramic seat where one might sit and be drenched, sprayed, doused, pummeled, misted, or otherwise afflicted by water under pressure.

Rho waved the cabin's door open. "All-sides atomizer and heavy spray," he told the cabin, "followed by three minutes of downpour and five minutes of deluge at 310 absolute—"

The misting began immediately, while he still had the door open.

That was extremely peculiar, because Rho had not given the "go" command. He scowled. "No, no," he said, annoyed, "just wait a minute—"

All the water stopped.

Rho stood there and stared into the cabin. That wasn't supposed to happen either. Had the machinery suddenly developed a fault? "Now *what* under the sun—" he muttered in the Speech, one of his father's preferred imprecations.

A fat drop of water gathered on the surface of the biggest of the applicators, the one embedded in the ceiling of the cubicle, and fell. *That one always did have a tendency to leak,* Rho thought as it came down, splashing into the small puddle of water that had already collected in the bottom of the receptacle.

And the splash said to him, as clearly as words, *What's the problem?*

Rho froze stock-still, thunderstruck. He was used to using the Speech for casual conversation with offworlders or with his mother and father. *But not with infrastructure, not with—*

There's always some problem with you, isn't there, the water said, pooling, and sounding rather put out. *Get hot, run downhill, it's enough for most people, but with you, nothing's ever good enough. So what are you expecting today? A different matter-state, maybe?*

Rho blinked and stared. *This is turning into a good tenday for shock,* he thought, feeling almost weak, and leaning one-handed against the wall of the cubicle. "What is going on here?" he said under his breath.

He was not prepared, not in the slightest, for the small, hot spark of light that appeared in front of him, hovering in the air, almost at the end of his nose.

And it was *looking* at him.

From the core of the light it seemed to Rho that he could hear a soft rush of whispers. Something *behind* the mere physicality of the world was whispering to him in the Speech. And as he listened he realized that the Speech itself was changed. Suddenly it wasn't just what it had always been to him before, words with meanings, like any other language. Now without warning there was something deeper behind every word he heard, something of far deeper import: the source of meaning, the fount of power, distant but present. Every word sang with the secret.

The whispering came in many voices, all saying different things, all to different purposes... but they all sounded like *him*, like Rho thinking. But he had never in his life thought anything with the kind of certainty he heard here in every word. Here in this little core of light he heard answers: *all* the answers.

For the first second or so, Rho stared at the fiercely-burning little light with as much astonishment as if it was one of the tiny flying biting *shisp* that sometimes, even with the protective force fields, managed to get into his rooms in the right weather. But the shock lasted only a second. He knew exactly what this was. Countless times since Rho was small he'd seen his father and his mother reach out and open a hand to have something exactly like this appear in it. Indeed, he'd first started picking up words in the Speech by hearing them speak to the fierce little cores of light held in their hands.

Rho actually sagged against the refresher cabin, staggering back a step to lean his back up against it as if the little burning light was going to jump at his face. It did follow, but just enough to keep hanging in front of his nose.

An Aethyr!

Rho opened his mouth and said to the little spark of light the words he never thought he would speak to another being as a wizard. *"Dai stihó,"* he whispered.

A chorus of greeting came back to him, in the same word, or words: one answer, and all the answers. In the response Rho could hear every word there had ever been, singing in the background of the reply. Immensities were bound up in that little burning light. All languages, endless knowledge of other species, all the secrets of wizardry—assuming he could figure out how to ask for them.

Because it wasn't just any Aethyr. It was *his* Aethyr.

I am a wizard, Rho thought, his mouth dry with shock and astonishment. *Finally,* finally *it's happened!*

He swallowed, or tried to, because that meant something else was finally upon him as well. Now would come the test—the Challenge, as his own people called it; though instantly many other idioms for what was to follow rushed through his head. *The Certification, the Nightwalk, the Ordeal, the Invigilation—*

Beyond all hope, and so very late, Rho's turn had come. He was a probationary wizard. *But now comes the proving,* he thought. And what would it look like? His father's, in so far as he knew anything about it —for Nelaid had always been shy of discussing the subject—had come during the last period of instability in Thahit's deeper atmosphere. His mother's had had something to do with the weather. Once when he was small, before he understood the proprieties surrounding such discussions, Rho had questioned the Queen about it. Miril had simply smiled and said, "There was a storm."

He instantly imagined his mother as a mighty heroine, standing on the sky with arms raised in a blaze of glory, forbidding the storm to wreak havoc on some distant settlement or populous city. "You had to stop it?" Rho had said.

His mother tilted her head in rueful negation, and said, smiling as if amused at herself, "No, my son. I had to let it happen."

Rho had gone away from that discussion greatly confused. But now there was at last a chance that he might understand, not just that, but so many other things—

Gingerly he reached up to the little blinding spark, still hanging so close to his nose it was making him blink, and pinched it between thumb and forefinger.

The voices that Rho heard singing instantly grew louder, but not deafeningly so. And they all sang now on one note, one tone. They were waiting, whoever they were—waiting to see what he needed. Anything he asked for, any knowledge, any word, if it was right for him to have, it would be given him.

The sense of the power locked up in that little core of light made Rho begin to tremble. *This is why our wizards came to call this instrumentality 'their Aethyr',* he thought. *As if they held the great Powers in their hand.*

Because they do.

I do!

And the Aethyr in his hand was waiting for him to *do* something. *Speak,* the voices said, *act, command! The worlds are waiting.*

Rho gulped. This was wondrous. It was terrifying. And he had *no idea what to ask for.* There he stood, gaping, while the knowledge of the universe, wizardly and nonwizardly both, suffered itself to be pinched between his thumb and forefinger, and looked at him—he could *feel* it looking at him—with considerable patience.

He opened his mouth, shut it again. And then it came to him.

All I want right now is out!

Rho went hot and cold all over with the sudden sheer *wonder* of the idea. To be Sunborn—at least, when one was of the Royal line and also a child—was to be guarded night and day and never allowed to go anywhere alone. His tutors in the royal household had spent his earliest years drumming it into him that there were people who would be happy to use a new young prince as a tool or weapon against his parents. Once he'd understood the threat, Rho had been most careful never to try to escape his supervisors or do anything else that would give his mother and father cause to fear for him on that account.

But even though they'd long since taken the childproofing force-fields off the balustrades of the high terraces in Sunplace, and he could walk home by himself from lessons through spaces normally felt to be secure, Rho wasn't all that much freer now. There was still always the chance that he might be taken captive to be used as leverage against them. Even so, he wasn't allowed to go about the planet by himself without the journey or errand being arranged far in advance, and security put in place. And as for going offplanet, that was simply out of the question. He had long since learned to stifle the terrible longing to just be somewhere else, someplace where the unbreakable chains of expectation and duty wouldn't bind him down.

Rho swallowed hard. *But they don't now. Not tonight! I could go— I could go...*

His imagination simply failed him in the face of the impossible breadth of the vista now laying itself out before him, possibilities that had never, ever been available before. It was as if someone had pulled the sky apart and revealed another sky past it, wondrous, endless, full of other worlds.

Which it *was*. How many millions of worlds existed out there, places Rho had thought he'd never see until some unimaginably far-off time when he would be grown up? If even then. But now no one could stop him... not even his parents.

I'd never want to frighten them, Rho thought. *But just this once, just tonight—it's my Challenge and surely this is my right, to have a few moments to enjoy this before the trouble starts! Whatever the trouble is. I'm a wizard now! I can go out, I can—*

Rho quivered all over with the opportunity. "I can, can't I?" He said to the Aethyr in his hand.

You can travel to any location for which you are willing and able to pay the price of transport, the Aethyr said, sounding utterly unconcerned. *Determine your desired location and a price and details of the transit spell will be provided to you.*

Rho stared in wonder as he realized the Aethyr wasn't going to act as a surrogate for his parents. It was just going to let him do what he thought right. *This is so incredible,* he thought, and hugged himself with glee.

Then his eyes went wide with shock and he threw his arms wide again, staring in horror at the Aethyr still held between finger and thumb. "*Sorry,* I'm so sorry, are you all right? I didn't hurt you?"

This instrumentality, the Aethyr said, sounding quite dry, *is fairly robust. You need not be concerned.*

"Good," Rho said. "Good. Then I want to go somewhere else."

Coordinates? said the Aethyr.

The image had fleeted through his mind a few moments ago, and now returned much more strongly— a place he and his parents had passed through some years back, ever so briefly, on their way to a meeting with a delegation of wizards interfacing with a group of planetary executives. The place had been huge and terrifying and confusing and loud, and it had haunted his happiest dreams for years. "The Crossings," he whispered. "Just for a little while—"

Worldgating costs for transits to the Crossings can be partially offset by parasitic debit-reference to the portal structure installed in this facility, the Aethyr said. *Otherwise, the duration of your visit to any off planet location is entirely elective, assuming there are no extraneous life-support requirements. Desired time of departure?*

He was tempted to say *Right now! Or ten partitions ago would have done as well!* But from many long discussions with his mother and father Rho knew that you needed to be precise in your language when dealing with an Aethyr—otherwise problems would ensue, and though some of these might be funny in retrospect, others could kill you. "Fifteen partitions," Rho said in the Speech, and then glanced down at himself in sudden horror. It would not do to appear at the Crossings in raiment that suggested he'd slept in it.

Starting countdown, said the Aethyr. And suddenly Rho saw a column of Speech-digits appear in the air and begin flashing downward through a count of fractional partitions of the Wellakhit hour.

It didn't take him fifteen partitions to make himself ready. It was more like five. Any prince worthy of the name often found himself faced with four or five ceremonials to attend to in the day, and precious little time to change between them... so he knew how to do this in a hurry. Seconds after the countdown began Rho was deep into his tiring-room, waving his frantic way through racks and shelves and hanging-space. Shortly he came up with a dark red-gold over-robe and darker red tunic and trousers and soft boots, an ensemble that looked quietly well-to-do but not flamboyant—as the last thing he wanted was someone from the Crossings contacting the Royal house or one of its equerries to inquire whether they had mislaid a prince.

Rho threw the clothes on and set them to rights in what for him would have been unseemly haste. *Well enough. Money—* Hastily he went scrabbling through a chest of drawers at the back of the tiring room. From it Rho dug out and pocketed a few cash-charged valuta plaques that had only anonymized contact with the Wellakhit world banking system—as, much to their credit, Rho's parents felt no need to know what he did with his allowance.

Hand baggage, Rho thought. Without having any in such a place, he would be too likely to stand out. He dug around in his presses and closets and came up with a simple strapped carrier bag, along the lines of what the Queen had brought the groceries home in the other day, though heavier and with touch-sensitive security fastenings on the flaps. *Because who knows, I might see something I want to bring back...* Finally he hastily brushed his hair out, pulled it back, and knotted it once behind in the simplest and most utilitarian way, a worker's or cleric's style.

Quickly Rho looked himself over in the mirror by the tiring-room door. Even if anyone recognized him as Wellakhit, he would most likely be mistaken for some kind of business person, maybe some household's official out on an errand. He glanced up to see the count-down digits (which had been following him around as he attired himself) flickering into the next sequence of five hour-partitions.

Rho headed out into his living area again, where the Aethyr was hanging patiently in the air, waiting for him. As he reached out to it he felt his pulse start to pick up again. *My first spell. Oh, in the Most Central's name, I can't believe it, I can't believe it's finally happening—!*

"Display the worldgating matrix, please," Rho said, trying to keep the tremor of excitement out of his voice. And there was just a little edge of fear there, too. *What if I mess it up? What if I get it wrong? What if I'm not really meant for this?*

—Except of course I am, they wouldn't have given it to me otherwise—

But this was still a probationary activity. His Challenge was about finding out whether he was good enough at this to survive contact with the Lost Aethyr, who in one form or another routinely turned up to eliminate new wizards if It could. And Rho knew, because over time his father and mother had told him, that there were wizards who *weren't* good enough. There were those who had the Great Art offered to them and couldn't bear the weight, or got something crucial wrong and didn't come back from their Challenge—

Please advise if prepared for early departure, the Aethyr said.

Hurriedly Rho reached out and took hold of it. Then something occurred to him and started him panicking again. "Do I have to keep hold of you? Or how do I—"

Just a touch of amusement was audible in the dry pseudovoice. *You cannot lose this instrumentality,* the Aethyr said. *Reach out and you will find me within touch. Now*— The countdown sequence flicked over to breaths and fractions of a breath, with the annotation under it in the Speech, *Time to termination of current CIWF receptor area booking.*

The room went dim around Rho. From the empty space where he stood, a complex diagram, chorded circles nested within circles and other more complex geometric figures, spread itself out all around from his feet, all full of words in the Speech. He had another moment of panic: there was too much written here, he didn't know where to begin reading, what if he said something wrong or in the wrong order—

But then Rho took a deep breath. *Calm down! You know what comes next...* Especially since he'd seen his father and mother do it countless times.

It was one of his very early memories—his father teaching him to write his name in one of the simplest of the Speech's recensions. "There'll be more of it later," his father had said, looking down with quiet satisfaction at the long careful vertical scrawl of curls and curves, "and it will mean more."

There definitely is, Rho thought as he looked down at the older-wizardly-Roshaun version of his name, all adorned with new outgrowths of characters he'd never seen before. *And it definitely does...* For he could feel the *him*-ness of it even at this distance, even from the parts of it he didn't thoroughly understand as yet.

Rho stood there for as long as he dared, scrutinizing the long chain of descriptors while the countdown kept sliding by. As far as he could tell the most basic version of his name was definitely there and correct: the newer additions to it would need study and analysis, but for the moment that would have to wait.

Flashing a little further along in the spell-diagram was a trail of softly-lit characters suggesting where he should begin to recite the spell. Rho took a long breath and began to pronounce his very first words in the Speech as a wizard.

He was in no wise prepared for the sense of exquisite, shattering *certainty* that flooded over him as he spoke words that had always before merely had sense and now also had *meaning*. And moment by moment Rho could hear everything around him going quiet as the meaning became more intense through being given voice by a living being on the Aethyrs' business. *Because I* am! he thought in growing triumph. *Even this little errand, this exploration, is on their behalf. This is errantry! More: this is the Challenge, the first act of the process that will prove me a wizard —*

—or not—

Rho gulped, steadied himself, and concentrated on speaking the words as they were laid out in front of him, more and more quickly working how to move through the reading of the spell diagram. All around him he could feel the forces building, and both feel and see the structure of his on-demand worldgate constructing itself on the matrix of hyperspace strings that interpenetrated everything, space and matter alike. With the words of the spell Rho was binding himself into the new substructure, making a direct connection to the place in spacetime where he now desired to be.

More and more intensely as he recited, Rho could feel that the words he was saying might possibly be more real than their mere surroundings—more real than the place where they were spoken or the being who spoke them. He was shivering with the perception, but not with fear. The words were older than he, stronger than he, endlessly ancient... but still fresh and strong and ready for whatever purpose he wanted them to serve. *Or that they want* me to—

Because it was all starting to get confused as the room dimmed around him and the power kept flooding into the spell diagram. Increasingly Rho wondered whether he was speaking the words or they were speaking him as the until-now silent rumble of the turning world beneath him started scaling up and up, deafening, complaining as he was pried out of its grip and matter-of-factly removed from this airt of the world and dropped down into—

Another!

RHO GASPED and blinked and stood very still on the sudden, shining floor, staring all around him.

He'd noted the spell's selection of his destination, a neutral arrivals area in the Crossings. And here he was, exactly in the center of a wide hex-paved space fenced off from a broad main concourse by a circular blue metal railing. The hexes were nonadjacent, spaced out from one another, and Rho was occupying one of his own, nearly as wide as he was tall. As he glanced around, elsewhere inside the railing other beings were appearing at intervals: here a hominid, there a jellylike creature all blue and shivering, over there a bright-carapaced arthropod of some kind—

Rho stood transfixed with delight, gazing around. Beyond the railings stretched more and more and more of that broad white floor, away off into the distance. And out there in the concourse every kind of being one could imagine was walking or crawling or sliding or slithering to and fro, winging it from place to place in the middle airs, gliding along on small personal transports or on one of the larger moving walkways that crisscrossed the vast space at intervals.

Above Rho, starting at about ten times his height overhead, floated elements of the daytime "elective ceiling" of the Crossings—hundreds of slabs of energy/matter matrix, some of them translucent, some transparent, some glowing slightly, floating serenely in many overlapping layers above the concourse and mercifully blocking out the view of Rirhath B's blinding, scalding day. Rho stared up fascinated at that impossible vault, getting no more than a glimpse here or there of the sky itself, fluorescing under the ferocious radiation of that alien sun.

And that was Rho's major concern—not the ceiling, not the sky. *That star—*

I can hear it!

Even here, even through the overdoming rayshielding built to

protect the many species who came here, he could hear the actinic
shout of it, the roar of the solar furnace. Thahit, dangerous and
unstable as it could be, did not begin to compare. Rirhath B's star was
a main-sequence giant, blue-white as a thunderbolt and millions of
times brighter. He could feel the texture of its gravity well from here,
sense how the air was almost thick with its neutrons. *I could get out
and feel that light on me without a ceiling in the way—*

Something began to buzz under his feet, pulsing. Rho looked
down and realize that his hex was flashing. The intervals between
flashes were getting shorter, and the vibration under his feet was
getting stronger as the transport management system let him know
that somebody else needed this hex very shortly. *So maybe I should
stop standing here like some gaping yokel and be about my business...?*

Rho laughed softly at himself and moved out of the railed area as
quickly as he could, and then went to have a look at that star.

It took some doing to work out how to get out of the Crossings facilities proper. Rho quickly realized that this was intentional. There were
too many ways for unwary transit travelers to come to grief on this
planet, considering the inherent dangerousness of the exterior environment. Leaving aside the radiation and the brilliance of the light,
for all he knew the atmosphere might be bad for hominids too.

Belatedly Rho found he also had to admit that he wasn't in a
terrible *hurry* to get out of the main concourse area, because there
was too much to see. The shops, the restaurants, the banking and
business facilities, the bars and leisure centers, even the sanitary
facilities, were all utterly fascinating—full of wares he could sometimes barely understand, foods he'd never imagined, businesses and
currencies and modes of fiscal exchange he couldn't even begin to
figure out at such short notice. And it was all *new*, a complete super-
fluity of things to wonder at. All around him moved beings of every
possible description, beautiful, bizarre, extraordinary, peculiar, delicate or gross, occasionally familiar but mostly strange beyond belief,

the din of their multitude of voices making the strangest music imaginable—

I could stay right here for years and never *understand all this,* Rho thought in utter joy. *And the cultures, the worlds beyond, the sources of all this— I can* go *there! I can be somewhere* else *than where I've been trapped all this while, I can see those worlds and meet those people and* understand *them!* Because that was one of the things the Speech was for, and though he'd been able to speak it before, it hadn't been anything like *this.* Now he could look even at the signs by the gate hexes, and as he read the prosaic workaday scheduling notifications on them he could also see in the very words themselves their ancient pedigree. He could directly feel in them the power of the Aethyr that had invented them in the deeps of time—

Rho had to stop himself and swallow, and once more command himself to calm down and cope. *Here I am standing looking at a gate information standard as if it's the Most Central manifesting in person!* "Outside," Rho said under his breath, not caring if anyone saw him talking to himself.

But now as before, "outside" meant figuring out how to do it. *Well, best go ask for directions, then,* he thought, and started looking for a sign that would head him where he wanted to go without first sending him into a philosophical tizzy.

He walked on through he concourse, trying to read the signs a little less immersively. Shortly Rho caught sight of a general-information pillar of some bright silvery metal with bands of glowing words in many languages rotating around it. At once, apparently responding to his attention, one of the bands began displaying messages in Wellakhit and the Speech; and the first of these were the words MAIN INFORMATION AND STATIONMASTER'S OFFICE. After them a pointer-symbol rotated into view, indicating that he should proceed to his right.

Rho headed that way, pausing only once when his attention was caught by a shop window where the management seemed to be offering integuments, carapaces and skins for sale, and advertising INSTALLATION WHILE YOU WAIT. He couldn't help but stand there for some moments wondering what it would be like to have true body armor grafted onto you—*jeweled* body armor, to judge by the rather glamorous samples on display in the window. *What would my royal mother say?* Rho thought. And then, *And what would they say at lessons!* But the thought of his mother's likely response (he could just see her raised eyebrows) drowned out the thought of what of his schoolfellows and instructors might think.

Regretfully he left the shop window behind and made his way down the long broad shining concourse toward what appeared to be some kind of giant nest knitted out of the blue metal that appeared frequently in the public space here. And moving in and out of the space were a number of long, shining beings, glittering in light that shone down on them from the open frame-network and from invisible sources higher above.

What are those?

Rirhait, whispered something in his mind. Rho started, but it was only the Aethyr. *The dominant species on this planet.* And without warning it spilled a great flow of data into his mind: details about the species' anatomy, physiology, history, interactions with other species, languages, literature, mindset..

Rho had to stand still again and concentrate to keep from simply being mentally washed away in the flood of information. *I'm going to have to get used to this,* he thought. "A little more slowly?" he muttered, as a crowd of blobby bubbly creatures made of some clear jellylike substance and filled with peculiar colorful squirming shapes divided around him and flowed past him, throwing annoyed looks at him as they passed. And it was extremely strange that he could tell that they were looking at him, when they didn't have anything like eyes or faces to do it with—

Chelicerae, said his Aethyr (in a slightly different voice this time), and immediately dumped what seemed like another bucket of data over Rho. They were called the Mafesh and they hailed from a planet of a small collapsed red star so cool that it actually had steam in its upper atmosphere, not that this bothered the inhabitants of its one world Maf, because their big core-heated world was completely covered by a complex-hydrocarbon soup—

"Will you *slow down!*" Rho said to the empty air. "I'm never going to remember all this if you just dump it into my head like that!"

Yes you will, the Aethyr said.

Rho made a face, because he was none too sure. "Just don't do it when I'm in the middle of a conversation with somebody, all right?"

Noted, the Aethyr said. But it sounded a bit smug for some reason.

Rho just shook his head and made his way on along the concourse to that complex blue-metal framework. Inside it was a crammed-in assortment of seating frames and data panels and nonphysical displays hanging in the air. Rho slowed down a bit on his approach, as the information center had seemed to be coming down with Rirhait a couple of minutes ago. Now, though, he could see only one. It was a long-bodied creature wearing a segmented silver-blue shell as metallic as the gleaming blue framework around it. With many of the legs attached to its front segments it was tapping away at some sort of apparently featureless data input console, and staring at this with a wreathing bundle of long-stalked eyes that were rooted in one end segment.

Rho made his way up to the most open-looking space in the framework that would allow him to see and be seen by the creature. He arranged his face into what he hoped would be construed as a courteous expression, and said in the Speech, "Gentlebeing, the Aethyrs' favor on you; will you help me? I seek the Stationmaster."

"Yes, naturally you do, what else is new," the creature said, turning not a single one of all those eyes toward him. And it kept on working.

Rho paused, not sure if somehow he'd gotten his phrasing wrong, or if he was dealing with a species that had difficulties parsing the speech. "Sorry," he said. "Perhaps I didn't make myself clear." And then he found himself actually shaking with the thrill of being able to speak his next words to another living creature for the first time. "I am a wizard—" he said.

"Yes of course you are, why wouldn't you be, the place is coming down with them," the creature said. It sounded less than impressed.

It occurred to Rho that he had forgotten something. "And I am on errantry," he said hastily, "and I greet you."

The Rirhait fixed its gaze on him. It was a progressive business, this—one eye turning its regard to him, and then the next, and the next, and the next...

Rho had no trouble holding still for this performance, partly due to its uniqueness, and partly because he was after all a prince and used to having a lot of eyes on him. What he was *not* prepared for was, when those eyes were all trained on him, to see every one of them sequentially rolled at him and shifted away in an expression of exquisite ennui.

When the eyes were all pointed in every direction that was *not* toward Rho, *"And?"* the being said.

Rho opened his mouth and closed it again, having absolutely no idea where to go from here. "Uh," he said. Then he rolled his own eyes, for he could just hear his royal father saying, *Truly, my Prince? Grunts? Shall we have it noised about that mere surprise can reduce the Sunlord-to-Be to take refuge in grunting?*

Rho's frustration tipped him over the edge, and he threw any further thoughts of caution to the five airts. "Excellent gentlebeing," he said, drawing himself up tall, "perhaps a misunderstanding is in progress. Be it known to you that I am Roshaun ke Nelaid am Seriv am Teliuyve am Meseph am Veliz am Teriaunst am det Nuiiliat det Wellakhit, Son of the Sun Lord, Beloved of the Sun Lord, firstborn of the Sister of the Sun, Prince and Ruler in Waiting to the Wellakhit lands, and Guarantor of Wellakh."

The Rirhait kept tapping away at the data input. Finally it paused, swung exactly one eye in his direction, and said:

"How lovely for you."

Rho couldn't prevent his jaw from dropping.

"So was there something in particular I can assist you with," the Stationmaster said, "or do you have a cultural imperative that requires you waste other beings' time?"

Rho closed his mouth and then opened it again.

"Or wait," the Rirhait said. And slowly one after another of the eyes came around and trained themselves on Roshaun again. "You *haven't* actually been put up to this by one of my broodlings. Have you."

The tone was bizarrely accusatory. "What?" Roshaun said. "No." And then, because he honestly couldn't think of what else to say, he added, "My apologies."

The Rirhait began to emit an odd scratchy noise like something mechanical that badly needed a service call. Belatedly Rho realized the sound was laughter: apparently even the enacture property that invested the Speech with wizardly power didn't necessarily enable one to automatically parse emotional responses. "You're *sure* he didn't talk you into this? You *are*? What a pity."

More eyes trained themselves on Rho again, and the front end of the Rirhait was vibrating a bit. "Well then, young prince from the back of beyond, you have found the one you seek. So my question to you is: is this a business matter regarding relations between your homeworld and the Crossings, or do you need assistance with infrastructure?"

"The latter," Rho said. "I would like to go outside."

More eyes fixed themselves on him. "Rather dangerous for thin-skinned species such as yours, by and large, unless you come with subcutaneous rayshielding."

"I have some engineered in," Rho said, "and I can add to it with wizardry if there's need."

"All right," said the Stationmaster. "Turn around and look back the way you came. See the second standard on your right there, with the crosscorridor just beyond? Those are the legacy 200-group gates. All those hexes have access to the the facility exterior. Choose any one you like and specify your preferred destination using your instrumentality. There's an observation deck up on top of one of the hard transport parking and storage structures, if you prefer a relatively unobstructed view."

"That sounds acceptable," Rho said. "Thank you."

"If you decide to go further afield, princeling," the Stationmaster said, cocking several eyes at a nearby data tablet which looked to Rho to be just a plate of blank blue metal, "I note that your instrumentality is equipped for unlimited travel for the duration of your Challenge, Ordeal or Invigilation—"

"Challenge."

"Fine. Just present it to the gate attendant or gate management system, or automatic hex for access to the master gating system. Please study any gate's associated schedule carefully as outbound gatings do not necessarily imply timely inbound or return legs. Anything else?"

"Ah, no," Rho said. "Thank you."

"Very well." The Stationmaster turned the attention of almost all its eyes back to the dataplate it was working with; but one eye remained looking at Rho. "So go well then," it said.

Rho gave it a small bow and turned away.

"And well met," the Stationmaster said, as if under its breath, "on the journey."

Rho half-turned, both delighted to be saluted with the Avedictory for the very first time, and bemused by the tone, which sounded as if the being for some reason didn't usually care to be heard using it. But the Stationmaster was already threading its way off among the bluesteel tubes toward some other data input pad.

Standing there in the bustle of the open concourse, Rho paused, then shrugged a hand and headed for the 200 gates.

THE OBSERVATION DECK was not (as Rho had half hoped) a solitary experience. People were transiting into the small dedicated landing space almost constantly, and no sooner had Rho himself appeared there than the hex under his feet was flashing and vibrating to tell him to get off it.

He spared this no more than a moment's notice, though, and simply did as the gating hex wanted him to... because immediately upon appearing out in the open Rho was half deafened by the untempered roar of what he'd come up here to hear.

The broad space around Rho was quite barren—the solid roof of this building paved in the same shining white floor-substrate as the interior spaces of the Crossings, and devoid of any kind of furniture. Visiting beings who'd already left the landing area were wandering about across the wide expanse, some of them pressed up against the forcefields at the edges of the roof and gazing out at the broad cityscape beyond, a low spiky forest of glass and blue-metal towers, spilling nearly to the horizon in all directions.

But Rho wasn't interested in the landscape. Indeed he barely noticed it as he slowly moved out into the center of that wide space and stood still, his face turned up toward the sky. His senses were already being overwhelmed by light and sound—or at least what his mind and body insisted on experiencing as sound. The voice of Rirhath B's great star was all around him, tearing through the atmosphere in pulsing waves of ionizing radiation and splashing into him, the sleet of its neutrons tearing ceaselessly through him and everything else in their path. Even here, three times as far away as Wellakh was from its primary, the intensity of the star's actinic light set the cloud cover above nearly on fire with green-white fluorescence. Even the great depth and density of Rirhath B's atmosphere could stop only so much of the incoming torrent of brute power.

Rho stood there and just let the vast deafening blast of power wash over him. What the star was saying wasn't so much spoken as shouted. He had yet to hear Thahit itself in this way, but by comparison it would surely seem like a whisper. Trembling in the down-pouring onslaught of light and other radiation, Rho felt tempted to laugh at his desire to commune with something so vast and insensately powerful. *But I'm a wizard now,* he thought, *and I've always wanted to do this, so now that I can—*

Still, he was shy about it, and briefly put the moment off. After all, he had an excuse. *Listen before you talk,* his father always said. So Rho stood there with his eyes closed—not needing mere physical sight for what he was doing—and listened for some minutes more, trying to hear patterns; established and carefully-monitored pattern being the heart of the business of stellar management.

The star itself for all its ravening power was actually quite settled. Its own well-established cycles beat through it, as easily felt for Rho now as a Wellakhit pulse. The sound of multimillennial certainty was wound deep into them. This star's changing cycles of magnitude and other radiation output had remained steady for tens of thousands of centuries. If he got any information about them from the blast of data pouring down on him, it was a sense of business-as-usual about it. *Maintenance isn't anything this star needs,* he thought. Which was a relief: the sheer power of it would have made its management a challenging task.

But Rho kept on listening because doing so felt sheerly ravishing —though he could hardly bear the intensity of what he felt. *Everything's changing,* he thought. *Just yesterday I probably couldn't have borne this. Even the Speech still hurt sometimes...*

He had been so small when he first began to learn the Speech from his parents as a language of discourse, and first found out how it was not to be able to bear something. Rho had learned the words readily enough, but all through that early time he'd felt as if something was *wrong* with them, something was missing. The glances he'd caught his parents sharing over his head had meant nothing to him then.

Now of course he knew what they'd been thinking. Sometimes young ones destined for wizardry could feel the lack of the enacture property in the stripped-down version of the Speech that served merely for communication. Mostly this was seen as a positive indicator, a sign of good things to come. But at the time Rho didn't feel positive about it at all. Every time he said a word in the Speech he could feel something itching at the back of his head, trying to *happen*. And the older he got without wizardry being offered him, the more he and his parents independently began to fear that it never would be. Seeing how it troubled them when he talked about his discomfort, Rho learned to keep to himself this sense that the whole world was saying to him every day, *You are incomplete, there's something missing about you and you'll never make it right!*

But he also kept silent about his distress because he'd begun to understand the looks the courtiers and staff leveled at him on the days when he complained openly about the emptiness of the Speech. The officers and politicians attached to the royal household were starting to perceive him as potentially a permanent non-wizard, and therefore both a liability and a tool or weapon that might be used against the King or Queen.

Horrified, Rho quickly schooled himself to start acting "normal". He worked to move with an imitation of his mother's certainty or his father's grace, and to keep his face very still... like someone completely untroubled. The effort of it was endlessly wearying, and it hurt him—though not so much as the thought of endangering the King and Queen would have. And if Rho seemed intent on making sure that every word proceeding from his mouth where other people could hear was in Kings'-speak, the formal recension of south-continent Wellakhit spoken in the court by everyone who lived or worked there, well, he was content to let them think he was being studious about the official language... *not* that whenever possible he was avoiding the other because speaking it hurt.

Now, though...! Now he stood out under the light of a stranger-sun, gazing up at it, his eyes watering a bit—not even a Royal-house Wellakhit could look unblinking at such a ferocious star—and was able to say to it, without any pain at all, *"Dai stihó,* mighty cousin: how do you do?"

It took a little while for an answer to come back. Stars have business of their own, and even thought takes a bit of time to travel such a distance. But Rho felt himself regarded from that distance—stars notice when they are noticed—and after a little, the answer came back, vast, leisurely, and thoughtful: *I, Kishif, burn. And what of you?*

Rho shivered all over at the sound—or the feeling in his bones— of a piece of the living world speaking to him; and a *huge* piece at that, gigantic almost beyond grasping and crammed with raw power.

"I, uh," he said. ...And Rho laughed at himself. There he was, the son of the Sunlord of Wellakh, reduced once more to grunting.

"Kishif my cousin," he said in the Speech, "I burn as well. If much more slowly."

Long may it be so, Kishif said.

"And for you also," said Rho.

For a little while he stood there while beings of many species walked and scuttled and slid and floated around him, paying him little or no attention, and he and Kishif chatted—if so small a word as "chat" can be applied to a conversation with a star—about how her atmosphere was feeling and whether the SunTap power source rooted in it was irking Kishif at all, and what Rho was doing there. Kishif inquired politely enough how her very distant cousin Thahit was doing (for regardless of the preconceptions of smaller beings, stars are highly social creatures and can easily tell when a wizard has been collegially affiliated, even sporadically or at a distance, with another stellar body).

Rho told her in a general way how Thahit was getting on— having the pattern data from the simulator to judge by—while trying to bear up against the immensity of the physical and mental reality of the tremendous being he was dealing with, the great weight and age of her. They spent a while asking and answering, Kishif apparently attempting to get a better feeling for the difficulties and challenges of an unstable star, Rho trying to clarify matters without becoming too specific (for it occurred to him that he wouldn't like to violate Thahit's privacy). And it was only when Rho's skin began to feel a bit hot that he realized that this discussion should probably be brought to a close, as his hereditary internal shielding against ultraviolet could only do so much about exposure to a blue-white giant.

"Most excellent Kishif," he said, "with regret, I think I must retire."

The response took a few moments to come back. *Yes, of course, you've much to do,* Kishif said, *Starsnuffer to foil, the usual sort of thing. Come back again when you've got matters sorted...* And she trailed off in a huge offhand mutter (or shouted mutter) of power and turned her attention to something apparently pertaining to her corona.

Rho blinked and staggered a little as he came back to full consciousness of what was going on around him. *It's not really that easy,* he thought, *talking to stars. Even when they're well-balanced and friendly...* Suddenly he understood why his royal father looked so wrung out and weary sometimes when he came back in from Sunplace's highest terrace, where he went to work with Thahit alone.

"ARE YOU ALL RIGHT?" said a voice from right behind him.

Hastily Rho turned and found himself looking at another hominid. There was no telling what world it came from—no surprise, in a facility this large. The hominid was a biped like him, and four-limbed; its hair was much shorter than his, and its skin was a peculiar sort of pale pink color. It had longer-than-shoulder-length hair that was surprisingly close to the red-gold color of his father's, and it was dressed in a tightly-woven one-piece garment with a surprising number of pockets all over it.

The being had spoken to him in the Speech, and so he responded in the same. "Yes," he said. "I was thinking of going in: the heat is beginning to be an issue."

"*Just* the heat?" the being said, and laughed. "How are you even out here without a protective suit?"

"Well, how are *you* so?" Rho said, looking the being over. "I can see none."

The stranger reached into a pocket and did something with one hand: twiddled a control, perhaps. Around it a faint skin of pale rosy light could now be seen shivering. "New model," the being said. "Selective plasma sine/wavicle occultation."

"Oh indeed," Rho said, interested. That was a fairly advanced technology, one of many to come out of the research-and-development side of the Interconnect Project—one of many ways to do small-scale shielding on planets that needed temporary protection from

their stars. "I didn't know they had spun out personal implementa-
tions of that already."

"Put enough valuta behind it and things happen faster," the being
said, and flashed a slightly mercenary smile at him. "Saw some news
feed that said the tourist authority based here commissioned them
for travelers passing through to rent."

"Handy," Rho said. "Such would certainly make it easier for visitors to visit other sites of interest on the planet."

"True," the being said. "I guess there must be some. They probably get a little tired of being in the Crossings' shadow all the time."

Rho tilted his head in agreement while saying in thought to his
Aethyr, *Can you tell me who this may be?*

Privacy lock obtains, said one of the Aethyr's many voices, a dryly
informational one. *Genetically of the stream of hominid heritage widespread in the Tashammeh Arm of the galaxy,* said another.

In the back of his mind Rho was promptly shown a map of his
home galaxy, concentrated on a region just beyond the spur arm in
which Rirhath B was located. A series of bright pointers flashed into
existence, displaying numerous starsystems in that area. *Sexual
cognate: species-orthodox female. Species: Archanin with post-initial species
diaspora genetic alterations. Physiology type BCAIFDFEHH.* The ten-
character descriptor system that Rho knew well from his father's
interstellar consulting work would break down into numerous
subtypes, but he didn't need to get into that right this minute: "oxy-
gen-breathing land-dwelling hominid" summed it up well enough.

*Public-information data stored in the Crossings transit system shows a
recent origin here,* said another voice, and one of the congeries of stars
scattered across that view pulsed softly. Its label said *Phaleron,* and
the view pushed in to illustrate the three hominid-inhabitable worlds
in the system, a singleton planet and a two-world gravitically-
conjoined pair—

"Sorry," the being said. "Did I say something wrong?"

Rho blinked and realized he was going to have to remember that
normal people would have no idea he was communing with the
Aethyrs, and the being—*the Archaint,* he corrected himself. *She.* —

wouldn't have been out of line if she'd taken offense. "No, not at all," he said, "apologies, I'm still—adjusting." He didn't feel a need right this moment to say what he was adjusting to.

"Oh," she said, and smiled again. "Good, I wouldn't want to offend anybody when I'd hardly just got here."

"Not at all." He'd long been schooled not to smile too readily at people he'd just met, but this once, for an alien, he didn't see a point in being overly stringent about it, and returned her smile.

Present intrapersonal emotional/intentional dynamic: curious, said one of his Aethyr's quieter background voices, so quiet that Rho almost missed it. *Overtly interested. Distress level: medium.*

Rho blinked at that. Most of the Aethyr's voices seemed more assertive about expressing themselves. This one he had to strain a bit to hear. *Not always easy when all this data is vying for my attention. I'm going to have to learn how to filter everything down... Meanwhile, show some interest, for pity's sake, don't be self-centered!* "You're perhaps between transits on your way to somewhere else?"

"Uh, no, not as such. I was looking for someone, and not finding her, and I needed a break. Came up here for some fresh air."

He had to laugh at that, as it took a very specific type of physiology to consider Rirhath B's air "fresh". "I mean," she said, "in life these days you get used to being stuck inside so often, that outside is kind of a treat..."

There was an odd thread of sorrow behind her words. *Lonely,* Rho thought. *She sounds lonely...* If there was a tone of voice Rho knew, it was that one. "If you've had enough of the freshness," he said, "perhaps you want to come back inside with me. I had thought some refreshment might be pleasant."

"It's not a bad idea," she said. The expression she was now wearing, if she'd been a Wellakhit, was one that would have suggested she was trying to master herself emotionally. "And I've got some time to spare. Let's go in—"

She paused, then laughed. "I don't even know your name."

Even at this distance from home, old habits learned on Wellakh meant he was not going to give a chance-met stranger more detail than necessary. "Rho."

"I'm Avseh. Let's go in, Rho."

DIRECTLY ACROSS FROM the 200 gate hexes was an open-seating area provided with what looked like every kind of seating furniture known to sentience, as well as a smart-floor area that would create custom seating for you on the fly. At the kiosk, Rho spent some moments of bewilderment trying to get to grips with the huge range of offerings laid out on the menu displayed across the surface of the counter. Finally he chose a flavored water with tailored additives that analyzed your body chemistry as you drank, so that the water shifted its aromatic-ester composition as you ingested it to a flavor state described by the advertising described as "nonstimulating and mildly agreeable".

"Only mildly?" Avseh said, tapping the image of some sort of pink juice drink and then pausing to dig around in the carrybag she wore slung over one shoulder.

"I wouldn't like to overdo it so early in the day," Rho said as he dug around in his pocket for one of his own credit plaques.

"Oh, no, no, Emissary," said the Rirhait as it waved at the drinks disposer and floated the containers up to the counter. "The charge is handled."

"What?"

It wreathed a few eyes at him in amusement. "The system sensed your instrumentality as soon as you walked up. Your charge and your companion's went on the the Crossings infrastructure account as per usual. Unless you require a charge reversal—"

"Ah, no, of course not. My thanks."

"Not at all, Emissary," said the Rirhait behind the counter, and waved all its upper legs at him in a good-natured way as it turned back to its work.

Rho discovered as they took their drinks and walked over to their seats that he was actually trembling with the residual thrill caused at being so addressed by a being who had never seen him before and might never see him again, but nonetheless recognized him as a wizard. It was heady stuff.

He realized Avseh was staring at him as they sat down. "Um, sorry," Rho said hurriedly, "did I do something culturally unacceptable, perhaps you would have preferred to pay for that—"

"What? No! But—you're one of *them?*"

"'Them?'"

"A wizard." She went unusually pink in the face.

"Yes," Rho said, and did his best to keep his disbelief at being able to say it out of his voice. He kept feeling as if one of the Aethyrs might suddenly descend in glory from more central regions and announce that there had been a horrible clerical error and Rho wasn't meant to be a wizard after all. *But no, surely they'd never be so cruel—*

"Really," Avseh said, looking at him strangely.

"Yes, really. And since you recognize me, your world then is one where the Great Art is practiced in the open?"

She laughed. The sound was somewhat bitter. "Yes," she said, "for all the good it's doing at the moment."

It surprised Rho how this response unnerved him. He was equally surprised to discover how little time it had taken him to make the jump from seeing this being as an alien to seeing her as a young woman, maybe fifty or sixty sunrounds old, truly only a little older than he. *But all by herself here,* Rho thought. *Upset and alone—*

"I am on errantry," Rho said, "and while I cannot go into the particulars—" *—because I don't know what they are yet!—* "if I can help you, I will. You said you were looking for someone?"

"Uh, yes. Her name is Mevseh. I guess she's why I spoke to you up on the roof there. I'd thought she might have gone up there herself and—" Avseh looked fairly embarrassed, if Rho was judging her expression correctly. "It's just—Mev kept looking at the sky like that when we were leaving home. Like she couldn't really believe what was going on." She looked bitter, now. "And who could blame her—"

"Why? What *was* going on?"

She shook her head. "Um. True, it's a big universe after all, but half the people from there are coming out through here—"

"I haven't been here that often," Rho said. "And I just got here myself. Very likely I missed the details of whatever's been happening."

"Well, it's been in the news. Our star, it's called Phaleron, it's in the next arm over and it's getting ready to flare. They think it might destroy all three of the inhabited worlds in the system if it can't be stopped. For a while we thought our wizards could keep it from happening, but apparently they can't."

She paused and ran her hands through her hair, a distraught gesture that suddenly reminded Rho of his father. "And finally all the governments got together and told everybody to leave the planets as quickly as they can. There's some kind of interstellar disaster plan that's being implemented, but it's just getting started and my family didn't want to wait. Our mother's in the government and she had warning of this months ago, so she started making plans. The week before the announcement was made there were already a lot of rumors going around that something bad was going to happen. The announcement of the crisis, our mother thought—which meant the gating systems would get incredibly choked up and we might get caught in it. Finally she said, 'No point in waiting, we should get our things together and leave.' And so we did. But there were complications..."

That bitter look again. Rho felt suddenly and terribly out of his depth. He was used to thinking of planetary disaster in broad strokes, because that was how his family had been dealing with it for centuries: vast swathes of infrastructure in need of rebuilding or repair, the replacement of whole atmospheres and ecosystems. But here was an aspect of such a disaster that was just as valid—one displaced person, all by herself and in pain. And Rho couldn't even think of what to say to her. To even suggest that he could begin to share her sorrow seemed shallow and stupid.

"I wish I could help," Rho said.

She looked at him out of that bitterness as if he'd said something completely unexpected. "That's very good of you," she said. "But I don't know how you possibly could..."

Rho tilted his head in negation of the idea that there might be nothing he could do to help. But for the moment he was confused that he'd heard no mention of this flare event, even as a *potential* flare event, from his father.

But then why would he mention it to me? Rho thought, feeling his own bitterness in retrospect. *Assuming he'd even heard of it. It is a big universe; stars flare all the time and this one, this Phaleron, is a long way away from us. ...And anyway, why would he have said anything to me? What could I possibly have done to help?*

But all that's over now! And the urge to help was certainly there. This is why I'm out here, after all, so why not?

Rho reached out into the air and pinched his Aethyr into existence. Avseh flinched a little, eyes going wide in astonishment at the sight of it. "What, what's that—"

"Wizardry," Rho said. And despite his desperate attempt to restrain it, a small smile popped out. He tried to hide it right away, but it was too late.

Avseh didn't notice: she was too busy staring at the little burning light in his hand. "Is *that* what it looks like? I thought it was supposed to be some kind of book you read out of, or— What does it, I mean how does it—"

"It tells me things," Rho said. "Let's see what it can tell me about this star of yours—"

Then he heard himself, and stopped, embarrassed. "Wait, I'm sorry, that's all wrong," Rho said. "The star can wait a few minutes more! Who were you looking for?"

"My clone," Avseh said.

That made Rho blink a bit: he had heard of such folk but had never met one. "Your clone-group was traveling," he said, "and one of you became separated from the others?"

"Yes," she said. "It sounds so idiotic after the fact. There was an incredible crush of people when we came in, though, so many folk from our old world, heading to the new one. Normally we can feel one another a good distance away. The bond's not just genetic: because we're Archaint, and most Archaint are empaths or telepaths, there's a mindlink as well. But we didn't realize how in a place like this it gets drowned out... especially when it's so much busier than usual. Too many different kinds of thought, too many different kinds of mind. Too much like looking for six other grains of sand on a beach. And we weren't wearing mechanical locators, we never even thought of it, because when you can always feel where all the others are, who'd bother?..."

She sounded utterly wretched. Once again Rho wasn't quite sure how to proceed. "I've heard it said that members of a clone may experience physical side effects if they become separated for too long—"

"The word you're looking for is 'die,'" Avseh said. "And if one member of the clone dies the bond between the others is weakened, and—"

Her voice was growing choked: she was seconds from weeping. *"No,"* Rho said.

Avseh looked at him in sudden confusion.

"There will be no dying," Rho said. "I forbid it."

Her look turned from despair to a kind of amused annoyance. "Oh really."

"Yes, *really,"* Rho said, and scowled his best I-am-a-Prince-do-not-dare-argue-with-me scowl. "No more of that for a moment. I need to think." He turned his attention back to the Aethyr. "Do you know your star's name?"

"Didn't I tell you? Phaleron."

"That's what you *call* it," Rho said. "Do you know its *name?"*

Avseh stared at him in confusion. "What? No."

Rho sighed. "Never mind... the identification will be positive enough with the system-primary name. Phaleron—"

The place in the back of his mind where the Aethyr displayed its images flurried with them. Rho let it get on with its sorting. "Once you find your clone-sister," he said, "where will you and the rest of your clone go then?"

"We're heading for a system a couple of lightyears away," Avseh said. "There's a planet there called Melesh; it's another of the Archanin worlds. Our branch of the Archaint exordium has 'right of return' there because our planet was originally settled from there. Melesh has been suffering from net offplanet migration for centuries, and so they're actually kind of glad to have people coming back. There's plenty of room for us, the climate and the atmosphere are similar..." She hitched her shoulders up a little and down again, a gesture that Rho didn't understand. *A shrug,* one of the Aethyr-voices whispered in his ear.

This is their star, whispered another of them.

It showed him Phaleron—another of those troublesome little yellow dwarfs that could have been Thahit's twin. Across the floor of his mind spilled a network of graphs, mathematical equations, luminosity curves, statistics of every kind.

It was something of a stretch to analyze them quickly without having the stellar simulator to feed them into, but Rho could manage. Just from looking at the light curves for the past few tens of Phaleron-sunrounds he could see something about them that made him feel a bit queasy—a morbidity that he little liked the look of. *Light bleeding away, irregularly, out-of-cycle...* The look of it pained him. Cycle was everything for stars: the lack of it or derangement of it was never a good sign.

Then (in the statistics and the historical reports) came the first of several truly bad patches of weather, borderlining on the "bubblestorm" state in which the star repeatedly coughed great gouts and bubbles of plasma out across its system: always a sign of a star getting seriously sick in the regions beneath its heliopause. And the wizards in the worlds around Phaleron tried to intervene, but the interventions were too few, too ineffective and had been left too late to affect what was happening... the long-deferred bubblestorm, building inexorably toward a serious flare. *No question but that it will seriously damage all three of those worlds, if not destroy them outright. A single day's rotation for each world would be enough to scorch them bare.*

"I don't understand it," Rho said, opening his eyes to find Avseh giving him a rather peculiar look. "Why didn't they call in expert help?"

"They did, it didn't work—"

His first thought at that was: *Not expert enough by half. Speak immediately to the King, take his advice on this!* But hard behind that idea came, not so much another idea, but a couple of feelings, quite intense ones: embarrassment paired with an intense unwillingness. He could just hear how the conversation would go. *My son, wait, you're a* wizard? *And you didn't come straightway and tell us? Instead you ran away, ran off to—*

Rho hastily clamped down on that line of reasoning before the guilt and frustration inherent in the scenario swamped him. *Besides, I have the tools now. I can figure this out. I'm a wizard now and I don't need help to manage this!*

And the joy of it—the longer he examined the problem—was that this opinion wasn't mere bluster: he really did *not* need help. Thahit had produced a very similar episode of deep-atmosphere pathology several hundred sunrounds before, and the Queen regnant at that time had dealt with it fairly quickly, leaving extensive notes after the fact. Rho had in fact re-enacted her solution and variants on it more than once in the simulator, with his father looking on, and had found it— *Well, not a* simple *fix*, he thought. *But manageable.*

As for the problem with this star, and that he should be here right now to deal with it, Rho was caught somewhere between delight and annoyance. The delight was easily expressed: *It's just as father and mother always said. There's a question to which every wizard is the answer. And by the Aethyrs' will I've been brought here to answer this one!* And the annoyance was straightforward too. *All the tales of Challenge I've heard have been so awful. Death and destruction, puzzles too hard to solve. Is this all I'm going to get?*

"Still," Rho muttered, "no point in complaining. Here's this mess and someone needs to *do* something about it..."

Avseh was gazing at him in complete confusion. "Yes, but *what...?*"

"What I was sent to do," Rho said. "I shall go to Phaleron and bring them the solution they need. But first of all I will handle a solution closer to home." He looked at her drink. "Are you done with that?"

She glanced from the container, to Rho, to the container again. "Uh, I suppose so."

He held out a hand. Avseh handed the drink container to him, watching while Rho wiped the rim of it where she had been drinking. Then he passed the Aethyr to those fingers and let it sit there briefly.

A few moments later Rho put the container down on the table and let the Aethyr wink out. "Come with me then," he said, "for there's someone we need to see."

SOME MINUTES later at the great central nest of blue metal tubing, the Stationmaster looked up from its endless data input and regarded Rho with numerous annoyed eyes. "*You* again," it said, with a kind of amused disgust. "What in the worlds is it now?"

"This being requires your assistance," said Rho.

"*Every* being in this place requires my assistance, it seems," said the Stationmaster, the disgust growing more pronounced. "There are days when I really wonder what we're paying the help for."

Avseh looked uncomfortable, but this answer left Rho feeling somewhat cheered. He was more than familiar with this kind of cranky-functionary response from years of interchanges with Sunplace's most ancient retainers, and he knew from parental example exactly how to deal with it. "Doubtless you do," he said. "No matter. Attend me. You naturally do covert genetic-material detection on all creatures entering this facility—"

Some of the eyes trained on Rho acquired an unusually sharp-edged look. "We never discuss ongoing security operations," the Master said.

"That's well, for I have neither time nor desire to enter into such a discussion. By Wizard's Right I require access to your system for a few programming microcycles, no more."

Once again all those eyes were staring at him, and this time it wasn't a look of lazy dismissal: it was serious annoyance. "For what purpose?"

"Genetic material tracking," said Rho. "Somewhere in the facility is a member of this being's clone-family. They have become separated and have no mechanical aid to assist them in relocation. Their genetic identity data will be near-identical within a vanishingly tiny tolerance, and its location will therefore involve no invasion on other travelers' privacy."

"You can get at the data from inside your instrumentality, surely," said the Master.

"Not the genetic-material data," Rho said. "Correctly, that is protected. I therefore require your assistance under the Right. There is certainly an unlock code..."

He extended the Aethyr toward the Stationmaster. It angled several eyes toward it, and then cautiously extended a claw into the brilliance.

Rho felt the information he needed snug into the Aethyr and run like wildfire down the lines of the little wizardry he had laid out ready inside it. "Thank you," he said. "Obviously this data will be deleted immediately after use."

"As if I won't be changing that password a millisecond later," said the Stationmaster.

"Of course you will," Rho said. He paused a moment, watching absently as the inner data processing functions of the Aethyr riffled through the entirety of the Crossings' genetic identification data. There was so much of this that it actually took several seconds before there was a result.

He watched with utter satisfaction as, one after another, six lights flickered into being on a map of the Crossings that the Aethyr was building in the back of his mind. Four lights together: one light at a considerable distance, right across the huge facility, over by the entrance to one of the methane-breathers' food halls: and a sixth one right by the single orange-golden light that marked Rho's spot at the Stationmaster's office.

"Now, worthy being, I have coordinates for you," Rho said, and read them off. "If you would be so kind as to program a convenient hex?"

"In the 200's again," said the Stationmaster, claws tapping away once more at its seemingly blank metallic input pad.

"Wait," Avseh said, breathless. "What are you—do you mean that—"

"She's a long way across the facility," Rho said, "but you'll be with her in a minute. Stay out of the methane, it almost certainly smells dreadful and will do you no good. After that, noble Stationmaster, once they're together again, if you would kindly transfer them to this location—" He read off the second string of numbers.

"Do I look like a gate podium attendant to you?" the Stationmaster muttered. "I need to have that looked into. Please Gods it's not infectious."

"I must go," Rho said to Avseh. "But go on: go to your clone-sister, and rejoin your family, and tell them all the Aethyrs greet them by me."

Shocked, astonished, Avseh stared at Rho—then threw her arms around him and squeezed him very tight. "Thank you," she said. *"Thank you!"*

And without a word more she took off at a run toward the 200 hexes.

Rho watched her go, fascinated, happy for her, glad to have been able to help. *But that star is waiting! And* there's *what I've been sent to do—*

"Is there anything else I can do for you in my incredibly ample free time?" the Stationmaster said.

"I could use a gating to these coordinates," Rho said, and began to read.

The Stationmaster snarled something in Rirhait that even knowledge of the Speech seemed incapable of rendering, and tapped at its input pad even faster.

3

So it was (he felt quite sure the songs would someday say) that Prince Roshaun ke Nelaid-and-all-the-rest-of-it went forth upon his Challenge-day to heal the sick star Phaleron—

At least that was how it *should* have gone. Typically, though, the business turned out to be not quite so straightforward.

Even wizardry has its bureaucracies... its etiquettes of cooperation, and its best-practice standards for various levels of wizardly intervention, with and without supervision. Rho knew—having been told so in no uncertain terms by his father—that to merely arrive on a planet and announce "I'm here to save your world" is seen, at best, as a touch gauche, and at worst as quite egotistical. Wizardry has reasons for its structures and its channels, and wise wizards observe them if they want to get anything done.

So before leaving the Crossings Rho spent a short time with his Aethyr determining exactly to whom he needed to make his case, and where they were. Perhaps unsurprisingly, most of the system's most senior and most gifted wizards and all those who had any experience at all with stars had been for weeks in practically nonstop conference sessions sited on the most distant of their three worlds, working out what to do to keep Phaleron from flaring until the planetary populations could be evacuated. So to that meeting Rho immediately made his way.

The people of Phaleron's three planets were, like Avseh's people, of Archaint-hominid descent, and (like many of them) empathic telepaths. This meant that under present circumstances, being around them when they were in such distress was, well, *distressing.* Though Wellakhit had something of a reputation for being mind-deaf, Rho nonetheless felt a headache coming on as he made his way through a large ornate room sited at the heart of a government building in one of the planetary capitals.

He had managed with the Aethyrs' help to make contact with the Planetary wizard in charge of the emergency endeavors, a planetary management specialist named Tarat. It took not much time to find him, as he was the tall shaggy-haired one in a sort of long silken wrap, standing at the center of a huge informational Speech-diagram showing details about the star Phaleron, a great aggregation of data and imagery. He was also the center of a crowd of other wizards who were both telepathically and vocally shouting at each other, while he attempted (apparently without much success) to keep them calm.

Rho immediately felt sorry for him. Without hesitation he went straight into the heart of that circle, took up stance there with the utter self-assurance of someone instructed by royalty in the art of looking certain, and waited in well-mannered but imperious silence until the wizards surrounding Tarat started to fall quiet at the sudden appearance of someone in their midst who was definitely not at all local.

"Cousins all," Rho said in one of the phrasings used by wizards bent on joining an intervention already in progress, *"dai stihó!* Greeting you in the Aethyrs' names, I charge you to tell me your trouble and make me part of its solution!"

They gazed at him in astonishment, and Tarat after a moment said, *"You're* the wizard who messaged me before? You're on Ordeal!"

The word wasn't one a Wellakhit would use, but he understood it as a cognate Speech-term to Challenge. "Yes."

"Well then of course we need to give your input extra weight! And you are here from—"

"Wellakh."

From the empty air Tarat retrieved what looked like a little book-roll, pulled it apart in his hands, and scrolled through it. *"Oh,"* he said after a moment, the emotions rolling off him quickly becoming divided between horror and a kind of stricken, impressed under-standing. "Oh, my, yes, I see why this would be something you'd know about! How is it that we haven't heard from you until now? — But sorry, sorry, you're just *now* on Ordeal, as of—what, the last *rotation?* You didn't waste your time, did you cousin! Never mind, thank you so very much for coming, in the One's name tell us what you have in mind, because we need help in a hurry!"

Rho immediately turned his attention to the reference spell circle on the floor beneath all their feet. "Well. Before I got here, I was having a look at your chromosphere figures for the last—what do you call it? Month?" He had always wished Wellakh had a moon: he resolved to have a look at this world's specimen if he had time. "And you see this curve here, this is all wrong, this shouldn't be—"

"Well of course it's *wrong*, the star's about to flare, isn't it?"

"No, you're missing what I'm saying, this is atypical! If you look down here, yes, the heliopause, look at these dynamics, see the skew on those numbers, why's the curve bulging like that? And look here at the heliopause, it's deranged, yes, but this looks rather short-term, doesn't it? Yes, here, let's have a look at the iron lines—"

It took Rho a few moments' work with his Aethyr to work out how to display a full chromatographic spectrum for the star, but once he had it hanging in the air before them, Rho saw clearly that his initial impression had been right. What was going on here was dangerous in the short term, indeed *quite* dangerous... but the effects didn't seem to have penetrated to the levels of the star's structure closer to the core. It was, at the end of the day, an upper-atmospheric phenomenon with only a moderate amount of mass and convection devoted to the ongoing morbidity dynamic, and so it could be derailed—

"All right, good, yes, look here," Rho said, excited and pleased that there was a possible response to the problem so readily available, "I know this is going to sound peculiar to you but it's not as bad as it looks—" He plunged into what his father would doubtless have dismissed as a fairly easygoing analysis of a case of diseased stellar chromatography.

Tarat meanwhile was all but goggling at him, as if the Aethyrs had sent him some kind of unstable genius. Rho found this funny—not to mention even headier than being called "Emissary" for the first time —and found himself having trouble not bursting out laughing at the sudden wash of amazed respect from the other.

Tarat was staring at Rho's diagrams. "And this will—" He sounded as if he hardly dared say it. "This strategy will put the whole problem right, won't it! Not just delay the flare, but derail it entirely!" An astonished look of sudden hope, of hope that its owner had plainly never hoped to feel again, washed over his face. "Powers that Be be praised, this will do the work that's needed, *this will stop it!*"

"Well," Rho said, "at least it will persuade your star to choose another path." No one simply told a star "You're going to have to stop that *now*" and expected results. The thought of trying such a stunt with Thahit, after hearing some of his father's stories, horrified him. You explained, you cajoled, you wheedled, and sometimes you got quite forceful, even physical. But stars were themselves quite physical in their outlook, and a good robust intervention was not only accept- able but sometimes expected as a sign of respect.

"Yes," Tarat said, "yes it will—"

"So what do we do now?"

"Well, we'll need to call in the other wizards who're working on this, and the planetary governments, and then we'll have to take some time to allow for decision-making—"

True choice is made in a flash, he could hear his father saying, *in a breath. Those asking for time to think in the face of a crisis are routinely looking for ways to avoid dealing with it. Once you know the right way to go, for all Aethyrs' sakes don't give them time to start arguing about it!*

Rho gave Tarat a long look across his book-scroll. "I'd say you're short of time for discussion," Rho said. "This approach will work if the management is implemented quickly. But within a matter of hours this situation will have progressed too far to be altered. Look at that set of variables there!" He pointed at one tightly nested group of core energy statements that was winding itself tighter and tighter as they watched. "And there, the convection transfer in and out of the upper chromosphere. If that energy gets to the surface and begins to derange things further, well—"

He did what was apparently in at least some places the local version of a shrug, with his shoulders instead of one hand.

Tarat's eyes went wide. So did those of many of the others standing around them.

And it was as if that simple gesture was what tipped them over into action. "We'll call the local specialists and the governments' representatives in," Tarat said. "You'll explain it to them?"

"It seems that's what I'm here for," Rho said, and had to bite his lip to keep a sudden grin of triumph from popping out. *Most inappropriate,* he could hear the King saying. *Restrain yourself.*

Rho did. But at the same time he found himself wishing his father was here to see this...

THE CALL duly went out to the various experts and dignitaries who had to be convinced that this was the way to save their lives, and those of their worlds, and their star. What ensued was a long session, and not an easy one. By the time it was coming to what felt like an end, Rho had lost count of the number of times he'd wanted to bang all their heads against the single small table in the middle of the big room where they all met to stand in a circle and have matters explained to them. The various beings and entities spent what seemed like endless time assailing him with annoying questions that were, he had to admit, completely understandable under the circumstances, even though from Rho's point of view they were fairly stupid.

The only question that satisfied him at all was when the king or chief presider or mayor or whatever of one of the smaller nations on the most sun-distant of the system's three planets said, at the end of the clearest explanation Rho could come up with, "How can we be sure this will work?"

King Nelaid would have said, *In this universe, no one can be certain of anything. Demanding certainty is demanding reassurance that what happened yesterday will happen today. The laws of averages alone militate against it*— Rho knew, though, that though his father was right, that approach wasn't what was needed here.

So he simply shrugged again, that gesture for some reason seeming to have a near-wizardly effect on these people. "It worked on Thahit," Rho said, "three hundred forty-one sunrounds ago. And the planet lived to see another sunround. Indeed, at least three hundred forty-one more."

Then he folded his arms and waited to see what they'd do.

To his utter astonishment, they *decided*, all of them, in a rush, and accepted his plan.

The tension in the great room, of course, didn't now relax: it got much worse, much of that increase coming from the wizards who were going to be expected to pull off this feat. "Will you come with us?" said Tarat.

"Of course I will," Rho said. He was very glad to be invited, and with so many natives of the star's system handy to explain what a stranger not native to the local stellar economy was doing there, he felt it likely that they need expect no more than the usual problems from the star itself.

It took a while more to complete the formalization of the agreement to intervene, and to pull together and fully brief the wizardly team that would step into the star to put its problem right, and to set in place what protections they could against the electromagnetic disturbances that would inevitably propagate through the system in their intervention's wake. But at long last they were all standing together inside a wide forcefield-enclosure poised over that burning, roiling surface, and Rho looked down into the turbulent fires and felt, peculiarly, satisfaction, even before any of them had done anything. It was his very first in-person stellar intervention as a wizard, the very first time in his life that he would do what he had been born to do, trained to do, intended to do, from the very beginning. He was, at long last, exactly where he was supposed to be.

Even if I fail, he thought— But he wasn't going to fail. This was actually going to be a fairly simple piece of work.

The star, whose name was Peklimut, resisted them. This was expected, since stars are as resistant to sudden change imposed from without as any other being. *And now,* Rho thought as the forcefield-bubble from which they were working began to sink into the star and be buffeted by the inner fluid turbulence of its upper chromosphere, *now comes what I've been waiting for!*

He knew that almost every wizard meets the Lost Aethyr at some point, or in some form, during their Challenge. And when the star began to rage at them as the wizardry meant to change its behavior set deeply into its structure, and some thousands of partitions of distance beneath the intervention group turned into a wildly raging battleground of forces, *This is it!* Rho thought. *This is the combat I always thought I knew how to imagine when I lay on my couch at home, thinking how it would finally be when I became a wizard.* Which was why he found it funny in a way how prosaic this seemed by comparison with his dreams; as if the Lost One should turn up in dark-flaming glory on your doorstep and then tell you that your Challenge was to clean your room.

Not that the star didn't try to flare right then, of course—and worse than Thahit had, in its day. But Rho knew what to do about that, hands-on. And in wizardly seeming, "hands on" was the modality he used to control the impulse, reaching down into the shrieking and rebellious roil of plasma beneath them and simply seizing hold of the forces trying to come broiling up from beneath the heliopause at them, holding them in place beneath it and *not allowing them to move.*

It was just as well Rho had no time to panic, plunged into his very first wizardry as he was almost without preparation. But wizardry aside, he knew what needed doing, having done it in the stellar simulator. And the Aethyr helped him by simply casting that work into wizardly idiom, and laying out the spell diagrams he needed to speak his way through. *Or shout!* Rho thought between breaths, for the roar of the angry star was enough to deafen anything living. *So concentrate, so that 'living' is a condition that endures awhile more!* And he focused on the words in the Speech and on feeling the wizardry come live around him—

Seeing that Rho's strategy was working, the other wizards were already following suit. Other hands were thrust down along with his into the burning maelstrom, and all of them hung on together while under them the star bucked and writhed and tried to burst out of its own gravitational confines, attempting in a spasm of insensate fury and frustration to blow.

But it couldn't—not with all of the intervention group imposing their joint will on its physics—and didn't. And when Peklimut had exhausted its rage and its inner atmosphere began to settle, there was leisure for Rho to step back a little and watch as the star's own native wizards reached down more subtly into the mathematics of Peklimut's physical situation, setting deeply into the star riders and provisos to its equations that would prevent further such flare events from having a chance to start setting themselves up in the first place.

Finally, after what seemed like hours—but what was actually only a space of maybe a thousand breaths—they were all able to step away from the work and rise to the surface again, leaving Peklimut regarding them with a combination of annoyance and relief, and a general sense of being glad its (admittedly) helpful intruders were all done with business now and well out of its mass, because it had had enough of this to last it a lifetime.

On the return to Varesh, the planet where the intervention group and the planetary dignitaries had met, that was when Rho finally felt —along with understandable and inevitable triumph—the equally inevitable weight of the energy expenditure spent on the wizardry he'd just enacted, as it fell down all over him like a wet blanket, seemingly dragging at both his limbs and his brains. *Oh, my couch, I want you,* Rho thought as he sagged against a handy chair and propped himself upright with both hands while people crowded around him, congratulating him. *Ah, to get back home and just fall down for a while!*

He could imagine the conversation that would ensue when he suddenly turned up in Sunplace, not just a wizard all of a sudden but *exhausted* by wizardry—and this too fit none of his previous fantasies about the event. There should have been a triumphant return, there should have been tears and laughter and hugging, the dignitaries of Wellakh should have been called in and bowed before the new wizard who would have laughed kindly at their discomfiture at finding all their whispered doubts to be invalid, now and forever. But instead all Rho wanted now was to stagger into his parents' chamber and show them his Aethyr and say *Yes, royal father, yes, queenly mother, I am a wizard now, and can we of your grace have this conversation later because I'm dead on my feet!*

For the time being, though—because his mother and father had drilled into him the meaning and uses of diplomacy—Rho had little choice but to stand there and suffer with a smile the accolades of the people he'd come so far to help, making as much nontechnical conversation as he could manage and accepting food and drink from them (at least the food and drink his Aethyr allowed him: once or twice he was nearly most kindly poisoned). But it was a relief when he felt he'd accepted enough of their hospitality that in good conscience he could finally say the formula his mother had taught him: "With regret, my cousins, all now being well, I will withdraw: and when I am gone, the Aethyrs be with this work and with you!"

Naturally this announcement was accepted with the normal invitations for him to stay a little longer—after all, he'd just helped save the world, indeed several worlds! But Rho held his ground, and finally someone escorted him back to the facility's excessively palatial worldgating suite, where his Aethyr showed him how to set his desired coordinates into the mechanism.

The thought of going straight home passed through his mind, but even as tired as he was he couldn't *quite* bear to lose that feeling of freedom yet. He'd pause in the Crossings long enough to have some kind of energy drink to wake him a bit, and something basic and Wellakhit to eat, and after that go home and face his royal parents.

That plan made, entropy naturally immediately asserted itself in the form of a scheduling problem. The local worldgating management system told Rho that for operational reasons (whatever *that* might mean) the gating previously scheduled for a hundred breaths from now had been rescheduled for *five* hundred breaths from now. Rho muttered under his own breath, chose the least comfortable looking of the seats in the overdecorated gating suite—being half afraid he'd fall asleep in it—and waited.

While he waited, his mind wandered a bit in a combination of fatigue and satisfaction. After a while Rho found himself idly returning in memory to that impression he'd garnered from Peklimut, that faint fleeting sense of its feeling that it was glad to be done with this annoying event, as it had had more than enough of it. Yet the impression, re-examined, now seemed to add: *in the recent past.*

Rho blinked. Who but these wizards had been working with this star recently?

...Or was the word he was seeking more like "meddling"? Or "tampering?"

Though I might have imagined that...

But what if I didn't? Is it possible that what I picked up was something its usual caretakers wouldn't even have noticed, normally?

In fact, was it the kind of thing that it would take someone who wasn't intimate with Peklimut to notice?

Rho had no leisure to take that thought much further, as right around then the hex cluster in the room flashed blue and a chime indicated its imminent patency for transit to the Crossings. But when he appeared once more under the great floating ceilings once more— above which the burning day had slid toward planetary afternoon— and strolled out slowly into the massive central concourse, a peculiar thought pushed its way to the forefront of his mind and took hold of him, impossible to ignore:

That was too easy.

Rho was so tired. *Is this just some kind of backlash from the expenditure the first time of so much energy? Am I trying to talk myself out of accepting my success?* And Rho pushed the thought away.

But it kept coming back.

Surely this can't be so, he thought, pushing the idea away again. *Every wizard is the answer to a question. Today was my turn at last to be the answer to the question, and answer it I did.*

...But who asked it?

Right there in the middle of the great concourse of the Crossings Rho stopped stock-still, oblivious to the traffic walking and gliding and crawling and humping and legging around him. The thought that had come to him was halfway to being sacrilegious, in wizardly terms.

It was impossible for a wizard to work consciously with the Lost Aethyr.

But unconsciously—

$\sim$

"RHO!"

The call from down the concourse went through him as if he'd touched an unshielded power source. He turned.

Maybe a couple hundred paces further along the concourse, to his great surprise Rho saw the young Archaint woman Avseh coming toward him. She wasn't alone, however. There were two of her.

He was tired enough after his exertions that it actually took a few moments for him to grasp what he was seeing. One of her was dressed as he'd seen her. The other was dressed differently, in a sort of long loose robe in bright patterns, and her hair was styled in a different manner (curly and fluffy instead of longer and pulled back). But otherwise she had the same red-gold hair, the same small light build, the same delicate features. *Her clone, of course. Her clone.*

They came hurrying to him together. Avseh was looking at him happily, her companion somewhat uncertainly and curiously. "Oh, this is wonderful, I hoped we'd catch you before you went some-where else, I wanted so much to thank you—"

"You thanked me already," Rho said, nonplussed.

But Avseh didn't seem to be listening, particularly. "But this is her, I wanted her to meet you and thank you too, this is Mevseh!"

"Greetings," said Mevseh, in exactly her sister's voice, though she sounded far more cautious.

"I greet you as well," Rho said. "Avseh, however did you come to find me here in this whole vast place? Obviously not by accident."

"The system logs the presence of any wizard who's in the facility," Avseh said. "I asked one of the gate staff to help me keep an eye out after you got me back together with Mev." She laughed with an air of slight embarrassment. "And you know, when I was first in trouble I really should have tried that kind of thing first. Except, well, I always had this picture of wizards as really important types that people wouldn't be allowed to just walk up and talk to…"

"Hardly," Rho said. "Did you go on to meet with the rest of your party?"

"Yes, we did, we have a little while, though, they had to reschedule our departure for Mevesh. Some kind of operational problem going on with the gates. Seems there's a lot of that going on today…"

"Yes," Rho said, "a certain amount of excitement."

"Come on, sit down, tell us," Avseh said.

"I shouldn't stay very long: my parents will be looking for me," Rho said; and it was true. It was wondrous, and a little unnerving, to have to have a care about what one said in the Speech, now that it had drawn enacture about itself and would no more permit itself to be used in even casual falsehoods.

Nonetheless there was a seating area not far away, and Rho couldn't find it in himself to be discourteous—not near the end of a day such as this had been. He allowed himself to be drawn over there, and this time Avseh got him a water of the kind he'd drunk before, and the same kind of pink drink she'd had before, for both herself and her clone-sister.

They sat there chatting for a little while, inconsequentially enough as it first seemed: about their reunion with the rest of their clone-group, news of the ongoing mass migration and the sudden turn of events that would make it unnecessary, strange and funny things they'd noticed in the Crossings between there and here now that they had leisure to see the area without being in fear for one another or the rest of their party. But Rho found himself first looking attentively into both their pairs of eyes, and then, strangely, finding that he was having trouble doing so. It was as if more attention than possible for just two people was being bent on him. And the two voices, too, were so alike. He was reminded of the many voices associated with the Aethyr, all of them sounding like him. But for some reason the reminder made him increasingly uncomfortable...

But Avseh was talking. "So you found me and sent me off and then—it seemed like just a few hours later everything had changed! There was so much about it on the news, it was all confused, but... was that *you?*"

Mevseh looked surprised. "They said that the planets' wizards had found a solution and *fixed* the star—"

"No one said anything about someone being involved except the people back home that we already knew about—"

"It did seem much better when I left it," Rho said. It was right, of course, to be cautious. "This, though, the events to come must yet prove."

"What *happened*, though?"

The desire to not discuss any of this that now rose up in him was surprising. Even yesterday, if someone had said to Rho *Tomorrow you'll be a wizard and will help stop a star from flaring!*, he'd have said he'd be ready right now to shout the news from the top of any available structure. But now Rho felt peculiarly exposed somehow.

"It's not easy to explain," he said, and thank the Aethyrs, that was true. Rho spoke for a little about the politics of it, the business of getting the governments' approval and so forth: material that he was sure would turn up on the newsfeeds in a matter of weeks if not days, as (inevitably) the nonwizardly contributors to the process tried to take as much as possible of the credit for the operation to themselves. Avseh seemed to be finding this boring—which struck him as sensible, as Aethyrs knew he'd found it so—but Mevseh seemed now to be hanging on Rho's every word.

This too he'd seen before at home: people who would attend a public or royal fixture and gaze at Rho as if the universe's secrets were coded into his pores. Sometimes the attraction turned out to be merely physical, which he found unnerving. *Because how in the worlds could anyone be interested in you that way without even slightly knowing your mind?* Sometimes it was political—people looking to curry favor with his parents through him—and it was an indicator of how disordered this whole business was that Rho found the attention of the "political animals" more natural and acceptable than the merely physical connection. *And who knows what it even means when an alien's attention is fixed on you this narrowly? Their whole psychology, it has to be different, how can one predict how to protect oneself, no telling what it means—*

Except by using wizardry. And that I really do not want to do right now...!

Rho snapped back into the moment and wondered with vague horror how much either of them might have noticed how much he *hadn't* been in it. That feeling of exposure kept getting stronger, and it was a challenge not to make an excuse and leap out of his seat and be gone. "...But you're not always doing spells and magic, surely!" Mevseh was saying. "What do you do?"

"'Do?'"

"Your, I don't know, work? When you're not out wizarding, or whatever you call what you do. I mean, everybody knows wizards can't just make themselves rich, it's against the rules, so you have a job, I'm guessing?"

It wasn't a question Rho was used to being asked at home—not least because everyone on the planet knew who he was and what he did. It therefore took a moment to find an answer that was both true (since they were working in the Speech) and wouldn't get him in trouble. "We call it being on errantry," he said. "And at home I work with my mother and father in the family business."

"Sounds boring," said Avseh.

"Too often it is," Rho said. "Desperately."

He allowed himself to fidget a bit, with purpose. *Quite shortly I could make that excuse I was considering.* What time would it even be in Sunplace right now? Were his parents up? They would check his rooms and wonder where he'd gone—

"Why would you even want to stay home when you could be doing all these exciting things?" Mevseh said.

Rho looked at her in some surprise, partly because he'd just realized something. *Why, when she first greeted me, did something so neutral and Wellakhit come out of my mouth in response? Why didn't it feel right to say* dai stihó *to her?*

But he was so worn out, and he was in a strange place, and nothing was going as expected today; why should this be any different? *It's not as if she was some unknown cousin and I slighted her.* Rho sighed at himself. *Once I thought wizardry would answer all the questions. Instead I get ever so many more...*

And something in the back of his mind whispered: ...*not a cousin...* It was so faint a whisper he almost missed it; more like an echo than anything else.

Rho didn't know what to make of that. He was distracted. Because, strangely, the question she'd asked was one he'd asked himself.

"I wouldn't say it hasn't occurred, sometimes," he said. "My father would say, the turf is always browner on the other side... And a lot of what a wizard does won't usually be exciting, or dangerous. It won't have the kind of effect that makes people praise you. Mostly it's about researching things, and working out what's right to do, and then building the spell to do it. Having the world work shouldn't be a high-profile business. Too much attention on you instead of the work just gets distracting..."

"You're right, it really does sound boring," Avseh said, sipping her drink and looking down the concourse.

Mevseh met Rho's gaze again. "But what you did," she said, "that means we won't have to emigrate at all. We won't have to lose our home, lose our whole *world!* We can go *back* after the power networks come back up and they fix the things that broke while the sun was being healed. *You* did that. And that was *absolutely amazing!*"

The sudden memory of arms thrust elbow-deep into starstuff, holding Peklimut in place while he and the other wizards kept it from going into self-destruct mode, thrilled once more down Rho's spine. *Yes. Yes, it* was *amazing!* If only all of wizardly life could be like that; on the edge, every breath a Challenge resolved, every moment vital! *But that's not the way of things, is it?* Even from watching his parents, Rho knew that.

"It worked out well for everyone involved," Rho said, rubbing at his eyes. *So tired... But don't be rude.* "Better than expected, in fact. That's hardly a bad result."

"But why shouldn't you want there to be more results like that?" Mevseh was looking at him as if it wasn't just his dreams at stake here, but other people's. "Why would you want to just have things keep on being the way they always have been? Why shouldn't your whole life be like it was just now? Because it *could!*"

Rho hardly knew what to do with such a question. And his first answer, the truthful answer, would have been, *Probably not.*

Because too clearly Rho could see what would happen to him next. He would go home, and his mother and father would celebrate with him, yes: and many Wellakhit people would be glad for him, and many others would be annoyed because their plans for how various factions in the government would interact with the royal family would now have to be adjusted. And beyond that... matters would stay largely as they always had. Sunlords tended to be stay-at-homes. And except for infrequent out-of-system business, Guarantors tended to stay settled within the circle of their world around its star. He would be expected to do the same...

It came as a surprise to Rho how long he must have been trying to avoid thinking about this. Yet here was the truth of how it would go, utterly at odds with all his childhood dreams of excitement and adventure. "I imagine," Rho said finally, "that kind of life would get kind of tiring after a while."

But Mevseh was alight with excitement at what she apparently considered Rho's prospects. "What? *Why?* It's just a shame. You could do this kind of thing for a long time, for years, and think how many worlds would thank you! *So many.* Way more than would ever even hear about you if you just stayed home with your family!"

Rho studied his drink and said nothing for some moments. Life without his family? What would that even be like?

But still...

The thought had come to him occasionally before, and now it rose up in new strength. To get away, out of the weary old frame of reference and never again to have to live up to anyone's expectations. No one following him, forcing him into proper behavior, keeping him on a single planet against his will. Nor would finances necessarily be a problem. If he chose to go freelance as a wizard—which some did —he could move freely and at will from planet to planet, and people who needed his wizardry anywhere he went would feed him, clothe him, give him a place to live. He was entirely within his rights to take his Art and go where he liked with it, making his own way. Unless and until the Aethyrs specifically sent one on errantry, *how* one used the power from day to day was one's own business.

Strange that this idea never really came up for me before, Rho thought. The "paladin" mode of errantry—the lifestyle of the wizards who chose to operate without a circle of friends and family around them, without a home, without anything but the Aethyrs' support— isolate, untethered, certainly heroic but essentially lonely— It had never particularly commended itself to him. But now—

Rho stared into his drink while Avseh gazed out at the concourse and Mevseh watched him, though he was only slightly aware of her scrutiny right now. The width of the vista that had opened out before him was dazzling. When he'd first become aware as a tiny child that his parents were wizards, that alone had made them like gods to him. They talked to gods, after all; the Powers that had made the worlds and kept them running gave his mother and father missions, sent them places. *Though mostly only places on Wellakh,* he thought. At the time Rho hadn't thought anything of that. Now he was wondering why this particular realization had been so long in arriving.

And what Rho had always wanted from his parents, in the way of stories, was tales of the distant worlds: the places that he heard about in the newsfeeds and in reference works at his lessons, the far-off places with strange alien names, inhabited by astounding, unbelievable beings. His mother and father had told him these stories gladly enough, but there'd always been a sense of underlying—not exactly *impatience*, but a kind of resignation. Under it Rho could just hear them thinking: *He'll get over it, get past it, when he gets older and comes to understand. Our work, our lives, are here.*

But it doesn't have to be that way for me, now, Rho thought in a tentatively joyous daze. *I could go elsewhere, be otherwise.*

Because he was *free.* He was a wizard and could do as he pleased. By ordainment of the Aethyrs this very day he was free: of Wellakh, of other's expectations, that for so long had felt like an unliftable weight around his neck.

And if Rho went home now and said, "My calling leads me elsewhere," both parents and planet would have no choice but to respect his choice. His royal father and noble mother would be heartbroken at first, yes, but eventually they'd find someone else on whom to settle the Great Watch over the Sun. *After all there are hundreds of our clan scattered around the world, and many of them are wizards. There have to be at least some of them who'd be far better suited to this work than I am.*

Rho took a long breath, let it out. It was strange to so suddenly, and for the first time, feel his soul beating against the bars of the cage.

Or rather, it had been beating so for a long time... but hopelessly. Now there was hope!

You could go, his imagination said to him. *You could go* right now.

Rho sucked in an involuntary breath at the truth of the idea, and the audacity of it.

You should go. Don't let anything slow you down. There's no reason even to go back. Anything you need on the road, you can purchase it, or it will be given you.

Staggering as the concept was, Rho heard it in his head in the Speech and knew it to be true. It was as if all the unfulfilled longings and desires of a difficult childhood and youth were speaking to him at once. Wild and wide and shining the prospect stretched out before him in imagination: journeying the worlds at will, going where his heart took him... facing down the Lost Aethyr in a thousand venues, a thousand forms, never the same battle twice. Losing sometimes, winning sometimes, it wouldn't matter which. Finding his own path, instead of following anyone else's...

The hunger for the mere possibility was for some moments nearly unbearable... the thought of a life outside of the trap he had been born into. *To leave that half-scorched world and never come back!* It had never been possible before, and so as a boy he had wasted no time dwelling on the desire to escape, because there was no way. He had been held planetbound by his powerlessness, by his duty to his House, by his love for his royal father and his lady mother. But now... *now.*

Now it could be otherwise. He could have a life in which which people would praise him not in hopes of advancement or political power, but because they valued him; not just for what he was what he represented or what he had been born into, but what he *did*—

Somewhere down inside Rho, a resonance thrummed softly, like a plucked string.

Trapped, Rho thought. *When was I thinking about that recently...?*

For all that he had just been drinking, his mouth started to go dry. *And who heard me thinking?*

"Sorry," Rho said, realizing with embarrassment how long his companions must have been waiting for him to say something. He looked up and saw Mevseh's gaze resting on him, patient, curious, waiting.

All at once Rho realized just who was looking at him and waiting to see what he would do.

He picked up his drink and closed his eyes and broke that gaze, focusing on the cold and wet of the drink.

The Lost One knew Rho's weaknesses because a fragment of It was in him, as in all other living beings. It knew his own desires could be made to betray him into a mad quest across the stars, away from something else he *ought* to be doing.

But what?

There was no way for Rho to tell. The Lost Aethyr could step in and out of the flow of time as it pleased, see his possible future time-line, and act as it wished to divert him from that course.

Rho was immediately certain that the course in question was important. *And I'm getting ready to go home, but it doesn't want me to do that. It wants me to run away.*

Why?

There was no way to tell. But regardless of that, the stubbornness that his mother used to despair of when he was little rose up in Rho now in full force. The stars called him, and he hungered to follow that call, so much. More than almost anything.

...Almost.

Because he wasn't going to do it. *Not if the Lost One* wants *me to!*

Rho now realized, though, why he and the other wizards had had so little trouble with their stellar intervention. It was meant to be easy.

And that's what was bothering me about the star. Peklimut tried to tell us that something was wrong. Something had tampered with it in preparation for this...

For me being here.

Rho was sure, though, that he wasn't meant to know that. He was meant to have had an exciting victory (which he'd had). He was meant to feel that endless more work of that kind lay out among the worlds away from Wellakh, waiting for him. *And doubtless there actually is such work. The Lost One tells truth along with Its lie to make the lie stronger.*

But now I see my Challenge. And its nature was simple.

Seem to do the Lost Aethyr's will... but *do something else instead.*

If only he could work out just what! ...And *quickly*. For thoughtful attention rested on him right now from across the little table, waiting to see how he would answer.

Rho had another long pull at his drink, and while he was drinking, listened hard. The Aethyrs he'd had a little practice listening to earlier had quieted now to a sort of murmur of background diagnostics, waiting for him to ask for something specific. But Rho paid them no mind, for what he was trying to catch now was the whisper of that one that he'd found hardest to hear: the one that seemed to suggest more sometimes with its silences than with words.

It was markedly silent now.

Rho put his drink container down and took a breath, doing his best to look thoughtful. Not that he *wasn't* thoughtful: but he very much wanted to look as if he was being thoughtful about the wrong things. *Wrong for me, at least.*

"It's strange to say this," he said to Mevseh, "but I think you're right. Who'll ever hear of me if I stay at home on my homeworld? One star, quiet now but watched constantly... It's not exactly a pathway to excitement or fame, is it?"

"I guess it doesn't really sound like it," said Avseh.

Rho pushed his drink aside. "But the Lost Aethyr is as easy to find on other worlds as on my own. Why not take the opportunity?" He gazed up toward the ceiling as if into that blazing day he'd seen above. "There are other people at home who could do the work I do. I could go out on my own... take the paladin's way along the High Road. It didn't ever seem possible before..."

"Don't you think it'll be dangerous?" Avseh said.

"It might be," Rho said softly. "But I can hardly let that stop me. It's not as if the Aethyrs have ever promised any wizard safety when they're out on errantry." He swallowed. "Anyway, no one at home would be surprised if I vanished now that wizardry has come to me. I've always dreamed of battling the Lone Aethyr on its own ground, out there..." He looked up again.

"But that's what they're always saying you're supposed to do," Mevseh said. "Follow your dreams...!"

Rho nodded sadly. "I need a little time to think how to go about this," he said. "Before I... do what I have to. Whatever that may be."

The two clone-sisters looked at him, and Avseh was just opening her mouth to say something when there came a soft chime, and the two of them glanced at each other. "Is that yours?"

"No, mine, I think—"

Mevseh looked up into the air, and a spill of text spun itself out across a stripe of color floating in front of the two young women. "Oh, look, after all these delays what do they do now but call the gate *early,*" Avseh said. "We've got to go..."

They stood up, and Rho stood with them. "And you're just going to go too?" Mevseh said, actually sounding a little forlorn.

Rho concentrated on keeping his true thoughts away from his face and his body, even away from showing too obviously in his mind.

"I think I must," he said very slowly, as if in struggle. "If my family learn that I'm here, who knows, they might prevail on Crossings security to send me back."

"Then you should go now," said Mevseh said. "Before anyone can stop you from following that dream!"

"Yes," he said after a moment, heavily. Then as if coming back to the courtesies of the moment, he nodded and bowed slightly to them. "Go well," he said. "And a good return to your home!"

"You helped that happen," Avseh said. "We'll never forget you..."

And they started off down the concourse. But as they went, Mevseh looked back at Rho... that thoughtful look again.

Rho swallowed. *Overshadowed,* he thought, with that same sense of touching a live powerguide. To act as if he recognized that state was one thing. To say it in the clear to oneself—thereby making it to some extent real— was quite another, for it ruled out any possibility other than the Lone Aethyr Itself being here to tempt him.

He could have laughed at himself if he'd dared, and it would have been most ironic laughter. *Did I desire more danger in my Challenge? Then someone on one side or another of the divide has heard me.*

Rho quickly bowed his head and turned away, standing for a few moments just gazing down unseeing at the tabletop.

The logistics of the situation, though frightening, were also interesting. To interfere properly with a living being, the Lone Aethyr (so wizardry lore maintained) had to temporarily enter into spacetime and be subject to its laws and limitations. If It was presently indwelling to some extent in the body of an Archaint (*and which of them? I think Mevseh but I could be wrong...*), that meant It presently possessed at least *some* level of telepathic sensitivity... but not necessarily enough to read the depths of Rho's mind.

In any case it was smart to take the most rigorous precautions he could manage quickly, while he laid his plans. *And what are my present power levels for if not the exigencies of Challenge?*

Not that what Rho had now to do would be easy. His mind was a whirl of frustration and confusion and anger and fear. But he had both talent and training in the art of focus, and had been taught by a master. *If you are in the midst of dealing with the inside of a star, my son, no matter how badly you might want to, you do* not *sneeze...*

The irony, though, remained painful. Rho had desired his Challenge to be a matter of terror and wonder, worth singing about. But mostly he felt like cursing. *That* art his mother had been the one to teach him, and though he wanted so much to indulge it now, he dared not. Later he would indulge himself with some of his mother's favorite invective, for good example was always worth following; and the cursing of Miril am Miril could raise welts on a stone wall even without wizardry.

Right now, though, what mattered was for Rho to get himself into a protected place where he could think. He had only a little time to choose a course of action and enact it.

As he considered how to do this, a memory arose into Rho's mind as if from a great depth, and speaking seemingly in his father's voice. *In doing what you must, fear not sometimes to do what it seems It wants you to do. But at all costs, do so in such a way as to produce a different outcome than the one It desires.*

And with those words came an image. In the back of Rho's mind he found himself gazing at something his father had shown him pictures of when he was very small: the disk of Thahit, all unstained, like a bright shield of bronze without a single spot.

Slowly Rho's eyes opened again, and he gazed unseeing for some moments into the air in front of him.

Then he turned and went to the drinks kiosk not far away.

The Rirhait tending it came over to him as Rho leaned over the counter, gazing thoughtfully down at the menu flowing past under the surface. "What's your pleasure, gentlebeing?" it said.

Rho thought about that. Finally, "Cousin," he said, "I need a great deal of something to drink with *this* chemical in it." And he pinched his Aethyr into visibility so that it could display for the Rirhait a diagram of the compound he meant.

The being focused a fair number of its eyes on what was displayed. After a moment it said something that sounded a great deal like "Wau", and wreathed its eyes at him. "All right. What you want is *fesh*. How much?"

Rho pinched the Aethyr again and got it to show the Rirhait a suggested dosage.

"*Wau,*" it said again, examining some readout of its own behind the counter and plainly investigating Rho's physiology to make sure what it was about to give him would be safe. "All right, gentle customer. However, please note: your eyes'll knot themselves right up if you try to have two."

Rho could only laugh at that. "One will be enough," he said, "or nothing will."

"Here, or at the table?"

Normally he'd have said *At the table, please*. But right now, irrationally, he didn't care to be alone. "Here."

A tall round stool promptly grew up out of the floor next to him. Rho sat himself down on it and waited patiently for the Rirhait to produce the drink from the the Crossings' master comestibles-supply system. When it arrived, sludgy-colored in a tall thin glass, Rho reached for it eagerly and took a big gulp.

His eyes almost rolled back in his head as he felt the first effects of the vital chemical almost instantly. *For a while,* he thought, *I am going to be very, very awake.*

And with the initial jolt of the chemical through his system, Rho irrationally began to hope. Possibilities were already stirring at the back of his mind. He didn't dare start thinking them through yet. *But one way or another I am of the Princes' line of Seriv, and if I must fail I will do it standing on my feet and doing my best! That will be worth singing about after I'm dead, if nothing else...*

Rho had another long drink of the *fesh*. It tasted truly awful, but he was getting more alert every second. That was good, because he was going to need alertness now more than he ever had before.

He glanced up at the Rirhait, which was leaning over the counter and gazing idly up the concourse with some of its eyes. At his glance, a few of them looked back at Rho. "I might seem for a short time to be meditating," Rho said.

A ripple of legs went down the Rirhait that Rho read as its own version of a shrug. "I've seen it before," it said. "If you don't want anyone bothering you, I'll keep an eye out."

Rho couldn't help it: he had to laugh. "Thank you."

The Rirhait wreathed some eyes at him and turned most of its attention back to the concourse.

Rho breathed out, pinched his Aethyr into presence again and gazed into that blazing little core of starfire until his eyes began to water.

Is it possible for you to create a space around me through which my thoughts cannot be overheard even by senior-dimensional entities?

Yes. Warning: such spaces can only be maintained for short periods, and the power outlay is considerable.

Is it possible to assemble a wizardry and enact it from inside such a safe space?

Yes. Again, power outlay warning.

All right. As regards the safe space: enable.

NOTHING VISIBLE HAPPENED AROUND HIM, but Rho was amazed at the total silence that fell all around. The never-entirely-silent din of the Crossings, all the sound of every kind of creature in the Worlds going about its business, was completely absent now. It was like a hint of how things might have sounded in the depths of time when the Most Central had been about to start work.

But he had little time to spend considering this wonder, as he could already feel the power running out of him in a slow steady stream, like water running inexorably downhill. Rho let his eyes drop mostly closed, so that almost all of his attention was directed toward the shadowy space inside of him where the immaterial image of his Aethyr hung in the emptiness, still as some distant star.

He began marshaling his thoughts the way he would have when he was about to present his royal father with a project to run in the simulator. *Starting position: plan of action: ways and means.*

The starting position was easily stated. Rho had been tempted by the Lost Aethyr, overshadowing the being Mevseh in one of Its many aspects—that of the Interlocutor, Rho thought, who had come to Wellakh in the time of the Choice long ago. *There It sat, right across from me, looking at me out of a mortal's eyes, asking me questions the way the legend says It asked them of the first Wellakhit and the first Wellakhit wizards.*

Having so been tempted, I must be seen to have fallen. For if I come out of this space and reject the temptation, my whole world will very likely suffer. The Lone Aethyr's attention was for the moment focused on him, waiting to see what Rho would do. If he went home, It would very likely follow him to watch the results of Its work. *And I have no desire to have its attention turned back to Thahit once more. Or Wellakh's people, or my parents.*

Nevertheless, It having tempted me, the temptation must now not only pay off, but be seen *to pay off.*

Not that the prospect of the possible future It had suggested to him did not possess terrible strength, even now. That freedom, that power, the excitement of that life... But Rho shied away from considering that too closely. The only thing standing between his will and the Lost One's at present was a short-term overdosage of a common Wellakhit stimulant chemical, and the Aethyrs' aid... assuming any of them were paying attention to the Challenge of a single wizard in the depths of a relatively large galaxy.

So never mind that, Rho thought. *Time to consider ways and means.*

He would need a course of action that was audacious enough not to be readily predictable. And considering that, some possibilities had begun to present themselves.

The Lost One is proud, Rho thought. *Everyone knows that. And in a paradox, to see another's pride subverted by Its own actions is therefore one of Its great joys. Therefore what action I take must be shaped by that outcome. I must be seen to have had my own pride broken... and to be doing Its will rather than mine.*

He considered the paths that seemed to be forking away from him and this moment in time. In one of them, he would reject the temptation and go back home to Wellakh, followed close behind by the Lost One's anger and enmity at having resisted It.

In the other, Rho would have to seem to accept the role it was offering him, that of a wandering paladin-wizard. He would go out among the worlds and do a certain amount of good in the service of the Aethyrs. But this subterfuge would mean he dared not return to Wellakh again for a long time, if indeed ever. And regardless of his taking this path willingly and as a ruse, doing so would still permanently divert from that other path that the Lost Aethyr somehow saw ahead of him and did not want him to tread. *And that other path almost certainly leads to something the Bright Aethyrs want me to do for the worlds' good.*

There in the darkness—and also sitting there at the kiosk— Rho dropped his head into his hands for a moment in despair.

But what can I do? There's no way out of this. I can't walk both paths. I can't be a paladin and go home. If I go home, I risk my star, my world, my family. If I go out on the High Road forever, I do the Lost One's will and... and probably die out there alone.

For a moment anger and pain flashed alive in him. *Haven't I been long enough alone?!* His eyes began to prickle.

But he heard an answer, then. His own voice in memory, speaking to imminent tears: *No.*

And as for dying alone: *No dying. I forbid it.*

Rho wanted to laugh at himself. *Such big words.* Now he knew the real size of them.

Except... did he?

He looked again at the statement he hadn't really questioned before.

I can't do both.

Without warning, an answer floated up to him from such an unexpected source, such an inappropriate one: yet another memory.

I want those.

You can have one or the other, his queenly mother said. *Not both.*

Why not? I am a Prince! Of course I can have both!

He could still hear her laughter, loving and amused. At the time it had infuriated him. Now it just made Rho smile. And then he realized that he might have been putting the wrong construction on the concept.

Not 'why can't I have both', but how *can I have both!*

Rho opened his eyes and had another drink of the *fesh*. He shivered all over as another jolt of the stuff went down his throat. It was starting to make him shake a little bit.

The Rirhait looked at him with a few spare eyes. Rho shook his head. "Sweet *Aethyrs* but that's terrible," he said.

"That's what I hear," it said, and went back to fiddling with the kiosk's data systems.

Rho closed his eyes again. Moments were running over him still like water running downward, but he thought he might be onto something. *Both,* he thought. *Both. Not one outcome, not one path... but two.*

Two!

Rho imagined himself once more in the darkness with the Aethyr hanging there shining. *I need assistance in the construction of a spell,* he said, *as the required level of complexity is beyond my present competence.*

Assistance is available. And Rho breathed out in relief, because otherwise he knew what he intended would be impossible. *Describe the wizardry, please.*

All the voices of the Aethyr seemed to be working in chorus now, as if for some reason unusually intent on what he was doing. After getting used to their multiplicity up to this point, the effect was a little strange, a little unnerving... but once more Rho reminded himself that at the moment he didn't have leisure to indulge in overanalysis.

I want to create a clone of myself, he said.

To what purpose?

Interventional, Rho said.

Describe the nature of the intervention.

He took a breath, thinking how to phrase this. *The clone will appear to visit multiple destinations, and then depart those destinations again. When visiting those places it will perform diagnostic wizardries on the stars. After performing each such diagnostic it will, after some delay, depart for the next destination.*

The Aethyr seemed to pause to digest this. *Is it your intention to invest the clone with enacture energy?*

Yes.

Is it your intention to invest the clone with free will?

Yes. With the stricture that it ought not depart from the specified planned path.

Will you desire to reclaim the experience associated with this clone at a later date?

If possible, yes.

There was a pause. *...Confirmed: this will be possible.*

Good.

Please confirm intention, the Aethyr said. *Your purpose is to direct this clone along a selected pathway in order to lay a false trail for a superdimensional entity?*

No names were mentioned. None needed to be. *Yes.*

He waited, almost in a kind of hope, for his Aethyr to tell him *This is impossible.*

But no such assertion came. After a moment, *Define the list of target stars,* the Aethyr said.

Rho swallowed again. *I don't have a list. But I want to create one by defining a set of conditions. Is that possible?*

Yes.

He began laying out the specifications. *Unstable stars with inhabited planets. Instability of these types—* Rho chose the types of stellar morbidity that he knew to be most common, and specified that the search include those with the worlds of highest population—places where even the interstellar organizations like the Interconnect Project, who specialized in dealing with this kind of disaster, would be seriously challenged by the prospect of handling them.

Define the desired volume of space, said the Aethyr.

In his mind Rho indicated a sphere of space centered on Thahit and approximately five hundred parsecs wide.

Noted. Other parameters? the Aethyr said.

Rho drew a deep breath. *This list needs to involve only stars that will not reach crisis levels in their morbidities for the next two hundred sunrounds.*

There was a pause. *Fulfillment of this parameter requires limited timeslide access in the information-only mode,* the Aethyr said at last. *Such access will require higher-level authorization. Authorization, if granted, implies significant energy outlay.*

I understand that, Rho said, and held his breath.

Silence ensued, one deeper than even that which already hung about him. Rho realized he couldn't even hear his heart beating in that silence. He waited.

Waited...

Approved, the Aethyr said. *Further parameters?*

Numbly he tilted his head in negation.

Compiling the requested list, the Aethyr said.

Rho sat quiet and drank his *fesh* and waited. After a little while the Aethyr said, *List completed.*

Thank you, Rho said. *Display the set, please?*

He was instantly surrounded by a tagged display of approximately three hundred stars.

Please indicate the order and approximate durations of visitation to each star, the Aethyr said.

Rho spent some minutes over this, doing his best to construct for the Lost Aethyr's benefit what would be a pathetic picture indeed. It would seem to see a Rho who would journey from star to star to troubled star, carefully investigating each one and then moving on... a sorrowfully peripatetic figure, always on the move, never at rest. Sometimes it would try to double back closer to Thahit, seemingly lonesome for sight of its homestar: but always it would be decoyed further out again by some twitch or threat in another star on the list.

If the Lost Aethyr troubled to look forward in time, It would see that none of these stars were truly in danger of going into crisis in the other-Rho's lifetime... and this ugly irony would please It well. Eventually It would most likely get bored with watching "him", lose interest—thinking It had won—and turn Its mind to other prey more immediately amusing.

Rho sat back wearily and examined his handiwork, and could find no flaw but one. *There's always the danger,* Rho thought, *that the Lost One might look in on Wellakh some day to see how my parents are taking my loss.*

But there's nothing to be done about that. In the short term, I have to save my world and my people from the Lost One's attentions now. *And this is the best result I can produce...*

Meanwhile the moments were slipping past, and his time in this protected space was getting short. It was time to start things going.

Complete? said the Aethyr.

Yes.

Final data on the prospective clone, said the Aethyr. *Is it to be sequential from your present timespace locus, or another one?*

This one.

Final disposition?

Such a cold word, such a painful word. But it had to be thought of, for the spell would not have infinite energy to power it, and could therefore only last so long. *When it is within one percent of expending its final energies,* Rho said, *it is to proceed to the next sun on the list, walk into its chromosphere... and die gloriously.*

There was a pause. *...Define 'gloriously,'* his Aethyr said.

Rho opened his mouth, closed it again. *All right,* he said. *It just dies. Painlessly.*

...Instruction accepted, the Aethyr said. *Construction of wizardry complete. Implementation of clone routine must begin immediately to occur within secured area.*

All right, Rho said. *Go.*

Trigger word in preparation. Please examine the price of wizardry and approve or decline it. And the Aethyr displayed a figure in his mind. It was an approximation of a certain amount of life energy, concentrated along a given temporal stretch.

Rho looked at it, and sucked in a breath. *It's... that's at least three sunrounds of a life.*

My life.

There was no way to regard such a number dispassionately. He felt cold, cold all over. Yet at the same time, the cold wasn't entirely fear. Rho could remember some of those nights when he lay staring into the darkness above his couch and thought, *I would do anything to be a wizard, I would give* anything—

Now the Aethyrs had called in that statement of intent.

Rho stared at the figure for a little longer and said, *I don't suppose there's any chance that this is a test, and that if I agree to pay the price I will be forgiven it*—

The answer was utter silence.

No, Rho said. *Of course not. Forget I said that.*

He took a deep breath. *Approve,* Rho said, and braced himself.

Nothing happened. *But then it wouldn't,* he realized. *I'm going to be paying that off a little at a time for a long while. The rest of my life. Forever...*

There was nothing to do now but manifest the clone and put it where it needed to be to start his journey.

The two beings I was speaking to earlier, Rho said. *Delay their gating.*

On what pretext?

I don't know... how about 'operational reasons!' He smiled grimly.

Length of delay?

How long will it take to construct the clone, manifest it, and send it to their gate?

Approximately thirty breaths.

Delay the gate patency for a hundred breaths, then. Rho had no desire to leave "himself" talking to the Lost Aethyr's one or two inadvertent puppets for any longer than another thirty breaths or so: "he" would be in enough discomfort at what he was about to do.

Shield activities about to occur in this area from outside observation, please, he said to the Aethyr. *Display only the present view.*

Understood. Shield period starting. Fifty breaths maximum. Though the shield had no visual component, Rho could feel it slide into being.

Spell trigger word preparation complete, the Aethyr said. *Please speak the word.*

The trigger word—actually an acronym of a number of separate spell activator sequences for the cloning routine—displayed itself in the Speech in the darkness before him. It seemed about as long as he was tall.

Rho took a breath and spoke it. And spoke it, and *spoke* it... and could not stop speaking it, for it seemed as much to be speaking *him*. When he was finished—or *it* was finished—he had no energy left for the moment except to slump forward on the kiosk's counter and lean there gasping for air.

And it still came as a shock to him when a hand came to rest on his shoulder. Rho gasped again, straightened, turned to look.

...It was beyond strange to see himself without needing a mirror. The other was absolutely as like him as wizardry could make it: the very image of him, to the last long golden hair.

It stood there. He looked at...

He couldn't say *it*. It was *him*.

The other him looked back, wearing the oddest expression—awe, amusement, a touch of sorrow. At the sight of him, all Rho wanted to do was apologize.

"You know why I had to do this," he said.

The other him tilted its head "yes". "And I understand it."

Rho gulped, trying to get control of that lump in his throat. "I will think of you *every day.*"

"I know," said the other Rho. "The same for me. But know this: I understand what I will be saving. You and I, we are victors over the Lost One together."

Rho hoped that was true. "You know that this situation... can't last forever," he said.

"I was there when you built the spell," his otherself said. "I do recall." Its voice was dry, but amused. "But you're running out of time. To have this work, we have to act now."

Rho echoed the other's tilt of agreement. He spoke the five words of a simple invisibility spell he'd prepared in the Aethyr earlier, and got off his seat.

The other him sat down in it.

"Ready?" Rho said.

"Ready."

He swallowed hard against a throat that felt suddenly tight. *"Dai stihó,* brother," he said.

His other self tilted its head in agreement. *"Dai,"* he said. "And give them my love."

Rho turned away and spoke to the Aethyr. "Kill the shield," he said.

It flickered out of existence as invisibly as it had come.

The other him looked up at the Rirhait behind the counter. It cocked a couple of eyes at him. "Another, Emissary?"

"Thought it would knot my eyes up," the other Rho said.

"So it might," said the Rirhait. "Could be interesting to watch." It chuckled at him. "But it's your call. Maybe you could use some of that tailored water instead."

"No," Rho said, "unfortunately I must depart." He got up. "Is our accounting sorted?"

"Gone on the master account as usual, young wizard," the Rirhait said. "Wherever you're going, go well."

"From your mouth to Their ears," said the other him. It was Rho's father's line. He lifted a hand to pinch his Aethyr into being, and turned just enough to catch Rho's eye.

And he vanished.

Rho breathed out and turned away; he too had other places to be. Very quietly he walked away and headed carefully down the concourse, looking at nothing in particular. He had to be cautious about how he went, being invisible. *And I can't be seen leaving, either. I will need to do a private gating using wizardry alone. There must be someplace here set aside for practitioners of the Art to use without endangering others...*

He consulted his Aethyr about this as he went, edging himself out of the way and over to the far side of the main concourse, where he would be out of danger of easy collisions with passersby who couldn't see him. As he did this he gradually became aware of something like an echo, half lost in the murmuring din of the Crossings' endless traffic. In the echo Rho found that he could discern the sound of someone speaking: yet another voice that sounded like his, but in a different way. *I wanted to thank you...*

You're going? Right now?

Yes, I've decided it's for the best. I wanted to let you know that you have made a tremendous difference in my life... and in the way I will be living it from now on.

Spoken in the Speech, all of it the truth. *Well, please be careful! And I hope you get home to see your people sometimes...*

That will be as the Aethyrs will it. But meantime I've accepted the Challenge, and you have helped me on my way to doing so. So whatever your reasons may have been, may you go very well...

Oh, our gate's ready... finally!

Yes. Take care, Rho!

And you as well.

A few more farewells from some set of gate hexes right across the Crossings... and then silence.

Rho stopped still where he was for a few moments and waited until he felt something he had no way to describe but would recognize instantly if it ever happened again—the sense of himself having been in a place twice, and then, suddenly, there just once.

With that the weariness that his urgency and the *fesh* had helped stave off began to settle down over him again. He pinched the Aethyr into existence, cautioning it to remain invisible.

About that private transport area...

You can walk to it from here, said the Aethyr, and tagged it in his mind.

It wasn't far: less even than the distance from his rooms in Sunplace to the Great Room. Continuing to keep well off to the side to avoid being collided with by the visible, Rho headed that way.

And what am I going to tell them! he thought. It seemed like endless change had befallen him in the space of just a few hours. *How do I explain what I did, why I did it,* how...

And then he sighed, because there, listen, still more voices. *How am I supposed to think?* The world had been so full of voices today. *Where are those coming from? A floor up? Are there facilities on some of the elective-ceiling installations?*

Rho looked up.

And stopped, stopped right where he was, without caring whether anyone might run into him from behind, or indeed run him right over.

He had completely lost track of the time. Rirhath B's great sun had set, and the elective ceiling had been decommissioned for the night so that the view could come through. And above him...

All unprepared for it, Rho stood still and looked up into the view called by some the Ninth Wonder of the Worlds. Above him spread a huge vista of night sky, and embedded in it were hundreds of very-short-period variable stars: a scatter of breathing jewels in every color possible for a star, all pulsing and alive—shrinking, swelling, shrinking again, all swathed in glowing clouds of their casually breathed-out emissions.

And Rho was equipped to appreciate them in a way that few visitors to the Crossings were, even wizards. He could hear their hundreds of voices—a great chorus of them, every one different.

Rho's throat went tight again at the sound. Their many differences were most welcome, for he'd had enough of sameness for a bit.

Silently he greeted them, hardly able to find words. In a little while (for even thought takes some brief while to cross such distances) they greeted Rho in return, one after another, leisurely, casual.

The sight and sound, after a day that already contained so much, left Rho simply dumbstruck. In a little while, though, he heard something even wizards would find heart-filling: the stars' amused laughter. Rho was given to understand that under the circumstances there was no need for him to come up with quick responses. They were not going anywhere (except in the placid gradual sense of galactic rotation). When he needed their voices, or a subject for research, or even just a sense of adventure and wonder, they would be here. In fact, they would be here whether he needed adventure or not.

Thank you, was all Rho could say.

No matter, the response came back again and again.

There's always time enough for everything.

What needs this time does not fulfill, another one yet will.

So go now, and go well!

And that said, there was nothing further needed except for Rho to go home.

HE REAPPEARED in the vestibule outside the Great Room in the earliest morning light, with everything around him perfectly still. There Rho deactivated the invisibility spell and stood breathing hard for a few moments as the energy-price for it deducted itself from him.

Slowly Rho managed to master his breathing and looked around him in a peculiar sort of recognition that found the things around him strange even though they were familiar. This high-ceilinged space, the carving of its stones, the design of the floor, the light starting to come in from the outer terrace— *I crawled on this floor when I was a baby. I bounced balls against those walls when I was small. How can just one day make all this look strange?*

But at least he was here now, and probably the effect would wear off. Granted, it was also funny to realize that what he'd seen as his great leap into freedom was in fact a great leap back to right where he had been, the place for which he had been intended, the job for which he was being trained. The irony wasn't lost on him. Yet he remembered a saying of his mother's about the Aethyrs: "Oh, they have a sense of humor. It is nothing like ours. But it's certainly there..."

A few days ago, even yesterday, he would have found the humor bitter. Now, thank the Aethyrs, everything was changed.

And in the meantime, the light outside reminded Rho that there was one thing he needed to do before he finally dragged himself down to his rooms for that sleep he so desperately wanted.

Quietly Rho went over to the doors that opened on the terrace, pushed open the one of them that he knew didn't squeak, and slipped outside. He had missed dawn by perhaps an hour, and behind smoky streaks of cloud all banded with crimson and gold, Thahit stood perhaps a handsbreadth above the red-and-gold dappled horizon.

Rho went to lean on the stone balustrade and gaze through the morning's haze at his system's star. For the first time in his life he looked across the Wellakhit morning and heard Thahit burn: *heard* the raw roar of the distant atomic furnace, seemingly filling all space from its core to Wellakh's orbit with radiation as fluid as water, burning like fire.

This was no mere simulation of that unending blast of energy by the machine elsewhere in the building, not just a mockup done in light and low-grade radiation, but something that burned with a splendid ferocity more real than anything else in sight. All that great sea of outrushing power sang with the utterly alien thought and intention of the body, the being, the creature hanging at the center of it, breathing, burning, *alive.*

Rho's sheer satisfaction at being able to feel it at last shook and rippled in him like the plasma and the radiation echoing through local space. "Finally," he said in the Speech, *"finally,* good morning, cousin!"

—and the whole upper atmosphere shivered in anticipation of how, in six minutes or so, it would be crackling with auroral discharge, the token of the star's sudden delight.

Finally, Thahit said, or seemed to say: *cousin, good day!*

Rho stood there for a few moments just bathing in that calm approbation.

And then, somewhere away behind him inside Sunplace, a door slammed.

Rho knew where. *Ah me,* he thought, *here it comes!*

He could hear the footsteps in the Great Room. A few moments later the room's doors were flung open, and out came his royal father in his sleeping robes, moving faster than Rho had seen him move in many sunrounds. "Noble and extremely ill-behaved Prince and son," his father roared at him, *"where have you been!"*

Rho bowed to his father as he came, then straightened up, lifted a hand, and pinched his Aethyr into life.

His father actually skidded to a stop, staring.

"The Crossings," Rho said.

Through the terrace doors right behind him came Rho's queenly mother, in casual trousers and tunic because she was always up before her royal spouse. She hastened to Rho, took him by the arms, looked searchingly into his face, and then pushed aside the one lock of his hair that kept getting into his eyes. "And that was all?" she said.

"Well..." Rho said.

His father looked at him piercingly. *"Well?"*

"I talked to some people," Rho said.

Nelaid and Miril exchanged a glance, then turned back to him. "And?"

"I visited another planet and helped heal its star."

Nelaid immediately produced his Aethyr and began scrutinizing it. His mother, meanwhile, looked at him and said: *"And?"*

For the moment Rho merely looked at her and said nothing.

The Queen smiled half a smile that suggested she would get the further details out of him eventually. But for the moment she simply embraced him, saying, "Your father has made breakfast. Come eat."

EATING WAS the least of what happened during breakfast. Rho told his tale in full—or as much of it as he felt able to, after such a day. He had felt half faint with hunger when he sat down in his parents' rooms and started to eat what his mother began, in plate after plate, to set before him. Now, though, he was feeling as sleepy from being full as he had been from the day's exertions, and much feared he would fall asleep in his plate if this didn't finish soon.

Rho described his challenge as well as he could, in broad strokes, quite willing to allow the more difficult portions of it to wait for another day. But the King, with his normal acuity, went straight to those portions and began to analyze them. "The Lost One..."

"My husband..." Miril said, pouring herself a third draft of her morning drink as they sat around the common table in the King's and Queen's rooms.

"Mother," Rho said, "it's all right."

"It is not omniscient, my son," said Nelaid. "It has access to one's thoughts and motives only when one has attracted Its attention..."

Miril sighed and nodded. "And it sounds as if by virtue of your wizardry, Its attention, as regards *you* at any rate, will be elsewhere for a good while."

"Which is as well," the King said. "Politically, matters will become somewhat more complicated, not less. Suddenly there will be a royal heir who someday will assume the Sunwatch in the full of his power, possibly even as the most senior wizard of our line on the planet..."

"I will be one more person to curry favor with," Rho said. "One more to blandish, one more to woo." A chill ran down his spine. "Or kill, if I refuse to cooperate, to behave as expected..."

"Not without coming through me," his father said softly.

"I had hoped this might *relieve* you of a little pressure," Rho said with some regret. It had occurred to him that this change in the local political economy could mean the tensions between him and Nelaid could very well increase, not decrease. *There will be ways I see my work, my destiny, that won't be the way the Sunlord sees them...*

"My son," the Sunlord said. "Stop that."

Rho had to smile at him. "Reading my mind, noble sire?"

"Reading your face," his father said. "You've had too long a day. Son, we will manage this for the best. What our political allies and enemies will make of it, we've long had our suspicions. Plans that have long lain prepared will simply need a little adjustment to suit present conditions." And he smiled a small feral smile. "The plotters and planners of Wellakhit politics have had enough trouble dealing with two wizards in Sunplace. With a *third* one in residence?" He waved a hand. "They have no hope. There may be excitement in the short term, but things will yet go well."

"When shall we announce this?" Miril said. "There will need to be celebrations."

"Oh mother *no...*" Rho said, hiding his eyes.

"The people cannot be cheated of an excuse for a paid holiday, my son," said his father. "Perhaps the beginning of next tenday? It will allow the employers time to start adjusting their schedules..."

"That will be then," Rho said, getting up and finding he was still wobbling. "This is *now*. And now is when I want my couch."

His father's face didn't smile, but his eyes did. "When you arise again, my son, come see me. Doubtless there will be much you've forgotten to tell me, since recollection of such events doesn't come all at once."

"Indeed not," Miril said. "I recall it took easily four sunrounds after we met before you told me the bit about falling down the stairs..."

The King of Wellakh threw the Queen of Wellakh a look. The Queen grinned at the ceiling.

"Royal father," Rho said, "you shall hear it all. For now... I beg you hold me excused."

His father got up and to Rho's complete astonishment, bowed to him: actually bowed. "Welcome on the Journey, my son," he said.

"Three times welcome!" And then Nelaid ke Seliv straightened up and pulled Rho to him and held him tight.

"And now," the King said, "to the planning...!" He turned and walked away for all the world as if he had something important to do. "Perhaps a parade..."

Rho hid his face again. *"Mother!"*

"Let him make his plans, my son," Miril said. "He has waited a long time for this."

There was so much love in her voice that Rho felt his couch could wait just a few moments more. He sat down by her again.

"I kept thinking of you," he said. "You at the door, the other day. And you as you are now, just around here... being strong."

She reached out and squeezed his hand. "And now," Miril said, "you may tell me what you would not while your royal father was here, for fear of upsetting him."

Rho looked at his mother and hid his mouth, the gesture of one amazed at another's wisdom, and not for the first time. *"Mepi,"* he said, very softly, "I paid a price."

She simply looked at him, and waited.

Rho took a long breath. "If you want to see the details," he said, "I give you leave."

Miril looked at him for a few breaths more. Then silently she lifted a hand and produced her own Aethyr.

Thoughtfully she gazed into it. Rho waited for her face to change, to crumple with pain when she saw the upsetting truth.

He was therefore most confused when she tilted her head at him in negation, and gave him a considering slantwise look. "So," she said. "You fear that you have lost some years of your life."

"Not a fear, mother," he said. "A certainty. The Aethyrs will not be cheated... and I did agree."

"Of course they will not," said the Queen. "But, my son... I do not see here, in the description of the price, time lost from your life's *span.* I see time lost from your *life.*"

Rho blinked. Miril was using two different words in the Speech, and one of them he wasn't sure he understood, enacture or no enacture. "Queenly mother, I think my vocabulary may still need work..."

His mother had often enough teased him about that, and she would have reason to tease him now: but mercifully she declined. "See here," she said.

She brought her Aethyr into phase with his, so they could both examine the same materials. The sensation was peculiar, but after a few moments he could see what she desired him to see.

In mind she pointed toward part of the log record of the wizardry. "The time period denoted here as the price would be... some three sunrounds, yes?"

"Yes."

"But look over here. Did you not think to check the record of the transaction after it was completed?"

Mostly I was really trying to avoid *doing that.* "I did think about it," he said. "But, mother..."

"No matter," his mother said. And that was exactly like her: always willing to save you face before you lost it. "Look closely, my son! The price you see in this column, yes, beyond question, it will be paid. The Aethyrs will no more be cheated than They will cheat. But there is no statement as to *when* this particular debt will be called in. And the mode of payment required—see it?"

Rho looked at the notation. *Assumption of Guarantee,* it said.

He opened his eyes and looked at her in confusion. "So this is not a deduction," he said, "a shortening of life. This is... doing something *else* with that period?"

"So it would seem," Miril said. "Being required to do something else, at Their pleasure." She let go of her Aethyr; it floated a little distance away and went out.

For a few seconds later they looked at each other. Finally Rho said, "Noble mother, I have *no idea what that means.*"

"No more do I, my princely son," Miril said, and leaned back in her chair. "I merely wished you to let this trouble go before you slept, for I saw you were troubled. But this I *do* know: at last my son is a wizard." And she picked up her drink and sipped at it, and smiled at Rho over the rim.

"You were both so sure this would happen some day," Rho said, standing up and wobbling again. This time the weariness was going to take him whether he liked it or not, and he knew he needed to get away.

"It had no choice," said Miril. "Now of course everything will change in this world, after we announce." She sighed. "But at the end of the day, our people will be no match for us. They owe us too much: and we are too good at not letting ourselves be used. What matters most is that the great majority of the planet will be glad a wizard of your father's line will follow him." She smiled. "He, of course, is already off being ridiculously proud of you. As am I! But you will just have to put up with that."

"And as for the subterfuge..."

"The Lost One is constantly seeking new playthings to assuage its hunger for what It gave up," said the Queen. "Either It will forget you, or It will remember. Indeed It would like well for you to live your whole remaining life in fear of what It might do if It caught on to your ruse. But what would be the point in that?"

Miril sipped at her morning drink again. "Let us therefore do our work as it presents itself to us, and leave It to do as It will. We have no choice but to do so anyway..."

He nodded. "Royal mother," Rho said, "I take my leave."

"Be off with you and lie down before you fall down," said the Queen of Wellakh. "And when you rise again... I saved that bark-bread for you."

Rho kissed his royal mother on the top of her silver-fair head, and then took himself away to obey her command.

EPILOGUE

When he finally collapsed onto his couch, after bizarrely yet lying wakeful a while staring at the ceiling (partly due to the excitement and the thoughts that wouldn't stop going around in his head, perhaps due to the *fesh*), Rho eventually dreamed again.

He was simply too tired to remember very much later on of the dream that later visited him. It was a strange disjointed business, full of darkness and fire and dust, quite a lot of dust; all most untidy. And everyone seemed to be shouting or crying, and there was a voice he didn't recognize yelling at him in the Speech; a young voice, he thought, perhaps a girl's. But twined strangely together with this noise, far quieter, in the background as it seemed, he could hear someone thinking—and was it him?— *The induction into wizardry did not come until you desired the power not for your own sake, but for someone else's.*

Those words echoed in the dream like a gong struck, strangely weighted with importance. Rho opened his eyes and found himself still resonating with them, as if the gong that had been struck was him.

For a good while more Rho just lay there staring up at the

patterned ceiling in the slantwise light of Wellakh's afternoon, now streaming in through the glass doors to the terrace. *It feels wrong,* he thought, *like it should be morning. Or midnight. I don't even know...* Too many planets in too short a time: "gatelag", his father called it.

And I'm a wizard.

Even after everything that had happened, it still felt impossible.

Lying there flat on his back, he raised his hand and pinched thumb and forefinger together.

Ever so gradually and demurely, as if teasing him, his Aethyr faded into view.

Funny, Rho thought.

There was no reply except a general sense of reciprocal amusement.

And now here I am, Rho said to the Aethyrs. *Here is where you told me it was wisest to be.*

After a good while, what seemed a possible answer came back. *It seemed you were the one who made that choice.*

True, but You hinted really, really hard.

...A matter of interpretation, surely. Very faint, that whisper: very hard to hear unless you were really paying attention.

Rho smiled. *And what do I do now?*

What every wizard does. What there is to do, day by day.

He thought for a moment of the version of him now making its lonely way among the stars. *And what of him?* Rho thought.

He is your sacrifice, said the Aethyr. *And sacrifice has its own power, even when it seems in vain. No sacrifice is ever wholly thrown away. Sooner or later the energy returns. All being well, the day will come when someone sacrifices on your behalf. Balance will assert itself.*

Rho sighed. *And as for the Lost One...*

Someday, all going well, It will not be lost. Every sacrifice made is made on Its behalf as well: for all is done for each. And balance will be asserted, though It may assert otherwise as It pleases.

There was a strange sense of satisfaction about the words. Rho began to wonder whether it was not merely an Aethyr he now possessed, but also one of *the* Aethyrs, occasionally presenting itself in the disguise of the instrumentality. *And is there even a difference?* he wondered. *Perhaps someday I'll know.*

He took a deep breath... and wrinkled his nose. *In the meantime,* Rho thought, *I need hot water on me. I smell like I've been in a ditch.*

He pinched the Aethyr away and threw his clothes off... then paused, picked them up, and draped them neatly over a chair where the day staff would find them and take them away. Then he headed into his sanitation suite—pausing as he did to greet the water. And having done so, and afterward having well cleansed and arrayed himself, then Roshaun ke Nelaid am Seriv am Teliuyve am Meseph am Veliz am Teriaunst am det Nuiiliat det Wellakhit, son of the Sun Lord, beloved of the Sun Lord, son of the Great King, descendant of the Inheritors of the Great Land, the Throne-destined, stepped out at last into Thahit's light to begin his life's practice of wizardry.

In the days and months to come, the outer circumstances of Rho's life did not change that much... though Rho himself changed, seeing that he would need to do so to make things work. His mother teased him about his sudden shift in behavior, but that, Rho knew, would inevitably be part of the future burden of his Art.

He became assiduous in his labors with his father in learning Thahit's subtler ways, all available to him now that he too could speak to the star without mechanical aids and hear him speak in return. He went out of his way to dress as a prince might be expected to dress, and punctiliously made his presence felt at all the royal and government functions he could reasonably be expected to attend.

In public he never spoke a word that was not in King's-speak, and insisted on using it even at home—because who knew who might overhear? Gradually to all viewers outside his family the Prince was seen to draw a redoubtable cloak of cool reserve about him that he would suffer none to penetrate. Many were the Wellakhit who for one reason or another—politics, intrigue, genuine interest— attempted to become friendly with the Sunlord-to-be, only to strike that shell of smooth hauteur for which he became well known, and rebound from it, rebuffed.

For his own part, Rho thought often, more often perhaps than he liked, about how he had been played—or very nearly played—by those strange pink-skinned aliens with their hair too like his father's in its shade. It had chosen such an innocent shape in which to hide Itself, the Lost Aethyr, and he had very nearly been caught out by its wiles... *nearly*. He went about his days intent on making certain that nothing similar would ever be allowed to happen to him again.

Most people took this response to be the result of some trauma associated with the Prince's entrance into his wizardry. None but his mother and father knew what truly underlay his apparently unbreakable aloofness. And even they only occasionally suspected something of the fierce awareness with which he went about his work every day, knowing that he had put himself in the Lost Aethyr's way... and would not be anywhere else.

Once or twice during his early practice, a fragment of a strange legend was heard on Wellakh: the tale of a journeying wizard, some kind of exiled nobility, endlessly making his way from one star to another away out in space, always returning to the dark after brief sojourns in the light. Whether anyone in the Wellakhit royal family ever heard the story remains unknown, but even if they had, it seems likely no one would have had any public reaction. After all, all kinds of strange stories come to the settled worlds out of the dark.

And if there was a day when the Prince met his royal mother and father for breakfast and said, softly and in pain, "There is just one of me again," they never spoke of it in any other being's hearing.

The Prince's mettle as a wizard, meanwhile, was tested often enough both on Wellakh and on other worlds, where he ran occasional consultative errands on his father's behalf. So he was not overly alarmed when some sunrounds later he passed through the Crossings on such an errand and found the place in an uproar— security staff running in every possible direction, and the remains of some strange *enth*-like creatures being carried away, occasionally in very small pieces, but mostly in buckets.

In the course of his gate-change he passed by the Stationmaster's central supervision facility, and saw that entity himself not too far away, walking along and having an intent conversation with a couple of nervous-looking hominids of some kind or another—possibly a male and a female if their secondary sexual characteristics went anything like the way Wellakhit ones did, though of course you could never be quite sure without consulting the Aethyrs. "Trouble? Oh, no trouble," the Master was saying, glancing about him at blaster scarring and various other signs of damage to the infrastructure. "Not really."

Roshaun ke Nelaid smiled slightly at the irony, saluted the single eye that was turned toward him as he passed, and went on by, heading for his gate. He gave the matter no more thought, for no mere civil disruption would ever be allowed to damage the Crossings in any serious way. His mind went back to the issue of the star he was meant to examine on his father's behalf, the possibility never crossing his mind that some connection might some day be forged between himself and a being from the distant world of those worried-looking hominids.

And what the Aethyrs might have known about this business, They never shared with Rho. For all is done for each, and—whether foiling the intentions of the Lost One, or fulfilling an agreement once made—sometimes surprise works best.

PART II

MAMVISH FSH WIMSIH

PRELUDE

Many species from this side of creation to the other and back again have at one time or another had a saying that involves perceiving the conditions then obtaining around one, and then pointing at them and saying in ultimate acceptance: "It is what it is." (Often with an added, or at least implied, "And what can you do?") And this attitude is often seen as very wise and the pinnacle of maturity.

Except that maturity isn't everything... as wizards will be the first to agree.

Every now and then in the course of events in the physical universe, the time rolls around for something particularly special to happen. When speaking of such occurrences after the fact, folksongs and carols and epic poems often describe a typical response to the approach of one of these event-nexi as "heaven holding its breath," waiting in high anticipation for the event to occur.

In the more central realms of creation, this description is sometimes accurate. But routinely the response is also rather mixed. There may be anticipation, yes... but usually running in harness with it is significant terror, of a type and intensity that would shatter beings originating in less central regions. This is because even the Powers that Be, regardless of their positioning outside the physical universe's timestreams, still cannot predict with perfect certainty what *will* happen.

Into all their calculations inevitably enter two sets of imponderables that do not easily submit to assessment accurate enough to allow prediction. One is of course the influence of the Lone Power. Its own behavior, routinely (and sometimes just reflexively) set against the plans and wills of the other Powers, can range through a broad assortment of responses from spiteful, amused *laissez-faire* indolence to an all-out hostility that in the past has as easily snuffed out stars and shattered worlds as it has crushed lives or blasted hearts. While Its former associates may have a general sense of Its present attitudes, the Lone One's rapid changes of mood have played havoc with such analyses many times throughout the aeons, and the Powers that Be have learned better than to depend on them.

The other set of variables—in a universe where even the vibrational rates of molecules may occasionally shift without warning—includes everything normally describable as "mere chance." The wizardly triusm holding that "There are no accidents" still doesn't render the intervention of random factors impossible: it merely suggests looking closely at what might have caused them. And though one great thinker of our own planet felt sure that God does not play dice with reality, others (even on this planet) have asked whether this is not more a comforting assessment than necessarily a true one. Even the Powers freely admit that the mind of the One is utterly unknowable by beings less centrally positioned. Is it possible that even the One may not always know for sure how the dice will fall... or (if knowing) might sometimes pretend *not* to know? For even the concept of "having everything turn out according to plan" becomes meaningless unless one has first accepted the possibility that things might *not* go that way.

In any case, when Heaven holds its breath, sometimes it's because chance *is* operating—the chance that the right being will happen to be in the right place at the right time to make something previously unthinkable happen. And this is most especially the case when someone suddenly comes along, looks at what *is* (and was and seemingly always will be), opens their eyes (or other organs of perception) wide, and says, "Well, that's just *wrong*."

BEGINNINGS

Wimst is one of those star systems that most people primarily interested in interstellar tourism would normally pass by without a second thought. The response of any of them who'd ever heard of the place—at least early on in its relationship with the greater galactic civilizations then extant in the Milky Way Galaxy—would've been "Wimst? There's nothing on Wimst."

And at that point, generally they'd have appeared to be right. At least from the point of view of other species along the same matter-substrate spectrum, the single planet that gives the system its name was not an appealing place. Judged as a home for carbon-based life, Wimst was (and largely remains) unusually bleak, unwelcoming, and hostile: extremely dry and barren, subject to both long droughts and bouts of violent wet weather that seemed to do the ecosystem little good except in the very long run. There would probably be some who'd say that it was a miracle that life had managed to burgeon there at all... except that life, as we know, usually finds a way without waiting around for miracles

Additionally, the system's location is not promising in terms of the longer-term development of a given species arising there, as normally in the long term most species go to space. Wimst and its star are buried deep in the middle of what astronomers from our part of space sometimes colloquially refer to as a coal sack. All this phrase normally indicates is a region with unusually high concentrations of interstellar dust, high enough when viewed from a distance to block out everything beyond it, and (from the inside) block out almost everything outside it. But the words do give a little sense of the dark, forbidding quality of such spaces.

As if this positioning wasn't already infelicitous enough, the space around Wimst is also something of a star desert due to its position in a backwater region between two great galactic arms. Between the already-sparse scatter of even distant stellar bodies and the obscuring qualities of the dark nebula saturating the region of the Wimsih star, the result is one of those skies which at nighttime tends to cause the beings living there either to believe that they are alone in the universe, or to wish desperately that they weren't.

In any case members of the dominant Wimsih species from earliest times generally paid little mind to the tiny faint lights that were occasionally visible in the night sky (and occasionally were not, as the interstellar dust changed its configuration from century to century and blotted out stars that might have been dimly perceptible before). Early commentators might have suggested that this blasé attitude arose because noticing the stars conferred no particular survival advantage. More sardonic commentators later on sometimes observed that from a Tauwff's point of view the stars would not have been worth paying attention to because nobody could eat them. But that joke could not acquire its bite until after one very important occurrence befell the Wimsih planet and its dominant species.

That species, the Tauwff, were endothermic, warm-blooded saurians of a type familiar across the galaxy in many carbon-based environments where climates are challenging. There are nearly as many beings of this type as there are of hominids—which says something about the inherent variability and adaptability of both sorts.

Initially, though, the adaptability of the Tauwff was not so much of an issue—as both their legends and their planet's crustal history make plain. But in understanding who and what the Tauwff became, possibly the legends tell a fuller or at least a more nuanced story.

IT SHOULD BE SAID (as a sort of prologue) that in the most central regions of existence the line between prophecy and game plan can be very thin.

Prophecy is at best a statement of intent on the part of some one, or even many, of the Powers that Be. At worst, at its most simplistic and easily derailed, or easily misunderstood, it's no more than a statement about the contents and appearance of a snapshot of a given moment in time. What that event or appearance actually *means*—whether it portrays a situation planned to be of long standing or of a duration counted merely in moments—is rarely clear simply from examining that single frozen image.

The Wimsih tell a story of one such prophecy, and how it came to bear on their whole world; how the prophecy failed, or (as some say) succeeded, and what finally came to pass.

Here, then, the tale in condensed form—as the most popular version, *the Canticles of the Great Subversion*, can take as long as three years to recite and might be a bit much for the tastes of a species whose lifespan doesn't routinely run to a decade of millennia.

THERE WAS in the ancient day a star new-formed—the star that would be Wimst's primary—and not long after its formation, the star heard a rumor in the heavens about the largest planet about to form from its accretion disk. The star heard how it was being whispered among the Powers that on this world to come would be born a species great in mind and powerful in their works, one that in its Choice would choose for the Powers that Be and not for the Lone Power, their old antagonist. It was murmured as well, as the tale of times and years rolled by, that one would be born in this world who would change many things, even to the fates of other worlds and of other species far away. So that star—a thoughtful and secretive being who would not then and does not now tell its name—having heard these rumors, set all its intention toward making of the new world to come a place that would be fit home for such a species and would fill all their needs.

Even when acting merely through the laws of physics, stars acting with such intent can produce great things. The vast disk of dust and slowly gathering elemental stuff around it came together and formed itself over long millions of years into a single mighty planet, one of the largest ever known to sentient beings. And the star, its kindling then well finished, shone mindfully on that world as it gathered itself into shape and settled in its new orbit, as its rotation slowed and its crust cooled and tightened, as its atmosphere stabilized and its first weather systems manifested and the very first rains began. Slowly the new planet's oceans spread themselves wide into the beds laid down for them, slowly the world's air grew deep and sweet, and the long, leisurely business of Life's manifestation there began.

As the world that would be Wimst came into its own, the whispers about it in the depths of creation became ever more frequent, and there was great anticipation of the species that would rise there and the world that would be their home. The planet would be a garden nearly from pole to pole, a place of great beauty and wondrous variation in its species. And of the species that would rise there to dominate that world, rumor whispered how it would be wise and long-lived and gentle-souled, patient and intelligent in nature, mighty benefactors and friends to all. This would be a species destined to leave its mark in the merely physical realms, an ornament to the galaxy that could claim it as its child; a world worth waiting for, which in the fullness of time would be filled with great works of joy.

But the innermost realms of creation are full of echoes. There far beyond those regions where the little local laws of time and space hold sway, a whisper may travel far. And at last that whispering came to the notice of the Power called Lone. In Its contrary heart, the Lone One thought, "So this new world a-borning will become a wonder for all the worlds around to see, will it—a place of peace and excellence and kindness as might be taken for a model for others far and wide? *We shall see about that."*

Many a long age went by while Wimst grew complex and beautiful, while life proliferated in its seas and across its continents. The Lone One, meanwhile, went off about what It had made Its business: corrupting and destroying and blighting and maiming, and otherwise deranging the One's creation in all the ways It might. In the fullness of time It came back to Wimst and, sure enough, found the most senior and highly developed of its species, the Tauwff, on the brink of establishing their first true civilization there.

The Lone One took bodily shape for a season and walked among the Tauwff, and was delighted to find them as quickwitted and kindly and wise as had been foretold... as well as innocent and not particularly perceptive of Its presence. And It waved Its Tauwff-ish tail in secret merriment as it went among them; for far from annoying the Lone One, this outcome filled It with glee. It could tell that the time of the Tauwff's Choice was close upon them... and therefrom It would get much entertainment.

It would, as was Its wont, enter into their Choice along with that world's people. And should the Tauwff somehow manage to stay true to the other Powers' designs, then It would punish them in so terrible a manner as to make them a byword and a cautionary tale through all that part of the galaxy. Whereas should It induce them to willingly accept Its gift, which is Death and the works of death, then for long ages they would be tools in Its claws to wreak much wickedness on all the species round about and on one another. And from that too, the Lone One would derive great satisfaction.

So on the day when it was destined to occur, to the place of the Choice of the Tauwff the Lone One came. Seeming at first to be merely one more of the many wise ones and elders and wizards gathered in the garden-like vale where they were met, sweetly the Lone One put forward its case to them, gesturing with graceful claws and wreathing its tail into sensible shapes.

Their greatness, It said to those gathered there, was yet but a weak thing without power to make itself safe and enforce it—and the

Lone One's gift to them, along with the mastery of it, would make them mighty. Using death and the threat of it judiciously and for the good of all, the Tauwff would come to wield great power over every species they met, imposing their way of life and the culture and wisdom of Wimstkind upon them even in the face of fierce resistance.

"For the only true power lies in likeness," the Lone Power said to them. "Only with those who are like us are we safe. Once safely made like us, they may be guided out of their destructive and benighted ways into the true paths of wisdom and action. And as for all who are not like you, you may either force them to become so, or else blot them from the universe as if they were a mere stain or spill of error. Thus you will make the worlds safe for yourselves and your hatchlings, and spread the wisdom and order of Wimst's people far and wide—an ornament to the galaxy that clutched it, and a people fit to teach unruly younger races the right way."

But the Tauwff, gathered together as they were for the purpose of Choice, were by virtue of that intention rendered far more aware of the Lone Power's presence than It had come to believe they would be during previous meetings with them singly or in smaller groups. Together they now understood whom it was that spoke, and roundly they rejected It.

"All your sweet-sounding proffers and blandishments, we do renounce them," the Tauwff said; "for we can clearly scent their source. Of your 'gift' of oppression and subjugation we will have none. We have no desire for empire, nor any wish but to manage our own world in our own way. What other worlds may do or not about their likeness to us is theirs to determine, as their worlds are theirs to rule. And of your desires we have long been warned by prophecy. With them, and you, we will have naught to do. Take yourself away therefore to some other world less well prepared for your meddling; we will have none of it."

The Lone One grew wroth at such bluntness. "I have heard overmuch of prophecy of late," It said to the Tauwff there gathered. "Therefore beware how you quote it to me! Your own ingratitude shall set the pattern for your destruction. Other worlds will yet tell in song and story of what Wimst had, and might yet have had, and what its people threw away. Not that *you* will hear firsthand of their pity, for what you have brought upon yourselves will follow soon enough."

With that the Lone Power departed from among them. But instead of visiting Its wrath upon them straightway, It made another plan. Into the distant cloud of leftover rubble and detritus that had never been included into Wimst's structure, It dropped a small gravitic anomaly that did no more than dislodge a few of those small distant bodies from their orbits.

The Lone One then departed that star system and went about other business, content to wait on events for a matter of some five or ten Tauwff lifetimes. As the palate-sharpener before a great feast, well the Lone One likes the fear that may arise when It threatens a species' viability and then withdraws, leaving them to live their days in doubt and unrest, always unwilling to enjoy any good thing for fear of the blow that promises to fall and bring it all to nothing.

And when It reckoned that enough time had gone by so that the edge was beginning to come off the fear, and the tales of that long-ago Choice were beginning to be ended with "but all went well regardless—", then It knew Its moment had come. The Lone Power came back to Wimst's system, and saw how some time in the last millennium or so one of the small dislodged bodies from out in the distant rubble-cloud had made its way inward through the system, and had slipped into unstable orbit around Wimst. Again and again the little oblong rock had dipped close to that world and swung out again, its orbit growing more perturbed each time. And at last, while the Lone One watched in much-anticipated enjoyment, that small rogue body arced in one last time, falling, and struck Wimst a deadly blow.

Swiftly Wimst's air went dark with upthrown dust, and the crust of the planet writhed and cracked in torment and emitted lava and deadly fumes. Wimst rides near its sun, and swiftly implacable heat grew and grew under the newly darkened skies. Wimst's poisoned seas began to steam themselves away into the new dark canopy, and the fouled air choked nearly everything that breathed, and most life on that world was extinguished. Soon all that was left was the Tauwff, and not many of them. And so shattered was their ecosystem that little or nothing was left for the few survivors to eat except each other.

"How like you your prophecy now?" said the Lone One. And It went away laughing, relishing the opportunity to step back into local time once more in a few millennia to see how many of the Tauwff were left, and in what state.

Yet broken and befouled and hurt nigh to death their world might be, the nature of the surviving Tauwff—perhaps five percent of the original population—remained as it was, unchanged. As years went by in their thousands and the atmosphere slowly cleared, as their now-barren planet was once more exposed to their homestar's blazing light, the remaining Tauwff were quite clear as to who had struck this blow at them, and why.

Then as now, the Tauwff were a hardy people and a stubborn one, intent on staying alive even in the bleak almost-lifeless waste their world had become. Great was their anguish at their awful fate; yet they would not simply accept it, knowing that surrendering to the Lone One's malice would simply make it stronger elsewhere, and fill other worlds with more fear.

So many of the Tauwff who survived bound themselves and their hatchlings by a mighty oath. They swore that those who were best able should surrender their lives and their bodies as food for those who were younger and might be able to keep their species alive; and those who so surrendered would do it willingly. "It seeks to turn us against one another," said the Eldest of the Tauwff, "that we may all die or struggle for life in hate and fear, preying on each other like beasts. But we will not suffer the Lone One to garner such enjoyment from our fate. If we must die, we will die doing each other all the good we may. We do this in Its despite; for by our action, something better will come of this. Though this fate seemed bleak to us, we are the Powers' people, not the Lone One's. Our choice stands."

And so it went on Wimst. That place which had been glad and full of life was now arid and bare and full of pain. The species that had been billions strong dwindled to a mere few hundreds of thousands over time, scattered far and wide across their planet in far-flung clusters, finally achieving a population that stayed stable at the barest subsistence level only by virtue of many of its people agreeing willingly to become one another's food—so that every life was potentially a sacrament.

And so matters went for many thousands of their lifetimes. The Lone One, true to Its intent, came back and saw what pleased It greatly; a beautiful world reduced to near lifelessness and a mighty species reduced to the most marginal of existences, barely clinging to life and at all times seeming just a claw's breadth from extinction. And seeing Wimst's great cultures wiped out—that garden of a world ruined and blasted and premature death now made a commonplace in nearly every life, only mitigated (if lucky) by another's sacrifice—the Lone Power was deeply satisfied that the ancient prophecy had been brought so neatly to naught. And was it not the Tauwff's own fault? For they had brought this fate upon themselves by refusing the gifts of Death and Empire It had offered them. If they were so unwilling to live lives of comfort and plenty, then that was on them, not It.

Seeing that all had gone as It willed, if not better, the Lone One went away well pleased and turned Its attention elsewhere.

And for many, many centuries, so life went on Wimst.

...Until something changed. For all inadvertently the Lone Power had revealed to the Tauwff the mechanism by which their species would be restored someday, and all Its ill works be undone; so that the Wimst would become greater than any mere Empire would ever make them.

But that is a different story.

THERE WAS DARKNESS, and for a long time that was all right.

Then she *knew* it was darkness, and for a good while that was all right too.

Then there was something else: faint, hard to make out for a long time, but slowly it became plainer. That was light; faint, diffuse, but definitely there. At first, by contrast with what had gone before, the light seemed peculiar; she was initially a little afraid of it. But as time went by, it seemed less strange, and finally the light became all right as well.

There was nothing to do, as yet, and nowhere to go—not that the concepts of "doing" and "going" would have meant anything to her at that point—so she just hung there in the faintly glowy nothing, waiting.

After a while she could feel something else happening where she hung. It was a sort of thumping sensation all along her skin, and not just there, but inside her too. Curious about what it might be, she tried moving around a little—having recently discovered that she could do that—and realized that the feeling and the vibration of it around her sped up slightly when she did. *All right,* she thought after a few more experiments of this kind, *that's something of* mine, *then!* It made her feel strangely excited and cheerful to find that she could change something. She started doing that again whenever she remembered to.

Things went on this way for a while, and then something happened that surprised her more than anything that had occurred so far, even the discovery that the light was brighter sometimes than others. Without warning in one of the slightly-more-shadowy times, she started to feel another bumping on her skin... and it *wasn't hers.*

A feeling rushed all over her: excitement! *If I do that,* she thought, *and that's not* me, *then there's...* another *somebody!*

She trembled all over with amazement, and her own bumping started to speed up because of it. And then the other one sped up too! She hardly knew what to do or think in the face of something so astonishing except to *be* there with it, enjoy it, be glad. *You're not all by yourself,* she thought, as if to whoever else was bumping: *I'm here too. We're together!*

That was the beginning of a happy time. Sometimes the bumping sound or feeling was fainter, sometimes it was stronger, but when she would drowse a little in the warm faint light, it was always there again when she would wake up. Another feeling began to become familiar to her: affection. She liked that sound, liked whoever was making it, hoped it could always be this way between them; that sense of reliable presence, so welcome, so different from before when it was just her. The warmth had been pleasant and her own sounds reassuring to listen to, but nothing like as enjoyable as the other's.

The warmth grew stronger and the light swelled and faded, swelled and faded, and she hung there waiting in company with the other who waited too. Slowly it became plain to her that something was going to happen to her, and to them. She hoped it was going to be something good. But what most excited her was the hope that that she was going to find out who or what that other presence *was...* and maybe even who or what *she* was. And if there could be something that was different from her, more than her, then, possibly, there could also be something that was different from here... *more* than here! All she could do was wait. *But I'm already good at that,* she thought, relaxing into the warmth, watching the light slowly grow out of the darkness again. *And so are you. Later on maybe we'll be good at it together!*

There was another realization she had arrived at lately which had been less pleasant than the earlier recognition of warmth and light and company. It had to do with an odd feeling of compression, of tightness. True, as that sensation had increased, so had the sound of the other's presence, that steady reliable thumping. But all the same the slowly increasing pressure was growing ever more irksome. She wanted to do something about it but didn't know *what.*

There came a point where she caught herself starting to move in response to the pressure, twisting and pushing, though she wasn't even sure what she was pushing *against.* There just seemed to be less room in the world, and what had been perfect comfort was less so with every brightening and darkening of the light.

Something else went wrong then, too. That steady reliable thumping so like her own... without warning, it went missing. One moment she was engrossed (to her great annoyance) in that pushing behavior she couldn't seem to stop, always feeling lately that she needed to find more room, more ease. Then the next moment she stopped, realizing how peculiarly quiet everything had become. All was bright around her, and indeed unusually warm, but the only thumping she could hear now was her own.

When did that happen? she thought, feeling suddenly lost. *How did I not notice before? How did I not notice right away? I don't like this!*

She concentrated on holding still and listening harder. *What if I just wasn't paying attention? It might come back. Let me listen!* But she was finding it hard to hold still. That urge to push and twist against the growing pressure kept getting in the way. And she could hear nothing of that friendly bumping, pulsing rhythm, even at her most still.

Her frustration grew, as did something else: a strange feeling, one she'd never felt before. She was *sad.*

How long that sadness lasted, she couldn't tell; it seemed like forever. Her sense of time was still very new, and resolving the finer shades between "always" and "not always" was still a challenge. But certainly that other bumping had been there for a long time, compared to the time she'd been aware of herself. That it should be gone now, without warning, without any way to tell if it would ever come back, was a blow.

There she hung in her sorrow through many darkenings and lightenings of the light, whatever those meant. She found it hard to care. But at the time when the sadness seemed strongest to her, another unusual thing happened.

She began to experience another feeling. It was nothing like the earlier ones. It seemed, like the thumping that had gone missing, to come from outside her. But it was far more direct, more specific; as if something else, something that had thoughts like hers, was speaking to her using those thoughts. It said: *Now. Now is the time. This is the where and the when that has always been meant for you: this is your place. Arise and do what you came to do.*

And she had *no* idea what that meant.

She considered for a while, there in the growing light and warmth in which she hung, but for the time being at least the words made little sense. *After all,* she thought, *arise* how, *exactly?*

There in the depths of her pondering she was distracted once again by that recurring feeling of pressure, of tightness. All of a sudden it felt much worse than it had before. Furious at having her thoughts interrupted by the growing discomfort, she squirmed against it, kicking—

And something *gave.* The shock of it went straight through her, disorienting, jarring her out of the feelings that had soaked so deep into the fabric of her mind. She lashed out again, pushing, arching herself, and felt whatever it was push outwards where she struck it.

That was when the light broke past her, indeed almost *through* her, such was its strength. Against the blinding force of it she found herself screwing closed eyes that a moment before she hadn't known she had. Something was falling away from around her in half-soft fragments that hardened and went fragile under her touch, shattering as her weight came down on them.

For a few moments all she could do was try to hold her own against the onslaught of input from senses that had never yet been matched to their proper stimuli. Her just-freed limbs staggered and bowed under gravity for the first time; her ears roared with the sound and even the feel of wind. She stared up into the harsh cloudless blue-green sky, briefly blinded by the color of it, while the knowledge came rushing into her brain.

Now she knew and understood that she was in the world. Now she knew and understood that she was just hatched, and that she was a Tauwff, and that there were many, many more like her.

But right now she cared not a whit for all of them. Two things were possessing her. One was something she had never felt before now: hunger. She was desperately hungry.

The other was a question that desperately needed an answer. There was no one here to give her any answers, though, for she was all alone: the last one left.

She glanced at the shards of shell scattered all around her in the rocky depression where the rest of the now-shattered eggs had lain, and then gazed, turning slowly, at the clawed footprints leading away from them in eleven different directions through the wind-drifted sand. It wasn't hard to understand what had happened to her brethren and sistern when they hatched. All had fled in every direction except toward the others, to save themselves from possibly being eaten before they'd drawn so much as a day's worth of breath.

She looked back to the deserted clutching-place, half buried in gravel and more sand. Next to the shell from which she had come lay another one, also empty: but its pieces were much paler, broken a good while ago... and not from the inside. The shell was partially crushed, and from the marks and gouges left on what was left of the delicate inner membrane, its insides had been picked out and eaten. Without any way yet of knowing how the knowledge came to her, she knew that the other one who had been with her in the dark, the one whose hearts she had heard beating in time with hers, had been in that shell.

Gone now, she thought, feeling that huge sorrow rise in her again. *Gone.*

But I will not forget them!

The sun—that was what it was called, she realized, the source of the light she had perceived even in the shell—beat down on her, hot and merciless, even slantwise as its light was coming so late in the day. The wind slid hot around her, and her eyes veiled themselves in an extra lid against the sting of the sand the wind carried.

She lashed her tail. Other feelings she had experienced before now—gladness, sorrow, loneliness. But now one arrived that was new. *Anger.* Because seriously, what kind of world treated you this way when you'd barely just been *born?*

She stared around her at the planet, and the universe at large, which had proven itself so immediately at fault. She was furious. But she had a plan.

"I am going to put right what is wrong with you," she cried, and whether the world or the wind were actually listening, she wasn't sure she cared. "Because plainly there's a *lot* that's wrong. So you'd better *look out!*"

NAMES TAKE LONGER to arrive than the basic knowledge that manifests itself in a newly unclutched Tauwff on its hatching day. The exact mechanism by which that knowledge appears was for a great many centuries uncertain, but understanding it was one of the motivations that drove the Tauwff to an understanding of the biochemistry of heredity nearly unmatched among species who turned their minds to such studies without first evolving highly technical cultures.

Over the many millennia after the disaster that turned their garden of a world into a desert, the Tauwff's desperate attempts to survive resulted in their already exceptionally adaptive physiologies gradually evolving their bodies into biochemical and analytical laboratories of astonishing flexibility and inventiveness. Even before the disaster, Tauwff bodies were already unique in their ability to store experience at the cellular level, in carbon-based compounds of exquisite and unprecedented complexity that interleaved in real time with the unique transmitter neurochemistry of the Tauwff brain. But the long desperation of the Doom drove the Tauwff, in their endless struggle to survive, into efforts and accidents of development that no one—plainly not even the Lone Power—could ever have predicted.

Much later research established that the pentahelically-compacted compounds holographically stored across the cellular structure of a Tauwff's body tissue were no longer merely archiving a given being's physical heredity. As the millennia of the Doom crept by, they had slowly begun to act, after the donor's death, like fossilized memory storage—backups of the original "hard data" on which the living being had acted, and from the evaluation of which it made its choices.

The practical implications of this situation, in an ecosystem where all life was under threat, swiftly became obvious. Tauwff who were better at survival stored that tendency in the fabric of their bodies—and those who ingested that tissue in turn became better at surviving. This being the case, it was only a matter of time before some Tauwff, better than others at exploiting their inner abilities for biochemical analysis, became able to sort for more effective food donors in the terrible ages during which (in line with the Doom laid upon them by the Lone One) there was little for them to eat besides one another.

Phenotype, genotype, somatype, overhide and underhide color, length and number of legs—all these markers in turn became signals that the bearer possessed greater or lesser aptitude for various traits that were of survival value, worth incorporating into oneself and passing to one's offspring. Some sets of traits were accordingly hunted nearly to extinction in the early millennia of the Doom, and it was many centuries before (reconcentrated or reintegrated by the chance eating habits of later generations) some of them cropped out again.

Given such an environment, the heredity inhabiting the beings trapped inside it inevitably starts looking for ways to game the system. Some strands of Tauwff heredity became expert at *looking* as if they would not be worth anyone's time to eat who didn't want anything but a fast meal. Some began perfecting the art of looking as if eating their host might make you sick. Taking the theme in the opposite direction, some early bloodlines came to look so delicious or otherwise advantageous-for-ingestion that the mere appearance of them was irresistible. The unwary would quickly be lured close enough to be unexpectedly dispatched by more covert "sport" evolutionary developments like poison fangs or powerful prehensile tails. Yet the temptation would be difficult to resist, for Tauwff who ate such gifted opportunists and were clever enough about managing their own biology could decide which of those ingested traits to keep and which to adapt further.

Life on Wimst throughout the initial millennia of the Doom therefore became a long, long series of episodes in a game that might as well have been called "Evolution in Action". No one won that game, or at least not for long. The most basic rule was to avoid being eaten for as long as possible. Initially the youngest Tauwff were the most disadvantaged in that game—and well the Lone One was thought to like the sight of the only hope of Tauwffkind, the next generation, being eaten when just out of the egg by those who did not accept the stricture that came with their kind's Choice.

But good parents among the Tauwff went to some trouble before they clutched to give their children all the advantages possible. With care they first located and incorporated (this being one of the commoner euphemisms for eating) other Tauwff who were willing to uphold the Stricture and willingly surrender their own lives for the sake of the new life to come. When one parent or another was ready to start the business of eggbearing (which any of the Tauwff's four sexes may choose to do), immediately after fertilization the sacrificing Tauwff became the parents' last meal—their intent being to pass the maximum value to their young in terms of nourishment, energy, and memory.

Then, just before producing the clutch, one or more of the parents would surrender their own lives for their children's sake. At least one parent would remain alive in order to stay close by and keep marauding nonparents away from the feast intended for the hatchlings. This intention was of course not always successful. Other Tauwff who had got wind of the impending clutch would sometimes attack the clutching site, devouring parents and other sacrificers alike, and even sometimes the eggs—though even the most depraved or amoral Tauwff often seemed to share the belief that eating eggs was for some reason likely to incur the Lone One's enmity.

But assuming the marauders did not find the clutching site, assuming that other predators did not (for though there were few other lifeforms left on Tauwff, the ones that remained were relentlessly hungry and could smell a clutch of eggs a great distance away), the hatchlings would in the fullness of time come forth into the light of day. Wimst's star's light would fall on them for the first time and Wimst's air would fill their lungs with their first breath; and activated by these, memories the hatchlings had never lived through would come flooding into their minds.

That was how it went for the last hatchling who stood among the rocks in the long low sunlight, and remembered her parents' names: Ehlmeth and Centif and Sishpeht. Their friend and sacrificer-by-choice Tivish would be somewhere nearby if she hadn't fled, driven away by predators or marauders. She could see in memory how her parents had prepared this place, hidden, walled about with stones, where she and her clutch-sistern and -brethren had been meant to take their first meal—and what might be their last one for many days, or ever.

She knew that she had to hurry, for though the heat of the day reflecting off the sand lent her for the time being some protection, once the sun went down those predators that tracked by heat would see her moving and make short work of her. Right now she had one duty only—to partake of the sacrifice that had been left for her and then to get away into the wide world and make what she could of her life.

So she went; but not without a last look at the egg with the empty shell, the one that had been broken from the outside. Away she whisked across the sand, breathing the new air deep, and hearing still in memory—her own memory—the sound of another heart just a couple of shells'-thickness away.

The Tauwff have a saying, "as sharp as a new hatchling's nose". Hers was as sharp as the saying suggests. More, the continuing inrush of memory from her egg-parents told her what she was smelling for: meat. The wind might blow as it pleased but the sand, even constantly shifting as it was, still kept strong traces of the trail purposefully laid down for her. The blood of her sacrifice-dam Tivish was mixed with this sand and trodden well into it, too hard and deep to blow away easily in a matter of just a few days. That blood had been changed before it fell so as to speak its nature to her nose while hiding itself from all others', and to her nose that trail stood out clearly enough to have been painted as a stripe of light across the empty world.

Before her first nightfall she found what she sought. It was another outcropping of stone rearing up out of the sand, identical to a thousand others that might have been found across any million square Tauwff-lengths of that part of Wimst. But this one, right up at the top, held hidden the flesh and blood of those who had died so that she and her egg-sibs might live. Even had she not been desperately hungry, she would have won her way up there to greet them had the slopes been made of glass.

Stones had been tipped down over the bodies to prevent any of the larger wingborne predators from ripping off large portions of the precious flesh and carrying them away. The only one not so fully covered was her sacrifice-dam, who had managed only to pull down one stone over herself before rendering up her life. Still, she had managed to cover almost all of the barrel of her body, where the organs richest in memory and lore were concentrated, and much remained of those despite the attentions of the smaller daytime predators.

The new arrival already knew at least this much of the Protocols: one ate first and gave thanks after, for time wasted could mean vital nourishment or enlightenment lost. So she went straight to her sacrifice-dam's body first and gladly took her nourishment from it— gorged herself on the delicacies laid aside there for her, and felt the knowledge slowly come rolling in over her mind like a strange internal restaging of the slow brightening of her world inside the shell. Words came in, understanding came in, peculiar concepts that would have had no way to occur to her when she was so new in the world came in. Finally she started to feel engorged in mind as well as body, and had to stop.

She knew she was going to need to sleep—that was brand new information, come of the flesh and the blood. She pushed herself down under one of the biggest of those stones, nearly into the body of her egg-dam, of which little was left after the birthmeals of her whole sib. Nonetheless she curled into those empty ribs and whispered, "I am here!"

Very strange she found it, then, and a little frightening, to close her eyes for the first time and slide over the edge of life into sleep. But as she did she thought, *This is part of putting the world right: I mustn't be afraid.* And so, surrounded by the reassuring smell of her egg-dam, she slept.

In the morning one of the wingborne predators came down not far from her. The scratchy sound of it moving on the sand and picking and scratching at the stones woke her; opening her eyes, from under the stone she could see its long thin legs, hopping around. The thought of this thing coming so close to her dam and sire, be they ever so dead, made her angry.

Let's see how you like what you're about to do when it's you *being done to,* she thought. Quick as lightning (which she remembered though she'd never seen) she shot her head out and caught one of those legs in her jaws and pulled the legs' owner under the stone.

There the two of them spent some time communing in a manner almost exactly the opposite of what the predator would have preferred. She found it had initially had little to tell her except some generalities about what flight felt like. But soon, as she licked its bones clean and crunched them up, she realized that the predator had incorporated into its nerves and its marrow a surprisingly detailed and expansive map of that whole region of the world. *If you ate enough of these,* she thought, *you would soon know where everything in the world was, or might be. That could be useful.* And she determined that she would devise a way to eat flying predators whenever possible, because if one was going to put the world right, surely it would be easier to do that while knowing where things *were.*

Then she came out from under the stone and went again to visit the body of her sacrifice-dam, her egg-parents' friend, who had walked behind them and hidden their tracks and finally, when they had won up here, covered them with the stones. She gazed at Tivish and thought it strange, perhaps a trick of the light, that her sacrifice-dam seemed smaller than she had the afternoon before. But then she realized that she *herself* was bigger, and this was by the sacrificer's gift. As they were alone and no more predators were in sight, therefore, she took enough time to say the words that she remembered but had never yet spoken.

"Know that I know the gift you've made me," she said. "It's one I won't forget. I'll take you everywhere with me in mind and right inside my heart. Together every day we'll teach the one who tried to make us enemies that instead It's made us Its worst dreams come true. All It's done in killing us is make us all immortal! So come be young again in me, and from now till I'm young in someone else, we'll dine together morn and eve, and all the meals between!"

Then she broke her fast on what fare Tivish still had left to offer her, and after that spent the rest of the morning with great difficulty digging under and around the stones that shielded the bodies of her egg-dam and egg-sire. They had not much of themselves left to share, for her siblings had had (she knew from Tivish's memories) some days' start on her. In fact her egg-parents had wondered what might be the matter with their last-clutched egg, and had feared her possibly damaged or dead, hurt somehow in what had happened to the egg that had leaned against hers until the morning the predators attacked—

She had to hold still and work to master herself as that memory, otherwise mercifully vague, surfaced for consideration, then faded again. But then she turned her mind to her task. It took her hours of pushing and nudging and digging in the loose gravel and sand under where her parents lay for her to be able to get at all of the last of the gift they had left her, and gratefully she made them part of her. She was too small to deal with the biggest bones except to crack them for the marrow, and when this task was done she had little energy left for anything but crawling out from under the over-roofing stones and out into the sunlight of a day already swinging toward its eve.

She went away from the rocks to the far side of the outcropping, a place of jagged stones and leg-deep fissures where some cracked bones had been dragged away by her brethren and sistern. These final parts of the feast were now being partaken of by multitudes of little manylegged lives—a thin, sometimes-parting, sometimes-rejoining, always-moving veil of a blue-green dark as the sky, made of a million tiny legs and bodies that clambered and crept all over the remnants holding the final and tiniest morsels of the repast her parents had set forth.

Other-memory immediately told the hatchling that these were *malfeh,* who lived in big colonies under the sand and came out at night to forage for whatever scraps of leftover life they might find above. Some of the flesh they would eat to improve the nest's intelligence, and some they would bear down below to serve as the growth medium for simple fungal life to eat when meat was scarce. They were the wounded world's way of making sure that absolutely nothing was wasted—not a scrap of food, not a whisper of memory.

She lay down beside one of the deeper crevasses that cracked through the top of the outcropping here, and watched the *malfeh* about their work. In the frenzy of feasting that must have been ongoing when numerous hatchlings had been here at once, a long bright green leg-bone that must once have had much luscious meat on it seemed to have got itself tossed away onto one of the upthrust jags of stone that were separated from one another by the network of deep cracks on this side of the outcropping. There the bone had lodged perhaps unnoticed, and now the *malfeh* covered it from one end to the other. To her it looked almost bare, but plainly not to the *malfeh's* eyes. With their tiny jaws they were industriously worrying away every last speck of the precious flesh, even dry and tough as it now was from being this long exposed.

As she watched them scurry about, the hatchling perceived something strange going on at the end of the rock where the bone lay. It seemed that a chain of *malfeh* reached down from there into the crack on the far side of the bone rock, and out of sight.

Curious, she got up and moved around to the other side of the bone rock, having to choose her footing carefully because of the width of the cracks. Looking down the other side of the rock, in the crack on the far side she saw something most unusual: her own silhouette against the brilliance of the sky. For the crack was half full of water, the first water she had ever seen, and (so her egg-sire's memory whispered to her) possibly the last she would ever see like this. Though water fell from the sky often enough, it was rare for Tauwff or any other life on this world to see it trapped or pooled, so swiftly it sank once fallen into the desperately thirsty ground. If she had but turned the other way when she got up, she might never have seen this small wonder at all.

Indeed as it turned out the whole bone-rock was a little island inside its crack, and all the *malfeh* who had come to it were trapped there. Except that, to her surprise, she saw they were not. Over on this side of the rock, and well down in the crack, she could see where that chain of *malfeh* led to the surface of the water. Other *malfeh*, some bearing food, were carefully climbing down the chain of their sibs' bodies. Then once at the bottom of the chain, she saw a sort of lump or cluster of the *malfeh* forming, all of them holding tight to one another. *But they are still trapped,* the hatchling thought. *This is very sad!*

The cluster of *malfeh* stayed as it was for a little while, maybe a few breaths of time. And then without warning the lump lost its hold on the chain, and lurched out into the water.

The hatchling cried out in surprise and distress, for she thought they were going to sink. *It isn't fair, you're trying so hard to get back to where you live!* But then to her surprise she realized that the little clump wasn't sinking. It stayed on the surface, and went floating across the water.

Little by little, propelled by the frantic movement of tiny legs at the edges of the cluster, the lump of floating *malfeh* made its way across to the wall of the crack on the other side. There it caught, and clung: and then the *malfeh* at the top and edges of the cluster grasped hold of the stone of the far side of the crack and started climbing up it. Those that went first didn't go all the way, but held the rock for long enough to make a chain of themselves, by which the rest of the *malfeh* who had floated over climbed up out of the water, and up the stone. Then at the top of the stone wall they turned sideways, as if following some trail the hatchling couldn't see, and vanished down a different crack, one that held no water.

That might have been an accident, the hatchling thought. So she turned back to watch the *malfeh* on the bone again, and saw the same thing happen several times more.

THIS MADE HER STRANGELY GLAD. *This is how things should be,* she thought. *It should be like this. We should all be helping each other, and putting the world right together.*

Of course she knew, even now, that this was not how things were. Just from the knowledge that her egg-dam's body had put in her own yolk sac to bring her this far, and from her birthmeal that had taught her much more, the hatchling already knew that it was the old Enemy of Wimst, the Power that some Tauwff called the Poison-Fanged and others merely called Lone, that had made things the way they were. It had dug Its talons into the planet's flesh and torn it open, laid its cruel Doom on the world and forced its people to devour one another to stay alive. And apparently as far as her egg-parents knew, no one had ever found a way to change that.

This annoyed the hatchling. *Someone should do better,* she thought. *Someone should find a way to change the world!*

And she looked at the *malfeh* again. *Even these little things are doing that! They could have eaten each other when they found they were trapped. But instead they found a way to save each other and keep on living, by using their own bodies all together.*

Then the hatchling wondered how anyone was ever going to convince all the Tauwff to come together and find a way to change the world so that they no longer needed to suffer the Doom. Her people were scattered all across the planet, mostly avoiding each other to avoid being eaten—coming together only when they could not avoid it, when desperation or hunger or the need to clutch drove them to.

The hatchling thought again of what the *malfeh* were doing, and by contrast the Tauwff's problem seemed hopeless. *They can't save each other just alone, or a few at a time. They need a lot of them, all acting together. The more the better.*

...But even with the malfeh, *there had to be a first one,* the hatchling thought. *Yes, maybe they found out how to do this floating-together thing by accident, the way it was an accident that I went over to look in the crack. But there still had to be one who got other* malfeh *to do it... maybe*

just a few others at first. And then the more of them who did it after that, the more who got away to do it again...

She crouched there in the low-slanting sunlight and trembled. It was partly from hunger again—she hadn't even felt the last hour or two go by—but also from something else she couldn't yet identify. She searched her newfound memories, but neither her egg-sire or her egg-dam or her parents' Sacrifice-friend knew what to call what she was feeling. It was a *new* feeling, and it was troubling to her, but she wouldn't have given it up for anything.

Finally she realized she was going to get no further with this at the moment—*and no further at all if I don't live to see the days after tomorrow!* For though by her parents' and their friend's grace tomorrow was seen to, and though hatchlings could go a long time between their birthmeals and the ones that followed, those birthmeals were still important.

So she went back to visit with her parents' friend again, and then with her dam and her sire, or as much of them as remained and could be dug out from under the stones. And after that was done and it was dark again, she burrowed under the heaviest stone and curled up where her sire's bones lay, and said, "I'm here!" And then she slid over the cliff of night into sleep again, thinking of *malfeh* all the way down.

Very early the next morning she heard scratching on the stones again, and waited to see flying-predator feet show just past the slab of rock where she lay hidden. This predator was no wiser or more careful than the last, though as she finished picking the fine shards of its crunched-up ribs from between her teeth, she was pleased to see it had internalized a map of the area that was far superior to the previous one's. *Bigger predators have better maps,* she thought. *It stands to reason: they can fly further. I must think of a way to catch the big ones.*

In the bright light of morning she returned to her egg-parents' Sacrifice-friend for the last time and concentrated on doing her justice. Once more, looking at what remained of her, the hatchling realized that again Tivish was smaller and she was bigger. She sighed in gratitude as she laid the Sacrificer's bones out for the smaller hungers of the world to find—this being seen as the proper way to complete the Protocols with someone who was almost finished giving of their best. The hatchling felt sad to do this, for it was the first of a number of farewells she must now say: in particular, farewell to the end of the first age of her childhood (or, as some Tauwff would have it, the end of childhood entire).

She went over to the other side of the outcropping where the cracks were, and gazed for a few moments at the bone, which was stripped bare and clean as if there had never been a Tauwff wrapped around it. There were no *malfeh* now. They were gone as if they had never been there, and the water that had been in the crack was all sunk away now into the stone.

It occurred to the hatchling to wonder if what she thought had happened had just been some kind of dream. But no: there was the bone, and it was cleaner today than it had been yesterday.

She turned away and went back to the stones that concealed what remained of her egg-dam and egg-sire. To them now she said the words of Gift and Acceptance, the last of their hatchlings who would say them. After that, she turned to Tivish.

"Now part of your name will be part of mine," she said: for Tauwff remember those they've incorporated and think of with affection by incorporating their names too. As for choosing Tivish for this intimacy, it was not that she was ungrateful to her egg-sire or egg-dam. But, as she knew from their own memories as well as Tivish's, taking a parent's name was so often done, even thoughtlessly done. And the hatchling could not get out of her mind the image of Tivish laboring with the heavy stones in the hot sun, and being so tired at the end of it that rendering herself up to the One felt like a relief and a solace.

At last there was nothing more for the hatchling to do but set out into the rest of her life. But something else was burning in her to be said, the way the sun, high now, was burning on her back.

"Now I go out to walk the world," she said. "But I do that to find out how to put the wrong things right. I will act and I will learn, I will ask and I will answer; and I will eat *every single one I meet* who seems likely to be able to help me put right what's gone wrong! I will do them due honor and add their strength to mine and make them young again. And with them in me I will walk a year and two years and five years and ten about this work if I must, until I've eaten wisely enough and well enough to be the strongest and wisest and bravest Tauwff there ever was. And then I will hunt down the One who did this wrong, *and eat It too.*"

The wind went whining by, and there was not the slightest sign that anyone or anything had noticed what she was saying at all. In fury the hatchling stamped all the feet she had, briefly wishing the day would hurry up when she had some more. "*I mean it!*" she shouted into the wind. "So you'd better pay attention!"

Nothing. The wind went hissing away over the sand, unhearing, unbothered.

"Well," the hatchling said. "We'll see about that."

Then Vish left that place, not looking back, climbing carefully down the sheer walls of the outcropping, and went forth into her world to put everything right.

THE QUEST

So Vish began her journeying.

In the beginning of her travels, Vish spent all the long bright days of Wimst walking across the sandy plains and through the rocky wastes, up the mighty dunes and down the lowland badlands. When the long dark nights of Wimst fell over her she hid herself away, digging herself in beneath big stones or deep under the sand. She grew skilled at this business, learning (by virtue of a few near-misses and scars that took many days to heal) that she was not safe until she was deep enough in the sand or below the stones to feel so cold she shivered. Her nights were not comfortable, but at least she woke again in the mornings. And she learned to tell the hours of the day without needing to see the sun, which was useful in places where the larger and more persistent predators lived.

For some days in the very beginning of her travels she had not a scrap of flesh to eat nor a drop of blood to drink except from various small incautious predators of the creeping and tunnelling kinds. This was because Vish's egg-parents and their Sacrificer-friend had walked many days through land otherwise unfrequented by Tauwff to where they could safely clutch without the danger of others of

their kind raiding the site for tender juicy hatchlings or the sacrificers' flesh.

Vish, though feeling increasingly empty, went about her travels
with a good and high heart; for she was about the business of putting
the world right, and what was a little hunger to that? Also she knew
her way better than most other hatchlings might, for the flying predators she had incorporated rode in her mind and behind her eyes and
told her which way to go (while complaining incessantly about
having to walk instead of fly).

Nonetheless she knew she couldn't allow the hunger to last long.
"If I'm to put the world right," she told herself, "and make the wise
and the quick and the brave and the strong of Wimst to be part of me,
I must first become strong myself. Therefore I must quickly find the
biggest, strongest Tauwff I can: and a place where there's already
good food is a good place to start that search."

With this in mind, Vish's plan was to seek out the nearest of the
places where Tauwff sometimes congregated in small numbers. The
closest of these, known of old to her egg-sire, was nearly a million
lengths away. It attracted people because a rare spring of water rose
up there in the midst of rocky foothills, and some of the planet's few
lifeforms that needed water (instead of getting all of it from what they
ate, as Tauwff did) gathered there too. Eating other lifeforms was for
many Tauwff far preferable to eating one another—if only for the
sake of a little variety in their diet—and therefore those who could
make their way there often did.

It would be a long walk there for a hatchling, nigh onto a Wimsih
year. "But I said I'd walk a year and two years and five years and ten to
put things right," Vish said, "and so I will." And so she began making
her way across the world, day by weary day using her egg-sire's
memories and the mind-maps of the flying predators she'd made a
part of her.

The seasons shifted as she went, the hot to the cool and the cool
to the cooler (in which one could actually feel the difference in the air
temperature of oncoming evening as much as an hour before the sun

set). And on her way Vish got to see what many Tauwff never did, not though they lived full lifetimes: she saw the rain.

The planetary climate, even in this latter day still much damaged by the Disaster that was part of the Doom, is a turbulent affair, full of weather patterns easily disrupted by even minor shifts in solar behavior. Long dry periods alternate with brief hard-hammering spells of ferocious rain that fill the air so full of water, one can scarcely breathe; flash floods tear viciously across erosion-savaged terrain and then sink away to nothing. Tiny against the huge surface area of one of the biggest "rocky" planets known anywhere, these thin sparse weather systems appear and vanish mostly unseen.

But Vish, unable to sleep one night because the cold in her dig-under-stone was too chilly for her, crept back up to the surface and saw a stormfront come rolling in—saw the lightning in the bellies of the clouds, saw and felt the rain begin, and clambered up to the top of the rock under which she'd dug. Perhaps the cold was lucky for her. As the water got deeper and started to slide by faster every moment, as (once more too curious) she clung to the spear of stone she'd dug beneath and put her face down into the water rushing past, she realized that while she could taste it, she couldn't breathe it. And the hole she had dug to hide herself under the stone was full of water now, its sides falling in.

That might have killed me in my sleep, Vish thought as the storm passed and the water sank away. Yet unsettling as this thought might have been, she set it aside as she watched the clouds pass over and leave nothing but darkness behind them. Except that up in that broad darkness, as if behind it somehow, there was a faint, faint light, almost too faint to see.

Where does the rain come from? Vish thought. *Where does it go? ... And what else might be up there? I wonder...*

There were no answers from any of the memories inside her, so she huddled down against the wet sand and gravel to wait for day, and when the sun was up, began walking again. Yet the thought of the clouds and rain, and what there might be above and beyond

them, kept coming back to her in the days that followed and would
not let her be.

At long last she came to the place she had been seeking, which in
Wimsih was called Bethesath. It was an old mountain that was made
of the bones of a mountain older still, one that had once been like a
mouth spitting out the world's fiery blood. But long ago the blood
had ceased running and turned to stone, and now what was left was a
sheer high rock with long ribbed sides running up to a broad flat top.

About the bottom of the great rock was a tumble and scatter of
huge jagged old stones that had cracked and fallen from it, and
among those stones rose the spring of water. Many small creatures of
Wimst hid among the stones and up on the slopes of the great Rock
of Bethesath, waiting for a chance to win down to the spring without
being eaten. And this was a challenge for them, as many Tauwff
people were down among the rocks as well, bedded in or prowling
about, waiting for some one of the small creatures above to be so
overcome by thirst that it could wait no longer.

Very cautiously and stealthily Vish approached this loose gathering, for these were the first living Tauwff she had ever seen. The
rubble field surrounding the Rock of Bethesath reached out a good
distance into the barren sandy ground around it, and Vish dodged
from boulder to boulder and did her best to seem small and thin and
unappetizing. And at this business she had good success, for the
Tauwff who caught sight of her as she moved toward the Rock mostly
favored her with expressions that her egg-dam's and egg-sire's memories registered as disinterest or disdain.

Good, she thought. *For I don't want them interested in me unless I am
first interested in them.* And she scuttled and crept among the biggest
stones near where the spring rose, and watched to see who came and
went, who spoke and was silent.

For three days and three nights she kept herself hidden, moving
no more than needed to keep from being noticed, wedging herself as
deep under stone as she could go by night, and mostly staying small
and curled-up and hard to see by day. Many Tauwff to this day have
the colorshift gift that allows them to be more difficult to see in some

lights and against some backgrounds, and Vish had it as well, though she was too young to be much practiced with it yet. Fortunately most of the stones around the Rock of Bethesath were its own color, a near-black veined with grey. So Vish mostly kept herself mottled in those colors and kept herself still, eating not a scrap of flesh and supping not a drop of blood, but watching the older Tauwff come and go.

When the fourth day rolled around Vish thought, *Soon I'll have seen enough to know what I must do.* Since she came she had seen Tauwff who were plump and Tauwff who were thin, Tauwff with ten legs and Tauwff with eight or six or only four, sharp-fanged Tauwff and blunt-toothed ones, bright-colored Tauwff and Tauwff whose color could hardly be told from whatever surface they stood against. She had listened to them speak and watched them be silent; she had heard some of them praise the Choice of the Tauwff and the Protocols, and others of them roundly curse both. And she had seen them both decline to devour one another, and set upon one another with every intent to kill and eat. These meetings Vish had watched most intently, seeing how either luck or skill could quickly turn the attacker into the attacked and the would-be devourer into the devoured.

It was on that fourth day that Vish saw again someone she had seen on all three of the previous days. He was a big Tauwff and a strong one, long-tailed and muscular, eight-legged and in hide-color a bright blue; and he had a kind of den or lair high up behind the biggest fallen stones of the Rock of Bethesath—a place from which he could look down on the spring and all those who came and went around it. Once each day he came down by the spring and joined the Tauwff there, and moved among them, speaking and listening, asking and answering. And on two of the days, Vish saw, after having words with some smaller or younger or fewer-legged Tauwff, the two of them would go up together between the rocks and make for the big strong one's lair. But Vish particularly noticed that though the big blue Tauwff came down among the stones again the next day, the Tauwff who had gone with him did not come back.

Now I know what to do, Vish thought.

So when things were quiet around the spring later in the fourth morning—for it was in the dusks before dawn and after sunset that the smaller beasts came down to drink—she made her way down to the water and waited there as if hoping for a scrap from someone's meal. And after a while, when she roused herself to move under cover near the heat of the day, a shadow fell over her. Vish paused, looking around in surprise, and then tilted her head back and back, for she found herself looking up at the big blue Tauwff.

"Whither away, little eft?" he said to her.

"The sun is hot," Vish said, "and the day has long to run yet. If I stay here among the small stones I'll bake my brains."

"I know a cool place up the mountain side," said the big blue Tauwff, "where you may shelter safe until the sun is low."

"Show me the way and I'll follow," Vish said. "What are you called?"

"Tarsheh I am. And what name might a little eft like you have earned?"

"I am Vish. Lead on, Tarsheh."

So Tarsheh led the way up the mountain, a steep climb even for a Tauwff with more than the minimum number of legs. As they went, the spring and all the other Tauwff fell away further and further below them, and Vish saw well how if she called for help she would certainly not be heard, and that if she tried to run away, any haste would likely make her miss her footing and be dashed to her death on the stones. Realizing this, she briefly felt as cold as if she were dug in deep, and shivered; but still she went on.

Soon enough after that the two of them came to the crevice or shallow cavern in the mountain's side that Tarsheh had made his den. It was shadowy enough, for the door was narrow and the sun could only come in for a short time each day.

"Come inside," said Tarsheh. "Here you can rest as long as you like."

Vish walked in and saw that there was no way out but the way she'd just come; and Tarsheh settled himself in the doorway as if to see what was happening below them. "Thank you for respite from the sun," Vish said, and settled herself on the floor of the cave.

Tarsheh stretched his neck up high and looked down at her with the jaw-stretch that her egg-dam whispered was meant to say he was amused, and his tongue worked in a way that made her egg-sire whisper, *He wonders how many bites you will take, and how much work they will need to go down.* "So tell me now," Tarsheh said, "how you come to be walking about all by yourself in the wide world?"

"I'm the last and youngest of seven clutch-kin," Vish said, "and I'm following the sun around the world in a great quest to put right what's gone wrong. And to do that I must become the wisest and strongest and quickest and bravest person who ever was. So I'm seeking out the wise and the strong and the quick and the brave, to make a meal of them and make them young again, so we may go questing together. You are very strong—that's plain to see. Will you give yourself over to me, brother?"

Tarsheh looked down at her as if he thought she was making a joke. "Why, you're hardly out of the egg to be bandying about such bold words," he said. "You hardly even count as an eft as yet."

"That may be true," Vish said. "But what do you say?"

Tarsheh uncoiled himself and stood up again, moving forward to tower over her, and letting her see all his teeth, which were very sharp. "I say that of course we should be together, and your youth and my strength will go very well together. But perhaps not the way you think."

Vish pushed herself right down against the floor of the cave and stared up at him with big wide-open eyes as Tarsheh moved closer. His jaw dropped wider open in his amusement at what he thought he saw—the dejected, scared-looking little Tauwff with her skin still shell-smooth, suddenly realizing that her big ideas were about to come to nothing—and a tender morsel to be sure, the flavor of her about to be made all the sweeter by her fear.

And while Tarsheh was still laughing at her and just starting to bend down over her with his mouth wide open and showing every tooth, from her coiled-down crouch Vish sprang up at him and fastened her jaws into his neck just under the jaw. With a scream of surprise Tarsheh tried to shake her off, but succeeded only in more deeply tearing the flesh there. Though Vish's jaws were still only small, it took only one more snap of them in just the right place to bite right through the soft unarmored throat-flesh and into the vital vein that pulsed there.

Tarsheh's heart was strong and it beat well and hard, so once Vish had bitten through that vein he had no more than a few shocked cries left to him before he toppled over. There he lay kicking every one of those muscular legs of his, bleeding his life out on the floor of his cave. And when he knew his last breath to be near, he gasped to Vish, "Take my name!"

"No, I won't," Vish said. "You used trickery on the small and weak to make your meals of them, and greedily ate yourself plump and strong when others went hungry within your sight. So if trickery's been practiced on you in turn, you're rightly served, and you're lucky your fate's been no worse. You may keep your name, and I'll keep the rest of you."

Before very much longer Tarsheh's soul unwrapped itself from around his bones and his last breath adorned the air, and Vish sat down to begin making Tarsheh young. Because he was so big and strong it was several days before Vish finished this business. Such was his reputation at the Rock that she was not troubled in her feasting even once, for no one wanted to take the chance of running afoul of whatever powerful and ruthless Tauwff had ended him at last.

Vish did full justice to Tarsheh, mindful of how he'd been the terror of the Rock for years and years, making his prey those who had themselves come there to prey on smaller and more innocent meat. Not a scrap of flesh did Vish leave on his bones, and her own teeth were visibly sharper and her hide thicker and her claws longer by the time she finished incorporating him. And then she spoke the words of the Protocols over Tarsheh, honoring his strength if not his wisdom.

"Because your greed and folly made you careless," Vish said, "it was well past time for you to be made young. Still, I thank you for your gift! For it means I'll be much stronger in my quest to put things right. You'll be part of that great deed, and together we'll deal with the one who has caused all this trouble! Therefore rejoice, and come away with me across the world. And as we go, tell me how you think we might best proceed."

But it was a good while before the spirit of Tarsheh's flesh would speak civilly to her, possibly because of anger at his own folly. Vish did not wait for him to make his peace with his fate, but went down quietly from the Rock in the dusk of the fourth morning, paying no mind to the little creatures drinking water from the spring. Out into the sandy waste she went, with the voices of her egg-dam and egg-sire and Sacrificer murmuring in her ears, and Tarsheh hissing complaint in the back of her mind and cursing her for a pernicious skinny measly little eft.

AND SO SHE walked for yet another year, and another year after that, eating what she could, drinking where she could, learning the wide wastes and journeying through them. Many strange things Vish saw in her solitude, many wild places, desolate and bare; yet her eagerness to put the world to rights bore her up through the thousands and ten-thousands and hundred thousands of long empty lengths. Many Tauwff she also saw, scattered far apart across the rocky hills and sandy wastes, longing for one another's company yet fearing one another lest they be devoured.

Many of these chance-met Tauwff wondered at Vish when they met, for by virtue of Tarsheh's gift she was become strong and tall for so young a Tauwff. To everyone who wondered, she would say, "I am on a quest to put the world right, and I seek the wisest and bravest and best of all Tauwff, to make them young and go on quest with me!" And she would ask all whom she met where to find such Tauwff, and those she asked would quickly tell her that they weren't the ones she was seeking—but they might know where she could find them.

Many such suggestions she was given, many tales she was told of Tauwff of amazing gifts; and one after another, with due care, Vish roamed the face of Wimst tracking each and every story to its lair. Most of these were rumors and legends spun out of control. Some of them were true but true too late, leading only to places where a few discarded splinters of bone or the crushed dome of a skull told the tale of a Tauwff long since fallen prey to illness or accident or (much more frequently) someone else's hunger.

Sometimes these disappointments left Vish stamping her feet in annoyance and frustration under the uncaring sky. "How long is it going to take to fix the world if things keep *going* this way?" she would shout at the empty waste. Then her egg-dam and egg-sire and the Sacrificer would console her, but Tarsheh would mock at Vish and call her an ill-tempered little four-legged worm with the resolve of a two-days' hatchling. And between the taunting and the comforting Vish would find her composure again and set out once more into the vast empty spaces of Wimst, following the slowly-increasing maps of the world that she was assembling by virtue of eating the flying predators, the *siefern*, whenever she could catch them.

On she walked, therefore, another year and another one after that, through wind and sandstorm and occasional blinding rain. And on these travels she met not one but two or three Tauwff who told her tales they had heard from others they had incorporated, or met while still living, of a Tauwff who had seven legs and could move faster than any Tauwff in the world.

"Seven is an unusual number for legs," said Vish. "Certainly this is worth looking into." So she examined the maps behind her eyes, where the *siefern* she had eaten lived and squabbled among themselves about who'd flown furthest, and set out toward where she thought the Tauwff of the Seven Legs might be.

And sure enough, Vish found her. The rumors and the *siefern's* maps took her far north into hillier country than she had seen before, a vista full of long barren ridges from horizon to horizon. Up and down she went along the ridges, and up and down between them, for days and days and days of travel. Then on one day like any other, she saw tracks going down from the crest of one of those ridges and up the next one, and so out of sight.

In haste, for fear the wind should erase those tracks before she could follow them to their end, Vish went down the ridge and up the next one, down along the tracks beyond it and up again. And the tracks grew clearer and deeper, and at the bottom of the next ridge Vish could see a den or lair dug down into the furrow between the ridges.

Vish made her way down there and called out as she came, "I am here!" And something moved in the shadows of the den, and an old Tauwff crept out and blinked up at Vish.

The old Tauwff had been red-brown once, but she was long bleached pale by sun and age. Her muzzle was thin and her eyes started bulbous-proud from her head, and she was thin and lean of belly and thin of leg: and in number her legs were seven.

She blinked up at Vish and said, "Who is the 'I' that you are?"

"I am Vish fsh Tarsheh," Vish said, having incorporated her first Tauwff; and though she would not use his name as part of her taken-name, she could use it as a given-name if she chose.

"So that is the who, and it's well enough. Whither away, young Vish?"

"I've walked a year and two years and three years and four, up and down and round about," Vish said, "seeking to put the world aright."

"So that's the where, and it's well enough. How do you come to be walking about all by yourself in the wide world, young Vish?"

"I'm the last and youngest of seven clutch-kin," Vish said, "and I'm following the sun around the world in a great quest to put right what's gone wrong. And to do that I must become the wisest and strongest and quickest and bravest person who ever was. So I'm seeking out the wise and the strong and the quick and the brave, to make a meal of them and make them young again, so we may go questing together."

"So that's the why, and it's well enough. But it's a mighty task for one hardly out of the egg," said the seven-legged Tauwff. "And for all you're big and strong, you're barely more than an eft as yet."

"Others have said that," said Vish, "and found out otherwise."

"That may be so," said the seven-legged Tauwff. "What brings you to me, young Vish?"

"You were the quickest Tauwff there ever was, so the stories say."

"And they say right," said the seven-legged Tauwff. "I could outrun the wind without trying. I could move faster than rain sinking into sand. I was so quick that I raced the Poison-Fanged One and beat her, and She bit my eighth leg off in revenge, and even then I was still faster than Her. 'But I have sharper teeth yet,' She said. And She was right, for every century is a hundred teeth in Her mouth. Now I am old and all the legs I've got left creak from shoulders to toes, and I don't have a single elbow that doesn't keep me awake with its aching all night."

"Then give yourself over to me, sister," said Vish, "and let me make you young again! If you make me as quick as you were when you had all your legs, together we can put the world right that much faster."

"That sounds very well, young Vish," said the Seven-Legged Tauwff. "And that I'll gladly do. But make me young again, and you make Her enmity against me young again as well. Be sure you won't mind that nuisance biting at your tail!"

"Let Her bite at me as she likes," Vish said, "but She'll have to catch me first; and I have some fangs of my own." And she bared them in a smile.

"Take my name then," said the Seven-Legged Tauwff. "It is Firtuth."

"No, I won't take your name," said Vish. "You deserve to keep it for your own. But I will make you young: so prepare!"

So Firtuth the Seven-Legged Tauwff went back into her den and lay down on its stones with a good will. There she composed herself and bade her soul unwrap itself from around her bones, so that her last breath adorned the air. Then Vish went into the den with Firtuth and set about doing right by her. Three nights and two days that business took her, for though Firtuth was thin her bones were strong.

The next morning Vish came out of the den and spoke the words of the Protocols to Firtuth. "Thank you for your gift!" Vish said. "It was well past time for you to be made young, and the Poison-Fanged One will wish She'd let your eighth leg be. You'll be part of the deed of fixing the world, and when that's done together we'll deal with the one who's caused all this trouble! So rejoice, and come away with me across the world. And as we go, tell me how you think we should proceed."

And off she went, with her egg-dam and egg-sire and the Sacrificer chatting with Firtuth in the back of her mind, and Tarsheh muttering that they were all a waste of his time.

SO ON VISH WENT, more quickly now every day, as she grew into the gift Firtuth gave her and learned the ways and means of speed. Even with only four legs she soon learned to run fast, faster than almost any Tauwff there was. *Not as fast as me, of course,* Firtuth would say from somewhere back in the space behind her eyes, *but you'll need more years and more legs for that.*

Vish laughed at that through her impatience and just went on, walking and running and walking again across the world for a year, and two years, and five years, and another five; eating where she could, drinking where she could, meeting as many Tauwff as she could. Every time she met others of her kind whose souls were still wrapped around their bones she spent many hours with them asking and answering, speaking and listening, seeking to discover the whereabouts of the wisest and the bravest Tauwff there were. Many a weary ten-thousand or hundred-thousand lengths' distance Vish ran, the journeys no less tiring to the spirit though she traversed them at greater speed. But she persevered, for there was a world to put right.

Many were the stories Vish heard along her way of Tauwff who were bold above and beyond all expectation, or cleverer than any others. One after another she followed every tale, through jagged stony sky-high mountains and across broad barren wastelands all covered with the tough pink springy caumis moss that nothing alive could eat. One after another the stubs of shattered bones half-buried in stony ground or tattered dried-up strips of ripped-off hide taught her that those she sought hadn't been *quite* clever enough. And if they had been brave, that too had been passed to others who had now moved on. Or (in the case of some poor mummified bodies she'd found half-buried in the endless dunes of the vast desert that wrapped itself all around the southern pole) they had taken their courage out of the world with them unshared, a fate more terrible to many Tauwff than the dreadful sharing the Poison-Fanged One had forced upon them.

In the last year of the second five, by virtue of scraps of gossip and rumor picked up here and there and the maps her incorporated predators displayed for her behind her eyes, Vish found her way to a place where a little far-scattered colony of Tauwff had gathered along the banks of a trickling brackish stream running down from a great stretch of high-plateau ground to the eastward. Among those starveling survivors, desperate with hunger but (as they were true to the Protocols) equally desperate not to eat one another, she heard tales of a Tauwff they told Vish was surely the wisest and cleverest person in the world.

His name, they told her, was Ashmesh. He knew the answers to every question you could think to ask him, and he lived high up on the arid plateau. From there he came down among them every now and then, and he had recently returned from a long journey and gone back up to the plateau again.

"Then I'll go there straightway," Vish said.

"You mustn't!" said all the Tauwff who lived by the river. "For his present cleverness doesn't suffice him. He's determined to become the wisest Tauwff in the whole world. He cunningly questions everyone he meets, and if he judges you to be clever enough, he'll devour you whether you surrender yourself or no."

"It's true you're big and strong," said the eldest of these Tauwff, a long lean gangly oldster with dust-yellow scales gone dull with her age. "But he's bigger and stronger far. If he thinks you're clever enough to eat, he'll tear your flesh and crunch up your bones and make you as old as he no matter what you do."

Vish stood and thought a while. Her egg-dam and egg-sire and the Sacrificer murmured behind her eyes, dubious about it all. But Firtuth laughed and said, *Can he run as fast as you can? The wise are often not much good at running, since they sit and think so much. Let him try to tear your flesh when you're a hundred lengths away before he can squeeze his eyes shut and open again!* And Tarsheh sneered with all his fangs and said, *Whatever else you've become, you're stronger than you look. Let him try to tear your flesh! If he bares his throat to you, you still might to do him what you did to me.*

Still Vish stood and thought. "If he's so clever," she said, "he'll know many ways to keep from having his throat torn. And he might well guess at my quickness by the way I move. I must think of another way to deal with him."

"If you'll be so daring as to try your luck with Ashmesh," said the old gold-scaled Tauwff, "you should go full-fed. I will surrender myself to you if you're hungry, for this life is nothing to me any more."

Vish lashed her tail "no". "It's to make lives more than nothing that I go," she said. "Because this is one of the ways the world needs to be put right! Maybe you should be made young again, but not for a reason like this! So let me go up to the plateau and see how chance favors my journey."

Vish then bade those Tauwff farewell and began to follow the riverbed up into the heights. She did not hurry, for she wanted more time to think. And though she dug herself deep and safe under stone by night, in the daytime Vish sprawled herself out among the rocks of the river's gully as if she'd fallen there, and kept very still under the sun. Sure enough, before long the winged predators came for her, thinking that because of illness or accident her soul had unwrapped itself from her bones.

But in her travels Vish had become expert at this ploy. That day and the next one and the one after that, as she made her way up the little river's course, she caught the predators and crunched their bones and drank their blood and learned the maps that were woven in their marrow. So it was that within four claws' worth of days she knew the lay of all the land thereabouts, and saw behind her eyes what the predators had seen: a lair or cave up on the high plateau by the riverside, where Ashmesh dwelt when he was not seeking out clever Tauwff to devour them and make himself wiser.

Though cleverness and wisdom are not the same, whispered Vish's egg-dam inside her ear; and Vish, as she came up over the last rise onto the great plateau, wrinkled her jaw in a grin of agreement.

So onward and upward toward the high plateau Vish set her path with a good and high heart. "If it's true that he's wisest," she thought, "then he'll be well eaten as part of my quest. And if it's not, then overcoming him will still be useful, at least for the people hereabouts, who sound like their lives will be quieter once he's eaten; and so the world will be done good. But I must be sure that this matter goes my way."

And there lay what was making her scales turn up at the edges; for she was by no means sure she could do so. On she went nonetheless as she had said she must, for there was a world to put right. And all the while her egg-dam and egg-sire and Firtuth and Tarsheh debated what would be best to do, while the Sacrificer was quiet. Only on the last night before Vish made her way up over the edge of the plateau did she whisper from behind Vish's eyes, *Where wiles and guiles may struggle or fail, persistence oft cracks the egg.* And Vish dug deep under stone that night and turned the Sacrificer's words over in her mind.

When the sun rose again Vish made her way up into the broad bright day that lay over the great plateau, and paused there at its edge to look behind her and out across the wide world. Even though she'd spent years now on her journeys it was rare for her to have so clear a view of the lands she'd journeyed across; and the width of the space that stretched in all directions between her and the edge of the world left her feeling very small. But after a while it came to her that perhaps the world could best be saved by something small; for if things went well the One who'd marred the world might not see its savior coming.

That thought so heartened her that Vish turned right about and began scuttling her way up the narrow stony watercourse that led into the heart of the plateau. And the sun had not traversed half the sky before she came to the place where the predators' sharp eyes had shown her the lair of Ashmesh the Clever.

Sure enough, there she saw him, lying in front of one of a number of small rocky rises that jutted up from the plateau. Ashmesh was long-bodied and thin-chested, narrow-jawed and slender-tailed, six-legged and most vividly green. His eyes were almost buried in his head and his teeth were nearly hidden away completely. All these taken together made him look hardy and wily and dangerous enough without him being wise as well.

But Vish sank her teeth into her courage and scampered straight up to him, stopping just out of leap-reach and ducking her head to him in courtesy.

"Whither away, little eft?" Ashmesh said to her.

"I've come seeking Ashmesh the Wise."

"I am Ashmesh. And what name might an eft like you have earned?"

"I am Vish."

"Well then, Vish, tell me how you come to be walking about all by yourself in the wide world."

"I'm the last and youngest of seven clutch-kin," Vish said, "and I'm following the sun around the world in a great quest to put right what's gone wrong. To do that I've become the strongest and the quickest person there ever was, and now I must become the wisest and bravest person as well. I've made a meal of the quick and the strong, and now I'm seeking the brave and the wise to make them young as well, so we may all go questing together. You are very wise, so everyone says. Therefore I've come to ask you: will you give yourself over to me, brother?"

Ashmesh regarded her in a lazy way. "You're tall and strong and quick for so young a Tauwff, I'll grant you," he said, "but you're still barely more than an eft for all that."

Vish smiled. "Others have said as much and found out otherwise."

"But I don't think I'll be one of those," Ashmesh said. "For I see broad and I see narrow: I see before me and behind me and all about from the height of my mind, as even one less wise might see all around with their eyes from this height where we stand. There's no direction you can find to attack me from that I'm not already guarding, little eft, for I am the wisest Tauwff there is. I have eaten Pevek the Deep-Thinker from the polar wastes far away, and Dilathsk the Golden from the Last Marsh, and Mehtharknishel of the Four Names from Undersark: and not one of them was a match for my wisdom or skill or could answer the questions I asked. Therefore give up your plan, young Vish, for not only will you not make a meal of me, but I will not even bother making one of you. So run along now down the river with you, and go save the world somewhere else."

Vish puffed up in annoyance. But in her head Tarsheh spoke up and said, *He's as vain as a suitor just after his pre-clutching dance. Just hark to his bragging and preening! The last thing someone like you needs is to eat that. You think too well of yourself as it is.*

And for all that Tarsheh's manner when he said this was as offensive as usual, Vish saw his point, and suddenly saw her way clear.

"But wouldn't it be fine to make a meal of me?" she said. "Think how much further you could pursue your travels to be the cleverest if you had my strength and speed."

Ashmesh snapped his teeth in bemusement at that, as if wondering why Vish would be so eager for him to eat her. "There's little meat on that bone for you, I'd think," he said. "Truly it's wise for me to save myself a meal if you're so witless."

"But I would then be part of the wisest Tauwff in the world," Vish said, doing her best to sound as if this was truly an exciting opportunity. "For truly everyone says your mind is without equal and a gift to the planet."

"Do they say that?" said Ashmesh, stretching himself in the sun, a pleased gesture. "Truly? That is unusually perceptive. And indeed they're right to say so."

"And that being true," Vish said, "think how much better it would be if you were young again in me! For even if I surrendered myself to you for the good purpose of making your body stronger and your life longer, and even if you ate every last scrap of me, alas, I could not make you young enough—not young in *truth*. Your heart would gain my youth and strength, but not your body. Whereas if you give your-self over to me and I did right by you, you would have both all your mighty wisdom *and* my body's strength and youth."

"This is mere idle chat and flattery," said Ashmesh after a few moments. "I cannot be swayed by the blandishments of a mere eft." Yet Vish saw the way his eyes looked and the way his jaw and dewlaps stretched when she praised him.

"Of course not," Vish said, looking shamefaced. "Yet where's the harm in repeating what so many people say is true? They all talk about your travels and the great ones you've bested to become the wisest in the world." And she made her eyes big and eager so that they swiveled with excitement. "Dilathsk the Golden knew every-thing about the shape of the world, they say, and what happens where the sky touches it at the edges! Yet you knew more than he? How did you best him? Tell the tale!"

And Ashmesh, nothing loth, leaned up on his front legs and back on his back ones and told the tale entire, from first greeting to last crunch of bone, and all the questions and answers in between. And when he was done Vish praised him and said, "How keen your ques-tioning was! How dreadfully he floundered! How kind of you to take his lesser wisdom into yours at the end and give him the chance to learn better!"

Ashmesh nodded at that and actually looked a touch abashed, and Vish said, "But then there was Pevek of the South, who everyone says knows the secrets of the ground and the deep places and every-thing below—"

"Knew," said Ashmesh.

"How did you best him? Tell the tale!"

Ashmesh told the tale from start to finish, glossing nothing over and leaving nothing out. The sun slid down the sky and the day grew cool and things began to go dark: and Ashmesh looked up with something like regret. "Tales must end when night comes down," he said.

"But more may be told tomorrow, surely?"

Ashmesh hesitated: but Vish's eyes were still swiveling. "More may be told," he said at last, and went into his lair.

Vish went off and found stone nearby suitable for her to dig herself beneath. And when the morning came, before the light of the Sun broke over the edge of the world, she was waiting with eyes wide by the doorway of Ashmesh's lair.

His eyes went wide too, but with surprise: and Vish knew in her bones that her gamble had paid off. But she was careful to show no sign. "Tell the tale!" she said.

So all that day she sat at Ashmesh's feet and heard him tell the tale: not just that of Pevek of the South, but of many another clever Tauwff or wise one he'd met and bested. And ever and anon Vish would say admiringly, "What a thing it would be to make such wisdom young!" And Ashmesh would scowl his eyes closed and mock her for an upstart hatchling gone delusional with hunger, or chaffer with her as if he was yielding to her will, and then laugh at Vish for a poor outmaneuvered fool.

Yet when she'd finished lashing her tail in frustrated sorrow, mere breaths later she would be begging him for another tale and praising the cleverness of Ashmesh. Each one being done, Vish would cajole him and praise him and speak him fair, and each time she did he would hesitate; but the hesitations grew shorter every time. As evening drew near again Vish once more begged Ashmesh for another tale of a battle of wits with some Tauwff to whom fame (in his always-available opinion) had attached itself with too little reason. Ashmesh laughed at her and took a breath's worth of thought, and then began the tale of Sesmef One-Eye, which even her egg-dam and egg-sire knew, and which was far too long a tale ever to be done by the time the sun went down.

Realizing that, Vish carefully kept her tail from lashing in triumph, but listened to the tale. And the sun went down in the midst of Ashmesh's tale, and she said wistfully, "More may be told, surely?"

"More of the tale may be told," said Ashmesh, and more quickly than he would have said it had he needed to think about the answer.

Then he went into his lair, but Vish could not miss the reluctance: and she dug herself in under stone and slept only with difficulty, for she didn't need her egg-sire's and egg-dam's and the Sacrificer's murmurs to know that Ashmesh was important to her quest; and even Tarsheh growled with annoyance at his cleverness and knowledge.

When the sun rose before Ashmesh's lair, Vish had risen before it and was there waiting. Ashmesh came out and greeted her by name, and then leaned up on his front legs and back on his back ones and began again to tell of how Sesmef One-Eye, who'd answered the deadly questions of the Clutch of Five and made them younger one by one, was (much later) made young in turn by Ashmesh.

The sun was high before he finished that tale, and when he did once more Vish praised his cleverness—for truly he was able to find creative ways to use his knowledge, and he was not afraid to put himself in danger to do what he felt he needed to do. And once more after that she said, "Be made young in me, Ashmesh! Do it now, and walk the world for another two thousand years! For the world can use you."

She surprised herself, perhaps, by how true it felt to her now. And in his turn Ashmesh hesitated, for over the past two days without his knowing it his will had begun to bend toward hers. Ashmesh was lonely up on his high plateau, and weary of being feared by everyone even though he had provoked much of that fear to keep himself from knowing himself alone. But most of all, Ashmesh found Vish's praise of him surpassing sweet—though he hoped he might keep her from knowing that.

For her own part Vish was willing to let him believe for the time being that she did not. *For the world needs to be mended, and what's a little guarding of one's thoughts against that?* For now she simply said, "Only you, Ashmesh the Clever, can be of so much help in this quest. Tauwff from now until the Sun stops rising will know your name and praise it; for you'll be one of the ones who helped put the world right."

Long, long he hesitated at the last. But finally, as the sun started to slide horizonward one more time, Ashmesh said: "It's true that I'm looking over the edge of life toward that time which not even wisdom can delay."

"All Tauwff would have reason to mourn when that day comes for you," Vish said. "So put it off for another lifetime's worth of years!"

"And if the world was put right, there would be many more people to be wiser than?" Now it was Ashmesh sounding wistful.

Vish did not betray her notice of this by so much as a claw's twitch. "And many more to praise you," she said, "as time went by."

He sat silent for some moments. Then he said, "I shall do that."

So as the sun went down they went into his den, and Ashmesh couched himself in his bed-place, and bade his soul unwrap itself from around his bones.

"Take my name!" Ashmesh said at the last.

"No, I won't take your name," Vish said, "for I don't know yet for certain if I want it. Your wisdom has yet to prove itself fully to me, and one should never take a name they're not sure about. But you may yet convince me; so let's see."

And seeing that matters would go no better than that for the moment, Ashmesh let his last breath adorn the air. That night Vish lay down by him and kept him company without starting to do right by him, for respect's sake and because there was always less waste if one had enough light to work with. When the sun rose again she set to work, and it took her four full days to do him justice. On the morning of the fifth day she stood out before his lair in the sun and said, "Ashmesh, I thank you for your gift! For it means I'll be much more clever in my quest to put things right. You'll be part of that great deed, and together we'll deal with the one who has caused all this trouble! Therefore rejoice, and come away with me across the world. And as we go, tell me how you think we might best proceed."

And she set off down the watercourse toward the way down from the high plateau, full of hopes that Ashmesh would be able to help her work out what her next move should be. But Ashmesh was already telling the others behind her eyes the tale of the Tauwff Trapped in the Cave of the Second Doom, and how he had freed him and learned his lore before making him young. And Vish's egg-dam and egg-sire and the Sacrificer and Firtuth all listened with interest, while Tarsheh muttered, *Vainglorious braggart, this next demi-aeon will feel like an eternity!*

So VISH MADE her way down from the plateau, and over the days that followed her egg-parents and the others, even Tarsheh, spoke with him much (though Tarsheh's speech consisted mostly of snorts of disgust).

Vish for her part also spent much time talking with Ashmesh, asking and answering. He was initially much distracted by the feel of her body and the way it moved with so few legs (*I'd almost completely forgotten. Once when I was out seeking after a sage of the Northern Sands...*). But after having heard about her quest every day in fairly broad terms every day for three days running, he now began to question her more closely about it, attempting to get Vish to explain to him exactly what "putting the world right" *meant.*

After several days of this Vish found herself becoming uneasy that, despite her years of journeying in this cause, she had never really thought deeply enough about that herself. She felt sure that the Poison-Fanged One, the Enemy of the World, was at the root of her troubles—that It was the reason the world went ill, the source of the Doom that had given Tauwff no choice but to prey on one another, and (secretly) she was sure It was responsible for the heart that had stopped beating next to hers so long ago. Though that was something of which she did not speak to Ashmesh.

But all the other reasons they discussed at some length. And finally, as Vish lay by a great boulder at the edge of a rocky plain some days away from Ashmesh's old lair, the Clever One said to her, *It would seem to me that what you should do now is seek out wizards.*

She stretched and yawned, and then lay still again, for she was just beginning to get past the satiety that had come of doing right by Ashmesh, and it was in her mind that another of the flying predators would taste good about now. "And what might wizards be?"

They are Tauwff with power, Ashmesh said. *I once did justice to a wise one from the eastern stonehills who had eaten a wizard. He said that her mind had been full of astonishing things, as well as a strange language that no one had ever heard; and she used it to speak to stones and moss and water and air, and even the very sky.*

"That doesn't seem like much use," Vish said. "I can speak to those whenever I please."

But the wizard could hear them speak back, said Ashmesh, *so the wise one of the Stonehills told me. And the dead things of the world would obey the wizard's commands, after she had spoken to them a while.*

"That might be of more use," Vish said.

The most interesting thing, however, said Ashmesh, was that all wizards, apparently, come to meet the One who made the Doom and laid it on the world. They face that One in combat, and best It if they can.

"And how do they best It," Vish said, unimpressed, "if the world is still as it is?"

The wise one couldn't tell me, Ashmesh said. *And the wizard he had eaten would only laugh at him, and would not tell him more.*

"That seems rude," Vish said. "Well, it seems that I must, as you say, seek out wizards. I will make them young within me, and they will tell me their secrets of how to meet the One who Made the Doom and discover how it may be unmade."

That may not be enough, said Ashmesh, *if the ones you make young are as stubborn as the one the Wise One of the Stonehills ate.*

"If things turn out that way," Vish said, "then maybe what's needed is for me to become a wizard. If one wants to be a wizard, what does one do?"

The Wise One could never tell me that, said Ashmesh, *nor could anyone else I've ever eaten.*

Vish scowled in annoyance. "Then I will have to find out," she said. And shortly a flying predator came down and she busied herself with catching and eating it; but the thought would not leave her mind.

She was greatly irked. It seemed to Vish now as if all the gifts she had sought out and made her own, all her strength and speed and even Ashmesh's wisdom, were as nothing compared to the prospect of becoming a wizard, which she had no idea how to do.

VISH AND THE WIZARDS

So on Vish went, running and walking and running again across the face of Wimst for a year, and two years, and three years, and five; meeting other Tauwff wherever she could discover them living, asking and answering, questioning and challenging, and telling them of her quest.

The difference now was that everywhere she went, she asked after wizards. Many Tauwff had no idea what Vish was talking about. Others, who had at least heard of wizards, told her that all of them were dead—long ago driven out of life by the Poison-Fanged One during the Doom, or else long since dead in the times between.

Still others told Vish that yes, there were still wizards, but they kept themselves hidden to avoid the Poison-Fanged One's attentions. Or else they lived very far away, east and north and west and south, a thousand thousand thousand lengths away—no one knew how far. Vish gnashed her fangs when she heard this, for it seemed to her as if the wizards were hiding from her on purpose, now that she needed them. "Why are they doing this?" she demanded of the air. "We ought to be on the same side: we want the same things! Why will they not meet me?"

None of the voices inside had answers for her, not her egg-dam or egg-sire or any of the others. There was nothing she could do but go on. And so on Vish went under the wide sky, and seasons came and went over and around her through another year and two years and five years and ten. Over the great Northern mountain ranges near the pole, she went, and southward again into the endless badlands under the mountains' slopes, up and down the rocky vales, where one was so like the one before it and the one to come that she often couldn't be sure where she was.

She came into one more of these endless sharp-bottomed valleys and scuttled down among its stones until, far away, she saw a glint of something bright red amid the round dun rocks.

Vish made for that spot of color, and saw that it was a Tauwff very wizened and withered and old, lean as a new hatchling but naturally much bigger. He saw her coming and said to her, "Whither away, bold young traveler, and why do you walk about all by yourself in the wide world?"

"I'm the last and youngest of seven clutch-kin," Vish said, "on a great quest to put right what's gone wrong in the world. And to do that I'm seeking out wizards, for I have already made young within me Tauwff who're wise and strong and quick, but they are not enough for my task." There was always a certain amount of muttering inside her head when she would say this, but Vish had come to ignore it. "I seek a wizard, to make a meal of them and make them young in me, so we may go questing together. So tell me, if you will: are there wizards hereabouts, and if there are, which way?"

"No—" said the old red Tauwff.

So annoyed was Vish that she was choosing the best of the maledictions she had learned in her years of wandering when the old red Tauwff said, "Not *wizards,* impatient traveler." And it stared at her in annoyance. "Just one."

Vish's mouth fell open. "Excellent brother," she said, *"where?"*

"Just over that next ridge," said the old red Tauwff, "in a cave under that slope, lives Podrist Short-Tail, who is a wizard and has been these hundred years or more. She is young yet, but she says that young wizards are strongest in the fight against the Poison-Fanged One."

Vish's heart began to pound. "We shall see about that," she said, and went straight up the slope toward the next ridge without bothering to say farewell in any of the prescribed ways.

And sure enough, she crested the ridge and hurried down the far side, almost falling several times in her haste, and so came to a place where there was a crack in the slope, like the one that had been Tarsheh's den a long time ago. And lo, down among the boulders and rubble that lay about the long tall narrow doorway, there was a Tauwff not much bigger than she, and as yet still only as four-legged though a bit heavier in the shoulders. In color she was a tawny dark yellow of a kind Vish had not seen before, but otherwise there was nothing much remarkable about her.

Vish came down to the valley floor and hurried to this Tauwff, who sat down on her back legs and awaited her. And when Vish came up with her, she wreathed what there was of her tail in greeting and said, "Whither away, sister from afar?"

"Are you called Podrist the Short-Tailed?" Vish said, out of breath.

The yellow Tauwff waved the tail, which was missing a third of its length at the end. "That I am, as you see. And what name might you have earned in your travels?"

"I am Vish."

"Welcome then, *hrasht* Vish."

Vish lashed her tail a little, not understanding; though the word seemed friendly, and for some reason sounded as if it meant the one to whom it was spoken was a clutchling of one of one's egg-parents' clutch-kin.

"I don't know that word," Vish said, though little used to admitting what she did not know.

"'Cousin' is how we say it," said Podrist. "Tell me then, *hrasht* Vish, what's sent you walking about the wide world all by yourself?"

"I'm the last and youngest of seven clutch-kin," Vish said, "and

I'm following the sun around the world in a great quest to put right what's gone wrong with everything. I've sought the quick and the strong and the wise to make them young so they could help me in my quest. And what wisdom has told me is that I need wizards to help me next. You're a wizard, your neighbor tells me. So will you give yourself over to me, sister?"

"I know your quest," said Podrist, "for righting the marred world is what all wizards seek to do. If you want to do that too, I say that you're well met on the journey."

"If all wizards seek to put the world right," Vish said, looking around her in a meaningful way at the waste of sand and rocks where they stood, "I would say you're not doing a very good job."

"Some things take time," said Podrist, "and some take power, and some take both. Not even the Great Wizard who leads all wizards in this world and knows what must be done has been able to achieve this task. Yet who knows, maybe with your help he will."

Podrist fell silent for a moment then, and looked at Vish. Vish looked back, uncertain what was needed.

Podrist sighed. "No matter. I both see your quest and hear it in my heart; for the Poison-Fanged One's clutch-kin speak to wizards there. The Bright Clutch bids me help you, and so I shall."

"Help me how?" Vish said, feeling rather confused by all this sudden helpfulness.

"You must unwind my soul from my bones and take this body if you can, for the Bright Clutch tells me you'll need it more than I."

Vish's mouth dropped open in surprise at that. "Well then, surrender yourself to me," she said, "and I will make you young."

"I can't surrender myself to you," Podrist said. "My Art forbids it. If you want my body, you may take it if you can: but you must fight me for it. You have not been tested yet, and I am your test."

Vish was not sure what that meant. "I am stronger than you," she said.

"We will see about that," said Podrist.

"I am quicker than you," Vish said.

"That may be so," said the wizard, "for you see my tail and how the Poison-Fanged One bit right through it when I first fought It for my power. But will being quicker than I am now be quick *enough*? We will see about that also."

"I am cleverer than you," said Vish.

"We will see about that as well," said Podrist. "But that won't help you today, unless your cleverness teaches you ways to fight me that can help you beat me. If you kill me and incorporate me, *hrasht* Vish, I promise I will be your loyal friend and help you find the Great Wizard and the answer to your quest. But you will not find him without first fighting me and unwinding my soul from my bones."

And Podrist leapt at her throat.

Then she and Vish fought. And where Vish was quick with Firtuth's speed, Podrist was quicker: and though Ashmesh hissed advice behind her eyes about how best to fight, Podrist was cleverer: and though Tarsheh's strength was bound into her bones and sinews, Vish feared it would not be enough, for Podrist's bones were like stone and the weight of her like boulders when it fell on Vish.

Together she and Podrist rolled on the stones and beat one another against them to make each other sore and weak. They kicked at one another's bellies with their hind claws, and tore at one another's eyes with their forelimb-claws, and bit at one another's armor with their teeth. Though Vish had had many fights in her days and seasons and years of walking, she had never had one like this, for every time she moved it was as if Podrist knew what she was going to do and did it first.

But at last Vish felt Podrist wearying a little, and knew that though her adversary was strong, her own journeys had made her stronger. And as they rolled across the rocks together and Podrist grappled with her claws for purchase, for just a moment she bared the spot between the right fore-shoulder and the base of her jaw, where scales are fewer and the great vessels run near the surface; and straightway Vish closed her jaws hard on that spot and tore it wide.

Podrist's heart was strong and beat well, so very quickly Podrist fell back limp as her bright blood pooled among the stones. Yet she laughed at Vish as she lay there, and at that Vish felt very strange.

"I will take your name," Vish said as she stood over Podrist, "for you fought most bravely."

"I thank you for that," said Podrist as her soul unwrapped itself from around her bones, and her last breath adorned the air.

But I have much more to give you than just my name.

And now it was Vish's turn to stagger and fall down limp, for with Podrist's freed breath a great rush and flow of knowledge poured over her like a flash flood coming down a ravine, and poured all of itself into her mind so that she hardly knew her own thoughts amid the thunder of it. She was deafened by words and spells, she was blinded by figures and diagrams written in the air as if scratched on stone. The rocks under her claws and the air in her lungs buzzed and burned with a great rush of *knowing*—knowing that the world was not empty, that the sky was not blank: that beyond it lay more, *other* worlds, more than this world, *endlessly* more, worlds full of strange creatures and languages and thoughts, worlds soaked in wonders unimaginable.

Vish was staggered and terrified by what she saw and heard and knew. Suddenly the whole of Wimst that Vish had walked and everything she had learned about it seemed small and negligible things in the face of what Podrist had in her time learned and seen and known. And the Great Wizard, Vish now realized, knew far more.

In her head now she heard the language she had not recognized when Podrist called her *hrasht*, but she recognized it now: the Speech, the one true Speech in which things were made and later marred. And in that Speech she heard Podrist speaking to her, and laughing. That laughter was the strangest thing that Vish had ever heard; for she had not even begun to do Podrist justice as yet.

Silence fell after a while, or something like silence: for all the space behind her eyes was full of that Speech, and her egg-parents and the Sacrificer and Firtuth and Ashmesh and Tarsheh were all abashed and silenced by it. So Vish got up, and not knowing what else to do, spoke the words of the Protocols over Podrist. "I thank you for your gift, Podrist the Short-Tailed! For it means I'll be that much stronger in my quest to put things right. You'll be part of that great deed, and together we'll deal with the one who has caused all this trouble!"

I was already part of that deed, said Podrist. And Vish was startled, for one does not normally hear one's new mind-kin until they have done them justice. *And I still am.*

Vish lashed her tail at that, not very much used to being talked back to at this stage, and a bit put out. "Therefore rejoice," she went on, "and come away with me across the world. And as we go, tell me how you think we might best proceed."

I could have told you that a whole fight and half a hundred breaths ago if you'd asked, Podrist said. *But when I waited for you to ask the next question, you didn't, and so I couldn't answer. So that fault is on you.*

This kind of judgment too Vish was not used to from someone she hadn't known a long time; and she could hear Tarsheh laughing at her behind her eyes. "Well, are you going to tell me now or not?" Vish hissed, quite annoyed.

Since you ask, of course I am, said Podrist. *I'm just one wizard of many in the world. What you propose to do in your quest is a mighty deed in truth, one that all of us have worked at for days and years and lives. Once marred, no world is made whole all at once! But if this one can be mended, the Chief Wizard of Wimst will know how that can be done; so to him you must go.*

"And where is the Chief Wizard?"

Right on the other side of the planet, said Podrist, *under another sky.*

Vish dropped her jaw in horror. "Walking and running there, even for me, will take a year and two years and five years and ten years *ten times over!*"

So it will, Podrist said. *And it's sad, for had you asked me how to find the Chief Wizard, we would not have had to fight. And if we had not fought I could have taken you to him quicker than you can twitch your tail, right across the broad wastes in a single step and halfway 'round the world from here, to stand under the other sky.*

"But you know how to do it! Why can't you do it now?"

Because my breath's adorned the air, you idiot, said Podrist, *and though you do me justice and incorporate me, still all that comes to you is my knowledge, not my power. Without both the knowledge and the power, there is no wizardry. And the power comes not from flesh and blood, but from the Powers that Be. They grant it and they withhold it at their pleasure; with the breath of acceptance it comes from them, and when the breath of life goes, to them it returns.*

And Vish roared and stamped all her feet and tore at the stones with her claws. *"You might have told me sooner!"* she cried.

Well, you'll know to be more patient next time, said Podrist quite cheerfully. *And now you'd best drag me inside and do me justice, for I can feel the predators circling even if I can't see them except through your eyes.*

So muttering under her breath, Vish did so. Three days it took to do Podrist justice, and for those three days Vish was quite curt and short-spoken with her, though Podrist spoke amiably enough behind her eyes with Vish's egg-dam and egg-sire and the Sacrificer and the rest.

Finally she was done, and Vish pulled the rest of Podrist's gift out into the open air on the morning of the fourth day so that the small things could enjoy it as well. Then she stood and looked around at the world and found it strange—for the new Speech was taking root in her mind, and everything had new names. And to her surprise Vish found that it was hard to be angry with Podrist now, for the ridges above her seemed fringed with a tremor of mystery that had not been there before, and the air seemed to be whispering things she could not hear. Even the stones beneath her feet felt strange and changed. *And is it them,* she thought, *or me?*

Behind her eyes Vish could feel Podrist looking out at her. "Whither away now?" she said.

To the Chief Wizard, said Podrist. *And it's well that you're the quickest Tauwff alive, now, for you will need to be if you truly want to meet him and put the world right at last. Now run!*

～

So BEGAN the longest of Vish's journeys.

She walked and ran and walked and ran again across the broad face of Wimst for a year, and two years, and five years, and ten, and ten years more after that, eating what she could, drinking where she could, asking and answering. But all her asking was about where the Chief Wizard was. Some had heard of him; some said he was a myth; some said he had died in the Choice of the World, and some said that though he had died he would someday come again to put Wimst right.

That last answer always put Vish out of sorts. "That's what *I'm* here for," she said. And Podrist would just laugh.

"It's not funny!" Vish would mutter. And Podrist would say, *Vish, it's not you I'm laughing at! The Chief Wizard will laugh, though, when you tell him how dead he's supposed to be.*

And Vish would mutter or growl or snarl under her breath, "Have we reached the far side of the world yet? When will we *be* there?"

And Podrist would laugh at her (as indeed she had been laughing at her for most of this time). *It's a long while yet to the far side of the world. You've got to walk for a year and two years and five years and ten years more, time and time again!*

But the snarling and the growling grew less frequent over time, for Vish was starting to learn the Speech. Having had so much of it poured into her head to start with, initially she resisted the Speech as one resists being rushed down a gully by a flash flood, possibly to be drowned. But slowly she realized that drowning her was the furthest thing from its intention.

And it *had* an intention. *That* was a most peculiar discovery, and she'd needed to come back to it again and again over an entire year, touching it and then shying away as if from a not-quite-dead predator that had turned in her jaws and bitten her tongue. What had filled her up when Podrist had released it, *meant* her to use it.

So Vish kept coming back to that long slow study as she ran, her mind filling little by little with words for which until now she had had no concepts. Slowly she was learning them. Slowly she was learning not only to see at will that extra layer of meaning that had begun to fringe all the physical reality around her, but to be able to see *beneath* it, and find the words that described what she now saw as clearly as the stone or water or flesh: mass, atomic structure, interruption of timespace, dimensional intersectionality.

Ashmesh's cleverness helped her here. Strangely, so did Tarsheh's strength; for the body sometimes reacts badly to the spirit when the spirit suddenly has access to more power than it had previously. Vish's muscles ached and her bones ached and her head and her jaws and even her *tail* ached, but Tarsheh always seemed to know how to stretch during the day and fold everything up by night when dug in so that the aches quickly faded.

"Why can't I just be a wizard now?" she would mutter to Podrist as she dug in under stone every night. "I know the words!"

You know some of the words.

"I know a lot of the words!"

There are always more. But anyway, it doesn't matter. You can't just decide to be a wizard. They *decide.*

"Well, how do I *make* them decide?"

Laughter, a bit sad. *You can't make them do anything.*

Vish scowled. "We shall see about *that,"* she would say.

For the first couple of seasons, for the first couple of years, Podrist would laugh at that. Then she stopped laughing.

On Vish went, learning the words, walking the world: another year, and two years, and five years, and ten, just as Podrist had foretold; eating what she could, drinking where she could, asking and answering, speaking and challenging. Late in that ten-year tranche, the walking stopped and the running began.

What's the matter? Podrist said to her at last, a season or so after Vish had started doing nothing but run at any time when she wasn't eating.

"It's getting to be time," was all Vish would say. She had come a long way in the Speech in the last few years, and though she knew she was lacking the vital property of enacture, the gift of the Powers that turned Speech and spells into wizardry, she could feel the fringing around the edges of things fraying strangely. The world was waiting for her. It was her time.

She remembered again, one night, that feeling from long ago, in the egg. *This is your time.* As she ran across the world each day in the blazing heat, or through rare brief ferocities of rain, the sense of time ebbing away had begun repeatedly to creep down her spine. *It's foolish,* she said to herself. *I'm still so young!* But the thought wouldn't let her be that there was something waiting to happen for which she needed to be as young as she could.

Vish ran.

And at last there came a day when things around her looked strangely familiar—so that she stopped and stared around at the peculiar rock formations throwing their long shadows over the sand. She'd seen their like elsewhere on Wimst, however many years ago... though not with this fringing of familiarity, as identifiable to her now as the Speech itself.

Podrist was looking around too, not as eagerly or with as much interest.

"Where is he!" Vish demanded.

Podrist shrugged her tail. *This is where he was when last he and I spoke,* she said. *But Vish, he may not be here now. He has this whole world in his care; he doesn't just sit in one place doing that!*

"If he's caring for this whole world, he's not doing a very good job of it," Vish said, annoyed. "Just look at it!"

One may care and do a good job of it, and yet have all things otherwise seem the same, said Podrist. *Sometimes the only way you would know otherwise is by comparing with how things would be if no care was being taken.*

Vish let out a long hiss of annoyance. "So what now?" she said.

We keep walking.

"Running," Vish said.

AND SO THEY DID: years more, millions of lengths more. Vish kept learning the words of the Speech, listened to the conversation of her behind-the-eyes kin, and wondered how she was going to put the world right if there was nothing more she could do now but run and run and run across the face of a wounded world.

Yet the Speech itself seemed to suggest to her, sometimes when she was just waking up after a long cold night under stone, that the running, in its way, was not just a way to get where she was going, but an important part of the putting-right. This seemed to her such a ridiculous idea that once out in the heat of the sun again, she began wondering if there might be something to it.

"As strange as these stories about other worlds," she said to Podrist on another day. "Why can't we see them?"

They were making their way down into a wide white salt-pan that seemed to stretch from horizon to horizon, making even the sky pale at the edges, more a turquoise than its usual dark blue-green.

They're too far for our eyes to see, Podrist said, *and the Beyond itself hides them. But not from wizardry. It knows the way.*

Vish knew that, and wreathed her tail with interest at the thought. "Why doesn't everybody go, then?" she said, "all the wizards? Why stay here, if there are other worlds that aren't marred and this one's so hard to put right?"

Because this one is, and it needs us. Podrist sounded grave. *It's not as if we can't ever* go. *But we know this world best.*

No answer came right back; but that was because Vish was squinting across the salt pan. "Is there something there?" she said. "A big rock or some such out in the middle there?"

It was hard to tell, with the heat shimmering all around the object. In fact Vish found it difficult to believe that the thing had been there a moment or three ago.

She stopped and stared harder. It was definitely there, the thing. And more: it moved.

Vish took a great breath and ran faster.

The dark shape out on the salt pan was no more than ten thousand lengths away, surely. It stood still and watched her come. It was a Tauwff, long-necked, eight-legged, massive of shoulder, long of tail. As she got close enough to see colors through the blinding whiteness all around, it was plain that this was no ordinary Tauwff, for he was a dark blue like midnight, and under his hide patterns and words in strange charactery swam and shifted, bright even in that blinding day.

Vish went straight to him, and then stopped, not knowing what to do or say. Podrist was keeping quiet, and her other mind-kin were mute.

"Well, Vish my little eft," the Tauwff said, "a long time I've been waiting for you to be ready; but here you are at last. Whither away?"

Vish said, "I've come seeking the Chief Wizard of Wimst."

"I am Mentaff, Wimst's wizard," said Mentaff, "and the one who stands on this world's behalf before the Powers and the One."

Vish stood there and looked at him. She was trying hard not to shake, for she could feel the power in him, like lightning in the bellies of the clouds before the brief ferocious rain begins.

"I hear tales in the wind and from the sand about how you've been walking about all by yourself in the wide world all this long while," he said. "How you've walked a year and two years and five years and ten, once and twice and three and four and five and six times over, to put right what's been done wrong to the world. But tales told by the wind and the sand are skewed by their own points of view. It's best if you tell me yourself why you've come."

Vish felt abashed, for the longer she stood before the Planetary she more she felt as if Mentaff knew everything about her and everything she was going to say before she said it.

Nonetheless, she said it anyway, because she'd said it to everyone else. "I'm the last and youngest of seven clutch-kin, and I've come right around the world in a great quest to put right what's gone wrong. And to do that I tried to become the wisest and strongest and quickest and bravest person who ever was, by seeking out the wise and the strong and the quick to make a meal of them and make them young again. So now I come to you—"

And suddenly it seemed madness of her to say anything more, for this Tauwff was plainly what she had been trying to become: the wisest and the strongest and the bravest... and a wizard as well, the greatest wizard there was.

"Yes?" said Mentaff. "You were saying?"

Vish's tail lashed in embarrassment. "I said to them, and I would have said to you: I'll make you young again, and once that's done you can come with me on my quest."

"But now," Mentaff said, "you're doubting that this is an offer I'll take kindly."

Vish gnashed her fangs in a sudden anguish of self-doubt. *Maybe I should just run away,* she thought, *and be a normal Tauwff from now on.*

...Yet I've come all this way and all these weary years to do this. And I will do it!

Vish held her head up. "That's as it may be," she said. "Will you give yourself over to me, brother?"

Mentaff looked down at her in silence for a few moments. Then he said, "How would you make me do that if I refused? For though you're big enough and strong enough for someone your age, compared to me you're still hardly more than an eft."

Vish felt abashed, for this was true. Still, "Others have said that," said Vish, "and found out otherwise."

"That may also be," said Mentaff. "Yet I have also made many Tauwff young in my time; and made many others my own age; older than young, and older than that. Some of them have given them-selves willingly: some have fallen in my path through their own ill doing, for as part of my work I do justice on Tauwff on the Powers' behalf."

Vish held very still under the thoughtful fixed stare of Mentaff's yellow eyes. "Once long ago I met one of this kind," he said, "one with blood on her claws, and incorporated her. When her marrow and mine had grown familiar, I heard a voice that she had not heard, and heard a heart beat that she had stopped from beating—enacting that which is crime even to the Poison-fanged One, incorporating someone not even out of the egg yet, one too small to say yea or nay to their incorporation. For even the Lone One demands that those suffering Its cruel gift have the right to agree or refuse: otherwise the evils or virtues of it are worth nothing."

"That is what needs to be put right!" cried Vish, her own heart aching inside her.

"Indeed it does," said the Mentaff, "for the heart that the wronged one's heart heard beating, until it heard nothing more, was yours."

Vish stared.

"Now what will you do, my little eft?" said the Planetary of Wimst.

She barely knew what to say. But finally she found the words. "I can't trick you, not being wise enough," she said. "Being quick or strong will not avail me here. And even if they did, I would not kill you, for you have my clutch-brother in you. He died—*you* died next to me once and I didn't feel it. I can't have you die next to me again and *feel* it this time. My heart will break as it broke when yours went still!"

"That is the Poisoned Fang," said Mentaff. "That is the fang that sinks into all our hearts sooner or later. So what will you do?"

"I want to put the world right," Vish said, very low in heart. "But I can't do it if killing *you* is the price."

And having said that, she could think of nothing else to do.

Vish lay down there on the hard white salt, and the sky above them seemed dark to her though it was day, and her breath seemed loud to her: too loud. At last she said, "Everything I desired has at the last come to nothing. I will unwrap my soul from my bones and let my last breath adorn the air; and perhaps some day I will come back and try to find my clutch-brother again."

A long time they stayed there without moving, the two of them, the great Tauwff and the smaller one. At last Mentaff spoke: and Vish did not understand his laughter.

"What there's no doubt of at all," said Mentaff, "from the stories I've heard, is that you are the boldest and most shameless Tauwff that ever was clutched. But it may be that you're also the bravest and most stubborn, and the least likely ever to have come so far so fast, or with such purpose. So we will find accommodation, you and I. For the Powers have said to me that it's time I was made young."

Vish stared at him again.

"And also the Powers have said to me that there would be born in this time a Tauwff of unusual gifts—" He laughed again. "One who was single-minded beyond all others, and fearless, and foolhardy and short-tempered; but one who might do unexpected things when loosed upon the Worlds. Yes, Wimst is marred. So are many other planets. Would you not be interested in setting some of them right as well?"

Vish gaped.

"So it was that the Powers sent all your helpers to you one by one —or you to them, to see what you would do. And finally they sent Podrist on errantry to you to help you on your way and test your resolve. Those tests I would say you have passed. Therefore I may safely recommend to them that you should have Enacture bestowed on you—for the Speech you already have, by Podrist's grace. And what happens after that... well, we shall see. Wimst is broken, as you say, and must be put right. But so must other things. We will see what you choose, and how."

"...Recommend?" Vish said, confused. "I thought no one could make them do anything."

"Make? Of course not. I cannot *command* them. No one can."

Vish's heart sank.

"But I *can*," said Mentaff, "make very strong suggestions. Which they will take."

Vish's jaw worked in astonishment. "But how will I run this planet? I don't know how!"

Mentaff blinked in surprise; then roared with laughter. "Isn't it amazing that you even think of such a thing? The worlds have *no idea* what is coming for them." And it took many breaths for him to stop laughing again. "You need not worry yourself," he said at last. "To be Planetary is a dangerous job, so there are always wizards ready to take it up. My apprentice Kasveth will be glad enough to take my place."

"Well," Vish said after a moment, "I suppose that's all right then."

Once more Mentaff laughed. "So by your leave, mighty one," he said, and lay down on the salt pan, "may we begin?"

Vish could do little but lash her tail "yes".

Mentaff looked at her with one stern eye. "Now, the *malfeh* told me," the Planetary said, "that even when you were just barely hatched, you always saw that they got their rightful share. So make sure you do so now."

And so the Planetary of Wimst composed himself to greet the One, and stopped his heart and laid down his head.

"Go now," he said, "and put the world right."

And his soul unwrapped itself from around his bones, and his last breath adorned the air. And as it did, Vish felt what cannot be described—felt Enacture descend upon her, the force that would turn all the words of the Speech that she knew into words of power.

"This then I promise," she said. "Life and the putting right of the worlds: that is my work until my soul unwraps itself from my bones! Nor will I eat anyone unready to be eaten, or make young those who don't desire it, for that's not our way. And wherever I go in the worlds beyond this one, I will serve the ones who gave me this power! ...And now it's time for something to eat."

She looked down at the feast Mentaff had left her, and then stamped her feet. "Why didn't you think this through?" she said. "Now I'm going to have to drag you all the way back to high ground before I can settle in to dine."

Idiot, said Podrist, and showed her a spell that would let her levitate Mentaff's gift.

Vish grinned and started back toward the edges of the salt pan, and her new life as a wizard. But the dreams of what was to come were nothing like as sweet to her as what she was already beginning to hear: the beat of another heart inside her, and the glad laughter of her clutch-brother Hwenmam.

ONCE WIZARDRY ENSUES, so the saying goes, the Ordeal follows hard on its tail, in company with the One who'll bite your tail off short if you're not looking.

But sometimes... just sometimes... *not.*

IT TOOK Mamvish five days to do justice by Mentaff, for he was unusually big and strong and heavy-boned. Quite late on the fifth day, after the sun had set, she left the rude cave where Mentaff had sometimes lived while in that locality, and went out to look at the sky.

It was blank to her no more. She already knew enough of how to use wizardry that she could see the stars, and hear, faint and far away, the songs and the lives of other worlds through the darkness. Mentaff had been right. Wimst must be put right, and she would help see to that. But there were many other worlds also that needed to be seen to, and all her soul was burning fierce with the desire to get out there and do it.

Not until I've had a little rest by my supper, however.

She sat down on her back legs and stretched her front ones, and tilted her head back to look at the sky.

Podrist looked through Mamvish's eyes with her, along with Hwenmam, who had been stretching his jaws out of shape inside her with smiling at their egg-dam and egg-sire and the Sacrificer. He had already bitten Tarsheh's tail several times, which had gladdened Mamvish out of all proportion. *Things may become dangerous outside,* she said to Podrist, *but inside, all goes well.*

Well, we'll see about that, said Podrist, for Ashmesh had been complaining that Hwenmam didn't treat him with proper dignity. *And there are other problems...*

"Yes," said Mamvish. "But they're not here yet."

Nor will they be, said a voice that did not belong to any of her mind-kin.

All of them froze still and silent. But Mamvish looked up and said, "Really? Why?"

Because you give me a headache, said the Lone Power, the Poison-Fanged.

"I do?" Mamvish said, not quite sure how to take this.

Yes. And therefore I will not be attending.

"I'm very sorry to hear that," Mamvish said. "The legends say that it is almost impossible to have an Ordeal without you."

Almost, the Lone One said. *We will meet often enough in the future. But right now...*

Mamvish shrugged one hind leg at It. *Go well, then.*

Things went quiet again.

Mamvish encouched herself and looked up at the sky for a while, considering, while the voices once more resumed their casual conversations behind her eyes.

Gradually she began to suspect something like the truth. For to be present in an Ordeal, at least in the Tauwff mode, the Lone One must be physically present. And Mamvish suspected—though wisely she did not say, or think too loudly—that the Lone One was a little afraid of her. For every other Tauwff she had chosen to make young again, she had done so, by strength or skill or wiles or (finally) by asking the other's grace. *And what—It must be thinking—will I do if she decides I am to be her prey?*

Theoretically, on the surface of it, the possibility might have seemed laughable. Theoretically a mere created being, tethered to flesh, could never overcome and devour the true being of one of the Powers that Be.

Theoretically.

...But was that *all* she was?

For all Its terrible power, for all that once upon a time and for aeons almost beyond counting it was Fairest and Highest, standing at the very pinnacle of created being... nonetheless the worlds have changed, and that was not how things were any more. The Lone One was excluded from Heaven, forcibly separated from its part in the great Order of things—an outcome that to Its way of thinking should have been impossible. Now It spent much of Its timeless existence mired in a frustration and rage of certainty that the other Powers were spending all their time looking for ways to frustrate It.

And from such a point of view, it was just barely possible that even a creature seeming as simple and obvious and transparent as this young green Tauwff... could be *more*: a power cunningly disguised beyond any expectation, a trick or trap designed for the Lone One's further humiliation. Though many beings might say (with reason) that more than anything else they fear the laughter of the Lone One, most of them would never suspect how It feared and despised, perhaps more than anything, *others'* laughter at *It*. For of all its weaknesses, the most dangerous is how seriously It takes Itself.

Mamvish stretched. "So by this Abstention," she said, "it's if I had eaten you! And therefore it's as if if I've made you young, which no one has done before and now can be done by others as well! Therefore I'll take your name, some day. When we know each other better, I will add it in with Hwenmam's and make some part of you part of me. I will make you young whether you will or no, as you made me older than I would otherwise have been and before my time."

And with that resolution made, she stood up and shook herself and said to the Powers that Be, "Very well: now I am ready. Let's begin."

Before the night was over she was standing under the vast moon of another world, setting a novel self-unfolding fractal spell into the crust of that planet (called Emidile) to burn it clean of a catalytic poison inflicted upon it by another world with which the Emidili had been at war.

The Emidili themselves, a crustacean species, would of course have to be moved off their world while the crust finished healing. But Mamvish was already making plans as to how that could be done. Her mind had gone back to the little *malfeh* she'd seen at her clutching-place, and how they had made rafts of themselves and floated away to safety.

Rafting, Mamvish thought. *That is what we'll call it...*

Behind her eyes there was a most aggrieved yelp as Hwenmam bit Tarsheh's tail again.

"Come on," Mamvish said to them all. "Work to do!" She
vanished.

AND SOMEWHERE IN the depths of reality, a Power all Alone rubbed Its
aching head.

PART III

RONAN NOLAN JNR

PREFACE

Attempting to describe (from a position in linear time) the thought processes of immortal hypersomatic beings far more centrally positioned than we in the vast matrix of the Pleroma is always going to be a dodgy business. Leaving aside their mutually interpenetrative relationship with and profound perception of the One at Creation's core, the mere structure of minds capable of operating in thousands of dimensions at once is never going to be less than starkly incomprehensible to those limited to working in a mere three or four.

And describing conversations between such beings is even more difficult. As linear time involves them only when they choose for it to do so, an overheard conversation—assuming the ability to overhear it at all—could easily, from our point of view, appear to begin after it ends... not to mention seeming to take either centuries, or some incomprehensible fraction of Planck time—or anything in between. Such a conversation might also have no middle... or seem to, as the most pertinent parts of the discussion may take place along other dimensional axes effectively as distant from us as if they were out beyond the creation-event horizon.

Nonetheless we know that such conversations between and among the Powers that Be do indeed happen. Among most of the

Powers, indeed nearly all of them, these discussions—be they casual or work-based, and regardless of the terrible energies or Pleroma-deep drama bound up in them—are normally positive and grounded in (almost literally) infinite good will.

But one class of these chats taking place at the white-hot heart of Things is not known for its good will at *all*. There is always an element of competition involved when dealing with the Power who first taught energy how to become scarce and the worlds how to run down. And it would be hard to find more competition between two Powers, even in conversation, even when one is so close to the Heart of Things and the other is so far away, than is the case when the two parties to the conversation are the Starsnuffer—the Kindler of Wild-fires, the Power who Walks Alone—and his brother, old associate and (now) immortal enemy, the Regent of the Sun, the Guardian of the Divided Name, Chief Prince of the Presence, known casually to his present associates as the One's Champion.

These conversations may normally be expected to be of dimensions-deep nuance and of terrifying complexity of bandwidth, data and emotion, such that their sheer intensity would simply evaporate to their composite quanta beings of less seniority who might blunder through such an interaction's fringes. However, since these two Powers are such close contemporaries in the great Scheme of Things, their conversations would to an eavesdropping being from someplace less central inevitably sound a whole lot like very young siblings having a fairly basic squabble.

So about this new one...

Which new one? ...Oh. He's nothing that special.

Come on, don't try that with me! You wouldn't be bothering if he wasn't.

You have no idea of why I'd be bothering.

Maybe I should look into it a bit more closely. Anything you're interested in is worth taking away from you and... Laughter. *Roughing up a bit.*

Don't even bother going there. He's mine.

Want to bet?

No. And he is! From the very beginning.

Actually, no.

You are so wrong. But you'll soon see.

You think so?

I know so! Just watch.

Don't be so sure...

You're insufferable. You're always so sure you're going to win. I'm going to make you eat your words this time.

We'll see about that.

And this conversation persists for centuries, or millennia, or fractions of Planck time, while elsewhere life goes its own way...

INDUCTION

"Ronan!"

Sitting at the breakfast table in their little kitchen, poking with one hand at the button on his phone that scrolled the texts while shoveling cereal into his face with the other, Ronan Nolan rolled his eyes. "Don't shout, Mam, I'm right here."

She was pouring out a mug of tea and didn't turn around. "Not you."

He glanced at the ceiling as if for help, not that any was going to arrive. "Not you": that was the story of his life, lately. He went back to finishing his cereal as fast as he could before it went soggy.

His Da—the source of the confusion, or at least a continuation of it—came down the stairs and down the hall into the kitchen, managing to both hurry and yawn at the same time. "You rang?"

"Traffic report."

Ronan's Da folded his tall dark closecropped self down into one of the little kitchen chairs and rubbed his face and yawned one more time. He could wear shirts and ties and work trousers all he liked, but with his long ironic face he still always wound up looking like some kind of hard man from a gangster show. "What about it?" his Da said, sitting down and grabbing for the toast Ronan's Mam had just put down on the table for him.

"They just said on the radio not to use the back road up to town this morning," said his Mam. "Somebody broke the gates at the DART level crossing again. It's all backed up."

His Da squeezed his eyes shut for a moment and made a kind of aggrieved hissing noise. "Idiots," he said. "Dual carriageway, then. Wonderful."

He started eating his toast at about twice the usual speed, since taking the M1 motorway up to town was going to mean he'd be an extra half hour getting to work at the Fingal County Council buildings. Ronan's Da worked as a mid-level planning commissioner with the county planning board. "Not a bad job", he'd always say, "except for the bit where I spend the whole day saying 'no' to people. Well, we can't all have everything…"

His Mam had visited the fridge for milk and paused halfway back from it to flip the eggs in a skillet on the stove. Then she put a mug of sweet white tea down in front of his Da, who grabbed it and more or less chugged it. "Got that history test today?" he said to Ronan.

Ronan shook his head. "Yesterday," he said. "We get the marks on Friday."

"Any predictions?"

"Pass," Ronan said.

His Da glanced up at him as the rest of the second piece of toast went down. "'Pass' as in 'not fail' or 'pass' as in 'don't be asking me that first thing in the morning?'"

"Second one," Ronan said, being unwilling to get into predicting anything when he genuinely had no idea what that grade was going to look like. It had been an essay test, and his history teacher's essay marking varied wildly depending on whether her very on-and-off relationship with her boyfriend was on or off at the moment. He couldn't wait to be out of his second-year classes in a couple of months and be shut of her and the history module and all the rest of it. *Summer,* he thought in desperate longing. *The weather may be shite but at least there's no school…* And even if the weather was generally bad at least the temperatures were higher, so you had a chance of getting in a decent hurling match with the lads without coming down with pneumonia.

"Fair enough," his Da said. "Keep us posted." And mercifully it seemed like that was all Ronan was going to hear about it this morning. Not that he normally wasted God's time praying about school business, but that test had got up to the "Please God just let me pass the fecking thing" level, and it really would be a relief to have it off his plate. There would be a few more tests that would get him this tense before the end of the year, but it was way too soon to waste time worrying about them. *Got a few weeks anyway,* Ronan thought, dropping his gaze to his phone again.

From down the hall came a *clunk* as the mail flap in the front door went. Ronan's Da looked mournfully at his eggs, started to get up.

"I got it," Ronan said, and pushed back from the table, dropping his spoon in the empty cereal bowl.

"Expecting a letter?" his Da said, amused.

The cheeky answer would have been *No, just don't want the morning half ruined by you complaining about your eggs going cold.* But Ronan kept that to himself. "Anybody wants me, they'll email me," he said as he headed down the hall. "I'm done, you're not. Problem?"

"None whatsoever. Well done that man."

Ronan bent to pick up the letters that had fallen on the wipe-your-feet mat by the front door and wandered back toward the kitchen, sorting through them. "Ronan L," he said (the electric bill), "...Ronan R," (his Mam's Granda, who had been dead for two years but was still getting mail here, usually something to do with his pension), "...Mary G," his Mam's mobile phone bill, "...Ronan L," the house phone bill, "...Ronan L..." —some stationery catalog, the third one this week at least. *"Jaysus* but these people use up a lot of paper on these things, you should tell them to stop some of them!"—"Ronan L..."

Not for the first time he wished there were a few less Ronans around: he felt kind of lost in the crowd. But the name kept cropping up in the Nolan family—on both sides—to the point where it looked like the whole lot of them had been out of the room when God passed out the name-imagining abilities. And the daily post didn't even begin to cover the seriousness of the problem. There was Mam's Granda Ronan (the dead one), Granda Ronan (his Da's Da, who lived in Little Bray), Ronan's Da Ronan (or simply "Ronan Nolan" to the neighbors), the middle-aged cousin normally referred to as Beardy Ronan (despite the beard taking occasional unexpected sabbaticals), and three other younger-cousin Ronans who were the children of his Da's sisters.

Finally he himself had come along and became (to his horror) "Baby Ronan." That had lasted for *years*. He'd had to reason, beg, or (in one memorable case) pummel his cousins out of it, one by one, until at last it was only the unmanageable oldsters clinging to the usage. *Nothing you can do about them anyway except not talk to them when they show up at Christmas...* Not that that helped. In fact it made it worse. ("Oh and here's the babby, will you look at ye, the height on you, I remember when you were just a wee dote and you..." Normally Ronan stopped listening at that point, as some reference to infantile bodily excretions routinely followed.)

Ronan handed his Da the pile of mail and flopped back down in his chair without passing any comment on the topmost piece, a plain white envelope marked PERSONAL AND CONFIDENTIAL. Ronan knew the look of those: it was something from the bank. Sometimes this was good news and sometimes not so good. When he was very small and had heard his father talking about "the overdraft" and how big it was getting, Ronan had for a while got the idea that this was some kind of cold-breathed monster living in the ceiling in his Mam's and Da's bedroom that might or might not creep out in the middle of the night and eat the family. While Ronan knew better now, he also still knew that discussing the overdraft without being invited to could lead to trouble.

For the moment his Da just pushed that envelope aside and glanced at the others, then returned his attention to his eggs and bacon. Mam had finally sat down across from him and was slathering orange marmalade on top of the butter on her toast, a bizarre behavior that Ronan could never understand. For him it was one or the other, never both.

"Nothing for you?" his Da said, giving him one of those sidelong looks suggesting teasing and being teased was okay at the moment. "Something some owl dropped off, maybe?"

Ronan snickered. "Probably a bit late for that." His thirteenth birthday had come and gone two months earlier with a small cake-heavy party that devolved (stealthily) into a cider bash in the parking lot up the hill. His fourteenth year had therefore begun with what felt like a near-fatal hangover and a resolution to leave the fecking booze alone until his eighteenth-party rolled around. If the kids at school mocked him for this resolution, Ronan didn't care: they hadn't spent as much time as he had with his throbbing head down the loo.

"Unless the post office lost it the way they lost the last one..." his Mam muttered as she bit into her toast.

"Wasn't your fault," Ronan said as he grabbed his bowl off the table and got up to rinse it in the sink and stick it in the dishwasher. "Way they've been going lately, it probably wound up on Mars."

His Da snorted. Thousands of pieces of undelivered mail had recently been discovered dumped in a local landfill: increasingly unlikely opinions about where even more could probably be found had been all over the media in the last couple of weeks. "Pity the bills can't go there too," he said, spearing the last quarter-rasher of bacon and the last bit of fried egg and gobbling them down.

Ronan's Mam snickered as his Da pushed back from the table. "Not the bills you need to send to Mars," she said. "It's the people sending them."

"Lotta work, that..." His Da headed down the hallway to get his coat. Even though it was April the weather had been running chilly and damp. "How many companies?"

"All of them," his Mam said.

"I'll get on it," said the voice down the hall. "Right after lunch."

"You're not even done with breakfast and you're on about lunch..."

But Da was back in the kitchen, looking around on the counter between the fridge and the sink. "What?" his Mam said.

"Keys. And this." He grabbed Ronan's Mam's chin and smooched her.

She smiled around the smooch. "G'way with you before you're late."

He got, trotting down the hall again. Ronan turned to follow him, as he was due to head for school in twenty minutes or so.

"Ronan—"

He paused, looked over his shoulder. "Me this time?"

His Mam gave him a dry look and put a hand on his arm, turning him toward her. "Is this one of the old uniforms? Thought we gave all those to the Goodwill."

He glanced down at the sleeves of his school uniform's jumper. "Nope, it's a new one."

She looked down at the navy-blue uniform trousers and shook her head in disbelief. "We just got this uniform last month..."

"Getting taller, Mam."

"Well, fine, but I wish you could, I don't know, *pace* yourself a little..."

Down the hall the door opened. "DART'll be late if that gate's broken again," his Da called from the door.

"I'll drive," his Mam shouted back.

"Okay. Bye!"

The door shut.

His Mam just stood still and sighed for a moment. She looked ridiculously housewifely: petite, blonde, with her cute little sharp-eyed face, wearing a little flowery dress with an apron over it—as if she'd fallen out of some laundry-powder commercial instead of being about to go be the IT lady at a four-star hotel up in Dalkey.

The laundry-powder-ad concept Ronan kept to himself, as his Mam could get pretty scathing about books not being judged by their covers. *And what do I know, maybe dresses with Hawaiian flowers all over them are hot in hotels right now.* "Gonna be late," Ronan said, picking up his phone off the table and glancing at the time.

She sighed. "Yeah." She went to him and kissed him. "Check up on Nana before you go?"

"Sure. When's her carer today?"

"Two o'clock. Theoretically."

They gave each other a resigned look. "Might happen," Ronan said.

"Even odds on pigs flying," his Mam said, untying the apron and chucking it across the kitchen into the laundry basket by the under-counter washing machine.

"You want me to check her at lunch?"

His mam sighed. "No," she said, "it's okay. This new one's good about calling if she'll be late, and if she does, there's Mary next door. Anything you need from the Superquinn? I'll stop there on the way home."

Ronan shook his head. His Mam headed down the hall and up the stairs to change: he leaned against the counter for a while, scrolling down texts from Pidge and some other friends at school.

His Mam bustled back in with her coat on, slinging her work bag over her shoulder. "See you later," she said, kissed him and was gone.

The front door shut. Ronan sighed, listening to the quiet of the house, and then went upstairs to see about his Gran.

ON THE WAY up he stayed on the right side of the stairs so as to miss the one step where the carpeting had pulled away from its nail and was coming loose; then hung a sharp right at the landing, switching back down the hall that led to the front bedrooms. The left-hand one was his Mam's and Da's. The right-hand one...

Ronan sighed, because the subject was always sensitive. Theoretically there were supposed to have been brothers and sisters. "I wanted a football team," his Da said sometimes, ever so wistfully, when he thought no one was listening (especially Mam). "Well, a five-a-side team, anyway..." The right-hand upstairs bedroom and the other back bedroom had been intended to contain at least another Nolan each.

Instead Ronan was in one, and the other back bedroom contained mostly junk and boxes and old furniture that his Mam was always meaning to get rid of—there was talk of turning it into a sewing room, or a reading room, or a den, or something like that: but it never happened. And the front right bedroom contained neither brothers or sisters, but Gran.

Is it Gran today, Ronan thought, *or Nana?* You never knew which of them she wanted you to call her, and somehow you always got it wrong. Ronan had long since come to suspect that she complained about this only for entertainment's sake, and he didn't often call her on it, because there wasn't a lot of entertainment in life for her these days to begin with.

Until a couple of years ago she'd always lived in her own little house up north of Dublin, in Skerries by the ocean. For the very young Ronan that place had been a kind of distant magical paradise where you could run around in the back yard and not worry about messing up the flower beds because the garden was halfway to wilderness and Nana didn't care: a place where when you came inside there was always fresh hot soda bread with sweet butter and Nan's own special marmalade that she made from the bitter Spanish oranges out of the can. His Mam still told everybody who'd listen the embarrassing story about how once when they were near Nana's house and couldn't stop in because Nana'd had some kind of Women's Institute meeting come up, Ronan had burst into tears of sheer heartbreak right there in the car. Even now he blushed at the thought of it. *Well, I was maybe* three! But that house had been special, and Nan had been its heart, and Ronan had thought things would be that way forever.

Then a while after her seventieth birthday, almost as if someone had thrown some kind of switch, Nana had started to "slow down." At least that was what the family called it. It wasn't as if she was moving all that fast to begin with, by the time Ronan was old enough to start noticing things. She'd always had trouble with her knees and her hips, and her constant mutterings of "Where ya runnin to, ya wee smidgeon, wait for me now, how'm I supposed to keep up with you…" had been part of the soundtrack of his life since he was six.

But gradually there came a time when keeping up wasn't even slightly on the menu any more: when Ronan learned at eight or nine that running away from Gran and getting her to chase him had stopped being so much fun, because again and again he had to circle back to her; that no matter what he did, Nana started tiring out faster and faster. And then there was no more walking for her, but mostly sitting, and very soon after that, mostly lying down because she said she felt so tired. And the stairway in her little house couldn't be fitted for one of those chair-lifts that take you up the stairs (and though Ronan's house could, it was expensive and his Da was still trying to figure out how they could afford it).

And suddenly the house in Skerries was being emptied out and most of the furniture sold off. The rest was put in storage, and the house was listed with an estate agent to sell. Ronan could still feel the echoes of the sick clench of his gut when he saw the FOR SALE sign hanging on its pole at the end of Nana's walk. Elsewhere in the little street the world seemed to be going on as usual—cars driving, people walking, everything perfectly normal. But to Ronan it had felt as if a world was ending.

Standing there in the hall in front of her closed door, Ronan suddenly realized he'd been there, unmoving, lost in the past, for at least a couple of minutes. He sighed and opened the door.

The head of the bed was up against the front window, which had its blinds pulled down this morning so the sun (if any) wouldn't come blasting in and overheat the place. The bed's brass-railed headboard was almost obscured by a triple pile of pillows. Against them Ronan's Nana was leaning back in her little pink bedjacket, her sunken eyes closed, her sharp little face relaxed, her soft curly white hair looking almost more pink than silver in this light (an illusion helped by the room's pink wallpaper).

Stronger than usual for some reason, today, what hit Ronan right away when he opened the door was the smell. It wasn't anything like

the smells he'd associated with her a forever ago, not the aroma of
fresh soda bread or the scorched-cottony scent of tea-towels hanging
drying on the handle of the kitchen stove or the scent of lavender in
bowls—real lavender it had been, too, from Nan's wild straggly
garden, not some plug-in air freshener. But instead, mostly drowning
out the tea-toast-and-boiled-egg scent from his Mam bringing her up
her breakfast, there was now that plasticky medication-bottle smell
and the sharp wintergreen scent of the salve the carer used on her
joints; the smell of personal hygiene that wasn't exactly as great as it
once had been because the shower was out of the question for Nan
more than a few times a week now. And under it all, the smell of *age*,
and helplessness. It embarrassed Ronan, and it embarrassed him *that*
it embarrassed him. The smell made him want to close the door and
get away, and it shamed him that he wanted to.

And here she was looking at him with her little bird-face but still
not quite registering that he was here, half dozing. "Lying down
beside her breakfast," she called it. *And me standing here like a stump.*

"Hey Gran…"

One eye opened and took him in. "I'm your *Nana,* ye wee dote,"
she said. "Chislers these days, they got no memories, it's them
computers' fault, they do all the remembering for ye…"

He rolled his eyes… but memory was an issue Ronan wasn't going
to get into with his Nan. Hers came and went, but when it was in
place it was like a razor. *And 'wee dote?'* He could've laughed out loud.
He was finally getting some height on him, after what seemed
endless long years of waiting, and he found it hard to care about his
Mam's complaints about the way he was going through clothes. *I was
the same size forever, he thought, it shouldn't matter if now I'm going
through a few in a hurry…*

He sat down on the bed beside his Nan. "Yeah, all my phone's
fault," Ronan said. "Who are you again?"

She opened the other eye and gave him a look that suggested It
was a bad move to give her sass so early in the morning, even after
she'd had her breakfast. "Somebody who still knows where your bum
is to swat it."

Ronan snickered at her. "Gotta catch me first, Nana."

"Not a long way to go to do that." She yawned at him. He was relieved to see she'd left her dentures in after breakfast. "You sleep all right, smidgeon?"

This was the first of the usual questions. There was a series of them, and his Nan wouldn't be satisfied until they were all answered. "Pretty good, Nan," Ronan said. "Didn't hear anything." This was normally her first concern. After decades of the peace and quiet of her tiny street in Skerries, where the only sounds to be heard were seabird-cries and the wind and the train going by and the faint hiss of the waves a quarter mile away, to Nana the outer fringe of Bray apparently sounded like one great big factory or building site.

"I heard the ambulance people go by..."

Ronan shook his head. "Missed that." The double glazing in the house was pretty good at cutting back on the noise, and anyway one more ambulance heading up the main road toward the nearby hospital wouldn't register for him.

"Nobody we know, probably..."

"Probably not." To Nana when she was in Skerries, any police car or ambulance or fire engine had been seen only secondarily as a sign of trouble and primarily as a cause and opportunity for gossip. In a town then still so small, everybody had known everybody and nobody's troubles remained their own for more than a matter of minutes. But here, in a town as big as Bray, it wasn't like that. People living just two streets away from you might be strangers. *Another thing that bothers her. The world here's just too big...*

Nana closed her eyes and breathed out, a sort of resigned sigh. Ronan just sat still and waited. Nana faded in and out, some mornings; the smartest thing was to let her fade back in again at her own speed. If you tried to rush her, the results could be erratic, or comical, or just embarrassing, and you never knew which you were going to get.

"When will Marjorie be here?"

Another of the expected questions. "Two, Nan." *Theoretically.* The carer's schedule seemed to change without reason and sometimes without warning, which was hard on Nan. Having things be pretty much the same from day to day was important for her, and sometimes when Ronan saw her he just wanted to say *Can you fecking get a grip and* be *here when you should?*

Except it wouldn't be fair, and his Mam would yell at him, and Da would give him that scowling disappointed look. Which Ronan couldn't bear, because though sometimes he knew what it was about, there were other times—more of them, to be honest—when he had no clear idea of what he'd done to disappoint his Da *now*. Most of the time he was apparently supposed to read Da's mind and figure out what it was, because explanations weren't usually forthcoming.

Ronan sighed, annoyed with himself. *Not like I've got the kind of problems some other kids at school have...* He sat quiet and waited in some discomfort for Nan's next question: "Did you look at the weather radar?" And that would be followed by "Can I sit outside today?" But his Gran just lay there with her eyes closed, the lids trembling a little as she breathed.

Ronan glanced at his phone and sighed. He had about ten minutes and then he needed to go. "I looked at the radar, Nan," he said at last.

"It doesn't look good."

He opened his eyes a little at that. It was his own don't-get-your-hopes-up phrasing for days when you could see the rain marching in across the island at you in broad bands. This morning the radar had looked pretty dodgy: patches of rain coming in from the west in unpredictable blobs and splotches, appearing out of nothing and then vanishing again before they hit the mountains between Dublin and the southwest. "Bubbling up," RTÉ's dark-haired chief forecaster-lady called it: the beginning of more summery weather patterns.

"No?" Ronan said, glancing around to see where the TV remote was. Sometimes she used it to pull up the text on one of the RTÉ channels, or the weather report on Sky, but he couldn't see it anywhere. *Might have got down in the covers again,* he thought; *she's always losing it down there.*

"I saw it," she said. "Before the eggs." Nan started fumbling around under the duvet. "He said it was going to get dark."

He? Ronan thought. "Oh, wait, I know. The guy on the new channel." TV3 had brought in a weatherman who was as jokey and casual as the RTÉ head weather lady was serious and on-message. The opinion around school was that he was also nowhere near as accurate, and spent way too much time on birthday wishes and people's landscape photography. "Waste of air, that guy," Ronan said. "You listen to him, you'll bring your brolly on all the wrong days."

"I don't mind bringing my brolly all the time," his Nan said, opening her eyes again and gazing over at the wall to her left as if there was anything there but a painted landscape of some mountains and an ancient framed print of the Savior in what Ronan's Mam referred to as Exposed Sacred Heart mode. "Bernie said to me just the other day that we're getting a lot more rain anyway because of the global warning."

"Warming," Ronan said, and then sighed, as his Nan's best friend, her former next door neighbor Bernadette, had been dead for the past five years. "Ah well, no point in arguing with Auntie Bernie." *Especially when she's in the churchyard and you're away with the fairies.* He got up and stretched. "Nan, got to go. You know where your button is?"

She pulled up the "panic button" she was wearing around her neck on its lanyard, giving Ronan a look that suggested she was considering turning him over her knee.

"Got your phone?"

She reached over to the bedside table, and with the air of someone being very purposefully kind to the mentally challenged, displayed to Ronan her special senior-phone-with-big-buttons.

"Got your book?"

Nana reached under the covers and produced the same copy of *Gone with the Wind* that she'd been reading for what seemed like the past year.

"Right. Mary next door'll look in on you in a couple hours, same as always." Their neighbor was a pensioner nearly Nan's age, but a lot more spry and always willing to check up on her during the day. ("Boredom," Ronan's Mam said. "Nosiness," said his Da. Ronan suspected they were both right.)

"Mary next door is a cow," said Ronan's Nana.

"And the apple doesn't fall far from the tree," Ronan said, recognizing his Dad's opinion coming from a different source than usual. He bent over his Nana and gave her a smooch. "You be good now."

"Do I have a choice?" Nana said, for that moment in time sounding a lot less away-with-the-fairies and a lot more annoyed at life. "Take your brolly."

"Yeah, yeah, the brolly," said Ronan, more than ready to make his escape. "Will do." *Because who knows, maybe she did see something on telly. And being where we are, the odds are better than fifty-fifty that it'll rain just to spite us.*

FROM SOMEPLACE ELSE—SOMEWHERE distant in time and place, or very close, depending on where one was standing—a snicker.

Oh, really. Come on now.

What?

I saw what you did there, brother mine. Or what you thought you did and got away with.

What?

You're all the time having these little deep-consciousness chats with him. Years, now, you've been at it. Well, two can play at that game. Can have been playing at it.

Perhaps they can. Perhaps they have. Yet here we are, still! And if we have been playing at that game, as you put it, and this is the best you can do to keep from losing—

You know what I can't bear?

Do enlighten me.

The smugness. You are so sure. *You think that just because you picked what you think was the right side, you're always going to—*

It wasn't a matter of thought, but of knowledge. Knowledge to which you were blind: self-blinded by your pride. And as for you trying to claim someone else's smugness as being a problem for you—

Problem? It's no problem! As you'll soon find.

Oh, I see. You believe you're about to inflict some kind of 'worst-case' event on him?

Him? As if I couldn't, if I cared to.

As if you'd be spending so much thought on something you didn't care about. On me, then?

Don't flatter yourself.

Why should I when you're doing it for me? Go right ahead. This should be amusing.

You— You actually think that—

I'm waiting.

A long, freighted pause. And then:

Not for very much longer.

RONAN GRABBED the dark blue parka that went with his charcoal-gray school uniform and threw it over his clothes. Then, glancing at the umbrella stand by the front door, he snickered and said under his breath, "Yeah, yeah, take the brolly…" Out of it he grabbed one of his Mam's half-size fold-up umbrellas and shoved it into the parka's pocket. He bent down to pick up his school bag, the backpack that held his textbooks and notebooks, and paused by the door to pat himself down. *Keys, phone, money…* He was sorted. He glanced at his phone. Twenty minutes till his first class.

He headed out the front door, locked it behind him, and trotted down the front walk to the footpath. In front of Ronan traffic streamed back and forth, cars coming down from the motorway exit up the hill, making for the main road into Bray. He paused by the front gate to take a look at the sky, thinking of Nana saying *It doesn't look good.*

Weird, he thought. The sky was clear: some high haze, nothing worse.

Ronan shrugged. *It changes real quick sometimes, who knows...* He glanced back at the house, having his usual early morning moment of *Did I remember to shut the front blinds?* His Mam was paranoid about that lately since there'd been a rash of burglaries in the neighborhood—hit-and-run thieves looking in people's windows, seeing something they wanted, smashing their way in to take it.

But the blinds were shut. *Don't know why anybody would bother with us anyway,* Ronan thought, turning his back on the place and heading down the road. *It's not like we're rich; we've got nothing special, no fancy cars, no fancy stuff...* Their house was like every other one in their block, a commonplace suburban neighborhood of stamped-out single-family houses: all with four bedrooms and a bathroom upstairs, a living room and kitchen and dining room and a toilet downstairs, a front hall with a walk to the street's sidewalk and a back patio from which you could hear everything else that was going on up and down the block... at least in the summertime, when doors and windows were open and people were outside trying to take advantage of what summer weather there was. If one family had a barbecue, every other family on the block could smell what they were having. "Togetherness," his Mam called it, always sounding as if there were levels of together that were all right and levels she could have done without.

But then his Mam had been a country girl from outside Athy— she would laugh and tell people that the only reason she'd moved here was for the broadband—and Ronan's Da had been born up in Clondalkin, west of Dublin, so that when he moved down here he thought *this* was the country.

Ronan snorted softly in the back of his throat as he got near the intersection between his road and the main road into Bray. Well, all right, you *could* see green space with no houses on it from here. Just look to the right and you were staring at the long green upslope of Bray Head, towering above the Irish Sea. But these days all the ground nearly to the foot of the Head had become suburban territory —rows and rows of houses. And while the higher parts of the Head were okay for climbing, when you *did* get up there mostly what you saw all around you, except for the sea, was suburbs. There was a brief spread of green farmland and forest on the southern side, but just a glance beyond it you started seeing the commuter belt that was swiftly spreading northward from Greystones. Only looking eastward past Delgany and the other townlands, getting increasingly built up, was there a view of more mountains. Off in the distance rose the sharp point of Sugarloaf, and closer than that the smaller hill, not quite a mountain, whose name Ronan could never remember so that he wound up calling it what his Gran did: "Shoogie."

Only the steep stuff stays clean, Ronan thought as he made his way down along the street full of parked cars, listening to the traffic getting louder as he got close to the intersection. *Anything we can build on... gets built on.* "So annoying..."

It was just one more of the ways it had occurred to him, lately, that life sucked. Or more to the point, that it had probably always sucked, and he was just now getting around to noticing it. *How did I never notice? I'm the noticing kind, usually.*

"Trouble is, you get used to it," he muttered as he got to the intersection and hit the button for the traffic light. "The suck level goes up real gradually and you stop noticing..."

The light's change-timer sat there ticking quietly to itself. Ronan glanced around him, a reflex: sometimes he forgot to check if anyone was near enough to hear him muttering to himself. But he was safely alone. Traffic ran back and forth in front of him, oblivious to one dark-haired kid in school uniform identical to those of a few hundred more a quarter mile down the road and on the other side.

The light changed and he sighed and headed across, paying the waiting cars no more attention than he had to—right then, not being overheard was more of an issue. Ronan had, so everybody told him, been a late talker, and then for a long time a very quiet child, to the point where they had him tested to make sure he was all right. Ronan couldn't remember any of this. And indeed he found the description pretty strange, because for as long as he'd been aware of himself, it seemed, he'd always talked to himself a lot.

While still very young he'd often wondered if other people had what he'd had when he was little—a sense that somehow or other, there was always somebody listening. This wasn't a feeling that had ever bothered him... just a sense that he was somehow being paid attention to even when no one was around. It was more reassuring than anything else, and meant that even when he acted a little strange and other kids left him alone, he was never specifically lonely. Or not *that* lonely. Feeling lonely turned out to be a reaction he had to be educated into, from books and TV and movies and other kids talking about it... when they ever did. He learned over time that loneliness wasn't something that anyone he knew would readily admit to.

As he got older, Ronan kept to himself any thoughts about his relationship with whatever he sometimes thought was listening to him. After all, it never said anything *back*, even when he was feeling most listened to. He noticed also that these "most listened to" feelings never came to him while anyone else was there, so he had come to consider them as extremely private.

This was just as well, since Ronan learned from indulging unusually expansive moods once or twice that telling people anything about the Listener was usually a stepping stone to getting called crazy or beat up—right up there with his Mam's opinion that he was eventually Meant For Great Things. That declaration he'd once made the mistake of sharing with "friends" when he was very young, and had been laughed at and sneered at for months. So Ronan had learned to keep his own counsel not only about his Mam's opinions, and his talking to the silences, but (gradually) about most of the other things that crossed his mind. As Ronan got older it seemed to him that just to make sure he didn't say anything that was going to get him in trouble, he spent more time talking to himself than to other people--

"Awright Ro!"

With a few exceptions, he thought as he turned. "Awright Pidge," Ronan said, as the tall lean gingery owner of the voice fell in beside him from behind. Pidge lived up in the Newcourt Road estate a little closer to Bray Head, and most mornings he had a game of trying to sneak up behind Ronan unseen. He was normally about as successful at this as he was at being called by his real name, Ronald, by anybody but one of their teachers. "Nice try…"

"Slow day," Pidge said. "How's your Nan?"

"Worried about the weather," Ronan said as the two of them fell into step. "Your mam better?"

Pidge shrugged. "Not coughing so much anyway," he said, unzipping his dark blue parka. This was new and too big for him—a desperate attempt by Pidge's Da, on their last clothes-shopping trip, to keep up with Pidge's own growth spurt. It was also heavy enough to keep him safe from temperatures in the Arctic, which meant that at the moment Pidge was always overheated whenever it was zipped up (meaning, in front of his mam, always: she was terrified of winter diseases, and twice as much as usual right now since she had a cold). "Outa sight now, thank God, I'm dyin' in here." Pidge shrugged his backpack back far enough so that he could get a grip on the sides of the open coat and flap them back and forth to cool himself down.

"Mind you don't take off," Ronan said.

"If only. You see the travel show last night on One?"

Ronan had. "The beach," he moaned, "oh God. What wouldn't I give up to go someplace like that on hols."

"Not just you." The show in question had featured a visit to an island with the kind of caster-sugar-sand-and-sky-blue-water Caribbean beaches that normally featured in movies about three-digit spies. "Not much chance, though." Pidge scowled.

Ronan nodded, making a sympathetic face. Pidge's dad was newly unemployed, his job lost when the hard disk company up the road closed and all its jobs went to Malaysia or someplace out that way. Pidge's mum used to stay home with his little sister, but now she did childcare three or four days a week and tended bar for two. So things were tight at the Culhanes' place, and for the foreseeable future holidays were going to be something that happened to other people. "Gonna be hearing all about it at lunch from some people," Ronan said.

"Bastards," Pidge said cheerfully. "Feck 'em. Life's hard enough without their noise. And can any of them even *swim?*"

They snickered together at the thought of some of the people in question—kids who came from more affluent families--floundering around in that sky-blue Caribbean and looking like right eedjits, since at the first meeting of their school's new mandatory swimming class some of the potential offenders had looked like they should never go near any body of water deeper than a bath or at best a Jacuzzi. "You can just hear them," Ronan said. "Murch'll say that beaches are only for hooking up on. Shawny'll start going on about unlimited rum drinks and O'Dorkley will tell us how all the babes are after his 'definition.'"

"Wherever he's keeping it. Sure he didn't let us see any of it at the rec center..."

They turned the corner into Putland Road and headed along the pavement past the church near the corner and down toward the school gate, where cars were backed up two deep as people dropped off their kids. "Any thoughts about that maths test?" Pidge said under his breath as they went through the doors into the locker-lined front hall.

"Besides being doomed?" Ronan rolled his eyes

"Oh, come on, Smidge—"

"Shut it," Ronan said without heat, and Pidge did. Ronan's for-a-long-time-short stature had been the original cause of his Nana starting to call the two of them "the Pidge and the Smidge", and it wasn't a nickname Ronan wanted anyone at school to know... especially these days when he was finally getting some height on him and what some of the teachers still thought of as "the schoolyard rough and tumble" was finally on the wane. The visits to the Headmaster's office, once a fixture in Ronan's life, were becoming mercifully rare as the kids who'd been the most cruel to him either graduated or learned the error of their ways.

They made their way through the press of unloading students and the noise of slamming car doors and turned right through the gates into the long drive that led down to the school. Presentation wasn't a huge place as schools went: one big building that was showing its age and was supposedly going to be torn down pretty soon—Ronan would believe that when he saw it, assuming it happened before he graduated—and three or four smaller temporary prefabs ones for the increasing number of classes that had overgrown the main building. Trees and some hedging were planted around the low outer walls to break the view up toward the church and the main street in Bray, and ideally to soften the general look of the grounds. *Not that it works...* Ronan thought in some amusement as they came up to the school doors.

"Which lunch you in today?" Pidge said as they pushed through the doors and headed for their lockers.

"Uh, it's Wednesday? Second."

"One-thirty, then?" Pidge started fiddling with his lock, which always stuck; there was no point in waiting for him to sort it out.

"Yeah." Ronan pushed him amiably in the shoulder and headed off for his own locker, wondering if his Nan might have been right about the weather and, if she was, whether he'd left a bigger umbrella in there.

THE MORNING WENT by the way it usually did: history, science, math (Ronan kept quiet and attempted not to be called on all through that class, and to his astonishment succeeded), religious ed...

He sat through that class with the usual resignation. It would have been a dangerous opinion to have out loud—especially in front of any of the more conservative or gung-ho teachers—but Ronan wasn't wild about religious ed. Oh, *church* was fine, it wasn't as if he didn't believe in the basics... mostly. But as he'd got older he'd started feeling as if there was something rigid and small and petty about a lot of what he was being taught, and if there was anything he really didn't believe God was, it was petty. Or small. His science classes only reinforced that opinion.

His normal tendency to keep things to himself had so far protected Ronan from letting anything slip about this that could have gotten him into trouble. It was an annoyance that religious ed was compulsory—in fact, the only compulsory subject in the school's curriculum—but he concentrated on just letting it pass over him. He wasn't alone. There were plenty of others concentrating on just keeping their heads down and saying the words when called on, passing the tests and mumbling not too clearly when they were supposed to be praying.

Ronan was lucky in that there wasn't a lot of pressure from his family at this end of things. The family went to Mass on days when everybody else went—the usual holy days of obligation—but besides that, it was pretty much considered optional. And yes, all right, his Mam had one of Nan's glow-in-the-dark religious-retro Blessed Heart nightlights plugged into a socket in the living room, but that was about the size of it. At least the thing kept you from tripping over stuff in the dark. And there was the Brigid's cross in the front hall over the door, four long arms and a central knot made of reeds woven together. His Da had picked that up from some tourist store up in Dublin. But at least everybody had one of *those*. It was the kind of thing you looked at without actually thinking about religion.

This was harder to do when you were actually stuck in the religious class, of course. Fortunately the class only happened a couple of times a week, and right now they were in a unit about the Gospels that was so dry and boring that even their teacher Miss Halloran had the grace to look embarrassed by it, and only laughed a little when she caught a couple of the kids in the back of the room falling asleep.

Ronan was going to be as glad to escape after that hour as anyone else. There had to be only so much time you could spend arguing about which of the four evangelists had been more accurate than the others. There was no telling how many people had rewritten what they'd written over the course of two thousand years. *And sure it's supposed to be God that's behind it all,* Ronan thought, *the writing and the rewriting too... but if that's true, then He's made an incredible mess.*

Not just of that: of nearly everything.

It was an uncomfortable thought, one that had been creeping in fairly often of late, and Ronan had no idea where exactly it was coming from. *Maybe just all the stuff going on at home...* His Da's overdraft, Nana's health, all the trouble that Mam had been having with one of her supervisors at work, some snooty guy at the hotel—they'd all been on Ronan's mind, darkening the local emotional weather. And on top of that, there was also the news, which Ronan had never paid all that much attention to when he was younger, but which now was becoming more of an issue due to his history classes. Ireland as a country had been pretty well off for a while. But a few of the big Irish banks had got themselves in the same kind of trouble a lot of banks had got into across the Atlantic, and without much warning the country had sunk tens of billions of dollars into saving them. After the fact, people here were getting nervous as the national stock market tanked and the world's financial agencies yanked Ireland's good credit ratings. Now everybody here talked constantly about the businesses already going under as a result, and how the bad times were coming back—when if you wanted a job, you had to leave home for some other country.

And not just everybody else, Ronan thought. *My time's going to come. Not long now.*

But the thought of leaving his family, being forced to emigrate, to become a foreigner in some strange land... *Feck no,* Ronan thought. *This is the place for me.*

Except what would happen when he couldn't find work? He'd have to go on the dole, his folks would have to go on supporting him, times would get bad for all of them. And the family he loved would start coming apart under the stress, as he'd seen others do. *And it'll be my fault—*

The sound of the kids around him packing up their books and starting to leave brought Ronan abruptly back to himself. Quietly he got up and did the same, trying to push the dark thoughts away. *But they'll be back. Sooner or later, they're always back...*

Lunch came right after religious ed, and Ronan went to it with relief, thinking about his Nan—despite his Mam having told him not to worry about her—and looking around for Pidge. But Pidge was nowhere to be found, and when Ronan texted him he didn't get an answer back. As a result he was reduced to grabbing a lunch tray and eating by himself. *Don't want to inflict this mood on other human beings,* Ronan thought, grumpy at the thought and grumpy about being grumpy.

The mood didn't improve after he'd finished his chicken sandwiches and salad, either. Lunch might have dealt with his blood sugar to some extent, but the school had gone on a health kick lately and done away with all the minerals; so as much as Ronan wanted a cola, he wasn't going to get one. And the Ballygowan water just wasn't cutting it (they hadn't even had the still water he preferred, only the sparkling, which had so much fizz in it that it gave him sneezing fits). So Ronan came rapidly, once more, to the conclusion that everything sucked. *When will this day be over,* he thought, dumping the recyclables off his tray into the green bin and stalking out of the cafeteria.

His next class wasn't for half an hour yet—there was no way Ronan was going to linger over his lunch by himself till the end of the period, looking like some kind of lonely loser—so he wandered out into the grounds around back of the main building of the school. At a distance across the mostly-green lawn he could see some junior phys ed class out on the football pitch putting on two colors of pinnies, and some of the guys doing stretches before starting a rotating series of five-a-side matches. *Not me today,* he thought with grim satisfaction, *thank you God for small mercies,* because it was his present kind of mood that tempted him toward the kind of leg tackles that would certainly be deemed illegal. *God, even football sucks today. Everything's really bad, isn't it?*

"...it's a rubbish beach," he heard somebody saying, the voice coming from behind the ugly temp building squatting about halfway from the main building to the back of the school property, "*anybody* can go there. You want a proper posh beach, Aruba, that's the place. They have these villas..."

Ronan rolled his eyes. *Why me,* he thought, *why now, why couldn't I have fifteen minutes of peace before what's going to happen happens?* But no, there was probably no avoiding that voice, or the person who owned it. He might as well face both of them head on.

Ronan walked on around behind the building. Back there on its blind, non-windowed side was a "dead spot" where the security cam stuck up under the building's low roof had a perpetually loose wire from when someone brought in to mend the guttering after a storm had cracked the camera wire's cable guide. If you knew how, you could come around the corner of the building unseen and jiggle the cable guide enough for the wire to get messed up and the camera's motor to fail. School being what it was, of course now *everybody* knew how; and people who absolutely couldn't stand waiting for a smoke until school was out would come out here after one lunch break or another and sneak a quiet fag.

You don't have to go back there, said a helpful part of his brain. But *Yes you do,* said a less helpful one, *because somebody away back behind you probably already saw you walking this way. If you change your mind now, word'll get around that you were avoiding whoever's back here. And everyone'll know who that is. So no point in it, none at all...*

Ronan slowed and shook some of the tension out of his shoulders, then sloped on around toward the "dead" corner. "Great place," that thin sharp voice was saying, "you'd feel right at home, Maurice, lots of *your* kind of people around, they bring you drinks and shit and fetch you towels and—"

The laughter that drowned the voice out wasn't kindly, wasn't funny. Ronan found himself getting hot under the collar, literally: flushed and sweaty with embarrassment and anger and the certainty of what was about to happen, because he wasn't going to be able to let it pass. He knew perfectly well who the "towels" line had been meant for. *Sure somebody has to stick up for him,* Ronan thought, furious. *It's not like it'd be hard if more than one of them opened their fecking mouths and said 'Enough!'* His mouth worked as if he wanted to spit. *Except they* won't. *Because they're scared they'll be the ones getting made fun of next.*

Ronan strolled around the corner. There they were: eight or nine guys, mostly his age or a year younger; and loudest and most self-assured among them, there was Seamus McConaghie. He was in Ronan's year, and because of that there'd been no getting away from him for what was starting to seem like forever. For a long time

Seamus had been one of the biggest and strongest kids in the year, but in recent months others had been catching up to him... which meant he'd been making up for it by being twice as nasty to everybody as he'd been since Ronan first fell afoul of him.

There were some mutters of greeting as Ronan ambled along toward the group, but just as many uneasy or hostile looks; and off to one side of the group, left a little by himself, was Maurice Obademi. He was taller than anybody else there, even taller than Ronan. But it never failed to strike him the way Maurice always stood with his shoulders bowed, as if trying to avoid standing out. *Not that it's possible,* Ronan thought. *So few African guys have made it in here as yet...*

Maurice was game, you had to give him that. There he stood, wearing a grim and bitter half-smile, just taking Seamus's bullshit... because he knew if he left he'd be accused of *not* being able to take it. He was standing with his head bowed, looking off to one side, and smoking his cigarette hard as if him inhaling deep enough might magically make Seamus choke.

Because something needs to, Ronan thought. Seamus loved riding Maurice. It had started as teasing him about his name. *How's a black fella get to be called Maurice? Bit posh for you, isn't it? Royalty in the family somewhere? No surprise there, I guess. Your dear papa probably goes by Prince Whongo or something when he's sending out all those emails.*

That taunt had made Ronan almost irrationally angry the first time he heard it. *Sure his name's not his fault,* he'd thought, *why won't they ever let him be about that?* Maurice was smart, he was good at sports, a nice guy, a kind one. *But the way they treat him any time he's someplace without a security camera or where a teacher can't hear—*

"Never get tired of it, do you Seamus," Ronan said. "So easily amused."

"Absolutely, Nolan," Seamus said. "Specially with the likes of you around. Letting wee Maurice here open for you now? If we were having a dull moment, it's over."

Some of the guys gathered around snickered a bit, waiting to see what Ronan would do. Ronan concentrated on keeping his expression casual, even though the back of his brain, the chicken-hearted part, was already yelling *Do you really need to do this now, just when things were getting quiet after last time? Why are you always sticking up for the oppressed and downtrodden, couldn't you let somebody* else *do it today?* ...Except he couldn't.

Ronan wandered over to Maurice for all the world like someone not having frantic internal conversations. "Got one I can pinch, Mo?" he said, nudging him with an elbow, mostly because it allowed him to stand beside the guy without being too obvious about it.

Maurice fished around in his pockets and came up with a battered white packet of ten. Ronan fished one out and took the lighter Maurice handed him. *I hate this bit but it's part of the game...* Ronan thought. He lit up and took a drag and concentrated on not coughing.

"Wouldn't think you'd be interested in smoking like us plebs, Mr. Great Tings," Seamus said.

Ronan flushed hot. *Yeah, there it is, couldn't wait three seconds, could he?* "Great Tings Nolan"— He'd never been annoyed by his home accent before, the way the "h" got dropped out: had hardly even been aware of it. Now he'd started to hate the sound of it. "I can take it or leave it."

"But you leave it, mostly. Can't afford it, maybe."

"Things're getting tough all over," Ronan said.

"Must be. Too tough for a smoke, too tough for a pint—" Seamus laughed his soft nasty laugh. "Not that your da's ever seen in the pub like a normal person, booze or no booze. Thinks he's better than everybody around the place..."

Coming from Seamus *this* was rich. His father was on Wicklow County Council and Seamus rarely forgot to let anyone who'd hold still know all about it, with the implication behind every word that they'd better be nice to him or "something would happen". *Never specifies what or to who. But he doesn't have to.* Because everybody knew that if somebody in the Council got on somebody's bad side, their application for their new conservatory or a medical card for a sick relative might go straight down the bog. Or get lost behind some sofa at the Council offices until whoever had stood up for themselves had to go to the offices and grovel to get something that should have been theirs by right.

"Opinion like that," Ronan said, trying hard to sound mild, "it's the kind of thing that usually gets somebody pounded."

"Why not then?" said Seamus. "Nothing stopping you." The implication hung in the air: *even here out of sight, you don't dare.*

Ronan scowled. "Could be that some of us aren't wild about beating people up any way at all," he said. "Maurice here, I heard that, what's the matter with you? He was born here just like you and me--"

"He's not, he's *not* just like you and me, what's the matter with you Nolan, you blind as well as stupid? He could be born here a hundred times over, he'll *never* fit in, just look at him! And it's fecking kindness to tell him so. Otherwise he'll be breaking his heart and wasting his life here trying to be happy, when he could just faff back off to 409 Land or wherever his mammy and daddy came from, and be all fine there."

"Oh, and you're all about having *him* be happy. This is going to be for his own good, is it?"

"Yes it is! At least he'll be honest about it, instead of like other people, sneaking in and taking our jobs and then sneaking off again now that things are going down the bog. Sure you see them all leaving now, now that they've got our money, all their little shops closing up, like that wee dump in Main Street, the *sklep* or whatever they call it—"

Ronan was losing whatever patience he had left. "That's the Polish shop, ye dim gob, does Maurice look like his people come from Poland?"

"Well he sure doesn't look like his people come from *here!*"

Laughter at that. Ronan scowled so hard he felt like his whole face was going to fold up. "If it's stupid we're talking about," he said, "it's somebody who's not gonna keep his place as a prefect long when the Year Head hears the kind of thing you come out with. The kind of thing that makes it pretty clear someone doesn't give a shit about the college's antibullying policy. Specially the bit about hate speech. You can stand out here in the dead zone all you like, but it's only a matter of time before when you've got your gob open somebody hits the button on their phone and catches you in the act. In a manner of speaking."

The way the look of smug self-assurance slid slideways off Seamus's face was worth something. But the nasty narrow-eyed expression that replaced it made Ronan have to concentrate on not taking a step back. *Nope, nope, hold your ground, here it comes.* "Like *you?*" Seamus said softly, moving toward Ronan. "Yeah, even a down-market last-year's crap phone like yours might have got a word or two of that. *Might* have."

And when I have to go into disciplinary for this, Ronan thought with almost a sense of glee, *my phone won't have had* anything *like that in it.* The teacher who ran the school's computer labs was way too expert at finding files in people's phones that they were sure they'd erased; Ronan was grateful he wasn't going to wind up as one of *those* horror stories. *Though maybe* another *one—*

"Won't know until it's too late, will you," Ronan said.

"Probably not, with a treacherous little snitch like you," Seamus said, eyes narrowing. "Specially with you coming over all Social Conscience Boy this last year. Friends with the likes of *him* and acting like you don't care what people think." Maurice scowled at the ground, sucking the rest of his cigarette down to a long bright coal. "And don't mind fecking 'round with history, either, when it suits you."

Seamus's face went suddenly grim. "Last couple years you seemed normal enough. But then all of a sudden you stand up with that essay in history last month. All nicey-nice to the Brits. Cromwell didn't kill every innocent Irish person he came across, it seems. Historians think it wasn't so bad, now. As if the people he *did* kill aren't dead enough, as if their blood didn't soak into the ground deep enough for you!"

Seamus was getting close, now, getting right up into Ronan's face. Ronan didn't dare step back, because it would give Seamus an excuse to take another step forward and then it would be all over. He could feel the spittle splattering against his skin as Seamus yelled at him from a about an inch away. *Okay, got problems now,* he thought. Seamus was a republican-fancier, everybody knew that, but this had more of an edge to it than Ronan would ever have expected. "Haven't we had enough fecking Brits here for the last, how long, eight hundred years now, crapping things up, maybe that's not enough for you? Going for nine? Bad enough they won't get the feck out of the Six Counties, you have to be making excuses for them?"

"I wasn't making excuses, we *know* more now, that's all, what's wrong with knowing the truth, what's your—"

"We don't *know* more, they're trying to make us think we know *less,* it's all about caring less, pretending the past didn't happen—"

It always came to Ronan with shocking clarity—and somehow, always as a surprise—that moment when he knew there was going to be a fight and nothing would prevent it, paired with the knowledge that walking away would just make it worse. Over the past year Ronan had begun to be a bit disturbed at how naturally at such times his brain slid straight into a mode of calm assessment—as if he was examining the situation from above, or between sequences in a videogame. *Those three, the younger lads, they won't make a move, they don't want to get mixed up in stuff out of their own year. Why get two Year Heads involved at the same time? Bad news for everybody. As for Seamus and his little friend, well, Bobby might pitch in but not unless it looks like Seamus is winning—*

"It's not like that," Ronan said. "Not at all."

"Well from the sound of you, you could have fooled me! Blood will out, me da says, and I bet he's right, I bet you've got some dirty Brit in your genes. Probably from your gran's side, the one in the upstairs room who's gone all feeble and drooly. Have to stick her in a home pretty soon, shouldn't wonder. But once you do, you and your lovely family can just take yourselves up off north somewhere, if you don't like how things are here—"

A wave of cold and a wave of heat ran all over Ronan within about a second of Seamus mentioning his Nan. "You just leave my lovely family out of it, Seamus," he hissed, and all his determination of just moments before about not being a jerk fell off him like rain off the unneeded brolly.

"Like that, wouldn't you? But it's no secret, because with your mammy getting all friendly with the boss up at that posh West Brit hotel up in Dalkey, heard all about that, who hasn't, when she—"

Something must have shown on Ronan's face at the shocked-anticipatory hiss around him from the other kids in response to "your mammy". And all of a sudden Seamus was just that bit closer to his face, eyes practically bulging out of his skull.

That's it, Ronan thought, and rammed his forehead right down hard onto Seamus's so-convenient nose. As Seamus staggered back Ronan kicked out and swept sideways with his good kicking leg, *pity it's not your head instead of a football, ya weasel!* Seamus's legs went out from under him, and down he went flat on his back without even a push to help him.

Seamus started rolling around and groaning and holding his face. "You fecking little arsewipe," he gasped between his hands, "when me da hears about this you're gonna—"

"But Da's not here right now, is he?" Ronan said. "*You* are. So better stay down and shut up, because whatever happens next, *you'll* feel it way before he does. And if it's arses we're talking about, whatever happens to *yours* next isn't gonna be wiping."

Seamus went still except for some moaning. The others gathered around started to snicker, but when Ronan looked at them one after another, they quieted. Finally he turned away from them in disgust.

"*God* these things are shite," he said to Maurice, dropping the cigarette and grinding it out under his shoe. "Honest, mate, you should quit, you can read the packet! Better than this lot." He glanced around at the others.

"Um, right," Maurice said, looking with some bemusement at Ronan, who was trying not to be seen gesturing sideways with his eyes in a suggestion that Maurice should get out of there. "Yeah, I should just... throw these away. Before class."

Ronan just nodded, staying where he was while Maurice headed around the corner of the building and away.

"Anybody else?" Ronan said in a friendly way.

He got some sullen looks, but no takers.

"Good. Enjoy lunch. If you've got the stomach for it after watching him bleed out." And Ronan peered down at Seamus in a fake-solicitous kind of way and then sauntered away.

Hope I don't catch something from him spitting all over me, he thought. As the adrenaline buzz died back his head started aching from where he'd hit Seamus's nose with it, and the saunter was very forced, as what he really wanted to do was run and hide in the bushes. *Because you know what comes next... Feck it all, why do I keep doing this?*

...No.

The faintest sense of amusement stirs the aether. *No what?*

This is the day, isn't it. This has always been the day!

More amusement. *It would be easy to see why you might think that...*

You played me!

You played yourself, sibling mine. You'll always complicate things to spite me, to prove that good isn't the same as smart; that good isn't smart enough.

The aether stirs again, with softly-voiced fury this time. *And how long have you been conditioning him to act like that?*

You've got it exactly backwards. He is as he is. If I tried bending him into another shape, he'd spring back eventually. Exactly, in fact, when it would best suit you.

Now if you're trying to say that—

And as for any thoughts of me seeking him out? It doesn't work that way. In fact you could make a case that he found me, rather than the other way around. And which of us is conditioning the other? I wonder.

We'll soon find out, I think.

Yes, we will.

Because whatever good you think you're going to get of him, it'll be simple enough to keep it from happening.

Oh indeed.

Yes indeed. Just watch—

"WHAT COMES NEXT" came soon enough; it'd been only a matter of time before the shoe dropped. "Somebody'll tell them if they don't notice themselves," Ronan muttered as he headed down the hall to his maths class. "Probably Seamus..."

All through Literature and well into the study period after that, Ronan waited in torment. It was almost a relief when the supply teacher who was minding the study period glanced down at her phone, which had just buzzed discreetly on her desk. *Here it comes,* Ronan thought, his stomach doing a flip as she got up and walked back to where he was sitting.

"Nolan," she said quietly, and showed him the text, from the school's front office. It said *R Nolan to Principals office at end of session plz disc.*

Disc was the unsubtle shorthand the front office ladies used for "disciplinary". *Seamus,* Ronan thought, *one of these days your diplomatic immunity's gonna catch up with you.* He sighed and nodded and went back to his book. All around him he could feel people's stares lingering on him, and for the time being he ignored them. They knew as well as he did what was going on. At least he was being spared the embarrassment of the get-up-and-go-*now* treatment.

At the period's end he made his way from the science library where his study period was held to the hallway holding the glass-walled main office. Past it was a wooden door with a polished wooden bench next to it: "death row", everybody called it. The bench was empty, though, and Ronan went to the door with its wired-glass window that said PRINCIPAL and knocked on it.

"Come in."

What followed was all familiar territory now: the windows overlooking the school's football pitch, the view downhill toward the water, the metal bookshelves full of files and file boxes and dictionaries (the Principal taught French and German when he wasn't lurking in here), the broad metal desk with the computer keyboard and monitor all piled around with stacked up books (more dictionaries, *jayzus, how many did a single human being need?*) and a framed photo of a middle-aged woman and a dog like a ball of fluff and a young fella in his twenties somewhere, wearing Irish Army camo and a blue UN beret, all of them smiling.

In front of the desk were a couple of armless office chairs. Behind the desk, sitting in a beat-up typing chair, was the Principal, Mr. Flannery. He was a lean, graying, pinched-looking little man with eyes set close together and a nose pushed a little to one side by some fight or rugby scrum in his long-ago youth, never properly fixed. He looked tired. That didn't surprise Ronan, who was certainly tired of seeing Mr. Flannery and suspected the feeling was mutual.

Ronan came to a stop near the right-hand chair in front of the desk and waited. Whether you were invited to sit or not was usually an indicator of how much trouble you were in. For the moment Flannery merely pushed the papers piled up in front of him to one side and looked at Ronan.

"Mr. Nolan," Flannery said. "I was living in hope that these little meetings had become a thing of the past."

"Sorry sir," Ronan said, and shut up. Over a number of "these little meetings" he had learned that there was no point in either trying to jolly the man up or act as if the world was about to end; neither approach did anything but annoy Flannery, who disliked both flippancy and theatrics. He wasn't a bad type, but he did seem sometimes to be stuck in some previous decade, and Ronan had realized there was nothing to do but let him get on with being that way and see whether he was going to act reasonably or unreasonably old.

Mr. Flannery sighed. "I wish you sounded more like you really were sorry," he said, "but maybe the honesty's preferable; I get little enough of that in a day. Let's hear your version of what happened out there and for God's sake keep it short so I don't have to be too late for my next class."

Not 'so we don't have to be late,' Ronan thought, not *'our* next class,' and got a chill down his back. His Da was going to be furious; he could see it coming. But there was no help for it now. So Ronan told his story, and kept it short.

While this was going on Flannery turned himself away in the swivel chair and left Ronan looking at his profile, absolutely immobile, just an expressionless silhouette against the bright window. When Ronan was finished, Mr. Flannery let out a long breath as if he'd been holding it.

"Right," he said at last, and turned back toward Ronan. His expression was peculiar: not angry, just his mouth drooping a bit at the corners. He looked disappointed, though at whom it was impossible to tell.

"I have to suspend you," he said. "I don't have a choice at this point; we've been down this road before, and anyway you picked the wrong target. Three days."

Because of Seamus's dad, Ronan thought, but didn't say. "I understand, sir."

"Problem is, I think you really do," Mr. Flannery said. "Mr. Nolan, not that I make a habit of passing comments like this where the subject can hear them, but you're not an unintelligent lad. Your grades are above average, which is disappointing when what I hear from your teachers is that you don't seem to be working particularly hard or for that matter showing much interest in anything. Either you're hiding your intellectual struggles unusually well, or we're not working you as hard as you deserve in order to come up to your full potential. ...Whatever *that* might be. Hard to get a sense of it when you mostly seem busy demonstrating how completely the worm's turned since you've put on three inches and half a stone."

Ronan could have said something pointed about none of the teachers doing that much to keep the worm from being stomped on previously, but for now he concentrated on keeping his mouth shut. In those few moments he became aware that Flannery was watching him do this, and seemed to be approving of it.

"You want to watch out for that," Flannery said. "Don't let vengeance turn into a habit. It's fun at first, but it's a drug. You start needing more and more and eventually you find no matter how much you get, it's never enough."

This time there was a sense that the man was waiting for an answer. "Yes, sir."

"All right, that's enough," Flannery said, standing up and picking up one of the dictionaries. "You're excused. You know I'm going to have to write to your parents about this."

"Yes sir." Ronan couldn't quite keep himself from making a face.

"Such is life," Flannery said, and made a face of his own, a grimace of faint disgust. "That's your cross to bear. Go on now. But Nolan? One thing." Flannery's eyes were hard as they caught him turning toward the door. "Your version of what happened matches all the others I've heard except McConachie's, which didn't mention so much as word one about what he'd been saying to make you go off pop. So good on you for showing him that that kind of garbage may fly some places but not everyplace. Get out of here now and keep a low profile for the rest of the term, and it's possible that letter I have to write will fail to make it into your permanent file at the end of the year. "

"Uh. Thank you, sir," Ronan said.

"For God's sake don't thank me, you're making my teeth hurt," Mr. Flannery said. "Just go now."

INVOCATION

So Ronan went to his locker and got his coat, and then did the only thing he could think of to do: he got out of town.

There wasn't that much choice about which direction to go, really. If he went anywhere near Bray's busy high street he'd inevitably be seen, and somebody his family knew—either just passing through, or in one of the shops—would tell his folks. If with some thought of lying low he went home, his Da would know he was there, because their house alarm was on text alert during the daytime, and Ronan's unlock code was different from the carer's. *And no point in making up some story about being worried about Nan, because Da's suspicious enough that he'll call the school and find out what happened.*

There was nothing for it but to go right out of town the back way, toward Bray Head. There were all kinds of tracks and outlook spots up there: he could sit there and wait until the school day was over, then make his way home on his usual schedule. When Flannery had said "write to your folks" he'd most likely meant by post instead of email: the school was still old-fashioned that way, something to do with email notifications not being legal enough. So if Ronan kept his mouth shut, he had at least a chance of one more quiet evening at home before the axe fell with the breakfast-time post. *Tomorrow morning early, before it arrives, I can tell them then....*

At that thought the feeling of immediate dread that had been twisting Ronan's guts up receded a little. For the moment, tomorrow morning seemed a long way off. Until then he could do what he liked.

Right, then. He cut across the grounds to one side of the drive, heading catty-corner for where the school's road hit the main one. There he hopped the low wall around the grounds and started heading off in the direction of the crossing he and Pidge had used that morning.

Of course he then had to deal with someone he always passed on the way to school. This morning, when the emotional weather had been fair and he'd been busy chatting with his friend, he hadn't even noticed her. But sure enough now as he came to the corner he felt her eye on him, and stopped for a moment.

It was the statue of the Holy Virgin, of course, that belonged to the church next door. Presentation College was after all named after the feast day of the Presentation in the Temple, and after Our Lady of the Presentation. So there Herself stood in one of the traditional statue poses, arms a bit out as if saying "Look what they made me stand on, could I ever have a flat floor for a change," and under her feet was the globe of the world. Between her and it was a fairly dispirited-snake, standing in for Satan and looking a bit squashed. The height and size of the statue, though, and the angle of the tilt of her head, made it look as if Herself was looking down at Ronan, and with a slightly severe expression.

"And what're *you* lookin at?" Ronan growled.

After a moment, though, he felt shocked at his rudeness, considering what his Mam would have said if she'd heard him. She always stopped and crossed herself when she passed the statue, and sometimes (if she wasn't in a rush) had brief conversations with it, always being careful to make sure no pedestrian was close enough to see it happening: as careful as Ronan was about not having his talking-to-himself overheard. But though his Mam's respect had rubbed off on him a bit over time, right now Ronan's foul mood left him unable to quite stop scowling.

The Blessed Virgin stood there looking unmoved by his snit, the statue's half-closed eyes and neutral expression leaving him feeling as if he was being not-too-positively judged. Ronan let out a breath and sagged against the low fence there, and glanced down at the snake. "Just wasn't your day when you decided to get troublesome, was it," Ronan muttered. "Mine either at the moment."

The snake remained squashed-looking and oblivious to this sentiment. Nearby the light changed and traffic started going by as usual, and Ronan just stood there feeling sore and raw around the edges—strangely bare and exposed for some reason.

It's because I'm not where I'm supposed to be.

Wherever the feck that is.

"Sorry," he said to the statue after a moment, not looking up. "Not your fault. Just a bad day. See you later, yeah?"

He turned away from the statue and started making his way up along the road, hardly noticing as it gently began to climb. Landscape too familiar to pay attention to—occasional houses and vacant lots and the small industrial estate that housed the old hard-drive place—fell away behind him unnoticed on either side as he walked and thought. His mood was darkening again; not so much with thoughts of what had gone wrong today—that was just a set of predisposing factors—but of things that were wrong generally: in his life, in the world.

It was something he usually gave no more thought to than he had to, but today the sad and angry thoughts seemed to be pressing themselves in on him, as if taking revenge for being too often pushed away. *No matter what I do,* Ronan thought as he stalked along with his hands shoved in his pockets, *no matter how I act... it's no use. I just don't fit in. Anywhere... anytime. I just don't fit.*

He couldn't remember when that idea had first come to him, or when he'd first realized clearly enough what was going on with him to express it to himself that way. It was so private a realization, so intimate, that he'd never mentioned it to another soul... and in a way it was worse because of that. But Ronan could just hear the easy denials that would come out of his Mam or Da if he said something like that to them. He could just hear Pidge's complete incomprehension. And there was no one else in the world who was anything *like* close enough for Ronan to dare to tell.

Because all of them, even the closest ones, they all have these expectations of me. All these ways they think I will fit in, eventually, if I just do what they tell me. He sighed, pausing for a moment at the roundabout where Briar Wood Road came up from his left to meet the main road, and stood there gazing up at the patched green and brown and stone-gray of the Head sloping steeply up and away from him. *Trouble is, when I do try doing the things people want, it never seems to work. They get disappointed, I get mad...*

A couple of cars came down the hill on the main road, heading down toward town, passed him by. Their sound faded into silence behind him. Ronan glanced up at the Head again, noting some tatters of gray cloud blowing past: not rainy looking. *Okay,* he thought, considering his next move.

When he'd walked out of Flannery's office and started planning where he'd go, Ronan would have preferred to stay in the school grounds and go straight out the back to Newcourt Road and then to Briar Wood Road, which led by small house-lined cul-de-sacs to the walking trail that climbed up to Bray Head Cross at the hill's top. That way he wouldn't have to pass the turnoff for his own house, and maybe have one of the family's near neighbors see him. But the wall between the school and the Newcourt Road neighborhood was too high to get over without drawing a lot of attention. Of course, the route he was taking right now had its problems, too. One of the roads he'd need to take to get up onto the Head went through the edge of the housing estate where Pidge lived. If anybody there saw Ronan, especially during school hours, they might tell Pidge's Mam, who'd tell *his* Mam... "Who needs security cameras around here," Ronan muttered, "we've got our own local intelligence community..."

He made his way to the left around the roundabout and on down Briar Wood Road. Briefly before the road curved and the view was blocked by houses, he could see the Irish Sea, looking flat and gray and unremarkable except for occasional sliding patches of light where the sun had managed to break through the low cloud. Away out across the dull pewter-gray surface Ronan could see a white scratch on the water: the wake of the big catamaran ferry from Dun Laoghaire as it started one of its daily runs to Holyhead in Wales.

The sight of it brought up in him a sudden irrational desire to be on that boat—to be going somewhere else, *being* somewhere else, *anywhere* else besides where he was and what he was stuck being and doing. But that was about as likely to happen as Ronan was likely to suddenly win a trip to the Moon. *I'm here,* he thought, scowling again, *and I get to go up and sit on the hill for the rest of the afternoon, and then go home.*

So on he went through the day's gray light, with every now and then a patch of sun sweeping by, there and gone again, always swallowed up again by the gray within seconds: a frustrating reminder of all the bright things it seemed just wouldn't or couldn't last. The houses Ronan passed looked gray and everything was dulled as he made his way around the curve and down to the cul-de-sac at the end of Briar Wood Road. It ended in a downslope and a hedge and a breezeblock wall separating the housing estate from the road up the Head on the far side: but there was no need to deal with those.

Off to Ronan's right was a field just sheening over in new green, the fresh grass coming up through last winter's worn-down, faded-beige stubble from when the hay was cut. He headed across that field to another hedge, hawthorn mostly, and pushed his way through it at one of the thin places, swearing at the thorns as he did his best to keep them from ripping his coat to ribbons.

A few of them got themselves well snagged into his coat regardless, and Ronan could just hear what his Mam would say when she saw the tears, even though they were only small. But that they'd happened at all just added insult to injury. *One more thing,* he thought, fuming. *One more thing I don't need right now.*

Even the few patches of sunlight now lost themselves in the high featureless gray of the sky as Ronan made his way across the field and toward the gravel road that zigzagged up the northwest side of the Head, toward the low nondescript County Council road maintenance buildings up there. He had no intention of being seen anywhere near there—it would probably just get him in more trouble. He worked his way eastward and upward along that road, and at one point where it doubled back on itself and kept climbing, he crossed it and ducked into the cover of the scrubby gorse-ridden woodland on the far side.

Here Ronan felt he could breathe a little as he got out of sight among the skinny straggly pines. There were a lot of places up here where you could avoid being seen, if you knew where to hole up: spots from which you could watch one or another of the network of tracks that ran up to the top of the Head, and be completely overlooked by the passing tourists and walkers even when they were practically looking at you. Even here, from so close by as the narrow hikers' track that ran alongside the woods, if you didn't want to be seen, you wouldn't be.

To Ronan's annoyance, he found the feeling of relief shortlived. Shortly it began to morph into something like loneliness. *Which is stupid, since I came up here to be alone!* But it seemed like almost the whole day had been like that so far, as if something was working to frustrate his attempts to change his mood. Ronan stood there under the eaves of the wood with his hands shoved in his pockets, feeling twitchy in his skin.

Feck it all anyway, he thought. *Holding still isn't going to work. Just walk it off.* He headed down to the east-running path, which was mercifully empty of any other traffic, and started to climb.

There seemed to be nothing interesting about the walk today, though, nothing that caught his interest: gray sky, gray sea, broken gray stones to either side, dulled-down half-brown grass and weeds to either side, gloomy woodland that hissed in the annoying sea wind that was hitting him in the face. *And yeah, a spit of rain on it too. One more thing I didn't need. Anything else going to go wrong? Because why not? Everything else has.*

Ronan fell into a grim marching rhythm as he slogged upward and eastward along the track, and in time with the frustrated rhythm fell into a kind of silent recap or recitation of all the things that were wrong with life, that were wrong with *him*. School, of course. But then came the things that were wrong with *home* life, too. He thought of his Nan upstairs, getting less comfortable and less Nana-like all the time. He was filled with fear at the thought of the day that would eventually come when she wouldn't be able to speak so easily, or maybe at all: when she'd look at him and not know who he was. The family would have to do what they'd been wanting so much not to, what Seamus had taunted him about: put her in a home. *And she'll die,* Ronan thought. *She'll hate it so much that she'll check right out.*

He could think of no way that this could be stopped...no possible cause for optimism. It was as if Ronan could see it coming a long way off, unavoidable, like the light at the end of the tunnel in the old cruel joke: not a sign of anything getting better, but actually an oncoming train.

He stopped short at a bend in the track and stood there staring out toward the water, upset enough at the moment that he hardly even saw what was out there. Ronan realized that he was shaking, and wondered how long that had been going on. Sea spray or the first hint of rain—hard to tell which, this close to the shoreline—sporadically blew fine and cold in his face, his eyes. All of a sudden Ronan felt like walking it off wasn't an option: he just wanted to sit *down* somewhere and try to feel stable again.

There were benches down along the cliff walk that ran along the east side of the Head, but the cliff walk was the last place Ronan wanted to go, because there were likely to be people on it, tourists and whatnot. And the last thing he wanted to deal with right now was people.

Up the hill, he thought. There was a place further along toward the coast side of the Head where some big cracked rocks stuck up out of the broom plants and the scrubby furze, half concealed by them and overshadowed by a cluster of the skinny pines. More than once he'd sat up there on hotter, brighter days and found some shelter. Unless it really started pouring down, he'd keep dry enough there while he got a grip on himself again.

Ronan had to scramble a bit to get up the steepest part of the slope right near him, but a few minutes later he was nearly around the shoulder of the hill and in among the rocks he'd been heading for. It was easy to mistake them as a bunch of boulders from a distance, but they were actually frost-shattered fangs of gray limestone that had been left exposed years before when some of the hill slid away in the middle of a wet spring. The rough sharp-edged slabs made a kind of three-sided enclosure open toward the eastern side, with the biggest slab at the back leaning a little forward and giving partial cover. Pine needles from the trees nearby had blown through the gaps between the stones and had piled themselves deep between them over time, a brown springy cushion now a foot or so thick.

Ronan flopped down onto that soft flooring and pulled his legs under him so he could lean back against the stone of the "rear wall." The space was snug enough around him to reduce the wind off the sea to an occasional breezy breath. His view of the world was here reduced to a narrow doorway that looked across uneven heather- and gorse-covered ground to what appeared to be a sheer drop-off, and beyond it, hazy and indistinct, the sea.

He sighed in a kind of relief at having the world be shut away from him even just this much, even for just a while. *No people, no noise...* Ronan thought; at least no noise but the soft susurrus of the sea whispering to itself, safely meaningless and distant.

That's the problem, he thought. *Getting any distance... any at all.* School was bad enough, the way it forced you into participation in activities you didn't care about with people you'd really rather have nothing to do with. Not that there weren't people Ronan *liked* being around, and classes that interested him. But usually just as soon as one of those tolerable classes was over, you were on your way to something you loathed.

If he could've spent half the day out in a field with a hurley in his hands and the rest of it studying music and maths, he'd have been happy. *But no,* Ronan thought, banging his head gently back against the rough lichen-patched slab where he leaned: *no, they've got to throw chemistry into it, don't they. And EngLit.* In which it wasn't the

Eng that annoyed him, but the Lit—any fiction older than a few centuries back bored him to tears. *And then the religion. And the history*—

He shied away from the memory of Seamus's taunting. Irish history was troublesome more or less from beginning to end; for every person who thought you were paying too much attention to it, there was another who thought you weren't paying enough. *And apparently it's my fault for doing too much research and coming up with an answer to the Irish Question that he didn't like...* He blew out a breath. *Last time I do that any more, then. Safer to toe the old party line and pretend that the Great Devil Cromwell killed everybody on the island and chopped down all the oak trees too. Safer to pretend that everybody who ever came here that wasn't Irish meant to take our stuff and do us dirt. Because half of everybody believes it...*

Ronan closed his eyes and concentrated on not thinking about Seamus and his ilk: concentrated on thinking about the hard grit of the stone against his head and the breath of breeze that swirled in and died away again, on the cocoa-butter smell of the blossoming yellow gorse on the hillside and the hiss of wind in the nearby pines. It took a few minutes of flat refusal to think about Seamus any more to acquire a bit of distance from images of that sneering superior face, and Ronan sighed again and looked at his watch.

Hours yet, he thought. *Hours before I can go home.* But even then there was no guarantee of things being all that much better once he got there... or not for long. Oh, it wasn't like big fights broke out or anybody got abused. But there were issues running just under the surface that kept coming up to get dealt with... and they *couldn't* be.

Ronan rubbed his face briefly in helpless pain that he could for once express because there was no chance anyone would see. *The other bedroom...* And its emptiness. It was the sign of another set of problems, one Ronan very carefully pretended he knew absolutely nothing about.

The trouble was that late at night he could hear his Mam and Da arguing—quietly, they thought, though the walls in that house had never been terribly thick—about whose fault it was that there wasn't a baby brother or sister (or two, or three). About his dad being afraid that other men in the neighborhood were mocking him as not being all that much of a man. *Won't drink, can't f—*

His mum would always try to stop him saying the next word, but his father's bitterness usually managed to get it out anyway. Then she would sigh. "Ah now. Come on, we've been over this a hundred times, you know it's not your fault."

"I *don't* know, Mary, that's the problem, the fecking doctor couldn't figure it out—"

"Well. Maybe the next one."

"Oh yeah, the consult, right, that'll happen in, what, five years at the rate the government's taking money off the HSE? And what it if *is* my fault and they fix it? What about you, by that time will you even be able—"

"Ro. We've talked about this before. There are possibilities—"

"Oh, don't start with *that* now! Best way to make all of them think I *really* can't—"

And then they'd be off on what Ronan now thought of as the Adoption Round of the Blame Game. It was no particular consolation that by the time they hit the Adoption Round they were usually neither of them willing to go on for much longer: its initiation signified that both of them were desperately weary of where this was going (or not going).

Their weariness about it was probably nothing on Ronan's at this point, but he would have walked into the kitchen and cut his own throat with one of his Mam's favorite cooking knives before letting on about that. But there didn't seem to be any chance things on that count would ever get better. *Even if they—*

His phone chirped noisily: a text. Panic shot through him. *Feck feck feck,* Ronan thought, fumbling the phone out of his pocket. *Oh God what if it's Da, what do I do? I am so screwed—* He stared at the screen.

Yr nan sad did u tak the umbrwllla?

Ronan stared at this for a moment. *Oh thank you God,* he thought first, because the text was from the carer's number.

It took him a moment to get his hands to stop shaking enough to text at his usual speed. *Tell her I'm OK, I have one at school.*

He'd already hit "send" before he started wondering guiltily whether that sounded too much like he *wasn't* at school right now. *Oh please don't let her get that idea, she'll tell the whole earth, not to mention Mam and Da...*

But the answer came back *OK thx.* And that, it seemed, was that: no more texts, though Ronan sat there nervously staring at the phone for the next few minutes, waiting for some new unexpected "other shoe" to drop. *I hate this. Everything sucks. Everything.*

Yet nothing happened. Finally Ronan slumped back and started working on breathing normally again. Staring out at the sea—flat, featureless for now, unexciting—calmed him a bit. He considered turning his phone off, in case someone should call and freak him out again. *But what if Pidge texts me finally? Or the carer wants me again. If I shut the phone off she'll freak, and Nan might freak too. And then the carer might call Mam or Da—*

Ronan shook his head and just stuck the phone in his pocket. There really wasn't any reason for any of those things to happen. And slowly the tension started to drain out of him. *Yeah, tomorrow'll be grim. But as for right now—* This little rare period of peace and quiet, *this* he could let himself enjoy. He 'd hear anybody coming long before they got anywhere near him—not that so many walkers or climbers were likely to come up here on a day that had started looking like this. Mostly people climbed the Head on days when they knew the sunshine would last long enough for them to take advantage of the view.

Ronan leaned back against the stone and turned his head idly to look, slightly unfocused, at the lichen spotting it—patches of white and pale green and (to his surprise) spots and dots of orange-gold. "Patriotic," he muttered, and smiled at the feeble joke, mostly because nobody was there to see him being irrationally amused by lichen.

He closed his eyes, letting out a long breath. It was funny, but with his cheek against it, he could feel the faintest warmth in the stone.

Apparently the early sun had managed to peek in here and rest on the stone for a while; and since the wind had dropped off, the sensation was even more noticeable.

Ronan blinked: then blinked again, concerned, because he knew somehow that more time had gone by between those two blinks than should have. He fumbled his phone out of his pocket and started thumbing at the buttons. *If I'm gonna doze off,* he thought, *better set an alarm.* Not that the idea of dozing off bothered him at all. In fact it was probably the best way to spend the time between now and when it would be safe to go home, because otherwise he would just lie here thinking of more ways that his life sucked.

And going-home time is when? he thought. *Three thirty, I guess. No sports on today, but I still wouldn't hurry back if everything was okay.*

He put 15:30 into the phone's alarm settings and shoved it back in his pocket; then looked out between the stones toward the gray sea, and sighed. Ronan folded his arms, shifted his shoulders against the stone until he got comfortable again, and leaned his head back once more. The stone was still warm.

Amazing how it holds the heat from so long ago, he thought. *Who'd've thought it...*

He blinked again.

HE REALIZED his eyes were closed, and there was a faint glow past them. "Sorry, lost it there," he muttered, blinking once more.

He looked up from where he sat on the low wall in front of the house, gazing at Bray Head. Its peak was hidden by cloud, as happened a lot this time of year, but the weather had been creeping toward that all day. Down here, though, the day was one of those weirdly luminous ones where you never see the sun, but all the landscape around shares in the glow, looking irrationally distinct despite there being so much cloud about. "It's okay," said the one sitting next to him.

For the moment Ronan was comfortable enough not to bother

turning around to look at him. "Couldn't be arsed," he muttered under his breath.

"To what?"

Typical that Pidge wouldn't get it when he needed him to. "Move," Ronan said. "Do anything useful. I'm just so fecking *tired* of it all. School. The idiots in it. Home. The world. Everything." He flipped his hands in the air. "What's the *point*, even."

"They were at you again," Pidge said.

"Seamus and his scurvy crew," Ronan muttered. "No avoiding them, and every single time they've got a new line in shite. You roll over and let them have their way, it just gets worse."

He rubbed his forehead: then caught himself—because that was the thing his Da did—and dropped his hand in his lap. "I tried texting you," he said. "Where were you?"

"Doesn't matter much if I wasn't where you needed me," Pidge said, sounding unhappy. "Sorry about that."

Ronan blinked. A lot of the time, Pidge could be pretty scathing about "getting all feel-y": it was rare to hear him be so open. But when he did it was worth listening to, and Ronan always made sure to let him know he was listening. "It's okay."

"Still," Pidge said. "Sorry."

Ronan nodded, reached out and patted him on the shoulder. "Okay. Lay off it now before I start freaking. Had enough of that already today."

"Um. Yeah, right."

They sat there for a few moments watching the traffic go by. Something about the image tickled the back of Ronan's mind, something off about it; but he couldn't think what just now.

"Because really," Pidge said. "Hate to miss a chance to catch up with you finally. Think think think every second, your brain's buzzin' like a wasps' nest all the time. Finding a quiet moment to get a word in edgewise, that's the challenge..."

"Is it?"

"You have no idea."

For some reason this didn't seem an unusual thing for Pidge to come out with. "Okay," Ronan said, amused, "say your piece then."

"'S nothing much except about you getting upset."

"Not at you."

"Didn't think so. But at what was going on..."

Ronan shook his head. "Did all I could," he said. "I just wish sometimes there was more. It's never enough."

"Though if there was a way you *could* make a difference—do something bigger?—something that really changed things—"

"'Course I'd do it. You kidding?"

"No."

"Well, yeah then! Because if you could change stuff, you'd *have* to. Can't leave things the way they are."

"No?"

"*Jeez* no, it'd be criminal. A fecking sin."

"Don't usually hear you getting religious."

"Feck no you don't," Ronan said. "You'd know better, I'd have thought."

"Mostly I do."

"Well then."

They were quiet together for a moment. "But yeah," Ronan said. "Religion's nothing to do with it! This is just about doing the right thing. Not like you should need religion to tell you that! If you could help in some big way and you didn't, it'd be like walking away from a hit-and-run, wouldn't it! If you can help, then you *have* to, really. Otherwise everything'll go to hell."

"It's doing that already, some people say," Pidge said. He sounded somber. "Everything runs down, no matter what you do..."

"Yeah, well. It does. But you still do what you ought to, yeah? Just letting it go because the odds are stacked against you, what's the point in that?"

"But if sometimes it got dangerous—"

Ronan shrugged. "My Da says you could get hit by a truck any time just crossing the street," he said. "If you were doing something that mattered and it got dangerous sometimes? Seems like it'd be worth it."

"Saving the world?"

Ronan snorted. "Like I could do *that.*"

"But if you could? Even just a little? Would you dare?"

The wording was odd, though no odder than some of the things Pidge said sometimes. "I'd dare a lot more than that."

"You sure?"

Ronan looked at him with affectionate scorn. "How sure do I have to be? You want me to stop and run a fecking referendum? Yeah I'm sure."

"What if you could, I don't know... have some kind of power... to help do the daring with?"

"What, like turn into some kind of superhero?" Ronan snickered. "Got a radioactive spider on you somewhere?"

Pidge laughed. "Think that was meant to be a one-off."

"Yeah, I'd have thought."

They sat quiet together for a few moments in the bright morning. "But what if there really was some kind of power? And not just for one person."

Ronan breathed in and out a little more quickly than he had been at the thought. "Have to be a secret, I'd think."

"It is, usually."

A strange feeling started creeping along Ronan's nerves. It was like the shiver that sometimes went with your hair standing on end... except that it brought with it a strange feeling of anticipation, of being about to hear something that could change the world. *And how does that even happen just sitting here on a wall?* he thought. Yet everything was suddenly freighted with that feeling that something more than usually meaningful was about to happen, was *already* happening, that you *could* change the world just sitting on a wall and this was what it looked like—

"Your choice, of course," Pidge said. "Some people let some others know, after it happens to them. Assuming they get through it okay."

Ronan sat quiet for a moment. "How many other people have this?" he said. "This power, whatever it is?"

"Considered one way, lots," Pidge said. "Considered another: never enough."

The words, the *difference* in Pidge's words, gave Ronan a bit of a case of goosebumps: but not in a bad way. It was like his body had a sense that someone else, not Pidge, was talking, at least some of the time. And this was someone way more, or different, or *other*—but that this was still okay.

"A lot of them here, though?" Ronan said.

"This world, you mean? A fair number."

"This country?"

"Same," Pidge said. "If you walked down Main Street from here to, say, where it starts to be Little Bray? Odds are good you'd pass at least a couple wizards."

"Really? *Real wizards?*"

Pidge shrugged. "Everybody's gotta shop *sometime...*"

Ronan laughed a little under his breath. "So you can't just stay home and magic up cash from the cash machine, or say 'Abracadabra let a trolleyful of stuff from the Tesco appear!'"

Pidge shook his head. "Not really the way it works."

Ronan made a scoffing face. "Pff. What kind of magic is that?"

"The real kind," Pidge said.

The goosebumps came up again. "Meaning?"

"You talk to the world in the language it was made in," Pidge said, "and hear it talk back. Tell it how you'd like it to change, and... if you can get it to say yes... *change* it. Understand what makes things work... and get them to work differently, because you asked them to."

Ronan swallowed, his mouth suddenly gone dry: swallowed again. He had to work at it, because the vista that had suddenly opened up before him was like looking up at the everyday sky and seeing it crack open and show you what was on the other side. In fact it was as if he could *see* that crack, somehow, in his mind: see how a world that had seemed little and dry and arid and hopeless had suddenly been hit by something, something from *outside*, and sprung ever so slightly open along that fault line to reveal a thin fierce gleam of something hot and deep and *real*. It was too narrow a crack for him to see detail through it... but it was *there,* and it seemingly laughed under its breath at mere physical reality and waited to see what he would do.

When he came back to himself a little Ronan realized that he was shaking, actually *shaking* in reaction to the sheer size of what he was apparently being offered—not so much a way out, but a way *in,* into something more than he'd ever believed possible. And Pidge was sitting there with his head cocked to one side, watching him, waiting. "You up for some of that?" he said.

"Up for it?" Ronan said, amazed by how rough his voice came out. "I was *born* up for it."

"Yes you were," Pidge said. "The basic requirement. Worth more than a whole boxful of radioactive spiders."

"Please," Ronan said, and covered his eyes with one hand for a moment. "An image I didn't need, thanks so much!" The ones he found in the bathtub some mornings were difficult enough to cope with, radioactive or not.

Pidge snickered. "Well. But even yer man in the red suit wouldn't have much of a skill set next to the one *you'd* have. That special language? It's *the* special Language. The Speech. Master it, you master wizardry. Takes a while to learn it. Some people spend their whole lives specializing in nothing else. Your first time out, the Powers that Be give you a bit of a boost—load in the basic vocabulary you'll need for your Ordeal. Later, in this part of the world, you have to do it the Irish way. Hold it in memory—the way bards did, the way druids did. But not on Ordeal."

"You mean," Ronan said slowly, "if you want to be a wizard, you have to go through a qualifier round."

Pidge nodded.

"And you're playing against...?"

"The Power that fell out with the Powers That Be," Pidge said. "... *Literally* fell out."

Ronan sat a moment and digested this. "What happens if you don't win?"

"Mostly," Pidge said, "you don't get to be a wizard."

"'Mostly.' ...Meaning there are other ways to fail out."

"It happens," Pidge said.

Ronan looked at Pidge hard. "There's something here you're not telling me. Like you're trying not to scare me or something."

"Well..."

"You're gonna tell me I could die, aren't you," Ronan said. "...So?"

Pidge put his eyebrows up in slight surprise.

"Stands to reason," Ronan said. "That kind of power, it's not gonna come cheap, is it? If the Bad Fella—it is him, isn't it? The Snake in the Grass?"

The eyeroll Pidge produced looked both resigned and amused. "He's been called that, yeah."

"Well, if it's him, and this lets people get up *his* nose instead of the other way around, doesn't seem like he'd just sit there and put up with it."

"No," Pidge said, stretching his arms up over his head for a moment to work a kink out of his back, then leaning back on them again. "No, you'd be right there."

"So what are the odds I wouldn't get through this thing—"

"Ordeal," Pidge said.

"Okay. This Ordeal: what are the odds I wouldn't make it?"

"Before it happens," Pidge said, "there is not a single way in the world to tell."

They sat there in the sun—there was some sun inside that brightness, or above it; Ronan could feel it —and jointly contemplated that for a while.

"Okay," Ronan said eventually.

"'Okay?'" said his friend. "That's it?"

Ronan gave him a shove, his shoulder into Pidge's. "What did I say about running referendums? I'm in. Where do I make my X?"

PIDGE TILTED his head back for a moment, as if feeling some of that hidden sun on his face, and a bit of a smile slid across it. But then he got more serious looking and started going through his jacket pockets.

"Okay," he said. "There's just one thing we've got to sort, because this is kind of a special case."

"Of *course* I'm a special case," Ronan said, running his hands through his hair. "Ask anybody."

"Not talking about your would-be crushes here, Ro."

"Excuse me, 'would-be'?" He put on an air of just-slightly-wounded indignation. "You *saw* Jackie drooling just yesterday."

"This is *not* a conversation we need to be having right now!" Pidge said. "Hold the thought till later, yeah? Got other fish to fry at the moment."

Ronan assumed an attitude of utter concentrated attention to whatever his friend might be about to say. Then he crossed his eyes.

Pidge looked at him sideways and shoulder-shoved him. *"Honest-ly,"* he muttered, "what to do with you."

"I'm all ears."

"Not since your mam taped them back..."

Ronan roared with laughter. It was a story only a very few people knew, and he didn't mind Pidge teasing him with it. "Okay," he said after half a minute or so, wiping his eyes while Pidge grinned at him indulgently, *"okay.* Say your say."

Pidge waited until he was dry-eyed again. "Here's the problem," he said. "Normally when someone becomes a wizard, the circum-stances are a little less unusual—"

"Can you even hear yourself. The words 'becomes a wizard' and *'less* unusual' in the same sentence?"

"Okay," Pidge said. "Fine, granting you that. But what's not so usual is that sometimes it becomes important that even the person committing to do something like this be, um, willing to have some parts of the situation be under cover until later."

"You said it usually had to be kind of a secret thing, yeah? No problem."

"But some parts of it would have to be that way... even from you. So that some of this setup... you wouldn't remember, later on. For a long time, till things change, you might think it was a dream, parts of it. If you remember them at all. *That's* unusual. And you need to okay it first."

Ronan sat there for a moment, scowling and kicking the wall with his heels. "Don't trust me with it, is that it?"

"*You?* You'd be trusted, no question," Pidge said hastily. "No question at all. But there's someone else... who might hear what you were thinking. And there's no other way to protect you from that."

"Ah." Ronan brightened. "Our friend Mr. Squishy McSnakeface."

Pidge stared at him... then spluttered with laughter. "That's a new one!" he said. "Thanks for that."

"So some of this stuff'd be, not just secret from other people...but secret from me, too."

"Yes. Not forever... but for a while yet."

"I'd be kind of a secret weapon, then."

Pidge paused, then nodded. "Yes."

"Sounds like it's about something important, then."

"It is."

"Yet still you're asking. If it's that important, why don't you just go ahead and do it?"

Pidge shook his head. "Not how we operate," he said. After a moment he nodded down the road toward the intersection. "Herself —" Ronan knew he meant the statue, or rather the being it was meant to represent. "The One could've done what It liked, that time, when It wanted to get into the world that special way. But that's not how things work. Beginnings matter. She had to give consent first."

Ronan snorted. "Yeah, and then the gossip started. All those people who thought she was the local Bad Teen Mum."

Pidge sighed. "Sometimes it's hard. Especially if enough info's leaked that there are prophecies that have to get fulfilled..."

Ronan rubbed his face with both hands. "Well, just so long as there aren't any about *me*—"

Pidge didn't say anything.

"Oh *no!*" Ronan said, and laughed again, as much in shock as from the conclusion he'd come to. "You want me to be some feckin' Chosen One? Everybody knows how *that* ends up!"

"If there's any choosing going be happening, it'll be yours," Pidge said.

Ronan sat there and frowned at the ground. "Well," he said. "You said things might get worse. But then everything gets worse. Runs down, yeah?"

Very slowly, very sadly, Pidge nodded. "It does."

"Well." Ronan let out a sniff of laughter. "No news if this situation might do the same, then. But it's like with Maurice before. You can't just walk away, even if it looks kind of ugly. Somebody has to put themselves on the line for people, stick up for them, yeah? Otherwise, what's it all for?"

The look Pidge gave him was interesting: as if something he'd said had somehow proven Pidge right. "That's it, right there," he said. "We're a good match, and this is going to work."

"Yeah," Ronan said, feeling suddenly more enthusiastic. "So come on, get on with it. In for a penny, yeah? So why not go in for a pound."

Nodding, Pidge started going through his pockets again. "There's a pledge to be made..."

Ronan snickered a little at that. "Yeah, saw that coming. Well, bring it on. And what are you looking for? I keep telling you you've got too many pockets in that thing."

"*Ah,*" Pidge said, and finally found what he was after in his front left jeans pocket. Ronan leaned close and watched with great interest and a fair amount of excitement as he pulled out...

...a folded piece of notebook paper.

Ronan stared. "Oh come on now, what's this?"

"What you've got to read."

"You wrote it on *this?*" He shook his head in disbelief. "Why don't you ever use that PD thingy yer mam gave you? That she spent about a million euro on at Christmas? You'll hurt her feelings. Also it's pretty cool."

"I *hate* that thing," Pidge muttered. "The keyboard's way too wee and I can't do the other input thing, the handwrite-y thing. It drives me crazy. And the batteries are shite." He scowled. "Also I keep losing the stylus, and they're expensive, those."

Ronan sighed and squinted at the crumpled paper. "Look at the state of this. How long've you been carrying this around?"

"A while."

"Sure it looks like it." Ronan rubbed at the smudges on it. "What's this gummy stuff?"

"Gluons," Pidge said, and nudged him with his elbow and snickered.

Ronan gave him a narrow-eyed look. "Do *not* tell me you're messing with substances. I'll stomp you flat and hang you up and beat you like a rug."

"Not glue, ya eedjit. Glu*ons.*"

Ronan rolled his eyes. "Yeah, fine, mister Aced My Science Test Last Week. Go on, rub it in some more."

Pidge snickered a little more, then sighed and smoothed the paper out over his knee so the folds were a little less prominent. The paper was the thin, wide-ruled kind you got in the cheap school exercise books they sold in the supermarket. Written on it in a rough square in the middle of the jaggedly torn-off page, apparently with a slightly leaky biro, were four or five sentences in a sloppy sort of upper-and-lower case print. You could see where whoever wrote it had tried to make the "square" even, but they couldn't get the spacing of the words right, and there were a few crossouts and a few places where a longish word had been squeezed into a space too tight for it.

"That's the Wizard's Oath," Pidge said.

Ronan rolled his head over nearly sideways and gave him a look. "This is the *least magic thing* I have *ever* seen."

"It's not magic," Pidge said. "It's wizardry. And yeah, sometimes it looks a little beat up around the edges. Because it is. And has been. For aeons."

The other's voice had gone a little edgy. "Beat up?" Ronan said. "As in... the other way?"

"Sometimes," Pidge said. "It's been a long fight. Sometimes you lose."

He suddenly sounded kind of tired. That made Ronan stop and look closely at Pidge, since "tired" wasn't one of his more normal modes of existence. When he was little (he'd once told Ronan very privately, and swore to kill him if he ever told anybody else) Pidge's family had for years called him "Tigger" because they couldn't get him to stop bouncing. Even now, he bounced most places when he wasn't slowing himself down to keep up with you.

"So good *doesn't* always triumph over evil?" Ronan said.

"If it did," Pidge said, "we wouldn't be having this conversation." At least there was a slight edge of humor on the response this time, but somehow Ronan still found himself feeling sorry for Pidge.

"Okay," Ronan said, "let's see what you've got." He took the piece of paper. "Besides awful handwriting. Janey mack, did you write this up against a *tree* or something?"

"Everybody's a critic," Pidge said, more amused. "Just see what you make of the content."

Ronan smoothed the piece of paper out over his own knee. "Okay. 'In Life's name, and for Life's sake, I assert—'" Then he stopped. "What's it mean by 'life'?"

Pidge looked absolutely gobsmacked, which made Ronan snicker. His friend looked hilarious with his wide mouth hanging open. "Sorry?"

"No, seriously. 'Life' like in life *here?* You said 'This world' before. *Not* just this world?"

"Nope. All the worlds."

"So there *is* definitely life on other planets."

Pidge gave him an amused look. "Even *here* they've suspected that for a long time."

"Yeah, well, suspicion isn't the same as someone handing you a piece of paper all covered with glue-y-ons and getting you to promise to protect something that might *or* might not be there."

Pidge looked bemused for a moment. "Uh, okay."

"'Okay' as in 'yes there is?'"

A long concerned pause. "You're not gonna call up the afternoon radio guy on RTE and tell him UFOs are real, are you?"

Ronan rolled his eyes. And then—taking in Pidge's look of growing worry—he snickered, and when he couldn't hold it in to just snickering any more, he burst out laughing so hard he almost fell off the wall. "Oh jeez, *your face,*" he gasped. "You should see yourself. No I will *not* call Joe if you tell me aliens exist. Which, it's too late, you already have, otherwise you wouldn't be giving me that look! But for feck's sake, just *commit* yourself here, yeah? No wonder wizards are in trouble if all the recruiters are like you, you're crap at it."

Pidge pulled a sort of 'excuse *me*' face. "Probably just as well they're not," he said. "I'm a little out of my job description here, no question. Keep going..."

"Right. So Life's got a capital letter on it. Like it's a name."

"And so it is."

"For... anybody in particular?"

"Probably Who you're thinking of, yeah."

"...Okay," Ronan said. "Not very personal, then."

"Or possibly *the* most personal word there is for anything," Pidge said. "If you *made* it. If it's yours, if it's still part of you, and really matters to you..."

Ronan thought about that for a moment. "Yeah, okay." He scanned a little further along the sentence. "'I assert'? Fancy word for just saying something."

"But you're *not* just saying something with this. Anybody can just say something, but when you *assert* it, you're saying 'This is true, this is serious, I believe in this.'"

"So okay, not a fancy word then. A specific one."

"Wizardry's all about the specific words," Pidge said. "The exact word, the word that perfectly describes something. Sometimes it's a name. Sometimes it's both. In fact, a lot of the time it is. Gonna wind up learning a lot of those before you're through."

"All right. 'Art?' This is an art? Just so you know, I flunked crayons."

"Anything can be an art if you're serious enough about it," Pidge said. He glanced up briefly in the direction of Bray Head. "Anything else you don't like in the first line, or can we move on?"

"Now now," Ronan said. "Me da says you've gotta be careful about what you sign."

Pidge's expression was resigned. "Actually, that's sound, he's got a point there. Next line?"

Ronan studied it. "Guard growth, ease pain," he said, "okay, those are good." He peered at the next sentence. "Seriously, I think I need to diagram this."

"Seriously," Pidge said, and snickered, "you're such a pain in the arse."

"Gotta be that way, yeah?" Ronan said. "If the Powers of Whatever need me, they've gotta know that's part of the package. Wouldn't be right to lie."

"That's sound too," Pidge said, and shrugged, and grinned.

"So then. 'Fight to preserve what grows and lives well in its own way...'"

They went through it line by line. It was strange, the way this process seemed to go on a long while, but also to take no time at all. But then time itself felt very weird to Ronan now, as if he was hanging outside it, somehow.

Finally they came to the end of what was written on the paper, and Ronan couldn't find anything to question about it. He'd always assumed the universe would end somehow, and he wasn't fussed right now about exactly how. *Wouldn't be my problem anyway...* He looked up at Pidge then and grinned a bit, turned the lined, wrinkled piece of paper over to check the other side. "That it?" he said. "Anything else I need to know about?"

"Ro," Pidge said, rolling his eyes.

"Terms and conditions apply? Ask my physician or chemist for advice?"

"*Ro.*"

"Okay," he said then, feeling sorry for Pidge, who'd been pretty patient with him until now (but that was his style). Ronan flipped the paper back over and got ready to read. He took a deep breath,

because suddenly it felt like he needed it. And also, a strange
nervousness had come over him, as if he was being watched, watched
by a lot of people. Except there was no one there...no one in the road,
no one on the pavement, everything empty and still and bright...

He shrugged.

"In Life's name," he said. *Quieter, it was getting so much quieter—*
"And for Life's sake, I assert that I will employ the Art which is its gift
in Life's service alone, rejecting all other usages." *Everything so still,
everything holding still, listening somehow—* "I will guard growth and
ease pain. I will fight to preserve what grows and lives well in its own
way—" *Silent now. When was it ever silent here? Even in the middle of the
night?* "—and I will change no object or creature unless its growth or
life, or that of the system of which it is part, are threatened—"

He was aware that Pidge was watching him, and there was something so strangely intent about it—but he couldn't stop to look more
closely just now, there was a sense growing on him that he needed to
hurry up, needed to finish this, that something was coming, something huger even than he expected. That narrow crack into something else was straining, wanting to jump wider, but it *couldn't* until
he finished—

"To these ends, in the practice of my Art, I will put aside fear for
courage, and death for life, when it is right to do so—"

Everything was silent, everything was waiting for him. Ronan
needed a big gasp of air for the last few words, and it was as if the air
jumped into his lungs, hurrying, wanting to be said in those last
words. "Until universe's end—!"

It was like finishing a race. Ronan felt wrung out, wanted almost
to bend over forward to recover, the way you did after a lap around
the track. He actually felt like he couldn't get another breath until he
got down off that wall, stood up straight, breathed. Hurriedly he slid
down off the wall and stood up in that light, clutching that piece of
paper, and beside him Pidge stood up too. Ronan saw, without understanding, the movement in the air of the light behind him, shivering
as if something too bright or strange to see flexed outwards and then
folded back behind Pidge; like a shadow, but bright.

The gasping took a few moments to pass off. "Remember that," Pidge said, kind of low, as if there was someone he didn't want hearing him. "Remember how it feels, that air, you may want it later."

"Kind of want it now," Ronan said, and took one or two more gasps of it before he felt right again. When he did, he looked down at the piece of paper again and had to laugh a little at how blotchy and ineffective the ballpoint writing looked. And then something occurred to him. "Y'know," Ronan said, holding out the paper to Pidge, "sure this isn't strictly legal."

Pidge blinked at him as he took the paper and folded it up again, shoved it in his jeans. "What?"

"Well, we're in Ireland, aren't we? There's gotta be an Irish-language version too. It's the law. Giving it to me in English, honestly? Makes me wonder if you did the homework..."

Then he got confused because Pidge started laughing at him. "Seriously," Pidge said after a good few moments, because he was practically gasping with it, "after all that, the whole bloody Oath, *that* brings you up short??" He wiped his eyes. "And what makes you think all this has been in English? *Listen* to you."

Ronan turned a withering look on Pidge. "Oh come on," he said, "give me a break—"

Except that wasn't how it came out. It was what he *meant*, yes. But the words came out differently... and nothing he'd ever said in his life before had shaken the air in his chest and the ground under his feet, so he could feel it vibrating right through his trainers. More or less of their own accord, his arms flailed out behind him to brace against the wall, and Pidge reached out and steadied him. *I'm my own earthquake,* Ronan thought, half in terror, half in delight. And also: *Did* I *say that? Or did it say* me?

...Whatever "it" was. Ronan discovered that he was shaking as he had been earlier, but for a whole different set of reasons now.

"Yeah," Pidge said, "now that you're *listening* for it, you're hearing it." He sounded satisfied. "When you speak the Speech to things, they pay attention. But then it was used to *make* them, so... it's all good." He grinned. "Meanwhile, far as the Oath goes, you're gonna have to wait for it *as gaeilge*. You've got other things to think about right this minute."

"Yeah, like how do I— Is that going to keep *happening?*" Ronan stared around him, suddenly and completely unsettled, as if someone had changed the world's rules on him and not told him what the new ones were.

Pidge's eyes glinted at him. "Count on it!"

"Then I need a dictionary, or a phrasebook or *something—!*"

"That's not how it works on this side of things," Pidge said cheerfully. "You want to know the word for something in the Speech? Ask it. Till you sort out what's coming, it'll be looking over your shoulder. You need a spell? Ask it, it's yours."

"A *spell,*" Ronan said under his breath. "Dear effing God *this is real—*"

"Yep, I was waiting for that one," Pidge said, and grinned. "Nothing will ever be realer! Well, maybe *some* things. But right now this is your very own version of the new real. Make it count, because for just this little while, you're the one who gets to say what it is."

Ronan shook his head and reached out to grab Pidge by the shoulders and shake him. "What the feck does that even mean?" he shouted. *"What did you do to me?"*

"Gave you what you wanted!" Pidge said, laughing a big laugh of sheer triumph like nothing Ronan had ever heard out of him before. Then he looked at his watch. "Whoa, will you look at the time," he said. "Gotta fly, Ro." And he grabbed Ronan by the shoulders and shook him in return. "Listen to me just for one sec, yeah?" Their eyes met, and Pidge's brown eyes were suddenly so much brighter than Ronan had ever seen them, so much more urgent. "Whatever you need: this first time out, *it's yours.* Take whatever you need and *don't be afraid,* yeah? Just do what you're going to do."

Pidge let him go. Ronan staggered—

And then something started bleeping at him.

HIS EYES FLEW OPEN. He found himself staring at lichen, his face against a rock.

What was that, he wondered. In his pocket, the phone was bleeping piteously, its alarm going off. *I fell asleep. A dream*—

Except that hadn't gone the way his dreams usually did. Usually, when he realized he'd dreamed something, the memory faded away within a matter of seconds. But this time there was no such instant fade. He *remembered*. The wall, the piece of paper, the words he'd read—

"*Ow,*" Ronan said under his breath, sitting up to stretch himself on the leaves that were now well packed-down under him. He felt stiff and sore, and could feel every single place the stone had been digging into him when he'd dozed off. He had to squirm himself around a bit to get the phone out of his pocket and shut it up. The digits 15:30 were flashing on and off.

Jayzus, he thought, *another sleep that didn't feel like any sleep at all. What's the point of a nap that doesn't even leave you feeling like you've had one?* He punched the OFF button and took a big breath—

Instantly Ronan was seized by sudden sense memory of how hard it had seemed to get a breath in that strange bright place. It was as if his lungs didn't know what to do with that air, with the brilliance in it, how clean and sharp and almost *fierce* it was. *It's not like the air's all that bad out* here, *really. But that, that was just so* different—

He sighed. It had been an odd dream, a good dream, full of promise. But at the end of the day, just a dream. And this, now, *this* was the end of the day, more or less, and Ronan found himself being assailed by thoughts of everything that was waiting for him out there, outside his little shelter of tilted stones. The walk home, his suspension, how long he was going to be able to keep it secret, the awful inevitability of tomorrow morning when the post came... Everything that had seemed just far enough away to ignore when he'd taken refuge here now, just a couple of hours ago, seemed an uncomfortable step closer.

He leaned back against the stone, letting out a frustrated breath, and gazed out past his feet at the bracken just past it on the hillside. A leaf of it twitched, not far away, and he held his breath and stared for a moment, wondering what might be out there, down low in the greenery: a hare maybe? But then some feet away another frond of the bracken twitched, and then off to his left another, and Ronan realized what he was seeing: the rain starting.

Great, he thought, morose. *Just one more thing.* One way or another by the time he got down off the Head and home again, he was going to be soaked to the skin. And then if anyone was home early, they would start quizzing him about why he was so wet, and where'd he been, and it was all going to start coming out. Even the little bit of peace he'd been hoping for between tonight and tomorrow morning would be over with already.

Outside the shelter of the stones the trembling movements of the bracken were becoming more widespread as the raindrops started falling more and more thickly and shaking the stems and fronds they fell on. Soon all the little patch of greenery that Ronan could see before him was trembling with the big fat drops of the beginning of a downpour. Ronan looked away across the bracken to the edge of the hillside and saw how solidly dark the sky had gone.

Maybe I should sit tight for a little longer, he thought. *Maybe I can wait it out, maybe it'll pass over...* But a good look at that leaden sky to the eastward dashed any hope that this rain was going to pass over any time soon. It was going to just keep on coming down. And for all he knew in a while there'd be flooding too, because the Head's ground was generally too stony to hold the water from a heavy downpour long. There was flooding from here and into the streets below all the time.

No point, Ronan thought, disgusted. Everything was conspiring against him to have a miserable time of it. *Might as well get on with it, then.*

He wriggled himself out of the shelter as best he could. It took a couple of minutes of pushing himself forward and outward more or less feet first, as there was no real room inside to turn around. Once out he stood up hurriedly at the feel of big raindrops starting to hit him all up and down his front. *Minimize the target,* he thought. But there was really no hope of that.

Frustrated, he thought *Oh who cares, gonna get soaked anyway...* and leaned his head back to look up at that gray sky. The first few raindrops drops struck him in the face. He flinched a little —

Wet, one of them said to him.

Wet, said another.

Wet. Wet. Wet, wet, water, wet, wet.

Ronan blinked in astonishment. The rain got into his eyes.

Wet, wet, other wet, tears, rain, skin, rain, wet, water, sky—

Ronan's mouth fell open.

—humidity, condensation, atmospheric convection, arcus, shear, ridge, core punch, inflow band—

They were falling on him faster and faster, pouring down with ever-increasing force, pounding on him: *words.* Not English words, and not Irish words either, but words in that other language, in the Speech, the one he'd been speaking without knowing how. But now he was going to know how to do it in the here and now, because they were falling all around him—

—tropopause graupel retrogression microburst anvil dome fractus helicity mesolow jet stream isotherm squall line stratoform rope cloud lapse rate—

The downpour of words just wouldn't stop; they were roaring in his ears all the time now, drowning out other sound. And the words weren't just about the things they meant, weren't just descriptions. They *were* those things. They were those things' *names.* Everything shook with them, thundered with them, inescapable—

Ronan stood there transfixed by astonishment, and by a weird kind of delight, as in drifts and curtains of meaning like rain the words came pouring and hammering down on him. *How can it rain words?!* But it didn't matter, because there was more of it, endlessly more, waiting for him, just waiting for him to ask for any word he wanted, any knowledge he needed, anything at all. *These are the words in which wizardry is conducted,* they told him. *All here. Waiting for you. Any time. Any place.* Life, the world, other worlds, unfathomable and unplumbable depths of existence, they were just waiting for him to ask about them, learn about them, find out how to act on them, learn how to change them and move them. The impossible made possible, endlessly, from now until the day he died.

It was as if a gateway had opened, like a door in the sky, pouring all this stuff down on him. Not just rain words or sky words or air words, but as the water started running down the hill, earth words too, *sedimentary inclination gneiss fossils conglomerate—* Ronan shook his head, shook the water out of his eyes and laughed out loud. *This is so amazing—!*

And it wasn't just that he was being given these words that was so wonderful. They brought with them a sudden storm of *certainty*, soaking him skin-deep and deeper. He'd never felt anything like it before: to be *sure* of things, to know what they were called, what they would do, *could* do. Suddenly Ronan realized how much of his life was spent—or even wasted?—being unsure about what would happen next. But this, *this* was certainty, right down to the bone, his bones and the bones of reality all around him; the ground had a name, had lots of names: the air had names, the water had names—

—he could hear the sea murmuring with them, a little distant here because the slight rise in the ground still protected him from it, *salinity, water cycle, ionic composition, relative molarity, circulation mode, conservative element, hydrophiles, chop, neap tide, clapotis, fetch, shoaling overwash backrush cusp—*

The words built around him like a flood, a rising wave, one that he'd have gladly waded out into except he didn't need to. An old memory rose dimly to meet him of being tumbled over and over by a wave when he was out swimming when he was small. There was something a bit uncomfortable associated with that, but it didn't matter right now, none of that mattered, he would gladly be rolled over under this wave and lost in it if it was made of words like this—

And all around him the thunder of words pouring down from nowhere just kept on and on. There was even something strangely familiar about it, as if this endless downpour was part of a huge undersound that had always been there, that he'd just never heard before... or had tuned out somehow. It was strange, but Ronan was starting to get the idea that maybe once when he was very little he'd heard it?... but had been talked out of it, somehow. *Sure it's nothing,* he could almost hear his Mam saying, soothing; *you were imagining it, forget about it now...*

Ronan found himself wondering, *Was that a real memory? Did she say that once when I was little, did I hear something?*

Most do, the something said back, though not in words. *Often when they're very young. Often they get frightened. Sometimes it's too big to handle, then. So they forget, and others help them to.*

And the sound just went on, scaled up, an unending hissing roaring blanket of white noise from the thousand dictionaries' worth of words that the new immaterial rain was bringing with it, a million libraries' worth of them, there were too many, too many—

Ronan collapsed to his knees under the weight of the onslaught of words, knowing they would never stop coming unless he wanted them to— *And I am* never *gonna want that!* He turned his face up into the rain again and it ran down his face and into his eyes and splashed into his nose and he didn't care, couldn't get enough of it: tilted his head back and opened his mouth and drank the rain, drank the words as they came down, he felt them soaking into him, all kinds of words! He wanted to jump, to yell, to run, to shout (and hilariously from the back of his mind came the image of Fred Astaire spinning around a lamppost and singing: now Ronan understood what the singing was about).

Because this was *real.* Magic was a reality, wizardry was a reality, *this was real.* The words just kept coming, hammering Ronan into the happiest kind of submission. Without this, he'd have been tempted to write off the whole conversation with Pidge—or whoever was being Pidge right then—as some kind of weird dream, a hallucination. But there was no mistaking *this* experience for anything but the truth.

Everything was there for him now... a vastness of knowledge that was his now to call on whenever he needed it: whenever the Powers sent him on, what was the word, errantry, or when he saw something that needed tending to himself. Ronan could just ask the world what could be done about a problem, and it would *tell* him. He could pick a method of intervention and the words would be given to him, the power put into his hands. *...Up to a point,* something reminded him: because the power of the moment wouldn't necessarily be with him at a later date. He'd have to make up for the lack of invincibility with brains. *Well, okay,* Ronan thought. *I can do that.*

I can do that.

I will do that!

And Ronan gasped, and gasped again, at the certainty, at the *truth,* when you said something in the Speech. It became *real.* He couldn't imagine anything more wonderful, or more dangerous. And that gift, that power, had been put in his hands. *His.*

And as the downpour of knowledge continued all around him, all Ronan could think was:

But now what? Who does this make me?

What do I do...?

AND ELSEWHERE IN REALITY, deeper in, one party regards another with a certain amount of puzzled disbelief.

What, just like that? Seriously?

Just like that.

A suspicious pause. *A little rushed, wouldn't you say? Not going to get the best response out of him under these circumstances.*

Now there's something I wouldn't imagine you caring about one way or the other! One more failed wizard? I'd think that'd be a positive result for you!

You know... I'm starting to wonder why you're so interested in my reactions, one way or the other.

Oh?

Yes. In fact I don't imagine we've had this long a chat about anything for...

Amusement, not at all thinly veiled. *You're going to try to work this out in terms of local time periods, are you? This should be fun. ...Then again, you were always big on trivia.*

...Years, it would be here, wouldn't it? Quite a lot of them. I have a

vague memory that something very large sinking into the sea would have been involved. What was its name again?

A slightly pained pause. *There would have been quite a few.*

Afállonë, yes, that was one. Atalántë, the Downfallen Land. Atlantis... And a pause not at all pained, but entirely too darkly pleased. *Death by water; so inevitable, one way or another. Such a lovely symmetry, when life arose from it.* And a smile. *I think I see some resonances here that I can exploit.*

Oh really?

Yes. You've shown your hand rather more than expected.

I rather doubt I've shown you anything that will do you any good.

Well then, maybe you won't mind me rushing things a little.

If you think it'll help you.

Oh, it will. Just watch...

INCORPORATION

He was never quite sure how he got home that afternoon. He had little memory of the walk. Because there was no one home when he got there, Ronan had plenty of time to check on his Nan (who noticed nothing about him odd at all, not a thing) and put himself into the shower and get into clean clothes, and put his that-day's uniform in with the rest of the wash that his mam would do that evening. The silent whispering that he started realizing he could hear all the time, even in the house's quiet, he wrote off as being something like the ringing in your ears you got after a long day at a music festival or a night with the headphones on too loud.

His Mam got home first, looking dead tired and fairly damp around the edges. "Oh when will this *stop,*" she said, shaking off her coat in the front hall and splattering water in all directions. "When do we get some sun? Isn't it supposed to be spring?"

Ronan had heard her car pull in and had gone to meet her with some vague idea of finding out whether she noticed anything different about him. He felt so marked-out, so utterly changed by the afternoon's events, that it astonished him when she breezed right past him down the hall and into the kitchen. "How was your day, Ro? You have anything to eat?"

He left the first question strictly alone. "No," he said, "thought I'd wait till dinner."

"Okay," she said, completely missing the omission—partly because this was apparently still Normal World (as opposed to the abnormal one he'd spent the afternoon in) and partly because in any conversation of his Mam's where food and other issues bumped up against each other, food inevitably won. "Pasta maybe?"

"Sounds good," Ronan said, wandering back that way to give her another chance to notice something different about him.

"Da's running late," she said, putting the kettle on and dumping the last of the morning's old tea out of the teapot and rinsing it. "Some meeting at work, he won't be home till seven maybe, with the traffic..."

She rattled on for a bit about work up at the hotel and things that had happened there, ridiculous guests and long-suffering staff, while Ronan stood in the doorway for a bit and then sat down at the kitchen table. He was astounded that something so ordinary and normal as this conversation could still be happening in a world where he'd had the kind of afternoon he'd had. The kettle boiled and his mam chucked the teabags into the pot and poured the water into it from a foot and a half above the pot, as usual—she was one of those "force and violence" tea-makers who believed that maximum pouring height got the best out of the tea. Then she went rummaging in one of the cupboards for some biscuits, and Ronan watched this with the detached bemusement of someone observing behavior on some alien planet.

When she flopped herself down at the table a few minutes later with a plate and some biscuits and a mug full of the new brew, Ronan realized she was looking at him a touch strangely. *That* was when the panic ran down his spine. "You okay, chuck?" she said. "You look a bit, I don't know... vague."

This was the chance, Ronan thought. Not to say anything about the wizardry—*that* was a decision he was going to wait a good while on: *because who knows if it'll work, if it'll last*—but about school, the suspension, the letter...

Ronan found that he really didn't want to lie to her. "Well," he said. "Got caught in the rain on the way home..." Because that was true. It was possibly the truest thing he'd ever said, on about six different levels.

"Oh jayzus, lovey," his Mam said, and patted his face, "sure you don't want to catch cold now, spring colds are the worst ones, did you take some vitamin C?"

He wanted to laugh. That was Ronan's Mam's response to everything that ailed you, and today in particular—when he instantly realized (without even having to look for them in his head) that he knew the eighty-three names for the seventy-two major variants of cold viruses and could talk any one of them out of troubling him—it struck him as particularly comical. "I didn't," he said. "Didn't think to..." Which was *beyond* the truth. Ronan had almost no idea of what he *had* been thinking: it was a wonder he'd made it home without being run over in the road.

"Well here," his Mam said, and jumped up and got all busy getting one of the fizzy orange vitamin C tablets going in a glass for him, and scolding him in a low-key though affectionate way about how he didn't take care of himself. Ronan sat there and made the kind of sarcastic-but-secretly-contrite noises he knew she was expecting, and drank the vitamin C. Then he accepted a mug of tea and let her start one of her long mild complaints about all the things wrong with her boss at the hotel.

For the next hour or so Ronan sat there and let it all roll over him, finding the boring familiarity of the scene strangely soothing after what he'd been through that day. When his Da got home, he too was in a sort of tired, nothing-new-happening-here mood that on a more normal sort of day might have set Ronan's nerves on edge, as just more confirmation that nothing interesting was ever going to happen in his life.

But now he'd learned otherwise. And slowly that realization began crowding out the normality, which just couldn't compete, wasn't anywhere near strong enough. The vast landscape of a profound arch-reality he'd never suspected of existing was having no trouble with beating the more commonplace stage set of "normality" flat into the ground. All the time, the whisper of words and words and words kept going on, getting little by little louder every half hour, every quarter hour... never deafening as the original downpour had been, but insistent in the kind of way that rain had when people said about it "It's settled in for the day..." Ronan started feeling as if with every breath the old Normal World and the new Abnormal World were rubbing against each other like bits of a broken bone, and he was never sure when one or the other bit was going to shock him with a surprise as acute as pain.

After they'd had their dinner and went into the front lounge to see what was on the satellite, Ronan found himself having trouble dealing with the way that the TV kept trying to show him things he couldn't possibly be seeing, just based on the way his mind was wandering as his Da channelsurfed. Words in English kept echoing themselves in his head as similar or associated words in the Speech, dredged up from the floods of Speech-words that were still sloshing around in there. And the TV—apparently capable of feats of band-width he hadn't ever imagined—kept showing Ronan alien scenes that nobody but he could see.

This started to cause problems. Once he laughed out loud in the middle of an episode of EastEnders that had nothing funny in it at *all* —another of their gloom-and-doom storylines, he he couldn't tell one from another these days—and his Mam stared at him as if he'd taken leave of his senses. "Um," Ronan said, and made some lame excuse about needing to do some kind of homework, and went up to his room. There was no way he could begin to explain the jokes the thing with all the legs that he'd seen had been telling; they'd been funny without Ronan even having to figure them out. There were all kinds of differences he'd thought having magic might make in his life, but improving his sense of humor had never been one of them.

Then after a while spent on his bed and finding the (non-)quiet (full of words, more words, *more words*) no more calming than the noise of the TV had been, he went off to the loo—and got the shock of his life when he turned on the faucet to get a glass of water first, and the stream from the cold water faucet immediately started shouting *Water water water cold hard wiggly tubes pressure (Navier-Stokes equations) exciting wheee!*

Ronan jumped so hard that he banged his head into the side wall of the loo and nearly knocked down his Mam's favorite little framed antique postcard picture of the Seafront Promenade. He had to stand there rubbing his head for a few moments and recovering himself as the water ran. *Probably just as well I didn't use the toilet first...* he thought.

Meanwhile the water from the tap was having itself a little party. Apparently it thought of the household pipes as some kind of thrill ride. *And how am I even hearing it* do *this!* Ronan thought. But then the water had been in the rain, and the rain had been in the town's treatment center, and who knew, it might have had time to get down the pipes into the water mains between when he'd been up on Bray Head and now ... Or maybe there was something weirder going on.

He braced himself and used the toilet (which mercifully seemed much more pragmatic about the joys of fluid dynamics, or maybe it was just that the water in its tank had had time to settle) and went back to his room, intending to settle in and read. But the air was still full of whispering, words and still more words and *ever more words,* hundreds of them, thousands of them, *tens* of thousands. *I'm going to have to* learn *all these?* Ronan wondered. *And how to use them? Put them together into—not sentences: spells?* Oh God.

Yet something in the back of his head, something that had been bored until now and finally saw a way never to be bored again, said *Yes!* at the prospect and pumped a fist in the air. No question, the prospect spreading itself out before him inspired something like the anticipation of a platform game that would take forever to figure out and really give you your money's worth. But right now it all just felt like too much to deal with. Too much had happened today, and he was exhausted.

Finally Ronan gave up, undressed, got into bed and turned off the light, hoping sleep would come for him quickly. It was a fruitless hope. The best he managed was a kind of vague directionless drift between sleep and waking, with occasional detours into dreams that made no sense, because they would start in the Speech and then segue into English or Irish, and then back into the Speech again. And memory was no better than the dreaming, in those times when he tried to hold his brain still and make sense of what had happened to him.

He took turns veering between delight and terror as he slid from having no words for what had happened to him, to having all the words, too many words, *every word in existence.* Those moments started to get longer as the night went interminably on. Endless vocabulary poured itself in and out of his head, as if he was a beach and the tide was coming in and going out, again and again, every time rearranging what it found a little bit, depositing another layer of the whispering freight it bore, and never once consulting *him.*

Once, just once, the thought *Did I have some kind of nervous breakdown up there, am I crazy?* inserted itself. But the words themselves seemed to laugh at that. And eventually Ronan felt he had to agree with them. He could imagine all kinds of crazy, but *none* of them included the jokes that that thing with the legs had been telling. As he understood it, crazy had to at least look like it had some relationship to things that might happen in your own head, and there was *no* way he could have invented something *that* weird.

Confusing and terrifying (and fascinating and, face it, occasionally delightful) as he was finding all this, though, the night wore on and Ronan realized what was coming for him. Sooner or later it was going to be morning. Sooner or later, that letter was going to arrive... and his life was going to turn into hell.

But wait. I have wizardry. What if... that letter just didn't *come?*

Willingly enough the Speech itself started to describe to him the problems he was going to have with that. One first had to learn the letter's location. One had to be able to describe its position in space-time, the materials of which it was made. And then one had to try to *convince* it to be somewhere else... not that easy a task, because once sent a letter had a powerful urge to get where it was going. The problems just kept mounting and mounting up, to the point where Ronan wanted to yell *Come on, this is magic, how hard can this be?*—and the Speech itself said something rather pointed and annoyed that boiled down to *This isn't magic, this is* wizardry. *Things don't just happen because you want them to. You have to work for it.*

"Oh great," Ronan muttered into the predawn darkness. "Just like real life."

Of course, the Speech said. *It is real life. What else would it be?*

He flopped himself over face first into his pillow and tried to hide himself from everything there. It worked, seemingly, for about five minutes... and then he was blinking gummy-eyed at the light through his window, and his usual alarm went off. Seven o'clock. Morning had come.

There was nothing to do but get on with it. So Ronan got up and showered, and got dressed exactly as if he was going to school as usual, and went downstairs. Then everybody sat down to breakfast, and Ronan simply sat there nursing his tea and keeping his face a mask, because his insides were sick with worry, terrified of the sound of the mail flap going.

And then it *went,* and the sound of it was like a tinny little bear trap closing on his gut. He started to get up and go for the post, but his Da waved him down into his chair again (he'd already finished his breakfast, despite Ronan willing him to for feck's sake eat slower so today would go like yesterday... *And then what?* he'd thought. *Gonna vanish the letter?*

Because he knew he could. The letter was *here* now. He could reach out with the senses that had spent the night (he now knew) waking themselves up and starting to bed down in his body and his brain. He could *feel* the letter if it was anything to do with him, and make it go somewhere else: up to his room, into the recycle bin outside, anyplace he knew for which he could provide coordinates—

But it didn't seem *right* somehow.

His Da was on his feet and nearly to the kitchen door. *You could do it,* Ronan's mind said to him, or part of it did. *Go on, hurry up!*

Wouldn't be a great start, would it?

But he'll never know! Neither of them has to know. Himself as much as said he was going to make it all go away if you did better this term. So you'll do better and it won't matter whether they ever see a letter or not—

His Da was halfway down the hall and the commotion in Ronan's head was getting ridiculous.

You could do it.

But should *you?*

Why are you wasting time trying to figure it out now, figure it out later—

Later's not the issue here. Now *is.* Now's where choice happens—

Ronan was starting to feel like one of those characters in a cartoon who's got an angel sitting on one shoulder and a devil on the other and they're fighting with each other. Not knowing what else to do, he stared into his tea and thought as loudly as he could, *Could everybody please* shut the feck up in here *so I can get a thought in edgewise?*

Everyone, or everything, shut up.

Ronan squeezed his eyes shut and just tried to get a grip. It was harder than usual. And now he couldn't get rid of the image of the cartoon angel and devil fighting over him, which was ridiculous. ... Though *this* angel was unusually combative and the devil was unusually agreeable and reasonable. In fact the angel sounded a bit like his Mam and the devil a bit like his Da, which was unfair, as his Da always seemed to come down on the winning side of any argument they had, simply by making Ronan sound unreasonable and stubborn.

Oh jeez what do I do. I've got to do something or it'll be too late.

He heard his Da picking the letters up from the mat.

But it, I don't know, it still doesn't feel right—

His Da was walking down the hall toward the kitchen again, starting to rustle through the pieces of post as he came. "Ronan L, Ronan L... Mary..."

Too late. Too late now. He'll feel it if I make it go away. And anyway I can't feel it, it's like there's nothing there for me, what if—

"Ronan L, Ronan L," his Da said, coming into the kitchen again,

"Ronan D—" And he frowned at the envelope. "*Who* the feck is 'Ronan D?'"

Ronan and his mam both stared. Ronan's middle name was Harris. "Who's it from?" his mam said.

"I have no idea." Ronan's Da stood there by the table and turned the letter over in his hands, and Ronan tried not to stare at it as if it mattered at all. *Just a plain white envelope.* Ronan swallowed as his Da ripped it open, and hoped the gulp of terror didn't show. *Plain white envelope, that could be very good or very bad—*

"What's the postmark say?"

"Um. Half a sec—" His da paused, turned the letter over and squinted at it. "Bray."

—Oh god oh god. What if the school got it wrong somehow, remember the time they had you mixed up with that other Nolan who was there, the one in third year, what was his name, Riordan, maybe his middle name is—

"Solar paneling," his Da said.

"What?" said his mam.

"What?" Ronan said, meaning to sound indignant but sort of squeaking the word instead. He took a hasty gulp of his tea to cover.

"These things used to just come addressed 'To the householder,'" his da was saying, sounding vaguely annoyed as he unfolded a brightly colored brochure that said SAVE NOW—GOVERNMENT GRANTS AVAILABLE! "Now they're actually posting them to real addresses instead of just getting them delivered in bulk?"

"Wonder which of the credit card companies sold you onto some bloody mailing list," Ronan's mam said. "See, this is what happens when you change banks..."

And his Da dropped the little pile of post on the table and they were off on *that* subject now, which had been a source of vague annoyance between his Mam and his Da for nearly a year. Ronan meanwhile just closed his eyes over his tea again and breathed out in terrified relief. The letter he was fearing wasn't there. It wasn't *there*.

There'd been a miracle. Or maybe An Post is just running slow. What a surprise.

Either way: Oh sweet Jesus thank you, reprieve!

...For a day. For *one* day. Twenty four hours. In fact, sort of twenty-three and a bit now. Fate was coming for him, no matter what he did.

Not a bad take on the situation, the cartoon angel remarked.

Ronan scowled. *Oh God this is all gonna be to do again tomorrow. Is being a wizard going to be worth this? I'm not so sure.* But the thrill that ran down his nerves at the concept of *being a wizard* made it plain that most of Ronan's mind thought he was talking shite.

All he could think of, after that, was escape. So he kissed his Mam goodbye and waved to his Da, and got out of the house to pretend to go to school.

W*AIT*. *Did you just interfere with the mail?*

More like one of your *tactics, I'd have thought.*

Aha, but you're not denying it!

If we get started on one of these accept-or-deny things nobody's ever going to get anything done. Don't you have, I don't know, something important to interfere with somewhere?

I'm doing that right now.

Except apparently not. A snicker. *Or not very successfully.*

I'd watch how you make fun of me.

Always, the answer came back. *I'm always thinking about that. Every Planck instant of my existence is spent on—*

It should be. It had better be. Because if you think you're going to get anything useful *out of this one—*

I already have. And I will again. And you know it, don't you! It's started already.

...Don't be so sure. The day is young. His life is young. And a lot can happen before the one or the other ends...

IT WAS ASTONISHING, and dispiriting, to find how little fun you could have when you had a day off school that you didn't want.

And just yesterday, Ronan thought, *I'd have given anything for a day or two off... Just not like* this.

He went out of the house and scowled up at Bray Head—which was practically shining in the morning's sun, here and there showing patches of that perfect so-fugitive spring green that when it appeared rarely lasted more than a day or two. *No way,* he thought, *not today.* Because who knew what lay under that innocent appearance? *Nope. Don't care. Gonna go to town today. Or maybe to Dublin.* He had enough money: he could catch the DART train in and lose himself among a few hundred thousand people who didn't have a clue who he was or care whether or not he'd been suspended.

He had to skulk for a while to make sure his mam and da were safely out of the way first. This he did by initially heading for the main road as if he was going to school as normal, but instead slipping hurriedly down the driveway of the house two houses down on the main-road side and concealing himself there in a little niche where they usually kept their bins. Those were out on the street today, though, and from that quiet spot Ronan looked out to see first his da and then his mam drive away, neither one any the wiser.

After that he resolutely made his way down the main street toward town, refusing even to look across the road as he passed the intersection where he'd normally have crossed for school. It was a mile and a half or so from there to the built-up center of Bray, and every yard of it that Ronan walked felt like *that* might be the one where his mam or da would have realized they'd forgotten something at home, and would drive past and spot him there.

But it didn't happen, and eventually it got too late for it to do so. Eventually Ronan realized he was free to just keep slogging his way downhill as the road twisted and turned past the convenience stores and the parking lots, the semi-detached houses and the strips of park that were scattered along the way. It took a while, as he didn't rush. He strolled slowly down through that relentlessly ordinary landscape as behind him the wind started to blow cooler and overhead the blue of the sky went grey, everything once more going dull and everyday and average-looking. Yet all the time words and *more* words and *still more words* in the Speech drizzled down around Ronan without pause, like a substitute for yesterday's rain; words that described the trees and the plants he noticed, and all the materials the houses he passed were made of; words describing the dogs and cats and birds and people he passed—words that *meant* them, could have *power* over them.

It was overwhelming, hard to take in... even after a whole night mostly spent trying to get to grips with it. Ronan liked to think he was good at coping with reality, even when it was unpleasant. But here he was suddenly weighted down with a whole new pile of it, and though he hated to admit it, he was struggling to find his balance.

So, great! he found himself thinking. *I've got wizardry! So why do I feel like crap?*

Because he did. *This isn't how I ever imagined it,* Ronan thought, *if something like this was going to happen to me. It would be terrific and wonderful and all my problems would be solved.* Instead the world looked a lot like it had yesterday, except that *now* he also had all this stuff he was going to have to learn if it was ever going to be useful.

He sighed, then, standing at what a lot of people considered the beginning of downtown Bray. It was the intersection where Vevay Road and Killarney Road came together in a vee—the angle filled by a weird old half-timbered building that once had been the City Hall and was now a McDonalds. Even the smell of the fries and the growling of his stomach (for he hadn't had the appetite for anything but tea at breakfast time) wasn't enough to distract Ronan at the moment. *I said I wanted this,* he thought, crossing over and heading down among the pubs and shops of Main Street. *And now I've got it. All these words...*

The whisper of them was always there now: even the late-morning traffic noise couldn't stop them. Whenever Ronan held still and closed his eyes, he could practically *see* the words starting to try to fit themselves together in his head in order to match whatever he was thinking about. *If there really* had *been a letter about me this morn-*

ing, and I'd had just a little more time to get used to this, he thought, *I could've made it go away.*

And the thought gave him a shiver. *What else could I do? What else should I do?*

Because he could still faintly hear the voice that had been talking to him all through that dream. *Making a difference. Making bad things stop happening. Help good things not get screwed up. Guarding growth...* There were a lot of things that could mean. *Easing pain...* That too.

Those words, the words of his promise, were burned into his brain and utterly memorable, even if some of the details surrounding the actual making of the promise were a bit dim. *I said that,* he thought. *I meant it. It's a good thing to mean.*

...So best get on with it, then.

There in the center of town Ronan stood looking into one of the plateglass windows of the local bookstore, not really seeing anything he was looking at: shiny covers, three for two deals, all the words on all the covers making less sense to him at the moment than the words he was hearing now in his head. Half of him was thinking, *Might as well stay here for a few minutes at least, because it's looking like rain again...* And indeed it was getting very dark back up at the north end of town, in the direction of the road back home. As he looked up that way, he saw a flicker of light in the clouds up there, followed a couple of seconds later by a sullen mutter of thunder.

That decided him. It was yet another good reason to go spend the day in Dublin, rather than hang around in Bray where he'd constantly have to wonder whether he was going to run into someone he knew.

He turned back to the window full of books and started going through his jacket pocket for enough change to deal with his fare on the DART. *Then I can sit down somewhere quiet, maybe get a burger or something, and get a grip and start working on this,* Ronan thought. *Because, okay, I kinda got caught by surprise.* And then he snickered at himself in mockery while the first big drops of rain started pattering onto the pavement around him and the first drops of rain tapped his shoulders. *Yeah, well, 'magic is real', who wouldn't be surprised? But here it is, looks like. So... time to make a plan. Let's get out of here and start making it happen. If I move quick I can get down to the station before this really sets in.*

The wind picked up in a gust as Ronan turned to his right to head back towards the intersection with Florence Road, which would take him down toward the Seafront and the DART station. The rain started pattering down harder, big fat drops that were going to mean another soaking if he didn't get moving. *Is it going to pass over fairly fast,* Ronan thought, glancing up to assess the clouds, *or is it—*

Just as he turned, another flash of lightning from the northward lit up everything in the street as blazingly as if someone had turned movie-set lights onto it. For just a split second Ronan was absolutely dazzled by the sharpness with which every detail jumped out at him, every bit of color and texture—the clothes of passing pedestrians frozen by that brilliance as brightly as if by a strobe, every edge or corner or surface perfectly defined. In the next split second that flash caught him right in the eyes and blasted the vision out of them.

He actually staggered as if struck a blow. The weird thing was that while Ronan was recovering himself, he didn't hear any thunder. *That can't have been* that *far away!* he thought, putting out a hand to lean on the shop window while he tried to blink some vision back into his eyes, which were showing him nothing but glowing afterimages. *Something that bright, it* should've *been practically on top of us—*

But there was still no thunder. And he couldn't find the window with his hand, which was weird. *I got turned around,* Ronan thought. *Okay, just stand here until the eyes are working again...*

The wind began to pick up once more; rain started splattering into his face. *Feck it all, this is just my week for getting wet, isn't it?* Ronan thought. He could have just started laughing out loud at the ridiculousness of it if he wasn't standing there in the middle of town where someone would come across him in a moment and think he'd gone spare. *Yesterday was all about water, and it looks like today's going to be that way too.* "Okay, come on," he said under his breath, "talk to me, what's the trouble?"

But for the moment, despite the fact that the water wouldn't shut up with him for most of the previous night, it had nothing to say right now. What Ronan could tell, though, was that it was scared.

Wait, what? he thought. That was just *wrong.* "Come on," he muttered again, knowing he was using the Speech in the middle of Main Street but not caring, because he was finding it upsetting that water should be scared about anything. "What's the matter?"

He didn't get any answer back that made sense. Ronan rubbed his eyes some more, blinked. *Yeah, better,* he thought, because much to his relief that afterimage was now fading. *Except, why's everything so dark all of a sudden, and wait, where are the—*

—buildings...?

Because there were no buildings.

Nor was there a street. Ronan was standing in the middle of a wheel-rutted muddy track that wound up to where he stood from the direction of the Seafront, and then wound away again, uphill in the direction of Bray Head. And he could see Bray Head from here, easily, because there was not a single building between it and him to obstruct his view.

He stared around him, open-mouthed. On all sides Ronan was surrounded by nothing but soggy sandy soil covered with scraggly bracken and sea grass, the kind that grew on dunes and hillsides close to the water. Further inland, in the general direction of Little Bray and the river Dargle, he could just make out through the mist and the down-pelting rain several large conical thatch-roofed houses that looked exactly like the ones in the Ancient Ireland theme park down by Waterford that he'd gone on a school trip to a couple of years ago. Penned in a rough enclosure of wooden pilings near one of the big thatched houses were some disconsolate-looking brown cows, all very muddy and raising up a pitiable racket of mooing at the weather.

"You and me both, lads," Ronan said, for all around him the rain was simply *hammering* down, the air hissing with it and water leaping up in muddy drops from every puddle. There were no people to be seen, which at the moment Ronan counted as a plus—since if the inhabitants were the kind of people who would logically go with these houses, or these cows, seeing him would probably just give them some kind of conniption. *This weather, honestly, they'd be smarter to be inside anyway...*

He looked up towards Bray Head again and saw the lightning flickering in the clouds above it, like a warning. *Or like a challenge,* Ronan thought—or something inside him thought.

He could feel it, too: that sense of something taunting him, daring him. His thoughts immediately went back to Seamus yesterday. Something up there, something behind the lightning, had taken up the dare that Ronan saying the words of the Oath implied. And from the looks of it, It had said, *Fine. Let's see how you handle—* Ronan looked around him and had to use the words: *Time travel. Let's see how you cope with that.*

And why do I get the idea it won't be just that? Because if Squishy McSnakeface just wanted to make my life difficult, he wouldn't have to go all timey-wimey with me. He's got something else up his sleeve.

Ronan pushed his hair back away from his face—because it was dripping in his eyes—and looked up at Bray Head.

"Okay," he said in the Speech, and not under his breath. "Time to get the lay of the land. Let's get on up there."

WITHOUT ANY WARNING, the landscape all around him was partly obscured by a diagram laid out in lines of multicolored light—like neon, but more alive. It was a diagram made up of interlocking circles that at first looked like a Venn diagram with a lot of writing inside it.

Ronan bent over to look at the parts of it that were nearest to him, for he was actually standing inside one of the circles. The writing was graceful and curvy, like a many-branched vine: it seemed to be some kind of cursive, its tendrils curling out on alternate sides of a central stem. As Ronan bent over to look at the writing he realized to his astonishment that he could read it. The long sentence that curved along inside one arc of the circle in which he stood was a number of words in the Speech that had to do with transport, moving something from one place to another. He saw a long word that he knew immediately meant *Bray Head,* followed by a string of words describing the location of the top of the Head: a coordinate set, like something from a GPS readout. *Okay,* Ronan thought. *And to get up there I have to read that—*

He straightened up. "Okay," he said. "Fine." And as the rain drummed relentlessly down onto him and he once more had to push his dripping, sopping hair out of his face, Ronan lost his temper and said, *"And can I please not be wet?"*

The sentence came out in the Speech, and forcefully, so much so that—as they had in his dream—the words shook the air Ronan used to speak them, and leapt out of him with enough force to leave him staggering. Feeling a little hurt but nonetheless cooperative, the water soaking into his clothes immediately removed itself three inches away from his skin in all directions.

Ronan startled at that, because now he found himself encased in what closely resembled a shell of pebble glass, the kind you put in bathroom windows. Except *this* "pebble glass" was apparently alive. It was shimmering all over from where the rain outside was hitting it— the rain, too, now cooperating by observing that three-inch limit. "Well, thanks," Ronan said then.

Welcome, the water said—and kept saying, repeatedly, in tiny ripples. He could see it saying so as well as hear it, which was interesting in and of itself: the movement itself apparently was an expression in the Speech, if you were water.

Right. Can we smooth that out a little? Because I'm not gonna be able to read through this.

Instantly the surface of the water around him went smooth and clear as window glass.

"Ta," Ronan said, and took a moment to get used to being dry again—*completely* dry, even the sweat of his initial shock was gone now. *So weird!* But there was no point in trying to deal with the details of all this right now. *Just get through it. One thing at a time.*

"Okay," he said under his breath, "let's see which bits of this I need to read now..." Because the Speech itself was making it plain to him that for any spell, the right words had to happen in the right order to produce a result. And transit spells, apparently, were notoriously tricky. Misplace the Speech-equivalent of a decimal point or a vector quantity at a time like this and you could wind up not on Bray Head, but *in* it.

In this case fortunately the two arcs' worth of wording he needed to recite were clearly marked for him. They flared softly in response as Ronan reached for the words that they meant in his head, found them, sounded them out without saying them. As he did numerous other notations and subclauses glowed faintly where they were embedded in the ancillary circle—protective barriers against remnants of older wizardry that might be lingering in the area.

Two phrases, he thought. *Room for a big breath in between. Let's go.*

He took a long breath and started saying the first phrase. The words were more under control this time when Ronan was taking more care over them and injecting less emotion. They didn't shake him so violently on the way out, but there was still a sort of buzzing and juddering in his body as each one was pronounced; as if someone had reached down inside Ronan and turned up the bass. And around him the incessant hiss of the rain was muting down as if someone was sliding some kind of master volume control downward; as if someone, or something, wanted to *listen.*

Speaking the words was an effort, though. Each one represented some fraction of the force that was holding everything in the world together. Each one felt *massive.* Every time he finished speaking one, Ronan felt like he'd lifted up a rock or a breezeblock and couldn't let go of it until he found exactly the right place to put it. Yet there was a kind of poetry in what he was doing, even if it felt strained and weighty and inherently dangerous. Every time he got a word, a stone, set in the right place, the act came with a huge sense of accomplishment, as if everything that existed was leaning in around him watching and applauding every time he got it right. The increasing quiet, as he put the second-to-last word of that phrase in place, might have freaked him out under other circumstances, but right now it just felt like a crowd going more and more still as you got ready to kick a goal—

Ronan came to the end of that first phrase and stood there gasping as around him the transit circles glowed more brightly in time with his breaths. There would be times, the Speech told him, when this would be quick and easy, over with in just a few seconds... but right now he was in a place where a lot of other wizardries had happened over time, and filtering out their influence was a problem. On understanding that, Ronan found that he could actually *feel* their traces deep-sunk into the earth, layered like strata of stone or sediment, and full of decayed or trapped energies as dangerous in their way as if they were radioactive. *Great*, he thought as he finished getting his breath back. *I'm living in a magical toxic waste dump...*

But the rest of the spell was waiting, and the rain was coming down harder; water was starting to run past him in little streams toward the seafront. *Better get to higher ground*, Ronan thought. He took a long breath and started in on the second arc of the spell.

It was harder. Things were dead quiet now despite the rain hammering down all around him so hard he could barely see through the fall of it—though Ronan's own little water-shell was doing its level best to stay still because he'd asked it to. Carefully and slowly he said the first phrase of the arc, which had seventeen syllables and was all about the actual coordinates of the flat bit at the top of Bray Head—and gasped. He said the second phrase, which was mercifully shorter and had to do with local shifts in the gravitational constant and matter density—and gasped. He said the third one, which (he suddenly understood) was several significant portions of his own name, and was therefore surprisingly easy to say—though a couple parts of it made him blush.

Then he said the fourth phrase, and this one was *really* heavy lifting and had to do with the speed of the Earth's rotation and how much that speed was going to change between the time Ronan said the last word of the spell and the time he arrived at his destination. Ronan was desperate for deep breaths of air now, but there was only one word left, the actuator of the spell, seven syllables long—one for each node of the symbol that finished the spell, a complicated Celtic-knot-looking thing. Ronan found that he was shaking all over with fine muscle tremors as if he'd just had a run round the school track. He locked his knees and clenched his fists and got those last syllables out—

And something squeezed the air out of his lungs so hard that for a moment Ronan was blind. Then the pressure let up again. Ronan gasped, opened his eyes—

And gasped yet again, because he was on top of Bray Head. And then the wind hit him and he had to concentrate on bracing himself until the gust let up for a moment and he could look around.

IT TOOK Ronan half a minute or so to finish getting his breath back, time he spent checking out the stony, muddy spot where he stood. The big cross they'd put up here on a concrete pedestal in the nineteen-fifties was missing. Well, *that* was hardly a surprise. But as he scanned around him through the blowing curtains of rain, Ronan saw that as far as Bray went, absolutely everything else he knew was missing too.

The landscape itself was almost exactly as it should be, from the rounded crests of the Wicklow Mountains to the southward, to the peaks of Sugarloaf and Little Sugarloaf behind him to the west, right around to the low soft rises and slopes of the Dublin Mountains northward and the bumpy crescent leading up the coast to Dun Laoghaire and out to sea. But they were all there was.

If things weren't already strange enough in the wake of the last day's events, this would have shaken him badly. But Ronan had had enough time to slide into a mindset where, since the impossible clearly *was* possible at the moment, he might as well roll with it. *Since I got here from home,* he thought, *stands to reason there ought to be a way to get back home from here.*

Immediately he understood the answer by way of the Speech itself: *Not until you've passed through whatever test is to come.*

"Well, okay," Ronan said under his breath. *After all, he did say 'Ordeal...'* "So let's see what that's going to be."

Assuming, of course, that the storm was going to let him get on with it. *Because people've nearly been killed in these mountains when they got caught out in weather that wasn't even this bad...* Ronan turned to seaward and was glad he was protected by the shell of water he was already wearing from the water that would have been lashing him otherwise. Out eastward, for as far as he could seen, slate-dark decks of solid cloud lowered over the sea from horizon to horizon, turning the day into a premature twilight lit only by incessant flickers of lightning up inside the cloud. The mutter and rumble of thunder was almost constant, most of it well out to sea at the moment but some rumbles getting closer, and quickly. The sea itself was in tumult, big waves plunging in toward the coastline. Ronan wasn't expert at judging sea heights—he wasn't into sailing—but the swells looked tall and ugly.

Have to feel sorry for whoever's gonna get hit by this, he thought. *Anybody living by this water is gonna be in big trouble real soon now...*

He looked out to his left, trying to get a glimpse of the thatched lodges near where he'd arrived, but then was distracted by the realization that there was a much bigger settlement much closer. Just down below him on the northern side of the Head, near its foot, was a cluster of such lodges, arranged in a rough double circle. The village—for the settlement was big enough to be considered one—was right where the southern end of the Seafront promenade would be, in Ronan's own time. Here, though, instead of a broad sandy beach, the little ring-village faced a stony shore that reached further out into the water than the modern Seafront did; and among the stones was a deep round little harbor that looked like someone had dug it clean out of the shoreline with an ice cream scoop. *Maybe, I don't know, a hundred people live down there? More?*

There was no telling. Sensibly, in weather like this, everybody was inside, and smoke curled sluggishly out of a few of the lodges' roofvents, only to be instantly beaten down out of the air by the relentless rain. There were some small oval-looking boats nearby, but they'd all been dragged up way up onto the shingled beach and lay there upside down, lumps that were already half covered with waterborne sand.

Won't be enough, Ronan thought, shaking his head. *The water'll be up around those soon... drag them away, smash them up.* And what happened to the boats would probably happen to the houses too.

The thought gave Ronan the shivers, dry though he was. He'd seen some seriously bad weather in his time. Bray, being on the coast, had caught some of the worst of the storms that came in from the European side of things when he was little. And everybody learned about Hurricane Charlie in 1986, when the river Dargle broke its banks and flooded half of Bray, killing people and causing millions of pounds' worth of damage that took years to repair. He remembered being shown ancient film and video footage of the chaos: Main Street under water, people paddling kayaks past parked cars, water cascading down over the DART tracks and past them, ripping up the Seafront's structures and dumping them in shattered fragments out on the beach. Now he looked out at that sea, where the wind was whipping the surface of the water into sharp scary-looking waves with whitecapped tops already almost hidden by clouds of blown foam, and he thought, *This really looks like it's going to be worse than that. Better get a last look at all this, because pretty soon there won't be anything left...*

Ronan gazed down sadly, thinking about that history unit in school, a few years back, and the way it had transformed the glamorized bright-colored Irish-myths landscape of his childhood into something more somber and difficult... and with a lot of mysteries buried in it that didn't have anything to do with stories of gods and fantastic creatures. He cast his mind back to what the historians down at the Iron Age village in Waterford had told them about life in Ireland back then. Those people had had a hard life, but an interesting one. There'd been trade with Wales, trade with places even further off—

Now, though, looking down at the double ring of lodges by its tiny harbor, into his mind by way of the Speech came flowing a great rush of knowledge that hadn't come from that school trip, from the hasty talk of raths and cashels and stone ring-forts. He wasn't just being told: he was being *shown*.

In a rush of sudden vision like a timelapse sequence in a documentary he saw for himself the wakes of little square-sailed ships making their way across from Wales and then running up and down the Irish coast, putting in at what natural harbors existed. He saw armed explorers go inland, seeking out the locals, contacting their leaders. He knew, without needing to see it, that money was changing hands: the trade with the Lands Outside was being built up as he watched. At first it was in dogs, then in cattle, later in horses: he saw them being led down to the boats and put aboard.

But slowly the cargoes changed. Ronan started to see lines of people going down to those boats, being put into them, and not returning. Then he realized with horror what the new cargoes were, and why so many fewer people were bothering to farm the inhabited lands any more. They had found a more profitable sort of merchandise. The Irish had discovered the slave trade.

Ronan had taken only brief note when it came up in his history class of the so-called "Irish Dark Age", a time between the second century before Christ and the fourth century after—when the pollen record in the bogs showed that suddenly people seemed to be doing a lot less agriculture, and no one was sure why. It was a mystery (one of his teachers last term had said) why this stagnation or decline in the ancient Irish Iron Age way of life should come at the same time as those centuries when the Roman Empire was at its peak—busily dominating southern Britain and starting to consider the opportunities that the next island over might hold.

It hadn't made much sense when Ronan had heard about it first. It seemed to him then that if nothing else, trade between the islands of Britain and Ireland might have done better, not worse. *More people, eating better, living better, more people, more farming, yeah? Should have been a cycle.*

But it wasn't. And now Ronan understood what there hadn't been proof of, because there hadn't been any writing about it, or any that had survived. People weren't farming as much any more because, instead, they were starting to raid each other's settlements, taking their food… then enslaving their former neighbors, selling them on, and living off the proceeds.

Ronan's mouth worked in disgust as the storm rose around him. *The slavery thing.* He had always hated it, and had been shocked to learn when he was small how Saint Patrick himself was a slave brought from Wales to Ireland. That was generally no news: everybody got taught about it in religion class. But that the Irish might be selling their *own* people into slavery—*that* definitely wasn't something you were taught in school. Ronan could just imagine Seamus's face, and his response, if someone told him about *that.*

Yet here it was, and it had been going on for a while. Not all the time, of course. Some of the stuff the wizardry showed him being traded through that little scraped-out port was gold and pottery and rough iron weaponry, and even baskets of puppies: *wolfhounds,* Ronan thought. *Or their ancestors.* But again and again those lines of twenty or thirty or fifty people chained together were prodded down to the water by men with spears, and packed cruelly tight into those little square-sailed boats like so much mobile merchandise.

Ronan's gut clenched at the sight of it, and he started to get angry. He looked away, out toward the roiling water, and could feel the size and power of the storm churning in toward him from out there. It would hit this coast and wipe out every one of these little settlements that might have been built next to the sea to take advantage not just of the fishing, but the business opportunities. It would kill the chieftains and the servants, the householders and yes, the slaves; and all their cows and dogs and cats and everything right down to the rats and mice… everything that lived there. Yes, the inland villages would probably survive. But there would be flooding and famine in a place where the weather and the climate were probably precarious enough already.

So let it happen, said something in the back of his head: a thought, a voice. *If they're part of the slave trade, maybe they deserve this. Walk away.*

If you walk away, said another thought, another voice, *who knows how history will be changed?*

Or how it won't be? said another. *Maybe this is the place where the trade stops, if you let this happen.*

Ronan was having trouble telling whether these were his own thoughts or whether the Shoulder Angel and the Shoulder Devil were back again.

Whether they were or not, they were both annoying. "Doesn't make sense," Ronan said under his breath. "Even if these guys all die, people inland are still probably going to do it..."

But if everyone here dies, it'll be a lot harder for them to carry on. The harbors will have to be rebuilt, new traders recruited—people who know how to sail in the open sea, who're willing to relocate here. Maybe it'll be too much trouble.

If everyone here dies, maybe the inward trade will stop forever too... and the slave boy who'll grow up to be Saint Patrick will never arrive. What happens to history here then?

Ronan stood there feeling the wind picking up. It too seemed to have voices in it—increasingly angry ones. Something was whipping it up, lashing it from behind the way a jockey lashes a horse, whipping it toward the shore. *If I don't do something,* Ronan thought, *we're going to have... I don't know... a tsunami or something come through here.*

It was strange that the thought *But what can I do about this?* never even occurred to him. For the moment he knew he could do almost anything he could think of... anything he could *decide* to do. It might cost him, of course, the way even the spell to get up here had cost him. But he knew he *could* change what was going to happen here.

Ronan swallowed as the roar of the wind past him started slowly to scale up toward a scream. He had little time to figure out what his next move should be. But what he'd said to Pidge now acquired an unexpected edge. '*Do you want me to stop and run a referendum...?*'

He could see the way the water was starting to pile up into huge waves out there. *Okay, maybe not a tsunami,* Ronan thought, *maybe you need an earthquake for that. But that's not natural, what's coming.*

This is going to flood way inland and scrape everything off the shore for miles.

And so what? said one of the voices. *If this storm doesn't do it, some other one will. You going to stay here for the rest of your life interfering with the weather? Nothing you do can matter here in the long run.*

It sounded very sensible. But that line of reasoning reminded Ronan of the issue of where he was, and *when* he was, and how he was going to get back... *if* he was. The wizardry had made it plain to him that there was no way out for him, no way back, except through this problem and out the other side... one way or another.

And Pidge had told him that sometimes people *didn't* come back.

Ronan gazed down at the little double ring of thatched lodges there by the foot of the Head, looking so crude, so primitive. From one possible viewpoint, this moment was so long ago. And his world was what it was: how could what happened *here* possibly matter to his world of computers and satellite TV and comfortable houses? *That* was the reality: the present, even the future. *This* was the past, savage and deadly even without bad weather—full of disease and danger and, yes, evil. Maybe it was better gone...

He was a breath from turning away and trying to figure out a way to get himself out of this when unexpectedly Ronan saw something moving down among the lodges. It was a little dot, almost black against the paler shingle and sand, and it was running away at top speed out into the wet and the wind. Straight for one of the boats it ran, and plowed right into the sand around it, and fell over.

The next moment, out from behind one of the lodges came running something that was almost a stick figure—boy or girl, Ronan couldn't tell—wrapped in uneven muddy-colored clothes that the rain and spray instantly plastered against the child who wore them. The thin little shape with long dark hair flapping and whipping around its face went pelting barefoot across the stones and sand, hopping a little because the stones hurt, making straight for the little black shape that had righted itself after running into the sand and was now cocking its leg against the half-buried boat, peeing against it.

It was a puppy. It finished peeing and then ran in a little circle of relief, giving the child who'd run out after it into the storm a chance to grab it, pick it up, and run back toward the lodges. The puppy was wriggling in the child's arms and trying to lick the face of the one who carried it. And a second later they were behind one of the inner lodges again, blocked away from Ronan's sight.

Just like that, his perception of what he'd been seeing flipped right around.

It's just people *down there,* Ronan thought. *And of course some of them are kids. There's no possible way any of this is their fault. And whatever else might be going on with the grownups, some of* them *are innocent too.* ...And more: even if they *were* involved in the trade, which seemed likely enough, how did he know that some of the people down there didn't hate the idea of selling people to make a living, but thought they didn't have a choice? Even if they were wrong, did they deserve to die for it?

For maybe long enough for three or four long breaths Ronan just stood there, half blind to the vista, hardly noticing the way the lightning in the clouds above was starting to flicker faster and brighter or the way the angry voice of the thunder rolled.

Okay, he said silently, because in this wind there wasn't any point in saying anything out loud: he wouldn't be able to hear himself even if he shouted. *You know what? It's not my business to figure out who deserves to die. That's all shite. This is about life, yeah? Let's just keep all these people alive and let them sort out the details themselves. This is their time, not mine. If there's going to be history, fine, let them be the ones who make it. But they can't do that if they're dead!*

THE WIND really started to scream now, and the wind was pushing at him, shoving him with intent, knowing he'd made his mind up. There was so much water in the air that Ronan could hardly see.

Except he had wizardry to see with; and the water itself seemed to be a little on his side. *Right,* Ronan thought, and glanced around him as he had a sudden nervous thought about how high up he was, and how exposed. *First of all, I'd really like not to be hit by lightning right now...*

The Speech showed him the spell: three interlocking spell circles surrounding him, with seven word-syllables glowing hot among them. *Good,* Ronan thought. *Thanks for that.* And he started to say them.

It was easier this time—a *lot* easier, not least because the spells were very different in type. Within a few seconds Ronan could feel, if not see, the grounding wizardry closing around him, ready to redirect any incoming lightning into the stones and soil of the Head. *Okay,* he thought. *That's a start. Now then...*

Ronan stared out at the storm. The core of it, he thought, was pushing closer and closer: the lightnings were flickering even closer together and more frequently in the clouds now, and out on the water he saw a lightning bolt stitch itself brilliantly against the livid sky and actually hit the water.

Not good, Ronan thought. *Time to get busy. Can't figure out how to fight what you can't see, though. What I need right now is the six o'clock weather report...* And for a moment he wished he had the dark-haired thoughtful RTÉ weather lady there to tell him what to do.

But suddenly he saw that he didn't need her, because he had the wizardry—which obedient to his request was now showing him, in a multicolored heads-up display seemingly half a sky wide, a schematic of the adjacent coastlines, with the overlaid imagery of the cloud and rain and wind, and all the isobars clearly displaying. Ronan put out a hand, and responsive to his gesture the display tilted until he was seeing something more like a satellite view, but exquisitely local and detailed.

Oh, this is great! Now all I need to do is figure out what to do— Because though RTÉ Lady talked about the weather all right, she wasn't in a position to *do* anything about it.

Ronan pushed his hair out of his eyes again, nervous. The schematic the wizardry was showing him contained layers and features that no RTÉ weather schematic was likely to show any time soon... and most specifically it showed the places where the shoreward flow of wind and the storm's heat exchange with the water were weakest, the places where a wizardry could most effectively make a change in the whole storm complex's direction.

But then he looked more closely at the numbers and Speech-characters embedded into the diagram... and as Ronan got a better grip on the amounts of energy that were going to have to be added to the system to stop the inward push, he was filled with dismay. The kinds of energy input required were what you might expect to get out of a hundred or so power plants in the course of a day. *Can't stop that,* Ronan thought, *no way... not even with all the power I've got! Useless—*

See, said one of those thoughts or voices inside his head. *You were told! This is a mistake. You can still get out of it, though. You can still walk away. Do it now.*

...But still, Ronan thought. And in the quiet between thoughts he didn't hear a voice, exactly, but a memory. *Take whatever you need, and don't be afraid.*

Ronan sucked in a breath.

To the wizardry he said silently, *Let's give this a shot. Maybe if we talk to the wind in—that area right there, yeah?* He pointed at one part of the schematic. *And push. Pressure's lower there. That curl there, the one that's coming in closest, it might just fall apart.*

And from directly above Ronan, without so much as a second's hesitation, lightning arced down and hit him.

Or at least it tried to. The grounding shieldspell filtered out most of the light and a lot of the noise, so that Ronan wasn't nearly as blinded or deafened as he might have been. But he staggered, and he had trouble seeing for a few moments.

Gasping from the shock, Ronan kept blinking until his vision came back. *Cute,* he thought, hissing with annoyed amusement—one of the noises his dad made when something went wrong but wasn't a total disaster. The bolt hadn't precisely been a feint: clearly whatever was behind it would have been happy enough if it had actually killed him. But at least Ronan knew his shieldspell was working.

And maybe, he thought, *that was a line of inquiry it didn't want me pursuing? Okay. Let's see about that.*

He found the spot again. *There*— The diagram formed up a couple of lines of the Speech for him to read, and an input spot for Ronan to make contact with for energy transfer, like a glowing handle.

He grabbed it, and read the words as quickly as he could. *Right there,* Ronan said in the Speech, *let's do it!*

Instantly he was reminded of the time when he was three or so and had managed to push part of one of his construction toys into a powerpoint that he'd pulled the "safety plug" out of. There was that sudden sense of being both frozen in place and violently shaken while you were stuck.

Yet this time there was a lot more going on. Ronan was consciously aware of having consented to be a conduit for the extra amount of personal power allotted to him for this first time out as a wizard. But though he knew the spell was protecting him against the worst of the side effects, he still felt like a heavy cable rated for one voltage and having to deal with a throughput about ten times higher. Uncontrollable tremors shook him as the power passed from him into the spell. Still Ronan hung on and gritted his teeth as he watched the numbers in the schematic changing, watched the swirl of cloud tremble as he was trembling, roiling like steam rising from a boiled kettle—

But it wasn't enough. And as for the power flowing out of him, it grew to be too much for Ronan to manage, second by second, just *too much:* he couldn't channel or direct it properly, not for long enough to make the change in the storm that needed made. Worse, even after all he'd done, the storm wasn't slowing up that much. That spot he was concentrating on—as Ronan watched, it just sort of melted away in front of him, and other parts of the curl of cloud and wind took up the slack. *Not enough...*

Finally he had to let go of the conduit-handle in the spell, and then stagger back and away from it, panting with exertion. On came the storm, and there was nothing Ronan could do, really nothing—

You were too stupid to take the warning, said that voice in the back of his head... and it was laughing at him. *You could've got away. But no!*

And now that storm's going to hit you head on too, as well as everything else here. With you all alone here, all exposed... And you saw how long it took you to get up here. It'll take you far too long to get away. What makes you think you'll survive what's coming?

It was the smugness that got up Ronan's nose, just as it had done with Seamus. The gust of wind that accompanied the self-satisfied, mocking prediction nearly knocked him over. But Ronan held himself pressed against that wind as if it was a wall, and concentrated on hanging onto his self-control.

Now you see your helplessness, that voice said, amused. *Put up all the brave front that you like; you're not strong enough yet to deal with the power that's been given you—and having discovered that, you've left yourself no time to run! How very choice. And now I'll pin you right here where you've trapped yourself, and crush you like a bug.*

The flush of rage that went through Ronan at that condescending, amused tone surprised him by its vehemence. He actually bared his teeth in fury.

"Oh *will* you," Ronan snarled. The anger was so intense that it pulled him back in memory to a schoolyard moment, so long ago, when he'd told those kids he did *not* want to run around that lunchtime, he wasn't feeling well, but one of them grabbed him by the hand anyway and pulled him away from the wall and—

And he *saw* it.

Ronan grinned.

T*HAT'S IT, that's absolutely it,* he thought. And before anything else could happen to stop him, Ronan leapt forward to grab the spell's power-conduit "handle" again, and said to the energy-channeling part of the spell, *Do that again, what we did before—hurry up,* just do it!

The power went flaming out of him and into the spell, and once more Ronan felt himself chained to the wizardry and shaken to the bone. But this time he did one thing differently as he pushed the power in: he reached out and added a different ending to one particular Speech-word where it was embedded in the diagram. The *lamesthae-* root was all about motion relative to a given axis, and force imparted along that axis. *Lamesthaetijh* had been the form he'd been using: *push, resist,* used of movement on an opposing axis. But now Ronan changed it. "*Lamesthaeturvh!*" he shouted. *Co-rotate—spiral —swing!*

The spell diagram shifted shape and appearance as he changed the word. What had before been like a pointed spear that he was thrusting at the storm now seemed more like a chain, curving, that Ronan was holding the end of as he started to turn in place. The spell channeled the power he was pouring into it into that movement, a spiraling movement, and Ronan gritted his teeth and *hung on* to that power input handle at his end of the chain of words, waiting to see if it would work. *Oh please let this be right,* he thought, desperate. Because it *had* to be. *Please let it,* please—

The immediate response of the storm was almost a hesitation, as if it had been caught by surprise because Ronan wasn't pushing it, *fighting* it, any more. Then, after some seconds, came the beginnings of resistance to the strategy. But it wasn't going to be enough to change what he was doing, *couldn't* be enough, because Ronan's unseen opponent already had too much energy invested in keeping the storm going the way it was going. And now Ronan wasn't trying to stop that. Stopping wouldn't have worked. Now, instead, he and the spell were *helping* it. The inward path had been a curved one to start with, calculated so that the storm's curving arms would strike the coast with maximum force. Ronan was just making it keep on as it had been doing—only *faster* than his opponent had originally wanted. *And so it's going to turn before it hits the coast full on. It can't help it—*

The storm started speeding up, and yes, its angle was changing. Ronan hung on to the word-chain of the spell, spun in place like one of those Olympic hammer-throwers and *hung on,* feeding power down the chain no matter how much he felt like his skin and his nerves were frying in the fire of it. Slowly his teeth-gritting started to turn into a grin. It was exactly like playing snap-the-whip in the schoolyard—that being the old furious image that had given him the idea. True enough that there was no way you could *stop* all those kids who were coming at you to grab you and drag you along. Yeah, you might have to hang on and go along with it at first. But as soon as you could find someone to help you and a place to dig your feet in and work to swing the *others*, unless they all stopped together, or dropped hands and broke the chain apart, they couldn't stop *you* snapping *them* around and into something else—!

Ronan leaned back against the motion as he spun, squeezed his eyes shut until he could see nothing but the chain of words he was holding and the knots and tangles of force they were attached to. The last six words at the far end of the chain, the ones fastened to the core of the storm itself, were the ones that mattered. He kept repeating them until he started to lose himself in the sound of them. *Just keep saying them, just keep repeating them, the spiral's in them, the swing is in them, keep it turning—*

And it was working. *Oh God it's working—* In his head Ronan could see the storm ever so slowly starting to shift off its original course, curving, curving more, *turning.* The worst of it was going to miss the coast, *it was going to miss—*

He wasn't at all sure how long that part of the wizardry went on. All he was sure of was that he didn't dare stop, because if he stopped too soon, it would all have been for nothing. The wind kept screaming at him for what seemed like forever, full of voices shrieking with frustration, rage, threats of revenge— But finally the blast and the noise of it began to drop off, slowly, slowly; down to a roar, down to a whine, down at last to a frustrated mutter, the noise you hear in your ears when you're running. Fits and gusts, at last... nothing better. There was still rage there, but it was exhausted.

Finally there was nothing more that Ronan could see to do. He let his contact with the spell fall away, and gradually it disassembled itself. As it did so he stood there swaying, the gray lightning-flecked world still turning around him because he'd been spinning so long, and finally he just sat down hard on the stones and held his head to try to get it used to the idea of being still again.

Did I just save the future? he thought, groggy. *Did I just make sure history was going to keep going the way it needed to for things to go the way they're going already?* It was too vast a prospect to take in, in all its good and evil: Ronan had to reduce it to something he could, for the moment, understand.

And wow, here's a thought. Did I maybe just make sure I'd be born? If I'd walked away from doing this, is it possible that I wouldn't have existed afterwards?

His mind reeled away from the concept, too shocked and wearied at the moment to deal with it in any detail. All he could do was laugh weakly at the concept. *Wouldn't the joke have been on me, then. Ha ha, very funny, McSnakeface. You should go into standup.*

RONAN PUT his head down on his knees for a few moments, relishing how the world no longer seemed to be spinning around, at least as long as he kept his eyes closed. But slowly he started to become aware that everything wasn't quite settled yet. A furious slow hissing growl was still coming from the waves and from the balked wind out beyond the roiling water. *He really doesn't care for being made fun of, does he...* Ronan thought. *...Well. Brought it on himself this time.*

Ronan opened his eyes, found that made him dizzy, and closed them again. *Give it a few moments yet.* He sat there concentrating on his breathing, and finally said silently, *So: was that it? Are we done here?*

Well... said one voice.

You may *be,* said the other. *I* am not.

Ronan got a strong sense that the fury he'd sensed in the power behind the storm was now looking for something else to focus on. And without any real reason for it, the hair stood up on the back of his neck.

I don't like this, he thought, and got up. Once more Ronan staggered when he was on his feet, and had to close his eyes briefly until his sense of balance settled down. *Absolutely* no *more spinning like that,* he thought, opening his eyes again. He couldn't remember having been so dizzy since that time he was six or so and his mam let him go round and round for as long as he wanted on that one playground thing, the wheel with the handles on it. *God was I sick afterwards. Never again just yet...*

When he was sure of his footing, *really* sure, Ronan made his way carefully over to the edge of the flattest part of the Head and looked out to sea. Those huge waves were still rolling in to land and crashing, *really* crashing, down at the foot of the Head. Yes, the wind had died away, but it had already transferred huge amounts of energy to the water, and all that had to go somewhere. *Have to be miles and miles of water stirred up like this,* Ronan thought. *Gonna be a long time before it gets rid of all this and quiets down...*

He stood for a few moments watching the water. There was something fascinating about the violence of it—the height of those waves, and the way that now that the wind was dropped almost to nothing, they were practically *sloshing* into one another, chaotically, like water in a plastic kiddie pool with people on all sides shaking it. And though the storm was now heading southward—much against the will of the one who'd started it going—the lightning that was jumping from cloud to cloud, or sometimes from cloud to sea, struck fiercely bright glints off the wavecrests. Ronan stood there staring at the vista for a moment, the bizarre movement of the water, the sheen of light down the waves when the lightning flashed—

Which was when Ronan saw something strange. There was a dark spot on one of those waves. For a moment he squinted, sure he was seeing things, as the wave flattened, curved up again. But no, on the wave behind it: that spot. A strange shape, oval, almost vertical as it slid down the face of the wave.

Another lightning flash went off, not too far away, and Ronan sucked in breath, horrified, as the shape ducked out of sight beyond another wave as it slid to the bottom of the present one. *Sails!* he thought.

There was no mistaking them as the little dark shape came up again and precariously crested the next wave, poising there a moment before starting to slide down the fore of it. A pair of square sails thrust out of it, one smaller, one bigger, both of them a dull salt-stained dusty red. They were flapping around slackly, because there was no wind in them now. But the general landward push of the agitated water was still driving the boat that bore them—pushing it closer and closer to Bray Head.

"Oh *now* what," Ronan groaned in sheer annoyance at a world (or a being) that seemed intent on throwing one thing after another at him. *Where had that come from? How long had it been out there?* "What are *you* lads doing here?"

Saying their prayers, for all the good it's likely to do them, the answer came back, amused.

And because there's no wind now, Ronan thought, *they've got no control. Ah God, this is my fault!*

Yes it is, the answer came back. And then came the laughter.

Another of those ferociously bright blazes of lightning lanced down out of the clouds and struck the water near that boat, illuminating everything about it in merciless detail. The little ship wasn't all that close, but Ronan saw what he was sure were human figures clinging to at least one of the masts.

"Oh come on now," he shouted, "not lightning *too*, don't they have enough problems, how the hell is that *fair?*"

And how would what you just did be fair? the snarling voice replied. *You and your little friend! Well, now you find out for yourself what your whole good-versus-evil nonsense is worth.* Nothing's *fair. Best you learn it now.*

Assuming that the angry power answering him was referring both to him and the owner of the other voice, Ronan had no time to spare for figuring out which one of them was "little." All he could concentrate on right now was the desperate and helpless little dark blot of a boat that was presently sliding down the face of yet another wave. Every time it managed the feat, Ronan was horrified at the possibility that it might not manage to do it again. And the number of times it would have to do it again was getting fewer and fewer, because the boat was getting closer all the time to the Head.

Ronan found himself absolutely certain that this was the reality of the abstract he'd been considering before: an incoming slaver. *Picking up or dropping off, who knows?* he thought. And the thought flickered across his mind: *If they're dropping off, is it better to be dead than to be a slave? If they're picking up, do they deserve to die for it?*

...Then again, thought I said I wasn't gonna make decisions like that.

Yet once more Ronan found himself hesitating. There it was right in front of him: the slave trade in miniature, made real. *And what if... what if I'm here because this is some kind of tipping point? If these lads die here, if they never get home, who knows, Rome might quit trying to make a go of it here. But if these people survive they can go back home some day and tell other Romans how good this country would be to take and keep, full of resources, and yeah, more slaves—*

Ronan stood there considering that for a moment. Regardless of Seamus's sneering, other countries' interference in *his* country's life had always been a sore point with him. *The hell with the politics of it,* he'd think when the subject came up (yet again) in history, *the hell with the economics of it and all the other shite, why can't everybody just* let us alone *and let us be* us?

And here was more of it, right on his own doorstep. *Stopping it, putting a stop to it right now, wouldn't that be nice...*

It suddenly sounded so *reasonable* somehow. Especially when Ronan really didn't have to do anything, when he'd already done what he'd been brought here for... yeah? He'd passed the test, the Ordeal?

But no answer came. All he could hear at the moment was a faint echo of that laughter that had made him so angry.

Ronan stood there quiet for a moment, and then another moment, while the wind muttered down to nothing around him and the water drove the small boat closer to the rocks that stood out a little way out in the water from Bray Head. *Crab Rock down there,* he thought, almost idly, *Periwinkle Rocks, those'll do for it. Big modern boats, way better built, have smashed to pieces on those. Everybody dead before the RNLI crews could get anywhere near them.*

It wouldn't take long. They wouldn't suffer long. After all, didn't everybody say that drowning wasn't the most awful way to die after you got past the first shock of the water in the lungs? *Just let this happen—*

Ronan shivered. *No,* he thought. *No, that's crazy, why would I think a thing like that??* And he gulped, suddenly wondering what had been inside his head just then, leading him along that particular train of thought. *Never mind it now,* he thought. *I can guess. What can I do now, how can I get them out of that—*

The transit spell—? But it would take too long. Think how long it took for just you. How long for a whole boat? And all the people in it? Even if you knew for sure how many of them were in there—

There wasn't going to be time, nothing *like* time enough to do something like that. And the boat was getting closer and closer to the rocks. And as Ronan had seen, the problem wasn't the wind— it was the water.

Something had to stop it. Some*one* had to stop it.

Okay, Ronan said, his guts clenching. *That would be me, then.*

He grabbed his hair and clutched his head to help get himself to focus, because all this had been coming at him so fast and he was wrecked from the last wizardry— *How do I get the water to just calm down, to stop this?* he said to the Speech. *I have a feeling just yelling 'Cut it out!' isn't going to do it.*

The Speech gave him to understand that he was exactly right. What he was proposing would have been like yelling "hey you" at a crowd and expecting the whole mass of people to stop moving. To control water, to control the sea, you had to use names. You had to name all the water, all the properties and elements associated with it, everything in the whole volume of an area you desired to manage. The question was... could you do it fast enough?

This is what all those words are for, Ronan thought.

But I can't possibly just say the words fast enough. There's no time. There has to be a bigger way to do this, a faster way, those guys are gonna get killed!

And then the Speech showed him a faster way. It was almost a reversal. It started with naming the most important names in the desired area, yes. But it didn't stop there. It was more of... an exchange.

Not just being in the water, Ronan thought, as a cold chill went down him. *Not just submerging yourself into it, getting lost in it.*

Being *it.*

INTERVENTION

nd the memory came back to him like a flash... like a flame leaping up, one that had been smothered down to the faintest spark for a long long time.

RONAN DIDN'T MIND SWIMMING, as such. He didn't mind being in the pool. But one day everything had changed.

The family had gone to the beach at Greystones. It was the pebbly kind of beach, where you could destroy your feet if you weren't careful, but it was nice there in the sun. The water had been cold that day, but sure the water there was always cold. You learned to cope with that.

The tide wasn't too high that afternoon, and Ronan had gone out into the surf happily enough and struck out into where the water was deep enough to swim. But at one point, when Ronan had stood up neck-deep in the water to rest himself and had turned his back on the water, then—when Ronan wasn't even slightly looking for it—came that one wave. It got taller than he'd thought, and there was no time to get away from it, and it came down on Ronan and rolled him over and smashed him into the sand under a ton of greenness with only the faintest bit of light around him. And the light was everywhere and he couldn't see the surface and he couldn't feel which way was up. There was nothing he could do, *nothing at all;* the sea was calling all the shots. Everything was roaring and he had to breathe and he *couldn't,* and he knew that if he once gave in to the burning in his lungs and opened his mouth that would be it for him, all over. And then—

—accidentally, completely accidentally, the water pushed him in a slightly different direction and he saw the surface and broke through to the air and the light, coughing and choking and spitting sea water.

Somehow Ronan managed to stagger back to the strand and up onto the pebbly beach and fell to his hands and knees there, coughing. His Mam ran to him to help him up, but his Da lay there on the towel watching him and said (loud enough for half the beach to hear, Ro thought), "Don't fuss him, Mair, you'll put him off, he'll get scared of the water."

Left it a bit late, Da, Ronan thought, for "scared" didn't begin to cover it. Ronan *knew* right then, beyond any possible uncertainty, that what had just happened had been *done* to him somehow. Not that he had the slightest idea *how.* But he knew in his bones and his blood that something had held him gripped in a cold cruel fist just long enough to make him think he was about to die. Then it had carelessly flung him up on the stony beach like a crumpled-up ice lolly wrapper, saying to him: *Remember this for next time.*

He'd known better than to make a fuss about it that day. As soon as he could afterward Ronan did his best to look normal, even to laugh about it and make fun of himself a little, which put his Da off the track. But starting that day Ronan began making it a habit not to go in too deep, and never again to put himself into a position where a wave could rise and he couldn't get back to the shore in time. He did it gradually so his Da wouldn't give him a hard time over it. Little by little he let it be seen that he wasn't that much into ocean swimming any more, that it was too cold (which was true) and that there might be anything in that water (which at least for one summer was also true, a fact that helped him).

Over time Ronan had successfully buried the memory, so that only in the most occasional dreams did he remember cold green darkness clutching him helpless in its fist while he struggled hopelessly for breath and life. He might wake up gasping once or twice a year, but always the light of day had been more than adequate to banish the message *Remember this for next time.*

And this *is the next time, isn't it.* Now Ronan understood where the message had come from, all that while ago. The Power that had caught him off-guard back then had been looking at this moment, *this* place, right here, right now. It had given him a warning, and a promise. *You want to get into it with me? You know what's coming. And this time you won't get off.*

Somehow, bizarrely, Ronan thought of Seamus and his little crowd behind the outbuilding at school. The tone was the same—that smug self-assured cruelty, that smirk of certainty peculiar to someone who had the upper hand and didn't need to be worrying themselves over *you*.

But this time, he thought, standing there in the hammering rain, *this time I know something I didn't know then.*

AND IT WAS that there was something about that experience the Lone One wanted him to be badly frightened of... so much so that he'd never do it *now*.

The loss of control, Ronan thought. The sense that something else was running everything, something that couldn't be stopped, something that might just possibly destroy him. *That's what's vital. It wants me to run away from that.*

So to win this, I have to invite that. I have to let it happen willingly. Squishy's betting that I'd never, never do that.

Ronan grinned in fury.

Bad bet.

To the Speech inside him, waiting tense, poised, expectant, he said, *Lay it out for me. It's all names, isn't it? I need all the names. The water, the shore... all of it. And what to do with them.*

Everything went dark around him. The view of the ocean went peculiarly abstract, so that what he was seeing was like diagrams of waves, not the waves themselves. But every bit of that curving, constantly-changing diagram was annotated in the tiniest Speech-script imaginable, words and phrases pulling and stretching, intricately interwoven and constantly interacting with one another. If the shapes of the waves were wire-framed, it was the tracery of the Speech that made up the wires— *Those are what the sea's matter and energy are hung on,* Ronan realized. *Those are the words that made them what they are. And what I've got to talk them out of for a little—*

He stood still a moment, looking out across the diagram and trying to hurry up and get a grip on what he was going to have to do, because there wasn't much time. Over the structure of the waves themselves, a secondary diagram spread itself out between one breath and the next, pouring the knowledge of how to read it into Ronan's mind.

It was a sequence of overlapping circles and ovals, seven of them, corresponding to the seven basic parts of the spell—its definition, invocation, incorporation, suasion, intervention, dissociation, and completion. The definition oval covered an area that stretched from the foot of the Head straight out into the water for about a kilometer, with the ship at the center of a short axis maybe a third of a kilometer wide. *Jeez, I've got to name* everything *inside that to save these guys? Better get started—*

But he had no choice. To save the ship, he had to calm all that water... which meant naming not just it but everything it was in contact with. *Right. Let's see where to begin—*

Nearest him, right in front of where he stood on the Head, was the part that was simplest to understand. In a circle right at the end of the the main ellipse, was his name in the Speech, the description of who he was. Ronan gulped as he went over to it and gazed down at what was written there. The Speech gave him to understand that in most Ordeals the wizard had more time to spend on the task, and in future he'd be expected to develop and lay out this data himself, but right now—

Yeah yeah, Ronan said, and simply read through his name-text as quickly as he could to see if anything about it jumped out at him as feeling wrong. Nothing did. *Which isn't to say some of this isn't enough to get you freaked,* Ronan thought, looking at his power levels: they read like there was more than one of him, and one of the more than one was seriously running hot. *Go around like that for too long and you could burn yourself right out—*

The Speech had nothing to say about that, which unnerved Ronan even more. But he didn't have time for it just now. *Fine, come on,* he thought, and set out across the structure of the spell. It rippled faintly under his feet, bouncing him a little. *Like walking on water...*

The definition ellipse had a wide sub-ellipse where the words necessary for invocation were laid out. Ronan crossed into the ellipse and started hurriedly sounding out the Speech-words in his head. Each one gave him chills down his back, the kind that his Da would sometimes shake his head and say were due to "somebody walking over your grave". But after the first ten or twenty of them, Ronan stopped himself. *Not enough time for a rehearsal on this stuff,* he thought. *Just going to have to do it live. Even as it is, time's gonna need to stretch... slow down a fair bit, anyway. Can we manage that?*

Yes.

Good. He stood there a moment and breathed in and out while the Speech poured what he needed into his head. All around him the rippling surface of the spell diagram flared bright with blue-green fire, while many meters below him the abstract sea-diagram roiled and tossed. Down one wire-frame wave he could see the small tight-written shape that was a ship with sixteen tiny life-cores in it slide down into the wave-trough and almost out of sight as it was driven toward for the offshore rocks.

Right, Ronan said. He took a big breath and then bent over and reached down with both hands into the activation region of the invocation ellipse, thinking of all the times since he was little when he'd

tried to hold water in his hands. Again and again he'd been disappointed.

But this time was different. What he was filling his hands with
now was more than just water. It was the *name* of water, the truth of it.
Ronan straightened up with his fists clenched full of words and
power, burning bright—then walked out into the invocation space of
the spell, out off the edge of the top of Bray Head and into the light-
ning-whipped dark.

Tell me the names, he said. *Tell me all the names. Tell me now!*

AND IT DID.

The Speech was coming more easily to him now, as if the effort
he'd made with the storm-handling spell had cleared a blockage. *Or
just pushed some door wider open,* Ronan thought. He was becoming
aware that there was a kind of channel between him and—whatever
lay beyond—through which the Speech and the great ocean of
knowledge associated with it flowed to him. Later on, Ronan understood, the channel would narrow down. Then he'd have to carry
more, or most, of what he got from the vast Beyond in his own
memory. But for the moment the passageway was fairly wide, which
was a good thing because that boat was getting closer all the time—

He said the first word: *shalathsh.* The sound of waves hissing up
onto the shore was in it, that simplest of words for sea water. There
were thousands of words for waters of other kinds and in other places
— highland waters, river water, icecap water, water high up at the
edges of atmosphere or locked in stone; but all of them had *athsh* at
their root. The word was powerful in and of itself—and therefore
difficult for Ronan to speak while maintaining full control over it—
but sheer power wasn't all he needed here: it was range and depth.
That meant invoking and associating with it quite a few more words
that would tell the sea how much of it he wanted to affect. One after
another Ronan spoke them and watched them attach themselves to
the core concept before he turned it loose.

When that long phrase was finished, and closed with an abbreviated form of the seven syllable word that looked like a Celtic knot, Ronan saw his pronunciation of *athsh* and its attached descriptors ripple across the spell diagram as if from a dropped stone and then sink into the water beneath it, starting to assert itself. What caught him by surprise was feeling the splash of it in his own blood, and being shaken by it as the ripples spread. *Right,* Ronan thought, and shivered. *This magic goes both ways. I can do it to the sea but I'm going to feel it too...*

Side effect or price, right now he wasn't sure which this situation was. And it didn't matter: this was the way it had to be. *All right, next phrase,* Ronan thought. *The minerals in the water, the salts and trace elements...*

He started identifying the words in the next ellipse of the spell that were the names and qualifiers of what was dissolved in the water, and reciting them. *Uliratha, shorrogyth-vallume, aloidia...* They should have sounded nonsensical, but every time he spoke one of them he could *feel* what it meant, feel the power from the deeper side of existence that had put the ability to make those words mean *more* into his hands. *Omryniaed,* the Speech whispered in his ear; *enacture.* Without that property, the gift that lay at the core of wizardry, none of this was possible. With it, every word spoken shook him from the inside out and became more real than seemed possible.

The names of the salts alone gave Ronan a fair amount of difficulty, not just because the Speech-words, though relatively short and simple, had great power wrapped up in them. But the more area the words described or the more matter they affected, the more difficult they became to invoke. Again there was that sense of being spoken by them, shaken by them. He might have been using them to impress his will on the ocean below, but it was going the other way as well. Those salts, some of them, were in his blood already, and elsewhere in him, stinging his eyes. It meant the Sea could have its way with him when he was done having his way with it.

Turnabout's fair play, Ronan thought grimly, and moved on to the next ellipse's worth of words as quickly as he could. These were for the ocean bed nearest the Head, the sand and the substrates. He could feel the words in his bones as he said the Speech-names of all the solid and (theoretically) unliving things under the water. *Sevit:* the fine sand washed in to sift down onto the granite of the near sea bed. *Defas:* the underlying bed itself, cracked, eroded, cracked again in some ancient earthquake, resettled, sloping down and out to the deeper water. *Gerassa:* the composite structures built up by sediments and the objects trapped in them over decades or centuries, the fossils, sunken ships, embedded garbage, bones...

Ronan shivered as the spell's parameters were expanded by that concept, and he could suddenly feel the age of the seabed in his own bones—the remnants of older life, calcified now but still full of its own memories, which by the power of the word and his wizardry were given something like life again. *And this is just gonna keep happening,* Ronan thought, shivering again. Every time he spoke a word or a phrase to the Sea, describing that particular part of it and taking it into himself so that it would understand his point of view—so that the suasion phase of the wizardry would have a chance to work—he could feel the connection between him and it getting stronger. Ronan knew that for the success of his spell, this was desirable. But now he was starting to wonder: *it's taking a lot of power to get into this spell. Am I going to be able to get back out?* Despite the fact that the rain wasn't reaching him, he was starting to feel wet again, and cold: from sweat. *Because I haven't even got to the live stuff yet. The plant life, the shellfish, the fish, the molluscs...*

And it was their turn now. The next ellipse held all those words waiting for him. He started work on them (*oleald, yboiveth, roinadethosien, onama,* who knew there were so many words for seaweed!). And though time was feeling dangerously elastic (or rather, fluid) at the moment, after those he still had to deal with the spell's littoral area between the breaker-waters and the Head, the shoreline. The big rocks and the small stones, the shingle down on the tiny steep beach at the foot of the Head, all those names had to be spoken too—

He shook his head and got on with it, because ahead of him there was one last big boundary to cross, and he had to keep his mind focused on that. And it was hard, with the feeling of water washing and washing at him. Not from the outside—the rain was keeping its word—but the inside. *Big stones, smaller stones, cliff scree, old glacial occasionals. Seiliu, killaid, tek, chorenn...* Ronan walked out a little further on the air to where it was easier to see what he was naming, and spoke those words one after another, more quickly now, because just ahead of him he could see the end of his task, the end of the naming. He stood there with the power he spent running out of him like water out of his hands, like blood out of his veins. But he didn't grudge it: this was the price he'd agreed to pay. If he was taking the Sea in, it was doing the same with him... which seemed fair. He wanted something of the water. The water wanted something of him. *Fair exchange is no robbery,* his Da would always say.

Well, we'll find out...

Ronan stood there in the dark, watching the things he was naming get more and more real, more and more defined, the diagram filling itself in with the enhanced reality he was enacting. He named and named and named everything the spell designated for him, everything he could see, until it began to seem to him that the Sea and the shore and the live things down in the water were all the real things there were. *He* was the dream, the figment, the construct made of words and air, slowly starting to vanish into the darkness as the green fire trickled away at last between his fingers and left his clenched fists empty.

BUT THAT OUTCOME, Ronan supposed, was inevitable. *Because that's what the Sea does, isn't it.* That was its nature. It was persistence. Though it was at the mercy of the other elements, of fire and air and earth, water got its revenge on them with every cycle through the biosphere; it quenched the fire, it dissolved the air into itself, it wore away the stone.

And if he wound up getting stuck in this spell with it, the Sea would wear him away too, Ronan knew—subsume the air in his lungs, drown the fire in his nerves, wear him away in a whole lot less time than it would take wearing away any stone. After all, he was mostly water himself.

The trouble was that the ocean was so *seductive* about it, so beguiling. He'd done his share of sitting up on Bray Head, in quieter weather, staring out to sea, lulled by it, thought and attention inevitably drawn away from himself and out into that vastness. Here, where all the words were doing their work and drawing them closer and closer together, even with all the drama and the violence roaring and washing back and forth below him in the shallows, Ronan could feel that vast mass of calm already starting to weigh him down into complaisance. And the longer he took about what he was going to do, the less chance there was that he'd ever come back from it.

...Which wasn't an attractive option. The thought of what it would be like to be stuck all the rest of his days with the crash and roar of the Irish Sea in his head, drowning out every other thought or wish Ronan might ever have, was terrifying. Or it would be if he allowed himself to dwell on it. *Could happen if you got careless. Might happen if you stopped concentrating on the job at hand. Just get past this and do the next thing that needs doing—*

Because the Sea's regard was already fixed on him, reinforcing what the Speech had told him about it. Though the Sea had life, it wasn't Ronan's kind of life. It needed something from living sentient beings, it needed something from wizards... and this kind of exchange, this kind of bargain, it didn't often get a chance to experience. There was life in it, but that life was not necessarily *of* it. That some life that didn't normally belong in the Sea should choose to do that, to *become* so—even for only a short time—held an irresistible appeal.

And that I can use. Because it's already kind of in my debt.

Now if I can just get it to see things my way...

The answer in the Speech took him by surprise. *And what way would that be?*

Ronan knew that he had some skills as a negotiator. But until now those skills had mostly been exercised in the schoolyard. Meanwhile there was something he was supposed to say first. *Dai stihó,* he said, *great Element's source.*

Be greeted, said the Sea, *young drop in My ocean.*

As greetings went it was casual, and a little on the superior side, but Ronan thought he could cope with that regardless. *Better get right down to it.*

Life's about to be lost, he said. *I want to save it. We can do a deal, right? Just say yes.*

Life is lost every day, the Sea said. *And engendered again a hundred times over for every life that ends.*

Sure, Ronan said. *But these guys, once they're gone, they're gone. They weren't expecting what happened; if they'd known the weather was going to be like this, they'd have gone anywhere else. This is all on me. I just want them to have a chance to walk away from this.*

And that's your desire?

For you to let them off? Yeah, Ronan said. *Let me help them get away from this alive.*

Why should I?

It was fascinating that something comprised of so many disparate elements should say "I". *No reason,* Ronan said. *Or just one reason. Because I asked. I did all this, all this naming, paid all this energy*—and it was a lot, he could see the figures written in the spell diagram and it was kind of a scary amount, who knew what kind of shape he was going to be in afterwards—*to save them.*

Why? You think they're evil.

He had to pause then—partly out of astonishment that his thoughts and attitudes were being perceived so clearly, and partly because he knew he couldn't lie. *Well, maybe. Yeah. But I might be wrong. I might not know the whole story. I*— He shook his head in the dark. *It's complicated. Just let them go, all right?*

And what price will you pay?

What price have I paid, Ronan said. *You're in me. Not something you get to do, or be, every day.* He swallowed then, seeing what he needed to do. *Go on, he said. Have a look around.*

He braced himself, half afraid that he was going to be subjected to some kind of watch-your-life-flash-before-your-eyes sequence. But that wasn't what happened. Instead his perception of that diagram-defined, wire-frame world washed away into something more indefinite. It washed away in the sound of rushing water inside his head and behind his eyes—everything gone dark green, a pale diffuse light wavering up above him somewhere, indistinct, beckoning but impossible for him to reach while he was held down under this weight of regard. The burning in his lungs was already starting, but struggling against it seemed counterproductive. *I asked for this. Let it run its course—*

The way time seemed to be stretching, Ronan had no sure sense of how long this went on. But he was surprised when one image started blurring itself into reality out of the rushing greenness; his Nan, in her bed, with her remote and her book and the sunshine (watery-looking at the moment) spilling in over her.

Also washing around Ronan was a peculiar sense of recognition. *...I remember her,* said the Sea.

Overlaid on this moment, as if reflected on other water, another image rippled into view: a young girl in an old-fashioned bathing suit, splashing into the water up on the beach at Skerries, diving into a wave and vanishing into it, laughing; coming up again, spluttering, shaking the water out of her hair, laughing again. *How many things does it remember?* Ronan thought. *How many people?*

All of them, said the Sea. *...When reminded.* There was a pause, filled only with the soft roar and rush of water coming in, going out. *Has she been like this long?*

A while, Ronan said. And then, though the thought made his throat tighten up, because it was the truth, he said, *Maybe not for that much longer.*

Water coming in, going out. *It's so brief, what we have,* Ronan said. *Such a short time. Those lads out there in their little boat? It's the same. Bet they've got people somewhere else who think of them this way. And it's not those people's fault what these lads do. Let their people have them a while longer, yeah?*

For an endless while there was nothing but the sound of water rushing up a shore, out again; up over the sand and back, like breathing. Up and back. Up and back. Ronan waited, silent.

...All right, the Sea said. *Do what you've prepared to do. I won't interfere.*

AND JUST LIKE that time seemed to snap back into place and start running again; and Ronan was standing in the middle of a spell diagram that flared bright in completion, the green fire of it flowing away from him, hitting the spell's outer boundaries, and immediately splashing back toward Ronan, the power ripping back toward him, ready to use.

He didn't hesitate. He flung his arms out in command and told the water underneath him, *Enough of that. Calm down right now!*

Even as he spoke the directive phrase in the Speech, Ronan was aware that "right now" was going to be relative. Huge amounts of energy were involved here, and since that couldn't be either created or destroyed, it had to go somewhere else. The kinetic energy he was removing from the immediate area was going to be dispersed up and down the coast. But for the moment his main job was to keep it from flowing straight back into the area he was calming.

As a result the arms-flung-out gesture turned into something more like holding apart a pair of walls that were pushing in against him and trying to crush him. Ronan braced himself at the middle of the spell and locked his arms, refusing to let those walls move *even one more inch* while his attention was trained on the scene below him. Slowly the waves were subsiding, going flatter. The boat was still driving forward toward Periwinkle Rocks, *but yeah, it's going a lot slower now, come on people, help me out here—!*

Standing there braced, pushing back with everything he had against the energy trying to crash back in and over him and the Sea

below him, Ronan could see people running around on the little
ship's deck now that it was safe to let go of whatever they'd desperately been holding onto to keep from being washed off board. And
those who'd been below decks were coming up in a hurry. *They don't
know why this is happening but they're not stupid, they know they need to
get off. Hurry up you lads, don't waste the moment!*

The sea kept calming but the ship still had the energy that the
waves had imparted to it, and it was heading right for the rocks,
sliding across the calming water like a skater sliding across ice.
"Come on come on *come on!*" Ronan shouted at the people on the
boat as it headed straight for the biggest of the rocks through water
that was bizarrely now as flat and still as a pond on a windless day. A
leftover lightning-flash from somewhere up in the clouds above illu-
minated the scene: the ship, the arrow-like wake behind it, the
mirrory surface of the water that reflected the lightning and the
clouds almost perfectly—

And the splashes of people hitting the water, breaking the perfect
calm of the surface, the ripples of their impacts to either side sown
behind the ship that continued straight for Periwinkle Rock. It was no
more than a hundred fifty yards away now and people were still
jumping out of that boat, *come on, how long can this be taking you,* a
hundred yards, *how many of you are in there, seriously? Twelve, thirteen*
— Ronan braced himself against the rebounding kinetic energy that
was trying to spill back into this space, that was trying to crush him
inside the spell, and he hung on, hung on, *fourteen, fifteen, come on,
just one more,* fifty yards maybe, *oh God here it comes—*

The boat plowed into Periwinkle Rock and collapsed in on itself
like an accordion folding up. The back of the boat pitched up and
over the front in a slow disastrous somersault and then crashed down
onto the top of the Rock, shattering like a dropped glass. Its masts
snapped off like toothpicks and bits of them came raining down into
the water.

But as he hung on, more of Ronan's attention was focused on the
narrow little rocky beach that ran down to the water right at the foot
of Bray Head. There he saw the splashes, reflecting another flicker of

lightning, as the last of the sailors to escape from the boat—the sixteenth lad whose jump he hadn't seen—swam the last few strokes that brought him to shore, and staggered up onto it among the stones and boulders there. Just a quick glimpse of him Ronan got, of a guy in kilt-y clothes that were plastered to him all over, and of a face upturned to him in the green fire that was burning through the rain: a glitter of eyes, a face with its mouth open in astonishment.

Ronan grinned down at him in pure triumph, and held up his arms with the fists clenched as if he'd scored a goal. Then he hurriedly turned his attention back to the spell. *Just a few minutes more, now,* he thought, feeling the walls of diverting energy still trying to crush in on him and his little ellipse of calm water. The boundaries were already starting to give way. But those other people were still in the water, they needed just a few more minutes to make it to land—

Except he was losing it. The walls of rebounding kinetic energy, even though that had been partly dispersed up and down the coast-line, were pushing back in on Ronan harder than ever now that he was running out of strength to push them back. He could see a few more of the sailors swimming in to shore, clambering up onto the stones, helping each other, shouting to the ones still out in the water.

Around him, the light was fading out of the spell diagram. Below it, the water was losing its mirrorlike quality, starting to shiver a bit as some of the rebounding kinetic energy started to seep back into it. *Still*, Ronan thought, gasping as he tried to hang on just a little longer, *didn't do too badly. Just—just a few more minutes—*

But it was going to be a few more seconds if anything. He was losing it. And he was having trouble breathing. He struggled to get one last gasp of the air around him. *Remember that air, you may want it later...* said a voice in his memory.

It was a good gasp: it gave him a last boost, a few moments more of hanging on. But the light was almost all gone from the spell now as the rebound started to crush him under it, pushing the walls together beyond his ability to resist any more, weighing him down. Ronan was staring to lose his visualization of what was happening below him in the dimness. *And now what? When the rebound, the backwash, washes me away... am I not me any more?* Though the situation was desperate, he had to laugh at himself. *Shortest wizardly career in history...*

Yet he'd been warned. *It wasn't like I went into this blind.* And though Ronan was desperate and terrified, there was still something about this that was almost funny, and he kept on laughing. *Well, yeah, blind, but it was the right thing to do, it needed doing, and this needed doing, this is life, saving this is what it's supposed to be about. Even if I didn't get it perfect, even if it was just one boat—!*

And here it came: the dissociation-and-completion stage—the end of every spell, so the Speech said, and definitely the end of this one. Everything was coming to pieces around Ronan, going dark, pushing him under. There was nothing he could do to stop it. But though the cold green weight that came down on him left him with no breath to laugh any more, there wasn't anything it could do about the triumph. *Because I did this,* he thought, catching one last fleeting lightning-lit glance of someone making it to shore, helping someone else do the same. *I did it. I did. Life—!*

...Though not alone. *Thank you, yeah?* Ronan said to the Sea, as everything faded completely down to darkness. *Cheers. That was good.*

Then everything fell apart... and he fell too.

...No way to tell how far, or for how long. But there came a moment when Ronan could see the cold hard ground coming up to meet him, and he winced at the sight of it, the way you wince when you're watching football or rugby in slow motion and you see someone about to get rammed good and proper. There was that same sense of inevitability, and you sit there going *Ow that's gonna smart,* and then it happens...

Except this time it was *him* falling, him getting hit, in the head, in the chest, half blind in the dark and not able to see what to do or how to avoid it. In a way it was like one of those falling-out-of-bed dreams when you snap awake and find you haven't really fallen anywhere. But Ronan knew he had. He went bumping and sliding painfully down into hard things, again and again, and then (when the bumping stopped and he just lay there in ridiculously grateful stillness) into a a slow numbing cold, and *wet, why the wet, you promised you'd keep it off me...!* he moaned to the rain.

The rain avoided him for as long as it could, and was eventually much relieved when the moaning stopped and the one who had spoken to it was no longer there, and it could let itself fall onto the salt-wet stones unconcerned about anything but being the rain.

IN THE IMMEDIATE aftermath of his first intervention Ronan was in no position to see or know anything about the half-dead bedraggled men who hauled their battered, salt-caked bodies up onto the rocks and lay there gasping in the rain. With surprising speed the ocean appeared to recall how to make waves again. Then even the downpour dwindled away under a firmament that swiftly tore its darkness to tatters and revealed, on its far side, a pure and tender blue, as if the world's sky had briefly been washed clean of all its ills.

Within an hour or so the boat's sixteen passengers had recovered themselves enough to struggle their way along to the little settlement at the foot of the Head. There they were given shelter and food and help for their wounds and bruises and broken bones by the villagers, who knew them well since they'd been acting as their middlemen for a loose-knit group of Irish slavers based in the midlands. There in that village the merchant seamen would remain for a month or so, until a ship from a different trading company in south Wales happened to dock at the village in hopes of taking some business away from the slavers that Ronan had saved.

While they stayed there they would tell, again and again, the story of the storm that caused their shipwreck, and of the strange dark young god who had appeared out of nothing, stepped off the cliff, and stood on the air above the sea, quieting it with his words and the power of the green fire he wielded, and saving all their lives. There was endless discussion over just who this god might have been. The sailors thought it was some demigod-son of Neptune or Poseidon or Set. The villagers were sure that it had undoubtedly been Manannán the Young, that mighty lord of the Tuatha de Danaan and ruler of the sea.

The question was never satisfactorily resolved. Eventually all the shipwrecked slave-traders returned to Wales and made their way through it to the more civilized (or at least more Roman) parts of Britain. Most of them eventually joined one or another of the larger trading companies working the Gaulish coast, and variously got killed in fights with other traders or tribes who'd turned treacherous, got drowned in the course of business, headed inland to take up employment less dangerous, or returned to their home tribes and retired on the profits garnered from the people they had sold. One survivor became a famous breeder of racehorses for the Roman professional racing circuit, amassing a fortune for which one of his impatient children poisoned him. Several other survivors were killed off the coast of North Africa, casualties in a battle between the flag-ship of a Sicilian trading fleet and a Mauretanian pirate vessel intent on stealing the Sicilians' cargo of arena sand.

One man, though, had been profoundly moved and disturbed by the events surrounding his shipwreck, and the sound of a young voice speaking and speaking and speaking all the names of the Sea. The night before the boat on which they would all set sail for Wales was scheduled to leave, that man went down to the foot of Bray Head and picked up from the shingly shore a small flat gray stone about two finger-joints long. He took that stone with him on all his travels ever after, pierced through at one end to take a cord that he wore around his neck.

In Egypt (where he wound up eventually, doing freight runs between Alexandria and Tyre as part of the murex trade) the man took the stone to an Alexandrine temple of Khepera and paid a priest-scribe there to scratch demotic characters on it saying I THANK THE GOD OF THE WORDS OF POWER AND THE GREEN FIRE FOR MY LIFE. The man wore the amulet all his life through all his remaining journeys, the last of which was to his homeland in Roman Germany, not far from the Rhine. When at last he died there peacefully in old age, he was buried with the flat gray stone around his neck—he never having suspected that its inscription actually said GREAT KHEP-RE PROTECT US FROM CHEAPSKATES WHO ONLY OFFER US A TENTH OF THE GOING RATE FOR CUSTOM INSCRIPTIONS.

And there the pierced stone lay in the ground among the bones of its owner, until some eighteen hundred years later daylight fell on the stone again as it was exposed in an archaeological dig. The archaeology intern who brushed the dirt away from it was understandably intrigued to find a post-Ptolemaic Egyptian demotic inscription on an amulet buried near Cologne, and he brought it to the dig's supervisor, a doctor of forensic archaeology from Paris, for further analysis.

The supervisor was surprised by the find too. She translated the inscription for her associate, and the two of them had a good laugh over it. But afterward the supervisor had to stand quiet for some minutes managing her surprise at having been shouted at by a stone that told her, urgently and with pride, *My name is Tek! The wizard knew my name!* And when the supervisor said silently in the Speech, *What wizard?*, all the stone could say (in some slight confusion) was, *I don't know. He hasn't been born yet.*

So those were the major occurrences in history that flowed from Ronan's actions in that long-past day. Of course, they may have served only to knit more tightly into the fabric of things other strands of history that were already well woven in. Only the Powers that Be, who see the fabric whole, can say for sure what was or was not or might have been different had Ronan failed to act, or acted otherwise.

This much, though, is certain: should he ever visit the Römischer Museum in Köln, something in the third display case on the right as you go in the front door will recognize him, and shout its name, and ask for his.

COMPLETION

That... was not... fair!

The rage that accompanied this sentiment was shattering. But the same rage has broken many times, over the aeons, on the good-natured resistance of the other half of this conversation.

I seem to recall you telling him that nothing was fair, or indeed expected to be. So if someone was unfair to you by winning, that goes squarely into the "self inflicted injuries" category.

A balked, furious silence ensues.

So you see, when I told you he was mine, and always had been... it wasn't just some idle boast.

More silence. *Trouble is, though, you're just not really a gambler at heart. Otherwise you'd enjoy these little contests more.*

Almost a sense of sputtering. *What? How do you mean I—*

You gambled once, and you failed. And since then you've always been all about fixing the game in your favor. And you know what? It's still not enough, and never will be... because the problem runs deeper. You just want to be right. *To have been* right. *And you weren't! Way back when, in that first moment of the new order, of your own will you made yourself all the things that weren't right—became the source of them, the fountainhead.*

You know it, too. But you keep telling yourself that the unfairness isn't your fault, when in fact you invented it. It's a pity you can't face that truth... because that would be the start of your journey back home.

The tone was almost pitying... and if there was something the other couldn't bear, that was it. *Home,* he said in vast scorn. *The last place I want to be.*

Yes, the other said. *It will be the last.*

This sentiment was ignored. *And as for* you, *nobody likes a sore winner,* he said. Without another word he removed himself a near-infinite distance from the Heart of things... far enough away for a casual observer to mistake the removal for something, or someone, being cast out into darkness.

The one who remained sighed, feeling the tiniest sensation of relief—like a breath that had been held in, being let out—when that conversation was over. Because here and there, up and down the labyrinthine ways at the white-hot Heart of things, every now and then—never shared or spoken openly, never more than breathed—a rumor has been oh-so-occasionally appearing. A rumor that something new is coming; and that at all costs, the One who presently Walks Alone must never, *never* hear of it... until it's too late for anything to be done about it; until the long soft breath of the New has had time to diffuse itself too deeply across and through the structure of existence to ever be dissociated from it.

Eventually all, absolutely *all*—the healing of the broken, the mending of the marred—may hang on that one secret never being discovered until it's too late. About that secret hangs a terrifying sense of possibility, almost of merriment. The matter is urgent beyond all urgency ever known... but it still has the chance to be just a little bit funny.

If only it works.

But the resolution to *that* conditional lies a little way further down the timeline of the world that many of its peoples call Earth. Outside that timeline, of course, it has already happened. In some parts of that timeline, the setup for the punch line has not yet occurred, and isn't even dreamed of.

Meanwhile, the one who'd been party to yet another phase of this very long conversation merely shook its head. *All right,* it said, *be that way...*

...Squishy McSnakeface.

And the One's Champion, laughing softly to Itself, went onward about Its lawful occasions.

OF ALL POSSIBLE aftereffects of taking the Oath, the one he'd least expected was that it might get the family to stop calling him "baby Ronan". And it got him a new bit of name as well.

Granted, to produce this result he *did* have to wind up in the hospital with severe hypothermia. But he knew he'd produced another result as well, one that wouldn't show up on any hospital's records: and that satisfaction made up (well, mostly anyway) for how fecking sick he felt.

It was Pidge, of course, the *ordinary* Pidge, who'd found him; Pidge who'd answered a text that the network had been late delivering and hadn't got an answer back, Pidge who'd got worried and suspected he knew where Ronan might have gone, Pidge who'd headed along the cliffwalk at the base of the Head on what had seemed at the time to be more a hunch than anything else. And it'd been Pidge who'd found Ronan there, collapsed, soaked through, and as muddy as if he'd somehow slid all the way down the seaward side of the Head.

Which should have been impossible, everyone agreed: *would* have been impossible. The impact onto the rocks above the cliffwalk alone would've been sufficient to kill him. No, he had to have been up on the Head earlier and tried to get down when the weather changed. Slipped and fell someplace—there was mud enough up there when it got wet—and then worked his way down to the rocks by the cliffwalk, and got himself blown off them by one of the huge gusts that had come up without warning late in the afternoon. Or washed off them by one of those huge swells that had hammered the coastline for an hour or so until the incoming storm went abruptly to pieces and gave the RTÉ weather lady something interesting to dissect at the end of the Six One news.

All this, including the ambulance ride, Ronan missed, being only barely conscious at the start of it and then later semiconscious and occupied with being wrapped in antihypothermia blankets and hooked up to warmed saline and otherwise examined and diagnosed on the trolley in the emergency room. But at least he didn't have to miss the details of the other very welcome side effect of becoming a wizard.

THE A&E admissions nurse was finding it difficult to deal with the two more senior Nolans who insisted on participating in the admission of the youngest male of that name. "Ronan Nolan," the nurse said.

"You can't call him that," the two men insisted in unison.

"Why on Earth not?" said the nurse. "It says that on his school ID."

"Because I'm Ronan Nolan."

"And *I'm* Ronan Nolan!"

"And we've both been admitted here so you have to call him something else so the records don't get confused—"

The nurse rolled his eyes. "All right, fine, how about Junior. You're the father, yes?"

"Yes, of course—"

"Junior, then." Busy typing commenced.

"Ought to be 'the Third', by rights—" the older of the two men muttered.

"Oh come on, Da, who uses *that?*" said the younger.

"Blood type?" said the nurse.

"A negative," said the occupant of the trolley. "And then can we shut them up and make them go away and get coffee or something? They're doin' my head in."

The nurse was struck by the laughter in the voice of the youngster on the trolley. Most people recovering from hypothermia as serious as what he'd been brought in with were either too physically sensitive or too emotionally wrung out to feel much like laughing. But he seemed to be recovering with unusual speed, which was a relief.

"You heard the lad," the nurse said. "Coffee machine down the hall. Jeannine, will you take Mr. Nolan Junior's vitals for me please? Need the in-house baseline so we can send him for the cranial scan."

And as he glanced sideways he saw the new admission put his head back down on his pillow with a visible sense of satisfaction far too marked for anyone who'd merely seen his da and his granda get sidelined. The nurse shrugged and turned back to finishing the paperwork as one of his colleagues wheeled the new admission away. *Family stuff,* he thought; *who ever knows what's going on with people? Not my business.* And he turned his attention to the next admission.

RONAN WAS ADMITTED TOO close to visiting hours to have any peace for a good while, no matter how his head ached. His Mam appeared and cried over him, and when he was allowed back in again his Da stood there actually holding his hand and looking like if anyone got too close to Ronan he'd fight them off. It was unnerving, in some ways, because there was no way to tell how long it was going to last.

The urge to tell them everything—because now that Ronan was done with it, he had to admit that it had frankly been brilliant and he was really pleased with himself—lasted about three seconds. *I've just had my head scanned for thumps and bumps,* he thought. *I start going on about 'wizardry' now, they'll think I've gone 'round the bend. Some other time maybe.*

Yet at the same time he had to tell them *something.* Rather to his surprise, Ronan's explanation that "he thought he'd seen some people in trouble down there" turned out to hold water—not only because it was true (which at the moment seemed like the important thing), but because there actually *had* been some tourists, Greek ones, up on the cliffwalk when the weather started to go south. They'd got themselves down off the Head just in time to avoid the worst of the huge waves that had started flinging themselves against the cliffs in the wake of the afternoon's sudden unexpected squall.

But there were other things on Ronan's mind. Not too long before visitors' hours were ending, and his Grandda took himself away to the pub to regale his cronies with the story of his grandson the hero who saved the tourists, Ronan found that one issue was weighing on his mind. *Gotta tell them,* he thought, *no point in putting it off.* "I got suspended yesterday," he said.

"Oh, well," his Mam said, as unconcernedly incredulous as if he'd just announced he'd broken a dish she didn't like. And to his astonishment his Da said, "Must've had a good reason."

Surprised, Ronan kept on going lest this sudden turn of good fortune should unexpectedly run out. "Seamus McConaghie was talkin' racist shite about Maurice Obademi and I laid him out."

"Good," his Da said with a look of grim satisfaction.

Ronan blinked. "Three days," he said, half expecting this to be the straw that broke the momentary camel's-back of good fortune.

His mam actually shrugged. "Well, they said they were going to keep you in here tomorrow anyway. So you won't lose any more school."

Ronan and his Da exchanged a glance. The logic behind this was eluding Ronan completely, and he thought maybe it was doing the same for his Da. "Okay," Ronan said.

At that point the bell went off down at the nurses' station and a soft PA voice started telling everybody it was time to leave. His Da kissed him—Ronan managed to hold still and just grin at him, because that kind of thing had stopped between them when he was about ten—and so did his Mam. "Kiss Nan good night for me, will you?" Ronan said. "I don't want her worrying."

"She wasn't worried," his Da said. "She said things were all right."

Ronan put that one aside to think about. "Good," he said. "Lunchtime then?"

"I'll drop by," his Mam said. "Too long a drive for some of us."

"I might grab the DART," said Ronan's Da. "They might be able to spare me a half day, I've got some flexitime days coming."

And as a nurse looked meaningfully in the door at them, they waved at Ronan and went away.

He let his head drop back on the pillow again (and then spent a few moments resolving *not to do that again* for a while because it ached and made him feel sick). He sighed.

That was it, he thought. *The worst thing... gone just like that. I should fall down a cliff more often.*

...And I'm a wizard! How fecking great is that...?!

HE MUST HAVE DOZED OFF, because when he was noticing stuff again things were dimmer, except for the not-really-Pidge Pidge, who was leaning over the rail of the bed, looking casually around at the machinery, the heart monitor and the blood oxygen thing on Ronan's finger and all the rest of it. *So, any last thoughts?* Pidge said.

About the complete heap of bleeding shite you just put me through? Oh no, no thoughts at all, get away with ye.

No, but seriously.

Well... Ronan trailed off, while the other watched him anxiously. But he couldn't leave him just hanging like that, especially when he wasn't really pissed off. *It was good for me, okay? Absolutely worth it all.*

Good, Pidge said.

How was it for you?

Pidge looked a bit stunned. *What?*

Well, I'm kind of your hire, aren't I? So how'd I do?

Pidge's expression went amused. *Pretty well. A lot of people're really pleased.* And he grinned. *One of them... is really* not *pleased.*

Our lad Squishy, yeah? ...Good, Ronan said. *Heard you two arguing. Didn't much care for his tone.*

Neither do a lot of other people, Pidge said, sounding quite dry. *...He may give you a wide berth for a while. It's not unusual, in these circumstances.* He sighed. *But it usually doesn't last... so take advantage of it.*

Right. Ronan looked up at the being who he was quite clear was masquerading as his friend to keep things easy. *And I'll see you again… when?*

Later on, probably. Usually not quite like this. Better to keep a low profile about this particular relationship for a while: even from you.

Ronan nodded. *Okay. Except—*

Pidge gave him a look. *What?*

We still need that Irish version.

The other looked at him in brief bemusement. *Of the* Oath, Ronan said.

Oh? Best get busy with your translation then, Pidge said.

Ronan was indignant. *You can't mean there aren't any yet! You said—*

There's plenty of Irish wizards, Pidge said, *sure there are. But you know whose translation's going to be the best? Yours. So you'd best be getting on with it.*

Tomorrow, Ronan said, leaning back. *Maybe the next day.*

Take your time, Pidge said, waving him half a wave, and heading for the door.

Ronan closed his eyes as he went, but then—catching something odd, a shiver of light—opened them again. *Huh,* he thought. *Fancy that. Wings.*

At first he thought it was just a visual pun. "Pidge," after all. But the wings, the more he looked at them, didn't seem to have anything to do with pigeons. He'd seen the like of them before, over Bray Head: the sharp-winged hunters, the falcons—fastest birds anywhere, piercing-eyed, deadly to whatever they hunted.

Without warning the half-seen image of the sharp wings blurred away into light, and Ronan found it hard to look at them. A few seconds later his visitor was out the door, and Ronan could just barely see the radiance of them against the wall outside in the hallway as the door sighed closed.

Never mind, Ronan thought, and let himself sink back into the pillow again, closing his eyes in utter satisfaction. *This,* thought Ireland's newest wizard, *is going to be* brilliant.

WIZARDRY KIND of took your mind off the more immediate issues in your life, sometimes: that was one of the first things Ronan found out as he entered into his practice. He quickly became—to no surprise whatsoever among those who could read Manual excerpts in the aftermath of his Ordeal—something of a go-to guy where water and its issues were involved, though the Knowledge (as he took to referring to it) let him know fairly quickly that that didn't have to be his specialty unless he wanted it to be.

Because he decided that for the time being it was wisest to keep his wizardry under cover, Ronan wound up enrolling in an increasing number of activities at school that gave him excuses to be away from home without actually having to participate in the whole session of whatever-the-activity-was. Some of these activities he actually found he liked, and others (like making the first-string hurley team) he'd liked already. So he was busy a lot of the time, juggling the business of dealing with coastline issues and away games without anyone noticing what was going on.

And if there were times when his dreams went dark green in their depths and he seemed to be looking up at flickering light far above while something else walked around in his body and looked out of his eyes, Ronan wasn't overly bothered. Eventually these experiences tapered off as (he began to suspect) curiosity elsewhere was satisfied. It was the sign of a debt being paid off in a normal way—or, at least, normal for wizardry.

It took Ronan a good while to realize that he was so busy being a wizard, he'd hardly noticed his life turning itself around. But then (one senior wizard told him later) lives are like ocean liners, some ways. "It takes a long time to turn the boat, unless you really want to mess up the heads of everybody inside it..."

He found that he no longer had time for the argy-bargy-with-other-kids crap he'd previously (and near-unconsciously) courted at school because it was a way to keep from being bored, and so sort of stopped being where he'd get involved with it... so that things almost accidentally started to look brighter. Because they started looking brighter, his classes started to seem more interesting to him, and his general performance in them started to improve—not that he really put those facts together for a good while, as he was too busy.

His principal, and those of his teachers who looked hard enough to notice, started to get a sense from watching Ronan that something had happened to him: that he was carrying himself, lately, like someone who'd been through events that had left him both more sensitive to what was going on with other people and less sensitive to their attempts to get at him—almost an air of "Are you kidding? I've seen worse." The principal, in particular, nodded to himself after noticing this, and removed Ronan Nolan—at least provisionally—from his interior list of matters requiring his concern.

Ronan didn't really notice this. He was too busy realizing, almost as an afterthought, that things were getting better at home... most especially since his Nan was starting to get better.

It happened so slowly, so incrementally, that Ronan didn't really connect the dots until a lot later. But after he was in the hospital, he had to do respiratory therapy for a few days after his Ordeal (because it was made plain to him by the Senior who "accidentally" ran across him in the respiratory suite at the hospital, the first day after, that it was generally stupid for new wizards to attempt medical wizardries on themselves)—anyway, his Mam met up at the receptionist's desk with a lady doctor from the geriatric medicine side, completely by accident, and they got to talking (because they had a common friend in one of his Mam's church-based charity groups), and they wound up talking about Ronan's Nan, and the lady doctor started asking his Mam questions about some symptom or other his Nan was showing, or not showing—

That was all Ronan could make of it later when he tried to get the whole story out of his Mam. And to be fair, she was a bit confused about some of the details herself. But the upshot of it all was that she wound up making some appointments for his Nan over at the hospital, and she went over there in an ambulance (which she found very exciting, they tooted the siren for her a couple of times and made her day) and had a bunch of blood tests done, and then they changed her medication. There was a lot of talk about inhibitors of some kind that Ronan didn't even slightly understand, but after a couple of weeks his Nan started—just sort of *coming back into focus* again. It was going to take more time, the new doctor said, for them to maybe do something about her legs—there were waiting lists and all. But now when she looked at you she *saw* you, all the time, and what that did to Ronan's head, just by itself, was worth everything.

It took him quite a while to start putting the various pieces of the puzzle together. For a good while all he had was a general sort of sense that the Universe was trying to make things up to him somehow. His area Senior, Mrs. Smyth, just nodded a bit when he told her about this, and she said, "You wouldn't be the first to think they saw that kind of thing start happening after their Ordeal, Ronan. Of course the Powers see Themselves as in debt to us, and try to make amends for the pains we're caused. But there's always more to it than that. The general principle is, 'All is done for each.' And for all that there's a great many of us in the 'each' category, there's also more than we can comprehend of 'all.'"

It wasn't until a few years later, when he met a not-particularly-Irish-regardless-of-her-name wizard by the name of Nita Callahan, that Ronan was unexpectedly introduced to the concept that he was not entirely alone in his head. It wasn't until the events of the Third Battle of Moytura were over for some months that he really finished getting his head wrapped around the finer points of the concept. And it was not until the events that surrounded the discovery of the Pullulus, and the strange and terrible fight on the world called Rashah that ushered in a new aeon of the Worlds' histories, that Ronan began to understand why so many things had needed to be kept secret... not just from him, but from the being he had been hosting inside him.

It took a while for him to recover from those events, as he wound up having to recover from injuries far more serious than anything that had happened to him off Bray Head. The physical part of the recovery was the least of his issues—that was handled, by experts using wizardry, within a matter of hours. But the mind takes longer than the body to recover from the kind of injury he'd suffered, and for a good while Ronan found the absence of what had become over time a familiar, if peculiar companionship, to be as strange and unsettling as its presence had originally been.

Ronan found it useful sometimes to go over to the cliff walk and listen to the water—which increasingly often had a lot to say to him —and just let his mind wander a bit; he slept better after such a stroll. One evening he went up the cliff walk and stood for a good while up above the shouting surf (the tide was coming in and there was a storm brewing out Holyhead way), just breathing the scent of salt and the iodine-and-tarnished-copper smell of seaweed, and then descended back into the orange sodium-lighted night at the edge of Bray. He didn't have a lot of homework to do that night, so there wasn't much to do but finish that (math again, increasingly a pleasure) and then watch some TV and talk to some people online, and finally head up the stairs and say good night to his Nan.

He got undressed and flopped down into his bed, pleasantly tired, with the sea still whispering in his ears, and read until he was tired, and then turned the light off and lay there gazing in an unfocused sort of way at the orangey streetlights through the blinds, until sleep came for him.

He had no sense of how long it took for the light to change quality from the brassy town light into that more silvery and sourceless radiance that filled all the air as he sat out on the sidewalk wall. For a change, he had company there.

First of all: will you forgive me?

For what? You were saving the fecking universe.

It's true that much rode on it. Very much. ...But still, even though you gave consent... it was an indignity: a wrong done to you. And I ask your pardon. We ask your pardon.

So now you, you guys I mean, owe me one? That's what you're trying to say?

Yes.

And I go about calling in that favor... how?

A shrug. *You call for it. You'll know when you need to. And we won't be small-minded about the response. Just... choose your time, all right? Be very sure you need it when you do.*

A long pause, starting out amazed and then turning exasperated. *Oh God. Do you even* hear *yourself?*

What?

You're already telling me that something big's gonna come up that I'll need it for. And not to waste this One That You Owe Me before I really need it. I cannot believe *you guys, you're so transparent.*

A longish pause at the other end. *Maybe I meant to do that.*

Ronan started laughing, because now it was just too silly. *Oh come on now. Level with me. You lived in my head for all that while, can we not just be straight with each other? Honestly.*

Well. All right. Your modes of perception are... unusual. But they seem to get the job done, by and large.

That is the *most bargain basement version of 'can't either confirm or deny' I've ever heard. Never mind... not gonna press you. But as for the rest of it, the way we used to be... that's it? It's all over now?*

Well. Can it ever be wholly over? By your courtesy, I was a part of you for a long time. The door swings both ways. Or to put it another way... there's always going to be some bleed-through. Of traits, of habits...

Good ones, you think? Ronan said. *Your handwriting, seriously, if I can help you out with that it's no problem, because yours? It was awful. And if you're going to show that kind of thing to other people, at least you should get a better pen.*

Laughter. *No, not showing that to anybody else. Only to you. In this generation, in this world, there won't be need for another to bear the burden you bore... as long as the weather stays set fair.*

And will it, you think?

For the short term, I'd say so.

Ronan laughed down his nose, knowing what 'the short term' looked like for his former houseguest. *Just as well, then. So... we're good?*

We're good.

Well, thanks, then.

Thank you. Always.

...Then nothing more until that older and endless light dissolved into morning; until Ronan woke up and got showered and dressed and had his breakfast, and then went upstairs again to say goodbye to his Nan, who was looking thoughtfully at a TV that wasn't on.

"You okay?" Ronan said.

"Fine," she said. "He says it's going to be nice."

"Yeah," Ronan said, "he does." He kissed her and headed downstairs again, and knew—regardless of minor bumps in the road ahead —that one way or another, that was going to be true.

PART IV

AEGOLIUS ACADICUS

OWL BE HOME FOR CHRISTMAS

FOREWORD

Every story comes in at least two versions: what seems to have happened, and what really happened. The better the story, the more versions of it make themselves apparent as Time's arrow flies. The very best stories come in so many versions you can't count them (and this is why we have parallel universes: there's far too much story to fit in just one).

It's usually easiest to start with the one that *seems* to have happened. Like this:

Once upon a time there was a small owl who had a big adventure.

...But reality is rarely so simple.

PART I

ONE

JD 2459186.50000 (2 DECEMBER 2020, 7 PM EST)

For the many citizens of New York City (and elsewhere) intent on seeing the traditional lighting ceremony for this year's iconic Christmas tree in Rockefeller Plaza, the day had started out looking promising. The weather was relatively mild for this time of year, in the mid-40s during the daytime because of the light cloud over the tri-state area. But the cloud had moved off as the temperature dropped. The National Weather Service was confidently predicting a clear dry night with temperatures in the 30s: no chance of snow, but at least no chance of rain either.

The tree itself was a particularly handsome one this year—a 75-foot Norway spruce from upstate New York. It had taken three days to transport it safely from its source to the streets of Manhattan and finally to the spot where it would stand, like eighty-seven other trees before it, in front of the handsome Art Deco skyscraper called Thirty Rockefeller Plaza, at the heart of the greater collection of buildings that made up Rockefeller Center.

Normally the streets around Rockefeller Plaza would have been crowded with people trying to get as close as possible to the upcoming lighting of the tree. However, this being 2020, normality was being forced into new and unfamiliar shapes. Nearly everybody who would have been watching the events live from the surrounding streets was at home watching it on streaming video. The entertainment that would lead up to the lighting was mostly pre-recorded on interior sets designed to blend in with the exterior reality of Rockefeller Plaza. A team of on-air talent from the local NBC affiliate was positioned up at the Fifth Avenue end of the brightly-lit Channel Gardens that led down to the Plaza proper. Here, optimally posed at the near end of a long double line of white-lit Christmas trees, they would deliver a more or less continuous and meticulously-scripted patter routine designed to segué smoothly through the numerous entertainment acts and the (far more numerous) commercials.

The Plaza itself looked more or less as usual—with the addition of giant rotating snowflakes projected onto the surrounding buildings, neon-limned columns and spotlights in constantly changing colors lighting the gilded statue of the ancient Titan Prometheus at the west end of the sunken Plaza. Above it all towered the tree, presently seeming unornamented by anything but a single many-rayed star of white Swarovski crystal at the top. The skating rink below it was covered with shining stage material for the live acts, littered with giant Christmas ornaments and yard-wide beribboned gift boxes.

The lighting-ceremony broadcast started at 7 PM. For the next two hours the extravaganza went forward with act after act taking place on video or live—this just a little eerie for lack of the shouts and screams of applause that would normally have followed every one. Earth, Wind and Fire stunned many people by reminding them how good they still were (and stunned some others by still being alive). A pre-recorded Dolly Parton sang affectionately about the Christ Child, her glittering white dress stirring in a wind carefully imported into the shooting set to match what had been predicted to be blowing outside. Masked Rockettes came out and danced their famous kick-line, split between two levels of stage and socially distanced, none of them touching any of the others. Various chart-topping pop singers of the moment (and hoping they'd last past it) emoted and harmonized, accompanied by pickup rock ensembles half-blinded by the color-changing light show going on around the stage. Commercial breaks came and went, as closer and closer drew the nine o'clock hour when the tree would blaze.

Throughout it all, hi-vis-vest-clad members of the production team who weren't in a control room or getting to grips with behind-the-scenes work in the underground areas surrounding the rink-turned-stage-space moved silently and purposefully around the edges of the Plaza both at the sidewalk level and down near the stages, any sound they made mostly concealed by the flapping of the many flags around it and the soft clanging of hoists against poles. These people were all far too busy to pay attention to one apparently supervisory group, also wearing high-vis vests, who stood companionably together across from the skating rink entrance with their backs against the side window of the Lego Store, intently watching the tree. But then who in that space wasn't doing just that, right then? It would possibly be inaccurate to say that no one saw them. They *did* go unnoticed.

During the commercial break at T minus three, the four long-serving on-air talent people got themselves onto their marks down at the Fifth Avenue end of the Channel Gardens and waited for their countdown cue from the control room, while their makeup people took one last run at them and hurriedly got out of shot.

The cue came. The cameras went live. Heartfelt sentiments appropriate for any holiday taking place during the disruptions and disasters of 2020 were expressed. On the stage below the divinely oblivious Prometheus, the Mayor of New York was revealed standing next to Rockefeller Plaza's landlord, their hands poised over a waist-high podium topped by a large gilded button. The brief, stagy count-down began—again a little eerie because there was no crowd to shout the numbers along with the talent.

Then came zero, and the Tree blazed. As always, there were no ornaments: just lights, fifty thousand-odd of them in many colors, shifting and shining as the slight breeze moved the Tree's branches, while occasional sparks of white light from randomly-firing LEDs glittered among the boughs. In the east-facing windows of 30 Rock, people started leaning perilously far out of their offices to grab hurried selfies against the newly-radiant backdrop.

An unseen chorus sang "Joy to the World" as the cameras lingered on the tree, and the credits for the lighting ceremony broadcast began to roll. The senior tech people tasked with keeping things running at the physical, Rockefeller Plaza end of things began to relax a little into the sense of *Great-we've-pulled-this-off-again* familiar to every production team that has repeatedly done a job well over half a decade or more.

This time, that sense was premature.

THE MID-HUDSON VALLEY NATIONAL WEATHER SERVICE weather radars at Poughkeepsie were the first to pick up something strange going on—an odd blurry collection of scattered echoes stretching nearly half a mile wide just west of the Woodstock area, drifting southward toward Kingston. As the signature approached Poughkeepsie and passed it on the westward side, it started picking up speed. The weather people for the local TV stations regarded this peculiar feature with increasing concern as it slid by over Plattekill, still west of the Hudson but now starting to overlap the course of the river. Clouds didn't look like that, but there were a few other phenomena that did, and none of them were good. Alarmed, some of the meteorologists emailed the NWS to pool their observations. Others got on the phone to the people down at the big FAA facility in Westbury on Long Island —the New York Terminal Radar Approach Control center— concerned about the possibility of bird strikes on incoming aircraft.

NY TRACOM immediately started alerting planes on approach to the five main airports for which they were responsible, and then began hasty consultations with the satellite Liberty Area airports at Stewart and Dutchess County. Radar coordinators there saw on their screens that the fuzzy slow-growing structure reported by the upstate facilities was spreading more broadly and reflecting more concentrated echoes, like a cloud growing thicker every moment.

The radar technicians immediately began running AI-based analyses to make absolutely sure that they weren't seeing something strictly atmospheric like an inversion duct, or some kind of radar interference artifact. But every analysis quickly came back negative. The structure looked something like bird flocks that had been sighted in the past, but much, *much* bigger... moving faster than any bird flock should have been able to, and growing broader all the time as it slid down the Hudson toward Manhattan. At TRACOM's LaGuardia desks, the sector chief hurriedly started ordering aircraft presently on LGA approach to climb one level higher in the approach "layer cake", break eastward toward the Deer Park VOR beacon halfway along Long Island, and circle there until advised otherwise.

In mid-Manhattan, people who were gathering (against police advice) to try to get a glimpse of the tree-lighting ceremony from the surrounding blocks now glanced up at the slightly unusual sound of jet engines changing their normal angles of approach to LaGuardia just across the East River. "Must be the weather's changing," some of those people said. And others standing around in the non-restricted side streets—in West 48th and West 51st, in the blocks east of Fifth Avenue and down by the Radio City side of 6th—heard over traffic what they started to think might be the wind changing; a low rushing sound coming from way, way uptown.

Within the police barricades keeping the tree-lighting area secure —because due to COVID-19 restrictions, the public had been encouraged to stay home and watch the lighting ceremony online or on the local NBC affiliate—the vast majority of human beings present in Rockefeller Plaza initially had no idea what the faint rushing sound was. The officials and camera people and local dignitaries stared around them, trying to work out where the sound was even coming from. It was the usual problem when you're in among the skyscrapers: sound bounces around and its originating direction gets hard to pin down. At first the sound was reminiscent of distant running water, and some concerned glances were thrown in the direction of the plinth where the statue of Prometheus lounged leisurely and golden in the evening cold, ablaze in the multicolored mood lighting. But the fountains around the statue were all bone dry, having been turned off just before Thanksgiving in preparation for the skating rink being commissioned for the season.

The sound drew closer, got louder. It started sounding less like water and more like wind; a very localized wind, but a strangely gusty one—sometimes nearly breeze-soft, sometimes rising to a brief soft roar and then fading down again. As it got closer it started to sound more like something breathing, slow and heavy: louder and louder with every breath as it drew nearer and nearer.

All of a sudden someone on the north side of the Plaza pointed upward. Heads all around tilted to see what was up there. At first glance it looked like vapor or smoke—but troubled smoke, trembling with obscure inner motion, and bearing with it an unnerving sense that though people in the Plaza might be looking at it, it was looking *back.*

Slowly the bizarre phenomenon dropped closer, where street-lights and building lights and the spotlights dancing around the Plaza could start to reach it. Inside it, shapes began to become visible... and eyes. Hundreds of eyes; thousands of them. *More.*

The cloud was made of owls.

A thousand owls? Five thousand? Ten thousand? Fifty thousand? *More?*

There was no telling: the cloud kept thickening, kept settling earth-ward. It was becoming so thick now that it was more like a snowstorm settling to earth, with every clump of snowflakes an owl. To someone who knew birds, the wide downward-sinking feather-blizzard now reaching right across from 50th to 51st and covering the whole long block between 5th and $6^{th,}$ contained every kind of owl that might reasonably have been expected to be living in the tri-state area. There were barn owls and barred owls and boreal owls, snowy owls and spotted owls, screech owls and long-eared owls, great greys and great horned owls, hawk owls and short-eared owls. And most numerous of all of them, scattered all through the settling soft-feathered flock, was a great cohort of saw-whet owls—mostly brown-feathered and diminutive, with cream-and-brown dappled breasts and round pale faces.

The flocking owls drew more and more closely together, the great assembly of them contracting into a cloud almost too dense to see through... a cloud full of eyes. They settled in toward the Plaza, nearly obscuring it. Here and there no more than a strangled flash of yellow made it through the flying bodies occluding the streetlights on either side of the Plaza. Soft blotches of feather-edged wing-shadow repeatedly blocked the downspilling spotlight-beams away and let the light out again, the huge spots flickering as some of the lights on the Tree were.

Slowly the cloud drifted toward the west side of the Plaza, briefly obscuring Prometheus's gold and the whole lower frontage of 30 Rock as the owls identified their prey. Then as one they closed in and dropped down.

Like snow they settled on the Tree, quieter now by the moment—for owls' wings are built for silence when they descend on their prey—and the Tree's lights went dim, reduced to occasional blurry blooms through downy feathers. Finally it was totally hidden, every branch of it from outflung skirt to peak. Inside the Plaza, an unnerved stillness fell as every human being there stared, amazed into silence.

A few moments later, as if it had been waiting for everything to settle, one final owl, a very small one, came fluttering down out of the darkness to flare its wings out and settle onto the treetop's Swarovski crystal star. It looked like some small and dangerous ornament, forgotten during too-hasty decorating—or like the actual intended tree-topper, come to reduce the present one to its proper subsidiary status.

All the cameras around the Plaza focused in on that smallest owl at the top of the tree. It stared at the nearest camera as if it knew what looked at it, and why. In what seemed very much like defiance, the owl opened its sharp little beak and began emitting high-pitched hooting sounds that could easily have been mistaken for a truck backing up.

The effect would have been comical if not for the expressions of all the other owls, who turned to glare at the cameras too... and as they did, seemed to start to settle chest-deep into the tree they concealed, as if sinking their claws into it. For a few breaths' time this went on. Then as if on a signal, all wings were raised. For that bare second the Tree's lights once more flashed out unimpeded. Then all together, all the wings began to beat.

Impossibly, the Tree began to rise. Its ascent was hesitant at first, the way a rocket seems to hesitate in the first few moments when the engines fire. But the upward surge gained speed. More and more quickly the Tree slid upward as if being lifted by a crane reversing some earlier one's action. Straight up it rose, steady, faster every second.

Everyone watching its ascent was held briefly immobile in the face of the Tree's mobility, caught in the tension between possible and impossible. *Obviously* it was impossible for owls, even so many owls—however many owls there were—to pick up a seventy-five-foot Norway spruce. Yet the owls appeared to have examined this news for evidence, found that insufficient, and discarded it as fake. It was as if they were being helped them somehow by some kind of intention that had decreed this tree to be free not just of Rockefeller Center, but of gravity.

Up went the tree, a multiplicity of relentless wings bearing it higher with every beat. The Tree's lights, astonishingly, impossibly, did not go out. They gleamed between the wingbeats, fifty thousand points of light trembling and wavering in the dark as the Tree's branches were tossed by the wind of the wings bearing them upward. Onward and upward the Tree soared, a conical blur of feathers and colored light and owl eyes catching it, with a few guywires and cables trailing behind like thin unregarded roots. The huge wing-blurred shape bobbled a little rightwards across West 50th Street as it rose, then lifted sharply upward so as to miss the top of the skyscraper at

45 Rock. Past that the Tree rose, higher and higher, finally drifting northward over midtown, higher upward still, and finally out of sight.

Slowly at first, then gaining urgency and volume, shouting started to rise from all around the rink and the statue, and from support staff for the on-air talent up at the top of the Channel Gardens. But one group of people, the ones leaning against the back windows of the Lego Store, stayed right where they were and watched all this happen, as they had from the start, with expressions far more impressed than shocked.

"Well," said one of them—a broad-shouldered middle-aged man with salt-and-pepper hair, wearing a parka and a high-vis vest, his hands shoved deep in his pockets and a thick book tucked under one arm. "*That's* something you don't see every day."

AND THAT IS how one of the more unusual news events of 2020 actually happened.

...Unless, of course, you're one of those who knows that it didn't happen that way at *all*. Or (if you're looking at the timeline in a different way, from outside) it did *once*—and didn't stay that way.

Now for *that* version of the story.

2

JD 2458941.25000 (SPRING 2020)

The owl first became aware of herself some time in the early evening of the world. It would have been hard to say just when; in the lives of most creatures so young, time isn't a thing that matters much. What she did know first, in that newborn twilight, was that there were owls who were bigger than she was, and who fed her and took care of her, asleep or awake.

The world had been warmer, then. Light and shadow had been more unpredictable, coming and going without warning. Shadow had been warm, the feeling of soft down pressing down, enfolding and protecting her nakedness. Light had been chill, when that sheltering shadow sometimes stood up or went away. In between times there was food— warm, soft with fur, rich with wet flesh. Greedily she snatched and gobbled it when it dangled down over her, and knew, for the first time, the sweetness of getting just what she wanted.

There had been other owls in that tight little space with her, as small and as naked as she, until everybody's first feathers started prickling in and then burst into down. Slowly the distinction crept into her awareness: there was *me*, and then there was *them,* the others. They would get between her and the food if she didn't move fast enough. She learned to move fast. If a sister or brother pushed her out of the way, she pushed them right back out, knowing every time her crop was filled that she was doing the right thing.

She ate and grew as fast as any of the others, and everything seemed fine for a while. Then, slowly, the owl realized that something about life felt vaguely *wrong*, and she didn't like that feeling at all.

It started to ebb somewhat—or at least the owl was distracted from it—when a second, more prickly set of feathers came in and the fledging-sheaths split off them. At that point the owl got a sense that if she worked her wings, the itchy aching feeling of something being *wrong* with the world would go away.

So, again and again, as she and the others in the nest got bigger, she clambered onto the narrow edge of the hole that led out of the nest and worked her wings, trying to understand what was supposed to happen next. Around her the world was shifting, as the nest stopped being everything and became instead a shadowy haven at the center of a much larger everything—the vast tree-pierced space with the half-seen empty sky arching over it, the wide realm through which the wind moved and breathed. In that larger space of being, the light-time was warmer and the dark-time cooler. But it was the darkness that felt most comfortable to the owl—the time where her eyes worked best and were learning to see the tiny movements down on the ground that made her insides feel pleasantly hollow, ready to have something warm and tasty put in them.

There, in that welcoming darkness, the owl learned to fly. At first she wasn't very good at it, with some unexpected tumbles onto lower branches that hurt her and made her angry, because she somehow knew the falling and the hurting were wrong. Something much better was meant to happen, something to do with how hard you beat your wings, and making sure you kept on doing that.

So she kept on practicing, while the other owls who'd been in the nest with her, her brothers and sisters, did the same. The female who'd spent her time sitting on them and keeping them warm until their feathers came in had gone, and her mate, who'd brought mice and voles to eat while she was sitting, now fed the young owlets while they got better at flying. Soon enough he started showing them other things—especially about how to catch mice and voles for themselves, and what other things could be eaten when those were scarce.

During that learning time the owl discovered other things that weren't so good... as on the night one of her brothers got out of the nest earlier than usual, just after the skyfire began to fade. Working on mastering his wings, he went flying out of the spinney of trees where their nest was. She had clambered up onto the edge of the nest-hole right after him, yet it was the merest chance that the owl was looking the right way to see something big and dark, far bigger than her, a broad-winged blot of shadow against the lighter night, come dropping swift and silent from above and snatch her brother out of the air exactly as he might have snatched up some mouse on the ground. The owl froze right where she was and kept absolutely still and silent, watching as the night-shadowed shape of the screech owl winged casually away into a tree beyond the spinney, settled onto a branch there, and set about turning her brother into meat.

The utter *wrongness* of it got down into the owl's insides and made her feel sick. But she knew better than to move or cry out or do anything at all until she saw that darkness take wing and fly away again, away from the spinney and out of sight. The owl sat there clenching her talons on the edge of the nest-hole and was *angry*—so angry that it seemed to fill the world. If she'd had words, they would have said, *Whose idea was* this? *Isn't it hard enough that we're hungry almost all the time and have to be on the hunt from dark to light? Do we have to worry about being somebody* else's *food now? This is* wrong.

The memory of that sudden, silent-falling darkness haunted every flight for a while afterwards. Watching out to catch prey while watching out to avoid *becoming* prey needed so much concentration, even as their father's gifts of food decreased. She and the three others who remained had to spend more and more time on their own hunting, or they would sleep empty in the morning and wake hungry in the dusk.

They grew uneasy and testy with one another as the lights and darks went by, while the dark-time slowly began to get longer and the food more scarce. Then one night their father flew away and didn't come back. The image of that wide-winged shadow against the night came back to the owl, and she wondered if it had taken their father as it took her brother. That feeling of wrongness rose up in her again. Once more things were changing, and she had no idea what to do.

The nest was too small for them all to share it any more, and the food around the spinney started to get scarce. The dark-time of the day got longer all the while, and even though there was more time to hunt, there was less and less to eat. The owl began to venture further afield, into new patches and copses of fir-trees. When she noticed she was eating better, she stayed in those places and no longer saw her former nestmates except by accident. Slowly, painfully, she learned the art of being alone.

Occasionally she saw other owls of her own kind that she didn't know, and found it very strange—unnerving in a way that was like the memory of the dark-eyed shadow that had killed her brother. So that one night, when she dropped off a tree branch toward a mouse careless about staying out after dusk and unexpectedly fell onto another owl who'd seen the same mouse, she was torn between fear and a great rush of that suffocating wrongness-anger. She took the other owl down onto the thick pine-needled mat of the forest floor in a tangle of grabbing feet and thrashing wings, and bludgeoned it into shocked stillness. Then she flew hastily up again, out from among the trees she knew well, and flung herself away through the dark air, determined to never come back there again.

So it went for some nights, as nights grew longer; she was eating better, but spending her days sleeping huddled against the boles of trees she didn't know. Sometimes she found one with an old nesting-hole in it, made and then abandoned by some other bird, and stowed herself away, safe from the painful brilliance of day. She would wake in the dusk, look out of the hole to get a quick sense of where in this new place the mice might be hiding, and then flutter down to a lower branch of the tree to wait for movement, or for the slight rustle of food.

The owl became busy in the way of all career hunters—focused on her craft and on improving it, discovering how to find bigger nests of prey or learning where by rivers or ponds the voles best liked to be. When the hunt went well, it was fun. When it wasn't going well, it wasn't fun at all. When you missed your catch a few times in a night, when morning twilight came and you tried to sleep with an ache of emptiness in your crop, then woke up in the dusk a little sick with hunger, that feeling of wrongness could be very strong. But it wasn't as if you could stop hunting. You got out of your hole (or off your branch) and got on with it, because that was all you could do to put things right again.

And by and large, things went well for the owl. Every night, under moon or cloud, in rain and wind or pine-scented stillness, she became more expert at dropping in perfect quiet on her prey— sinking claws straight in to stun them with pain, snapping their necks with her beak before they had a chance to know what had happened to them (for she found their meat tasted better that way). If her increasingly expert ears caught even the most distant whisper of screech owl or cry of eagle, near or far, she knew to hold absolutely still right where she was in the shelter of the tree-branches... and then, sometimes having stayed up late into the hurting sunlight, to fly away and find a new place, a new tree and new air clean of the memory, the wrongness, of that old shadow.

ONE SUCH SEARCH-FLIGHT was how she found the tree. It wasn't all about her unease over the presence of larger owls. Nights were becoming longer and longer, and they were getting colder, too. And though those longer nights meant more hunting time, which should have been better, the prey didn't see matters that way. Every night there were fewer of them. Increasingly the owl flew further in search of food than she would earlier have done—even into places where there were more of the strange unwinged, two-legged creatures that sometimes turned up in the forests where she ranged.

There were many strange hard paths used by the twoleggers and by the large hard shiny beasts that repeatedly ate them yet always spat them out again unharmed. Close to one of these paths, prominent in a small bare field, stood one of the blocky things the twoleggers roosted in. A tree stood right alongside, one with gracefully upcurved branches and feathery flat needles that clumped thick and gave good cover. The owl fetched up in that tree after a good early evening's hunt. She spent a while resting in its upper branches before going out again, and took some time to idly look it over.

With great speed she realized how very *good* a tree it was. It was taller than any tree in the nearest patches of conifers. The lower branches were a bit sparse, but the upper ones were close-set and symmetrical, perfectly hiding the tree's bole. Better still, many woodpeckers had been at it over time; they'd driven some nice and unusually deep nesting-holes into it. About halfway up, two of those holes were so close together that the insides butted together, and the woodpeckers had pecked through the thin separating wall of wood to combine them.

The owl thought she'd never seen a better nesting-place—ample, roomy enough to stretch your wings in—and found herself considering the hole with some obscure sense of eventually using it for something besides sleeping. Meanwhile, as she stayed there for one night, and then another and another, the tree also turned out to be unusually good to hunt from. At first its nearness to the hard path and the hurtling shiny always-in-a-rush creatures bothered her. Normally (having seen not just prey but owls lying dead next to those paths, unwitting prey to the roaring shiny beasts) the owl avoided such places. But perhaps because of the brushland off to one side, this spot seemed to attract a lot of food—not many voles, but a great plenty of mice and rats.

The owl had already been feeling restless, needing to go even further afield, in a direction she hadn't gone before—the direction where the skyfire again and again soared slowly across the daytime sky, lower and lower all the while.

That way soon enough, she thought. *But not right now. Right now, the food's good here. And this hole is very good. I like this tree. This is my tree. For now I'll stay and just eat a lot before I go anywhere strange.*

This she did for some days, as the skyfire swung gently lower every day, and was above the world's edge each day for less time. She came back to the hole every morning with her crop well filled, slept long and well till the dark came again, and rose again in the twilight to go hunting. Everything in the world, she thought, was going very well.

...Until suddenly it wasn't.

JD 2459164.91667 (11 NOVEMBER 2020)

B ecause the tree was near the hardened path, and that got chaotically busy with the roaring hurrying shiny beasts during the light hours, the owl's light-time sleep was troubled by more noise than was ever normal in the woodland where she'd been reared. For the sake of this perfect spot and this excellent tree she put up with it and, as days went by, grew used to it. The noise was never a constant—sometimes louder, sometimes quieter, sometimes as unvarying, hour by hour, as the sound of some rushing stream. So when there came an evening when she woke and everything seemed unusually quiet outside, it didn't alarm her.

What did concern her—after a few still-sleepy blinks—was opening her eyes and looking around to realize that the light outside the nest-hole had changed. It was much darker than usual. And though the owl could hear the shiny beasts running toward the tree and away from it as usual out on the hardened path, she couldn't see any of the light from their eyes at all.

She had no idea what that might mean, so she shook her feathers out and preened a little, and then stepped up on the inner edge of the nest-hole to make her way out onto a branch just below. But that branch was no longer there, or at least it wasn't where it was *supposed* to be. Something had bent it until it pressed right up against the outside of the hole. The owl pushed against the branch and other narrower sprigs of greenery caught in the hole by it and blocking her way.

It wouldn't give.

She stared at the blocked nest-hole, bewildered. This made no sense. Branches didn't *do* this kind of thing. Sometimes—after a wind, or because they had rotted through from disease, or if woodpeckers had been at them—they might fall down. But she'd never seen one fall *up* before, and she'd certainly never seen a branch get stuck against its tree this way. The owl stared at the part of the branch that was blocking her nest-hole, picked at some of its needles with her beak, and then tried pushing at it again.

It went nowhere. She couldn't understand what had happened. She couldn't understand what she was going to need to do to put this right. So, in her confusion, the owl fell back on what she normally did when faced with what she didn't understand. She held very still, stayed quiet, and waited a while to see if the situation would change.

It didn't change. Outside, darkness grew deeper; outside, the sound of the hurrying creatures on the hardened path seemed to get louder in the following night. Again and again the owl's patience failed her, and she went back again and again to try pushing harder against the barrier of wood and smaller fir-branches pressed up against the hole from which she could now not escape.

She had no idea what else to do. All that night the owl tried to get out, growing wearier and wearier with the useless labor of it. Sometimes she flung herself hard against the barrier; sometimes she just shoved herself against it and tried to pull it apart like prey; sometimes she flailed at it with her wings, other times tore at it with her talons until the bark on the branch frayed and her feet were sore. But nothing did her any good. She was hungry, she was thirsty, she wanted to *fly!* But there was nothing to eat, and nothing to drink, and no way to get out and spread her wings.

Slowly it grew lighter outside. Just as slowly, just as steadily, the noise of the shining beasts on the hardened path grew louder as more and more of them ran together on their path. And still she couldn't get out. The owl was angry, *angry*—but it did no good. It didn't help. *What's the matter with my tree?* she would have screamed, if she'd had words. *It's not supposed to do this. I want my tree back. I want it back the way it was!*

But all the time she'd spent waiting made no change. The tree didn't go back the way it had been. The owl's anger changed nothing. Outside the hole the light was getting brighter, but she was far too restless and upset to sleep.

That turned out to be just as well, because shortly things changed again, and not for the better. Outside the tree, she could hear a noise of the kind that the shining beasts made, a roaring that was deeper and louder than usual. It came right up by the tree—maybe even right under its lower branches—and sat there, roaring constantly.

The tree shuddered. The owl did the only thing that made any sense: held very still and stayed quiet, waiting to see what would happen.

And what happened was the worst thing she could have thought of. Another sound happened, a high thin screaming that made her ears hurt. She could feel it right through the wood of the tree. And then, horribly, the tree leaned over—*right over sideways*.

It didn't lean the way it did sometimes when wind pushed against the top of it, bending and then coming straight again when the wind stopped. Instead it was as if the whole tree was being blown down, though not as the owl had seen happen to a thinner tree during a storm out in the woods. That had been fast; this was slow. Soon the bottom of the nest-hole wasn't a floor any more, but a wall. Bits of old bark and nest and old coughed-up fur-and-bone pellets fell over on the owl as she scrambled to work out which way was "up", trying to find purchase in a space and a world that made no sense any more. *How can* down *stop being* down? *What's* happening?

There were no answers. Soon enough the tree lay on its side with her in it, as trapped as ever. And then, horribly, it was somehow wrenched further along the new "up", and swung sickeningly around

so that the light outside spun and swung too. Then the tree fell down
onto something hard, and the owl reeled with the force of its landing.

She clung to the nest-hole-floor-that-had-been-a-wall and
listened in sick terror to the roar of the beast outside, and the voices
of twoleggers that suddenly seemed to be all around it too. The tree
was moving again, lurching side to side, turning and then going
forward, top-first even though what had been the tree's top was now
down on its side. The going-forward happened faster and faster until
the owl could feel wind, even through the blockage across the nest-
hole, and her wings stirred helplessly with the desire to get that wind
under them and get *away* from here.

But it was all in vain. She couldn't get out to fly, to flee. All the owl
could do was try to be still, and to do that she was having to cling to
the wall with her every talon. Gradually she understood that
somehow the tree was making this move away from where it had
been. And now, trapped inside it, she was borne along to whatever
horrible impossibility the tree sought.

The movement and the shaking went on for many hours—
throughout the day, and into the fading-light time again, until the
skyfire vanished again. *That* at least was normal, even though the owl
couldn't see the sky where that was happening. Finally, not long after
the darkness came again, the movement stopped, and so did the
roaring of the beast that had been close by all day.

Do some of these beasts prey on trees? the owl wondered as she
shook her head to try to get her proper hearing back; she was half
deafened by the constant noise. *This isn't just wrong for me! This is
wrong for you. You ought to be in one place! You ought to be still, with your
branches properly spread out for the wind! I wish I could make this stop for
you, for me, for both of us!*

Around the tree she heard more of the cries of the twoleggers,
ahead of it, behind it, on all sides. Finally they too went faint, went
away. There was still noise from whatever hardened path was nearby,
a never-ending rush of the shining beasts, a river of them, never
silent.

The night went by. The owl's empty crop reminded her of it hour by hour, and she itched to be out, to fly, to hunt; but she could do nothing. She fell asleep a few times, waking in desperate hope to find herself and everything else back to normal again. But everything was still sideways; the world was still broken. *My tree, my poor tree!* she thought. And crowded up against the blocked hole, she drowsed once more and then woke again to the sound of twoleggers' voices in the dawn, to incomprehensible slams and groans and the shining-beast roar. Once more the tree lurched and shifted, and the owl hunched down into a small tight ball and squeezed her eyes shut in despair.

THE HOURS that followed seemed to go on forever—the owl trapped between sleep in which she found no rest and waking in which she found no pleasure. By dark or light-time she was hungrier every moment, but there was nothing she could do about it. In the middle of the rocking and the increasingly deafening noises, as the light bizarrely changed directions from one moment to the next, as she drifted in and out of a troubled doze, the owl remembered what it was like in her first nest.

She didn't think often of that time when she wasn't the one who took care of food and shelter, but the one who was cared for—the time when others gave you food, kept you warm and, if you got stuck or if your claws got hung up in your wings, would help you. They'd get you unstuck, and give you what made you feel less hungry, or less thirsty. She wished there was someone like that for her now. *I wish you were here,* she said inside her to that someone who wasn't there. *I wish you could help.*

But there was no answer. That was hardly a surprise. She didn't know what she was expecting to happen. There was no one with her any more, no sibling, no mate — not that it was time for that, anyway. There was no one to answer if she called out. She sat listening, the way weeks back she'd sat listening between hunts for any sound of her brothers or sisters, or her egg-mother or egg-father. But she heard nothing.

Hopelessness, that was all she had now: a feeling of things gone very wrong and impossible to put right. For who could make a fallen tree stand up again? She had seen enough of those; they lay on the ground in the woods, going slowly all to pieces as the world turned them into dirt. The tree that had felt in a strange way as if it welcomed her, as if it was glad to have its emptiness filled—that emptiness was no refuge for her now, but a prison. It was somehow broken. And how could such a brokenness ever be put right?

And this *tree,* the owl thought, suddenly furious as the tree and the world lurched again, throwing her against the inside of the too-roomy nest-hole. *This one! Why* this *one? There are trees and trees,* forests *of trees,* all *the trees there are that such a thing could have happened to—but* this *was the perfect one! This was* my *tree! Why did this have to happen to me? This is* very wrong!

The world around her paid no heed to her protest, and soon the owl laid herself down on what was now the floor of the hole and tried to stretch her wings and just *not be* for a while: not hear the noises, not feel the shaking or pay any attention to the fading light... because night meant nothing different. No chance at food or water, no hope of flight through the welcoming dark that was her proper home...

The sickening motion continued, and the owl slept through some of it; there was little else she could do. For a long while she knew nothing until the light once more came back, and with it the shuddering movement of the tree, now so irregular that there was no bracing against it. For a long time it flung the owl about in the nesting-hole, too weak now to resist. Her insides felt empty as an eggshell with its insides eaten, and her thirst was a constantly growing soreness in her throat.

After a while the movement grew smoother, though it didn't stop. A little strength came back to the owl, and once more she flung herself at the blocked-up entrance to the nest-hole. It made no difference, but it had become a habit. She was stubborn. Again and again she struggled with wings and feet to work herself free.

It was no use. The weakness made her lie down again and sleep a little, even though she was hungrier and thirstier than ever. But when she woke into the new night, she struggled up to her feet again and went to flail at the branch in front of the hole. *I will not give up. Something may change.*

But nothing did. The long painful night went by and passed into painful day again, during which the tree moved and stopped, moved and stopped. The beast-roaring went on all around, louder than ever, and the surrounding air smelled bad. Open or shut, the owl's eyes hurt her; it hurt even to blink. Even breathing hurt, now. And the realization came to her then that if something didn't change, she was going to wind up like her sib who was eaten, like the dried bird-bodies she'd occasionally seen by the hardened path. No movement about them, no life, bones stripped by crows; nothing left but glued-down rags and tattered feathers that occasionally jerked in some passing breeze.

The thought made the owl shake as if some icy wind had breathed on her. She was going to become the prey of something she couldn't see, but could feel; hovering low over her, big-winged like the screech owl that took her brother, as silent in flight as she knew how to be herself. It was death, coming for her in the shape of the branches that hemmed her in and kept her from flight and food and drink, from all the things needed for life.

It will end, she thought. *I will end.*

And when the movement stopped, at last, in one more newfallen dark, and the noises and twolegger cries outside the tree mostly stopped too, the owl lay there faint and weak for a long time before she could push herself up and try one last time to get loose, to get free. It did no good. She was still trapped. And somewhere outside, in the strange too-bright darkness, now she was sure she could feel watching her—as if from somewhere nearby—the eyes that went with screech owls' wings. They were glaring, waiting for the right moment to take her, as soon as she gave up completely, as soon as she lay down to surrender and let herself go. What watched wanted to see her *agree* to become prey.

All at once the steady ugly patience of whatever waited made the owl angry all over again. She snapped her beak with the anger, just as she'd have snapped it closed on a mouse's neck to kill it the best way, quickly.

This is wrong, she thought in absolute fury, weak and helpless as she was. *And it's* wrong *for things to be so wrong! Meat I may be about to be, like the dry flat broken-boned things on the hard paths, like my brother when the talons tore him. But that changes nothing. What I know is* true. *Let what waits take me if it likes, but I won't go willingly. I will pull against its talons even if I tear myself apart on them, and if I can I'll put my beak in its eye before it swallows me down!*

Then she fell down, faint and gasping harshly, on the wall-that-was-now-a-floor of her nest-hole. Breathing hurt her so much now that she wasn't sure how much more of that she could do.

Something made a sound, then. At least the owl couldn't understand what else she was hearing inside her, saying:

You desire Life.

I won't willingly be the prey of That, the owl thought, still angry. But the strength was going out of her breath by breath, and she had no way to make what she said become true.

What would you do if the world helped you not be Its prey?

She realized then that the thought she'd just heard was nothing of her own, but had come from *elsewhere.* And it was as if, on being spoken to, she understood the idea that others, some others anyway, could actually *tell* her what they thought, what they wanted.

This was the strangest thing that had ever occurred to her. Yet it was also somehow very good. The owl's feathers tried to rouse in pleasure at the sheer wonder of it. The question seemed strange, though. And with the concept of questions, came the idea of answering. *You mean, what would I do to make* this *stop? Anything!*

Would you help other creatures in like case? When it was wrong for them to be prey, would you try to stop that?

What? Of course I would, what kind of owl do you think I am?

Then make your promise.

It was odd that she now knew what a promise was: but she did. It was as if the word itself had told her what it meant. *I'll help!* said the owl. *That is my promise. But I'm hungry and so thirsty, and I feel so sick! I can barely move. If the world's not to make prey of me first, I need help now!*

No answer came back, though she waited. And after all that strangeness, sheer weariness bore the owl down beneath its weight and left her once more lying on the nest-hole's floor. Slow but inexorable, an utter darkness fell over her—a thing of the mind and not the world outside, a great weight of irresistible endings. In it the owl lost herself, and knew no more.

AND THEN THERE WAS LIGHT.

The owl blinked. She was no longer in the nest-hole. Now she was clutching crookedly onto a branch of her tree, outside the hole. And the tree was upright again, which she didn't understand.

She had no strength to do anything but lean against the tree-bole and stare around her, concentrating hard despite her weakness on not falling down and re-enacting the embarrassments of her young days. Looking down, the owl could see that some strange substance had been wrapped around the tree, pulling all its branches in tight. The stuff was still wrapped around the tree's lowest branches. But the upper swathe of the wrapping-stuff was gone from around the tree now. With it gone, the branch pressed up against the nest-hole had fallen away from up: had fallen *down* again. When that happened her body had toppled out of the hole onto a branch, and though she'd been unconscious, her body had felt the branch and gripped it as if it was her last chance.

Gazing past the branches, blinking hard to see out of hurting eyes, the owl could make no sense of the high hard walls of stony stuff that surrounded the tree on all sides. The noise that had accompanied her and the tree here, the rushing, hooting noises that the shining beasts made, was here still, echoing on all sides. Her head rang with it. At least the owl could once more feel the wind, though it was much broken by the walls all around...

And that was all she had time to consider. She was already

wobbling on her branch, and would have fallen in just a little more time had something not stopped her: the strangest thing so far. Up in the tree with her, clinging onto some kind of metal branch of its own, was a twolegger. It was all covered in—not feathers, but something smooth, like what had been wrapped around the tree—in a color so bright it would have made her eyes hurt even had they not been hurting already. With big soft feet that had no talons, the twolegger reached out for the owl and took hold of her, pulling her away from the bole of the tree and off the branch.

The owl was both too weak to struggle, and too shocked by the utter strangeness of what was happening to her to try to move at all. She could do little but fall back on what she normally did when confronted by something frightening or strange: hold still and wait.

The strategy turned out to be a wise one, for strangenesses now piled themselves one on another in such variety and abundance that there wasn't much else the owl could have done. Shortly the twolegger was down on the ground, still holding her, and the owl realized that she could see her whole tree again, though all its lowest branches were missing. She would have raged with indignation at that—those had been the *best* branches to hunt from!—but had no energy for it. *Later. Later I'll find somebody to peck for that.*

In the meantime she found herself placed in a small space like a nest-hole, but with sharp corners. There were some fronds from her tree in there, which were some slight comfort for the familiarity of their scent, though they were no good to sit on. Twoleggers in their bright colors came to stare at her, and she stared back. Then the top of the hole closed up.

This event repeated itself several times until any curiosity the owl might have had about twoleggers was well beyond satisfied. She was relieved when the hole stopped opening for a while—especially since light and dark changed places so frequently now.

The owl gave up trying to make sense of it. She was in the little sharp-edged hole for a long while, it seemed, and for a while the hole was closed tightly enough around her that she wasn't troubled by changes in the light, and fell asleep again. The next thing she knew, the hole was open again, and outside it was nothing but a comforting dimness. Another pair of those big soft twolegger feet reached in and wrapped around her. A moment or two later—or so it seemed—the owl realized she was standing on a leafless branch.

Weak as she was, she sank her talons into it in sheer relief and stared around. The branch was enclosed with some strange half-solid stuff that she could dimly see through, but there was no understanding what lay beyond it. In any case the owl realized that she didn't care, because there was something else besides her on the branch where she stood. It was a little pool of water inside something hard, and next to it was a dead mouse.

In all her life the owl had never been so glad to see a mouse, dead or alive. She pinned it to the branch with one foot and tore it in two and gulped it down in two bites. Then she drank some water, which was not a thing she would normally have done except for being *so* thirsty. She really wanted to drink it all, but she felt strange inside, so she stopped.

The odd unbroken twilight around her lasted a long time, but the owl was weary enough to not really mind. She dozed and woke and dozed again, and every time she dozed there was another dead mouse handy when she woke up—sometimes two—and more water. Now and then she realized one of the twoleggers was watching her from outside the strange see-through walls of the large hole they'd put her in. They moved slowly and quietly, and did nothing that much bothered her; so she ignored them.

After a while the owl felt well enough to try to explore the hole she was in. She fluttered at the sides of it without effect. It was made of some unyielding stuff like very thin fronds from her tree, but cold and hard. A little ways below the branch was what seemed like a hard little patch of ground with some soft chips of wood scattered over it. The owl wasted no more time trying to figure all of this out, because that was when one of the twoleggers started coming inside the hole with her.

The first time this happened the owl went as far down her branch as she could and just held still against the side of the hole. When she

did this the twolegger came to her, making soft noises, and took hold
of her feet with its own foot, so that the owl had to stand on that foot.
This was hard to get used to at first. But the twolegger kept distracting
the owl by (with its other foot) giving her mice.

The owl quickly decided that she didn't mind this kind of distrac-
tion *too* much. How many mice she ate, how much water she drank
out of the strange little pool, how many times she fluffed her feathers
out and settled down to roost and sleep on the branch, she had no
idea. But she started feeling much stronger, enough to try to fly. This
didn't go well for her; she kept crashing into the walls of the hole.

But then the light changed in the hole, growing a little brighter;
and the creature that kept holding the owl by her feet came into the
hole, picked her up, and walked with her to another place. It was a
bigger hole, much bigger, with bigger branches in it. And through the
walls of it she could feel and smell the wind.

The owl felt something strange inside her; something good,
something the opposite of the anger she had felt when she was dying.
But beyond that she didn't know what to do or feel... so she held still
and waited. Presently the twolegger with the soft feet came into the
bigger hole and brought her more mice. At first it put them on the
branch for her, and she ate them gladly.

But then the owl saw that the twolegger had a mouse in its foot
and was simply holding it: not eating it, but simply holding it where
the owl could see and where it would be easy to take. It seemed a
waste to just leave it there, so—since there was room to fly in here—
the owl fluttered warily to the twolegger's foot and snatched the
mouse. But she went back to the branch again before she ate.

The two of them repeated this odd business numerous times,
while the world got bright and dark and then bright again, until the
owl began to get both amused by it (another feeling she hadn't felt
since watching her brothers repeatedly fall out of the nest) and also
bored. But then that bright time started sliding into darkness again,
and without warning things changed.

The One Who Held Her By The Feet took the owl off the branch
she'd been flying from and put her once more into a small hole that

had parts she could see through, a little, but couldn't get out of. Then came some jostling and bumping and the dimming light sliding past her and the hole that held her—sometimes in very odd ways. The owl kept having to close her eyes so she wouldn't have to look at what was happening outside the hole.

But this uncomfortable time didn't last too long. The sense of headlong motion, such as the owl had felt before while trapped in her tree, now ceased. The little hole in which she was presently imprisoned was picked up and moved, and then suddenly she could smell the wind again, as The One Who Held Her By The Feet reached into the hole and picked her up in the usual way.

There were other twoleggers in company with the One Who Held Her; but there'd been others with the two of them before, and none of those had ever done her harm. So the owl held still a moment and looked around, and waited to see what would happen.

For a few moments, nothing happened at all. The soft-footed twolegger was still. The owl gazed around her, holding still, waiting, trying to work out what was happening. But the wind was breathing in her face again, speaking of water and trees and things living around and beneath them; and the sky was over the owl, the clear twilight sky she had seen only dimly for so long now, only at a distance.

It was there. She could fly. In utter astonishment she stood on the twolegger's soft foot and stared up at the sky: then stamped her feet on the one that held her. As she did so she realized she wasn't being held any more. She could *fly!*

A number of times during her captivity the owl had thought something like this and had tried it... then embarrassingly found herself wrong, flapping about in the twolegger's foot, as helpless as a chick. But that wasn't happening now. Her feet were free. So she stretched her wings out, and beat them, and leapt into the air and *flew.*

Almost too soon a tree loomed up in front of her. As much out of reflex as out of choice the owl dove in among its branches and sat down on one, not far from the trunk. It was all so *normal* that she hardly knew what to do for some moments. She wasn't hungry or thirsty, so neither of those conditions made her want to do anything. She didn't know where she was, but even in normal times she often didn't know that, so for the moment it didn't bother her one way or the other.

She flew again, then, and caught another mouse or two that she heard in the sparse dry grass under the trees. Then after flying a few times more she found a tree with a good-sized bole, the space around its trunk well shaded with close-grown branches and fronds thickly needled. The owl clambered into that dark-green dimness and tucked herself up against the tree's trunk as light started to creep into the sky again. With great relief she closed her weary eyes and roused her feathers out into a warm fluff against the daytime cold. *Finally* she was free of the twoleggers, free to fly where she pleased. She was full. She had shelter and time to rest. Everything was fine again.

...Except for one thing. It was an ache inside her, like being hungry; but it seemed to the owl that nothing she could catch or eat would assuage it. It was a soreness, a painful again-and-again rasp at the edges of her being, like being thirsty: but nothing she could drink would slake it. It was the one thing that had been perfect, but was perfect no longer: gone beyond ever getting back. Of all things wrong with the world, it was the *most* wrong.

Her tree was gone.

Before, she had not had words. Before, she hadn't known what words were, and she still had no name for them. But now (without knowing *that* she was knowing, really) the words for how to speak her anguish and anger to the world came to her.

I. Want. My. Tree. *Back!*

PART II

TWO

4

JD 2459186.04306 (2 DECEMBER 2020, 0702 EST)

I n the reality we all share (whether we choose to believe in that reality or not), it's a truism that the one thing magic was *never* designed for was exclusivity. There is too much in the world that's gone wrong, and too little time to put it right, to limit access to the great Instrumentality that makes the never-ending wizardly Work of mending-the-marred possible at all. Therefore—by design—what most people would casually call "magic" is all over the place, if you only know where to look for it.

With so much of it lying around, it stands to reason that all kinds of problems can arise when magic is applied to reality in unstructured or disorganized ways. This is one of the main reasons for the existence of wizards: to assist the Powers that Be in imposing some kind of order on a tremendous, universe-spanning force that without management and supervision could easily spawn total chaos.

But even taking into account the near-constant efforts of all the many millions of wizards scattered across the planet (and many others), sometimes things still get out of hand. Of the three hundred eighty-one thousand, six hundred sixty-seven non-probationary wizards practicing the Art in the New York metropolitan area as of December 2, 2020, all of them who heard it were caught by surprise (the first time, anyway) by a voice that spoke suddenly in such emphatic and furious tones that not even the normally-irresistible forward flow of time could constrain what it had to say. Such was its power that this voice was heard both after it spoke, and before. And the words it spoke were these:

I. WANT. MY. TREE. BACK!

IN THE NEW YORK suburb of Nassau County on Long Island, a wizard sat bolt upright in bed, jolted awake by the words he'd just heard in a dream and which were still thrumming in his bones.

"... What the hell's *that* supposed to mean?" he muttered; for what he'd just experienced hadn't been some casual moment out of nightmare. The demand—it was nothing less—had come in the Speech with which the world was made, not something any wizard could ignore however sleepy they might be.

From a couple feet away, a muffled voice said, "Mngff?"

"Did you hear that?"

"...Hear what?" said the man who still had the covers (as usual) pulled up over his head.

A second later the covers were yanked down with shocked speed, revealing someone with truly world-beating bed hair and a shocked expression. "Now *what* in the—"

"Yeah." The first man held out his hand. A book, hardbound and about the size and thickness of a fairly comprehensive dictionary, appeared there and weighed it down. "Go get in the shower," he said. "I've got a feeling we're on the clock."

IN THEIR MODEST bungalow tucked away in a relatively obscure corner of the Town of Hempstead, two Supervisory-level wizards—presently on a scheduled rotation as managers for North America's East Coast region—spent the morning doing what an uneducated observer (or someone who didn't know they were wizards) might have mistaken for "not very much." Coffee was made, and drunk. Toast was made, and burnt only once when the wizard in charge of the toaster was so distracted by something he was reading in the wizard's manual on the countertop that he forgot that the pop-up lever on the toaster had been misbehaving.

By the time the burnt toast had been over-buttered and consumed (because no wizard likes to waste things, and one of them didn't mind toast that was half charcoal if there was enough butter on it), they had made the joint determination that whatever had awakened them hadn't actually happened yet. Their manuals weren't at all forthcoming about the cause.

They had moved business into the dining room where they could use the dining table to spread out the manuals into as many viewing/reading expansions as they needed. There, for most of an hour or so between nine and ten AM, the two men wandered around the table, reading a great number of situational précis documents filed by other wizards around the world and sifting through them for any clue of what was about to happen. A lot of their colleagues were asking the same question of the local universe, though as yet no one had anything but vague intimations of detail. There was agreement that *something* unusual was about to happen, it was about to happen in the US northeast, where the wizards who'd heard the strange declaration were overwhelmingly concentrated, and that it involved a tree.

But beyond that?

"Nothing," said the dark-haired one, dressed now in sweats and a grey athletic sweatshirt that said DUKE. "Which means that whatever it is will be fairly major." He scowled down at his manual, which had spread itself into a broad fold-out display of the New York metropolitan area.

His counterpart, wearing jeans and a polo shirt with a fleece vest over it, was leaning against the table beside his partner and eyeing the map narrowly. It was presently displaying a hazy blue-glowing balance-of-probabilities interventional-locus region apparently spray-painted over midtown Manhattan, its boundaries irregularly expanding and contracting, solidifying and going vague, like some kind of giant ghostly amoeba.

"...Right. Look, Carl," he said, "most of the time if someone started talking to me about trees in this part of the world, I'd be looking up here." He reached across the table to tap the representation of Central Park. "But the loci of potential incidence don't seem to be particularly emphatic up that way. Down here, though..." Now he gestured at the area where the hazy light representing the loci looked thickest, in a rough oblong between 42nd and 57th Streets and 7th and Lexington Avenues. "It's looking a lot thicker."

"And that being the case, there's one tree that might be at issue." Carl pointed at the block between 49th and 50th.

"Is that today? I thought it was Friday—"

A mobile phone face down on the table began buzzing insistently. "Uh oh, here we go," he said, reaching for it. "Well, at least she let us finish breakfast." He picked it up. "Tom Swale—"

A brief pause. "Good morning, Irina! —Yes, we did. Would've been hard to miss, yeah! —Somewhere in midtown Manhattan, but the indicators are still— No. —No, I wouldn't say— Not inimical at all. Not a direct manifestation of our old friend, no. Something quite different. If you—"

He stood there listening intently for a moment, his eyes on the spread-out glowing map. "I take your point, of course. But I don't think this is ripe yet. I think we should allow it to progress before attempting to intervene. That's normally best practice with these—"

Another thirty seconds or so of quiet. "All right," he said, "we wouldn't have a problem with that at all. —No, the city's shutting down Rockefeller Plaza and the surrounding blocks, and they won't be permitting anyone in. The ceremony will be a streaming broadcast, both live and recorded content, and— And, well, your guess at this point would be as good as ours. From what I've seen in the manual, not even the visionaries have been able to get a reading on this... which by itself is unusual. I don't think we have much of a choice other than to wait..."

Another silence. Then he smiled. "No. There's that, at least. We'll put together an assessment group, people who know the area—" A pause: then a chuckle. "Well, why not? They shouldn't be strangers. —So we'll view it in realtime—" He glanced over at Carl and mouthed the word *Timeslide?* Carl nodded and made an *Of course, what else?* gesture. "And once we've made an initial risk assessment, Carl will fix an up-timeline view timefix for the team. Once we've run through it onsite, we'll start examining intervention options. Does that—"

A last brief silence. "All right," Tom said. "I'll drop you a debrief package with imagery and synced-up context when we're done with our first look. Anything else you want to add? —All right, then I'll talk to you later. *Dai,* elder cousin—"

He put the phone down. "That didn't sound too traumatic," Carl said, straightening up and stretching a little with his fists in the small of his back.

"Any conversation with a Planetary that leaves your hide in one piece is a good one," Tom said.

"So what now?"

"We make some calls... do some manual messaging. Find out everything we can about what's scheduled to happen. And then..."

"We wait and see."

WHICH WAS EXACTLY how things went until seven P.M., when the two of them settled down in their living room to observe and assess the imminent whatever-it-was. They had their wizard's manuals handy— not for viewing the events, though wizards' manuals have been capable of streaming video even when they were still manifesting themselves as carvings on stone, slabs of cuneiform-pressed dried clay, rolls of papyrus, or wax tablets.

Tom had passed the NBC streamed video to the big 4K screen on the living room wall, augmented by timestamp and graphic annotations from their Supervisory manuals that illustrated and classified the wizardly power-influx and power-expression in the target area. Carl, meanwhile, came in with an ice bucket full of cola bottles (the bucket had a small wizardry applied to it that would keep the ice from melting) and sat down next to Tom with his manual in his lap.

Their attention, at least in the early stages of the ceremony, was less on the ceremony's performances (excellent though some of them were) and more on the maps and charts that showed what energies, wizardly and otherwise, were presently at play in the tri-state area. The two Supervisors could see brief flashes of fire all over the maps, power-signatures of wizards presently on assigned errantry, or simply attending to the minor interventions that were every wizard's bread and butter.

Then, in an upstate area about eighty miles north of Manhattan and west of the Hudson River, one spark flared with unusual brightness, several orders of magnitude brighter than anything else they'd seen so far.

"Time fix," said Tom, leaning forward. "Start a clock." The manual display on the TV marked the time—*JD 2459186.59622 | 20:13:33, 2 DEC 2020*—and another display appeared directly below it, counting seconds upwards from the fix-marked Julian date.

They watched that spark drift slowly southward toward Woodstock and the Bluestone Forest, flaring again occasionally as it went. In every moment that followed, other sparks flared and began slowly to drift toward the brightest one.

There was—at first—a tentative quality to what they were viewing; a sense of some unusual process feeling its way through the unexpected, the new. At one point it paused for some seconds, and the energy-influx indicators wavered, dropped off...

Then that brightest spark flared, and flared again, higher. The power-influx and -expenditure indicators on the display started spinning their values up.

"Now what was *that?...*" Tom murmured.

Other glitters of light began to manifest themselves around the bright central one, drifting in closer. The movement southward started to speed up. The display lit with a faint webwork of fuzzy lines interconnecting the gathering glints of light as more of them appeared, closing in around that brightest source.

"Look at that," Carl said under his breath as the lines of light intensified, multiplied, grew denser. "What's going *on* up there?"

Tom eyed the six-digit readout at the right of the screen as the digits spun up and up through higher and higher values. "Not a new probationary talent. Or *just* a new probationary. Too low for an inhabition..."

"Bets?" Carl said.

"Figures don't really support it..."

"We'll see. Graphing for later analysis..."

More and more sparks of light were drifting inward from both sides of the Hudson and clustering around the bright power core that was heading south at an ever-increasing speed. "*Significant* physical component to that," Carl murmured. "That's gonna show on some-body's ground radar pretty quick."

Tom flipped a few pages in his manual, nodded. "It's happening right now..."

"Aaaaand course-correcting," Carl said as one of the associated compass-heading indicators shifted all at once, with abrupt certainty. "Heading straight for Manhattan. Somebody's got their own tracking routine running." To the manual, he said, "Tighten in..."

The view on the screen pushed in. The tangle of glowing inter-connections among the incoming phenomenon resolved into lines and sparks again, then gradually once again became too dense to make out particulars as the aggregate of compelling power and subsidiary forces slid more and more quickly south. "TRACOM's noticed," Carl said. "No alarms yet, though—"

"Good. Rather not have this be another of those NORAD things where they almost nuke the neighbors over a flock of geese..."

"No sign of that. Small mercies."

"Yeah," Tom said. "Flock, yeah. Geese, no..." The glowing cloud slid downwards out of Westchester and crossed the river into the airspace over Washington Heights.

"Split it," Carl told his manual. The wall-screen's view immediately divided between a view of the incoming cloud of objects and the countdown toward the lighting of the Rockefeller Plaza Christmas tree.

It was as well that their Manuals were recording everything that happened, for the two men spent the next ten minutes spellbound (so to speak) watching the output from the video stream as the cloud of eyes descended; as a very small owl sat down on the star at the top of the tree and stared her infuriated defiance at the cameras; as the wings lifted and beat and took the Tree away, up out of Rockefeller Plaza and high into the light-polluted night.

On one side of the screen, on-air talent was babbling ad-libbed nonsense, helpless to add any context to what had just happened. On the other, tracking was showing the same network of power, with one bright star at its core, heading for upstate New York, and finally vanishing into it.

The two wizards stared at each other, speechless for a few seconds. Carl found his words first.

"*That,*" he said, "was the damndest thing I've *ever* seen happen in that town."

Tom gave him a look. "Oh? *Not* the time the dinosaur ate Luciano Pavarotti?"

Carl laughed… though somewhat grimly. "We sorted that out," he said. "We'll sort this."

"Maybe so." Tom fell back against the sofa and rubbed his eyes. "But now all we have to do is figure out one thing.

"…How in the Powers' names did she just *do* that?"

5

JD 2459179.48264 (25 NOVEMBER 2020, 17:35 EST)

After she'd been freed, it had taken very little time for the owl to feel back at home in the world once more, now that she was away from the twoleggers. She hunted; she ate and drank and flew; she did all the things that were right for an owl to do in the normal course of life. But none of them left her *feeling* right. And this wrongness she felt most keenly every day as dawn drew near and the world grew light... when she woke and found herself, every time, in the wrong place.

She knew—because her bones told her so—that when the fierce light in the sky swung this low, it was a normal thing to follow it south and go where there was more and better food. The time for her to do that had been drawing near when the normalcy of her life had been upended. But now, day by day, she felt less inclined to do what her bones were suggesting. Warring with their continual uneasy murmur, as food got steadily scarcer, was an equally deep-set feeling that if she left this part of the world, she would lose the only possible satisfaction for some hunger that mere food would never satisfy.

And it came to her again and again, in the evenings, when she woke: *I want my tree. I want my tree.*

I want my tree back!

It was like seeing prey escape from right under your talons, that want. It was like drinking water (when one did that at all) and finding it foul. It was like having to hold still for what seemed like a whole night when you heard the cry of one of the bigger owls that would be glad enough to make a meal of you if it could. Very slowly that emptiness and that anger grew, though there was nothing the owl could do to change the longing, to make it stop.

Some days she found herself sinking talons right into branches where she sat waiting for prey, clenching and clenching again with the growing frustration of wanting *this one thing* and not being able to have it—the tree that had been hers, and that she was sure had been *glad* of being hers. She missed the tree. She missed what they had been together. She missed the tree's groundedness, perfect complement to her flight. She missed being home... being *part* of a home.

Days went by; hunt-time and light-time, hunt-time and light-time again... and matters did not improve. She was full-fed and comfortable, but everything was still *wrong*. For all the strange and awfulwonderful things that had happened to the owl, waiting had made no difference, *holding still* had made no difference, to the one thing lacking. Now she woke in the dusk of yet another evening that was like all the others had been, and in which things were still all wrong... or wrong as regarded that one great lack that made everything else wrong, because all other things were seen in its light.

The thought of the strangeness that had come to the owl when she was trapped in her tree—the strangeness that spoke—had recently come to her now and again. In this particular dusk, as she sat on a lower branch of the tree that was not her tree, watching the ground for prey, it came to her again. But the speaking had done nothing since then: *nothing!* And at the thought, a great flood of anger rose up in the owl at all the things that were wrong, *very* wrong, and needed to be put right.

Without warning that anger caught in her throat like prey swallowed sideways. It swelled inside her until it felt like it filled her right out to her skin, leaked out past it into every barb of every feather, right down to the needly points of her talons. The owl was *furious* at the lack of her tree and all the things about it that had made life right. But one thing she had now that she hadn't had before, until the words were spoken to her. Now she remembered that she had words of her own.

So now she used them. She caught the anger in them the same way she would have used her talons as she dropped onto a fleeing mouse. She sank the words in hard. She gripped with them, and would not let go. And the words were:

I. Want. My. **Tree.** *BACK!*

And instantly the knowledge came to her of *where the tree was.*

As if she hovered at a height and gazed down on prey that was huddled still, knowing her about to drop onto it, the owl could see a great expanse of ground made small enough to see. It lay out before her, a long narrow island to the southward, with very little forested or open land, but with those strange straight hardened paths running all up and down and across it. Just off one of those wide paths, in a great patch of tall thin sharp-edged stony things rearing up as close together as some choked pine-spinney, was a narrower pathway surrounded by more of the skinny squared-off stones and ending in a kind of broad pit. And on one side of that pit was her tree.

The owl's breast expanded with excitement and satisfaction as she saw it, and she shook herself until all her feathers stood out in pleasure and anger and warmth. She could *feel* her tree there. The sense of it—sight, feeling, whatever it might have been called—made the owl's anger flare up higher.

And when it did, through the anger she could hear the challenge of something bigger, stronger, older, crueler:

Come and get it, then.

The owl clenched her talons into the branch, hard, and shivered. Sudden fear of that voice, of what used it—of what waited, unassailable in Its certainty—breathed through the feathers of her face and made her shiver the way one did when one's body-feathers weren't enough to cope with the cold.

But she was *angry.* The mockery of the dark-feathered voice with the great curved claws hidden in it just made her angrier still.

The owl snapped her beak in defiance. *All right,* she said. *So I shall!*

She launched herself out of the tree and fluttered across the clearing to the first copse of firs, and perched on a branch of one of them, thinking.

That—*whatever* it was that had challenged her: it was strong, and old, and much bigger than she was. She wasn't going to be able to do this alone. She was going to need help.

There is a way to call for help, said whatever it was that had spoken to her in the tree. Its voice was very soft in her ears, like the merest rustling in the grass of something that didn't care to be heard. *There is a word to bring it to you... if you have the strength.*

The owl flew into another tree, and rested for a moment. *Tell me.*

What came into her mind then, sound by sound, seemed to wind itself into her bones, hot as blood, as she heard it. She knew immediately, without having any idea how she knew, that any owl uttering that call would be infallibly be followed by any owl that heard it. Even those that could not hear the sound of it would feel that same demand in their bones to seek out its source and follow. The anger and desire of the one who uttered that call would make it all the stronger.

There is a possibility that you might not live after you speak this word, said whatever had spoken to her. *Is this danger worth your life?*

The owl knew that what this voice said was true. The way it spoke to her, the words it used, made not-truth impossible. For a moment she hesitated...

But then she thought of the tree, *her* tree, and all the anger came back at once. *I may want it, but it wanted me too! And it has no voice to say so. I'll speak this word for both of us!*

And the owl opened her beak and spoke her first word aloud: spoke *the* Word.

It seemed to take forever. The owl had few calls of her own—a repetitive hooting noise, and a few other softer sounds. What came out of her beak now was more like a song, and in a voice she'd never known she she possessed. Uttering it took more than one breath.

Indeed it took a second, and a third, and seemed to want to take *all* the breaths—all the ones she'd ever breathed, and all those yet to come. That knowledge frightened the owl. But along with it came a certainty that this word *had* to be spoken, that it had been waiting forever for her to speak it; that it was speaking *her*—

Then it was gone from her, and let her go. With its departure the owl felt all her strength depart her. She sagged against the bole of the tree, weak and befuddled as a new-hatched chick, and gasped for air as one does who's just realized for the first time that it might be taken from them.

It took some good while for the owl to start to feel better. At last she was able to stand up on on her feet again. *Now I have to fly!* she thought. *But first I have to eat.*

So she flew a short distance to another tree and turned her attention to the ground beneath it. Soon, but not nearly soon enough for her, she heard a mouse scuffling among the deep-piled pine needles. She dropped from the tree, seized it, snapped its neck with her beak, and made her meal.

The owl had rarely bolted her food so quickly, for already she could feel what the Word she had said was doing, and she wanted to get on the wing to meet it. Already she was beginning to feel something strange. It was as if, though no other owl was near her, yet somehow owls *were.* She felt the way she had when her sibs were shouldering up against her in the nest-hole long ago, sharing the warmth of fluffed-out feathers... a familiar presence that she had nonetheless never felt in *this* way before. Every moment that warmth grew, and it was both a comfort to her and a cause for alarm. But the comfort outweighed that.

She hadn't quite finished eating the mouse and was in that comfortable post-main-gobble, tail-still-hanging-out-of-your-beak moment when another owl came floating silently out of the deepening evening and perched on a branch above hers. Normally such an occurrence would have filled the owl with alarm and jolted her into instant flight. But not this time. She could feel that strange connection, shoulder-to-shoulder, feathers-to-feathers—though the other owl, a horned owl, was easily three times its body-length away from her, and was one of those who'd normally have considered *her* small kind of owl an entirely acceptable meal.

The horned owl looked down at her, and as the owl gazed up at him, she realized that she knew what he was thinking. *You called me. I'm here. What are we doing?*

We're going to get my tree back, the owl said, and took a moment to swallow the mouse's tail. *We're going to put things right.*

That sounds good, said the horned owl (while looking a bit startled that it had words at all). *I'll go with you.*

As usual, eating made the owl need to excrete something to put herself in balance before flying again. She was just doing that when another owl landed in the tree, a barn owl this time, and stared down at her curiously. *You called me. I'm here. What are we doing?*

We're going to get my tree back, the owl said. *We're going to put things right!*

That sounds good, the barn owl said. *I'll go with you.*

By the time the owl had finished putting her feathers in order for what was going to be a longish flight, there were perhaps fifty more owls in the trees around her. At any other moment of her life such a situation would have thrown her into utter panic, certain that she was about to be made meat, as her brother had been. But now the Word she had spoken—or which had spoken her—left her in no doubt that she was safe; that all these other owls (for the time being, anyway) were her kindred, and they would all fly southward together and help her achieve her desire.

So she knew it was time. *Let's go now,* the owl said, *and get my tree!*

She jumped off the branch and flew; and in a flurry of wings, all the other owls rose and flew with her.

What happened next seemed to go very quickly. It didn't feel to the owl as if she was flying any faster than usual, but the landscape around her shifted with unusual speed. And every few wingbeats, it seemed, there were more owls around her, asking the same question, almost in chorus sometimes: *You called us. We're here. What are we doing?* Always she answered them: *We're going to get my tree back. We're going to put things right!* And readily all the other owls agreed, and flew with her.

Their numbers grew and grew as they flew south along the great river. Well above the trees they mounted—the owl leading them higher, so as to better know their way—and then higher still, until the gatherings of twolegger places spread out below them in glimmering splotches of golden light. The darkness fell more deeply around them as they flew, but other light grew at the edge of the world, to southward; a low haze of more golden light, brighter—the light of the place where the owl's tree was. Down the dark road of the river they flew, more and more swiftly.

Presently ahead of them the owl glimpsed something coming in the air to meet them. *Another owl,* she thought. *But all alone, and so big!* And as it drew closer she realized it was easily the biggest owl she had ever seen. It was dark-feathered, hard to make out in the deepening shadows of night, even for an owl. Its wings melted into the sky when you tried to see them clearly, and its eyes burned in a chilly color the owl had never seen before.

You called Me, said this new owl. *I am here. What are you doing?*

The question seemed for the owl only, and those eyes dwelt on her, hungry and patient, the way one looks at prey. *I'm going to get my tree back,* she said. *I'm going to put things right!*

Not without Me, the dark owl said. *You need not fly this long dangerous journey at all. I am the Lord of Owls. I will put things right for you in a better way, and give you your desire. Abandon this quest, therefore, and give over your mastery to me. Then all things will be well.*

The owl wasn't sure what the dark owl meant, but she didn't much care for its tone. *We're close to where I want to be,* she said as she paused, hovering in the air; and all the others slowed to hover with her. *Why should we stop now? We'll do what we need to do, and find my tree, and put things right ourselves.*

How can you be sure you will succeed? the dark owl said. *You are the smallest of owls! You are not great or strong. Give this task over to me, and I will accomplish it easily. All you need do is surrender your mastery to me. Then I will give your desire into your claws.*

For a moment, while it spoke, the longing grew in the owl—to go back to the way things were, *exactly* as they were, before all this trouble started. *You could have that,* the dark owl's thoughts seemed to whisper inside her. *Time may be turned back. All can be as it was. Accept the offered gift!*

Yet all the while the owl felt herself somehow being closed in by the dark owl's words, as if moment by moment they were enwrapping her in the hard cold stuff she hadn't been able to get through while the twoleggers had her. The owl snapped her beak in annoyance, for she'd had more than enough of being in places she couldn't get out of. *You came at my call, but I don't know you,* she said. *Who are you to offer me things? How do I know you mean me well?*

The dark owl, its wings spread wide as it too hovered, glared at her in momentary impatience. *Because I am wise. This power that has come to you will do you no good, bring you no rest! Other owls will envy you for it, and seek to kill you.* The dark owl's tone turned wheedling now, like that of a chick who wants the bigger scrap of meat that another one got. *But what do you need such power for? All you desire is your tree! I will give you that. Your tree will be yours forever, to own. None but you will ever roost there. If you like, it's even in My power to give you all the trees you can see from one edge of the world to the other; all the trees there are! None will roost in any of them without your leave. You will rule all owls as I rule you—*

The owl snapped her beak again, feeling suddenly how the passing moments were pouring through her feathers like wind. She felt the urge to be flying again before that wind shifted somehow and denied her the path to what she wanted. *I don't want to rule all owls!* she said. *And I don't want all trees. I want my own tree!*

At which point something else occurred to the owl. *Anyway, who are* you *to give it to me? The tree's itself, and no one else's to give! And even so, it* liked *to be mine. Who are you to give me what's mine already?*

Those cold eyes widened, going colder still, going angry. The owl, hovering kestrel-like in the moment with all the other owls, could feel a strange pressure in the air about her—a whirlwind of possibilities, waiting to break free. *Enough of this!* she said then. *It's time for us to fly. Be one of us and help me put the world right. Or be off out of my way before I* make *you!*

The dark owl stared at her in astonishment. *You'll make* Me? And it began to make a ridiculous cawing noise, almost like a crow. Great cruel amusement and disdain were in that noise, and it brought the owl's hackles up.

She had heard this kind of thing before—sometimes from other raptors, sometimes from other birds who thought her size made her a joke, and who then amused themselves by mobbing her. *Yes, I will!* the owl said, feeling her anger start to rise hot again. *I'll fly at you and fasten onto your face and put my claw in your eye so that you fall right out of the air down onto the ground and lie there going cold! I'll pull the feathers off you and strip your breast meat off and bolt it in four gulps! And when I'm done the little things of the wood will pick your bones clean, and when* they're *done the ants will run in and out of where your eyes were, carrying off whatever's left!*

That anger was swelling greater and greater inside the owl again, overflowing her. This time it also flowed over into those who hovered all around her, waiting to see what she would do. She glared at the dark owl, and all around her more and more of the owls who'd come at her call turned their gazes to do the same—hovering still, but all flexing their talons like they wanted to sink them into something.

So get out of our way right now, the owl said, *or that's just how it will be!*

The dark owl's only answer was to scream, a horrible screech-owlish shriek that promised death and destruction to them all. It flung itself at the owl.

But she was already out of her hover and winging forward. Quick as if she was catching a mouse, the owl did just as she'd said, reaching out with her feet and fastening her talons into the dark owl's face—

At that, the screaming face pressed up against the owl's breast began to grow, and its big beak snapped at her. That was horrible, but the owl's rage grew too, and she hung on and kept on beating her wings and clenching her talons tighter, feeling inward for an eye.

Then another owl's feet, bigger than hers, fastened into that face along with her. And right after those, another pair of feet, longer-taloned—a great brown owl's, possibly—hooked in through the dark owl's head-feathers from behind, and reached for its skull.

One after another, more and more pairs of razor-sharp talons pushed in out of the night, clenching into the dark owl's great body and gripping around its flailing legs and feet. The more the dark owl grew, the more owls came to fasten themselves to it, gripping tight, talons working inward toward its vitals. Huge as it was now, there were still more owls than it could deal with, though by comparison they might seem small as mice.

And what talons alone could not do, beaks now started doing. Swiftly the screams of the dark owl changed, turning at first from mere rage to rage and pain, as the sharp beaks of all that great gathering of owls dug into what the talons held, and started to tear. Soon enough the screaming became all one howl of pain as the owls ripped dark feathers away and let them fall; as the flesh beneath the feathers was rent off the flailing bones.

Nor could the tormented, diminishing shape now even fall. As it dwindled, the owls bore it up in the air over the dark river, ripping what life it had away. The dark owl's screams shifted into a strange high anguished keening—the aggrieved complaint of One who'd only become this physically real for the sake of having a conversation, and was realizing (now that the conversation had gone so utterly, unexpectedly wrong) that It might have miscalculated.

Finally the screaming faded away, and the owl felt what her talons held go still, then start to go unsubstantial. She let go, and watched the scrap of feathers and flesh she'd been gripping fade away into the darkness as they fell—the night now every moment growing more clean of those huge wings' shadow. All around her, all the other owls hovered and did the same. The last night-black fragments fell out of their claws and into a river now glowing faintly under the risen moon as a patch of high cloud slipped away. Untroubled, the light and the water swallowed those last scraps, vanishing them.

All right, the owl said at last. *Let's go on. We've got things to put right!*

And all together, bound by the one purpose, the owls flew.

WHEN THEY ARRIVED in the air over the stone-overgrown island and dropped down toward the pit-like place that held her tree, the owl realized the dark owl had done her a favor. She hadn't been terribly sure how she was going to take the Tree back. But now she knew that the owls who were with her had been enough to hold their enemy up in the air while they dealt with it. *And surely my tree won't be that heavy! We'll manage.*

Yes you will, something whispered in her ear—and with some humor, as if there could seriously have been any doubt on the subject.

Nonetheless, the owl had missed enough kills in her time that she knew better than to celebrate the mouse's taste before it was in her gullet. *There it is!* she said to all the owls who'd come with her. *Go sit down on it and take a breath or so. Then we'll get it out of here and go home.*

The other owls were perfectly willing to do just that. In a great cloud of beating wings they settled on the tree and gazed curiously around them.

The owl found herself glad of the covering they lent to her tree, because the twoleggers had somehow managed to turn it into an eyehurting tree-shaped aggregation of glaring colored fires and little sparks like tiny confused seeds of lightning. *That's going to have to be put right too,* she thought, *but we'll leave it as it is for the moment. Right now, getting it out of here is the most important thing. So let's take care of that.*

In the wake of the other owls she drifted down to the top of the tree and managed to get a grip with her feet on the prickly, overbright object the twoleggers had fastened there. Then she too looked around.

Instantly she felt something unusual. Glancing from one side to another at the smooth-faced stone cliffs surrounding the tree, and then more closely examining the pit it stood beside, the owl realized that eyes were watching her—some sort of strange twolegger eyes that didn't need to be inside heads.

She couldn't say that she particularly cared for the feeling. Staring is something predators do to their prey, and no predator likes being stared at that way. Still, it seemed right to let whoever was watching know what she'd come for.

The owl looked into the one of those glinting, expressionless eyes that was nearest. *I've come to take my Tree back!* she said. *I've come to put things right!*

All the twoleggers who were standing around in their bright plumage stopped and stared at her. *All right,* the owl thought. *They heard me. Is anyone going to object?*

She sat and waited, but heard nothing to make her think that any other creature nearby was inclined to argue the point. So the owl turned her attention downward to all her many colleagues who were sitting on the tree.

All right! she said. *Sink your talons in. We'll do what we did before, and go back the way we came.*

All over the Tree she could see the other owls doing as she'd asked. Soon it could hardly be seen for their fluffed-out feathers, and it gleamed all over with the reflected light of their eyes.

And you now, the owl said to the Tree. *Is this all right? Is this what you want?*

There was a long pause. Then from the Tree she slowly gathered that this was more than all right, *much* more, if only it meant getting away from all this fuss and noise, back to someplace quiet and dark!

Yes indeed, the owl said, in emphatic agreement. To all the other owls, now settled in and waiting for her, she said: *All right. It has to go up now. All together—!*

And up it went—not least because the Tree knew the owl, and

was more than willing to do what was asked of it even when no one had ever asked it for anything before... indeed, perhaps *because* no one had ever asked anything of it before. The owl could feel the Tree trying to make the work easy for them... and indeed it seemed surprisingly easy, as if whatever normally held things down was making an exception in their case. Up the owls went, and up the Tree went with them, rising high above the staring, shouting faces below.

Soon enough all those grew tinier, too tiny for even an owl to see, until the twoleggers and their shiny cliffs were lost in a crosshatching of golden and colored lights—all of it dropping further and further behind and below them, more quickly every moment. Finally the night closed around them as the owl and her people crossed the sideways rivers between them and the north, and passed at last into the beginning of the welcome dark beyond the island. The lights on the ground grew fewer and fewer as they rose, obscured by the mists of early winter, until finally the brightest thing left to be seen was the rising moon's light in the great river, shining on the path back home.

PART III

THREE

6

JD 2459186.58472 (2 DECEMBER 2020, 21:02 EST)

In the wake of these events, on the South Shore of Nassau Country, two wizards were sitting in front of a Manual-augmented flatscreen TV and watching several split screens' worth of output from various sources.

One of them had completely forgotten the bottle of cola he was holding in favor of staring at six different networks' and news agencies' bulletins about the suddenly empty spot in Rockefeller Plaza. The other was swiping through news pages on his iPad and cursing good-naturedly in the enacture-stripped recension of the Speech that was set aside for human swearing.

"So?" Carl said.

"Social media? About what you'd expect. Facebook's experiencing traveling Tree-gossip-related outages. North America's worst at the moment, but it'll spread. Twitter would've FailWhaled out at least four times between now and the initial time fix, if they still had the whale. Between the app and the servers, they just don't have the scaling to deal with what's happening here." An amused pause. "As for Tumblr, there are at least ten or fifteen threads' worth of owl memes already—"

He stopped, staring at the iPad.

The silence was telling. *"What?"* Carl said.

"Just you wait." Tom doubletapped the screen he was viewing.

It mirrored itself to the main display, which promptly showed a palely generic-looking male reporter in a navy blue overcoat and a star-spangled-and-stripy wool scarf. This worthy stood in front of the suddenly tree-less Rockefeller Plaza space and was attempting to project excitement, stern disapproval, and a sense of delicious scandal all at once.

"Stories have been going around for a while now that the antifa were attempting to weaponize *animals* in their struggle to destabilize our nation. So-called mainstream media pundits pooh-poohed the very idea. Well, tonight, right here in Rockefeller Center itself, we've seen evidence that animals do indeed appear to have been drafted into the liberal War on Christmas—"

Tom eyed his partner, who was now doing a fair imitation of a famous starship captain facepalming. "Is it speeding up entropy to *wish* those guys and their whole broadcast establishment were in the East River?"

"This is wizardry, not magic," Tom said. "Wishing doesn't make it so. Just mind your recensions and you'll be okay... Meanwhile, I'm thinking we've done enough assessment."

"Yeah." They both stood and collected their manuals and other equipment. "Whatever way this gets handled, there's no point in letting the first run of this mess embed itself any deeper into the event substrate."

"Precisely. Since we're the Regionals on call, Planetary's going to drop this in our laps any minute now. So let's have the manuals pull an oversight team together—at the very least, we'll need an inhabition specialist and a substrate expert. Then we can meet up with whoever Irina's office sends around... say, in the Plaza, half an hour or so before the time fix?"

"Seems right. We're going to need a whole sheaf of timeslides for this, but it can't be helped. I'll sort it with our senior cousins one level up."

"And make sure they freeze other timeslide requests from the time fix forward!" Tom shouted after Carl as he went for his coat. "Last thing we'll need is having to correct some other timeline before we've sorted this one."

Laughter from the side room. "I've only been doing this for two decades, you know..."

"Thought it was three."

"Are you *trying* to make me feel old?" Carl emerged from the side room and tossed Tom's parka at him.

"I seem to remember telling you I liked older men..." Tom grinned as he shrugged into his coat. "Vests?"

"Yeah, protective coloration never hurts." Carl gestured at the empty air, reached into it, and pulled out two hi-vis vests: chucked one at Tom. "Gating? Or personal transport circles?"

"Personal, I'd say. No telling how this is affecting the City gates."

"Yeah. I'll ask the Twins to shut down the 48th-50th-Street subsidiary gate; there's always a chance of contagion. Better more caution than less until we work out what's to be done."

"...Okay, ready. Inside? Outside?"

"Outside's probably better—too many people target on the living room when they're inbound. I'll go set the alarms."

A few moments later their patio door was closed and locked behind them, and they were standing out in the near-dark and the cold clear air.

"Over by the hedge?"

"Yeah. One thing, though," Carl said.

He headed over to the concrete koi pond on one side of the yard and just stood there a moment, watching the ripples. Then in the wizardly Speech he said, *"We might be in and out a lot this evening. Just so you know..."*

For a few moments there was no response. Then, after a moment, a pale shape whose sides glinted here and there with bright scales like mirrors drifted toward the surface, putting its head up out of the porch-light-sheened water.

"On a drying branch," *it said,*

"A lone bird is alighting:

"Nightfall in autumn..."

Carl nodded. "Right on the money," he said. *"Arigato,* Akegane-sama. See you later..."

The fish drifted down into dark water once more. "Right," Carl said, and went back to join Tom by the hedge. "Ready?"

"Ready. Let's do it."

A symbol-written circle flared into life in the grass around the spot where they stood. A second later it vanished, and so did they.

7

JD 2459186.61250 (2 DECEMBER 2020, 21:42 EST)

As the wizards who'd initiated the meeting, protocol dictated that they should be the first to arrive. After that, new arrivals would be expected to turn up fairly closely together, temporally speaking—the individual timeslides themselves mandating enough physical offset to keep anyone appearing at those temporospatial coordinates from accidentally impinging on one another's space in more than just the idiomatic sense.

To an observer unfamiliar with what was happening it would have looked enough like social distancing not to arouse suspicion. But then observers who were actually able to notice the arrivals would have been thin on the ground... since all those who appeared, one after another, were wearing vests or other items of clothing over-written with Speech routines designed to make the non-wizardly either not notice the wearers at all, or (if they did) promptly forget they had.

One after another the expected arrivals appeared by the west-facing back window of the Lego Store, and each time for some moments nothing much happened except introductions among those who hadn't met yet, and greetings among those who had.

"Dai stihó!"

"*Dai,* cousin. Carl Romeo— "

"Lissa Dalwhinnie. *Dai!*"

Carl peered at the tall curly-haired young woman in the long furry-hooded parka and leggings, and frowned, an I-ought-to-know-you expression. "Wait! I remember. Didn't we meet at the Invitational back in 2011?"

"In kind of a hurry, yeah..."

Laughter. "When is everybody at an Invitational *not* in a hurry?"

"Yeah, now that you mention..."

"Are you our inhabition person?"

"Oh no, I'm the scrubber! I'll be tidying the scene of leftovers from the original timeline after we concur on what needs overwriting." Then she smiled, glancing sideways. "If I'm not very much mistaken, *that's* your inhabition guy..."

Off to one side, a tall young Hispanic man wearing (under his own hi-vis vest) a long navy woollen coat and scarf, and a perfectly cut navy suit, was checking the ground around him to make sure his transit circle had vanished. He looked up, and his grin flashed out as he saw the Supervisories.

Tom laughed out loud. "*Mars boy!*"

"Are you *kidding* me!" the young man said, and strode over to Tom and hugged him hard. "*When* are you going to let that go?!"

"You'll need to make sure no one saw that," Tom said, over Kit Rodriguez's shoulder, to Lissa.

"With these on?" Lissa plucked at her vest, laughing. "Trust me, no one will!"

"Not that the bug can bite anybody on errantry anyway," Kit said, and headed over to Carl: hugged him too. "It's been forever! You promised you were going to come visit. When exactly does that happen?"

"What can I tell you?" Carl said, post-hug. "You know how things've been this year! And other work gets in the way no matter how many worldgates you manage." He held Kit away a little. "Nice look, Kit! Kind of dressy, though? I thought billionaires let all their employees wear sweats to work these days. Or at least to Zoom in."

"Mmm, no. Sometimes it's useful to misdirect a bit. Or indulge in protective coloration... depending on who's on the call. Makes life easier..."

"I'm not sure what's 'easier' about wrangling some of these self-made-money types into more responsible channels."

Kit developed a small vertical line between his eyebrows. "Might be that's too much work for even a whole crowd of wizards. Anyway, not my job. Some errantry's more about damage control."

"Controlling the damage before it happens, you mean."

"Well, what's *tonight* going to be about, then? You don't always need timeslides to be proactive. Keeping stuff from happening in real time has its challenges, but if it gets the job done..." Kit shrugged, glancing up into an evening sky half blanked-out with sodium-vapor streetlight glow and nonetheless locking onto a specific spot with the certainty of someone who knows exactly where something is without needing to search, or to see. "It's a nice planet, these days. Hate for anything to happen to it. Or happen the wrong way." He grinned. "And if I have anything to do with it, it won't."

Carl nodded. "How's the family? How's your Mama holding up?"

Kit sighed. "She's okay." He looked away, rubbing the back of his neck. "It's been tough," he said more softly. "But she's tough too. She just keeps on picking herself up, you know? She says, 'I can't fall over right now. My patients need me. And my colleagues need me more.'"

"That's our Marina," Carl said. "Give her our best."

"I will."

"How's your sister?"

Kit shook his head. "Haven't seen much of her this last year."

Carl looked concerned. "Nothing to do with... *you* know?"

"What? Oh, no, no, she's fine! All that's pretty much water under the bridge now. But she's been spending a lot of time in space."

"Chocolate?"

"Strangely enough, it's more about diplomacy." Carl gave him a look. "No, seriously!" And then Kit grinned. "Well, *some* chocolate. You'd have to talk to Sker'ret. He's been using her as kind of a secret weapon. That Imivi thing, for example—"

Widened eyes. "She was tangled up in *that?* My God. And got out of it all right?"

Kit glanced to one side, at Tom. "Yeah. Long story. After this, if we can sit down—"

"For certain values of 'after'. We may get through a few of them before things settle—"

"It's *never* gonna settle if you three don't stop with the Boy Gossip and get down to business," said a voice from just around the corner of the Lego Store as the parasitic light from another transit circle died away.

"We're on the good side of a timeslide," Tom said. "Business won't start for four minutes yet. And as for *you*—" With a smile he turned toward the startlingly blue-haired, grey-eyed young woman in jeans and a snowflake-covered sweater and a long dark shawl who was ambling toward them. "*You* set this little reunion up somehow, didn't you! And here I was thinking we were going to wind up with just one more of the newbies that you keep shoving out of Irina's office to see if they'll fly."

Nita Callahan snickered at Tom as she wandered over to give him a hug. "What? Not a chance when I've got other fish to fry. I get all *kinds* of things delegated to me now. And *you're* due for your half-yearly evaluation!"

Tom guffawed as he patted her back. "Oh, Juanita Lou*ise,* you're going to have to try harder than *that!* Like I'd believe something like that coming from *you* that didn't come out of you in the Speech. You just like poking me to see if you can get me to jump."

She grinned at him, but made no attempt to deny it. "Tomás," she said, "the L word? From *you*? What a transparent attempt to get *me* to jump."

"What, isn't it applicable? My sources tell me—"

"Way too much as usual," she said, elbowing him genially in the ribs. "Shut *up.*"

"See that?" Tom said. "That was assault! Right here in front of the Powers that Be and *everybody."*

This assertion was greeted with numerous snorts or shouts of unconvinced laughter.

"All right," Carl said over the ruckus. *"Cousins!* ...Not that we don't all feel the need for more socializing than usual, under this year's circumstances, but let's get local matters sorted out first."

Everyone quieted down and gathered together a bit, though not so closely that it would attract attention if the blanket don't-notice-me wizardry their vests had coded in should start to fray around the edges. Kit glanced over at the as-yet-unlit Tree. "Has the sitrep changed at all?"

Carl shook his head. "Further downstream in time? It's as you saw it, and getting worse. City's going out of its mind, the whole country and half the world just saw what happened. The rest will know within minutes."

"So as usual when we're considering timeline alteration," Tom said, "three questions. What just happened here? Who are we dealing with? And what do we do to fix it?"

"Define 'fix,'" Nita said, with an expression of good-natured skepticism.

"One thing at a time," Carl said. "The manuals go into a lot of detail, but what seems to have happened is this: There's a new power in town who is at the very least a wizard, and may be considerably more. Our cousin-of-interest is, to all appearances, an owl. She is the same owl who was discovered trapped in this very tree—" and he waved at it— "a couple of weeks back, starving and dehydrated; was rescued and rehabilitated in an upstate New York facility; and was then released into the wild. She remained there without apparent incident for some days, moving from place to place in upstate New York, in what could have been mistaken for normal pre-migration patterns for a saw-whet owl. And that pattern continued until—at approximately the time point where we're all standing—half an hour 'ago.' At which point, this owl spoke the Strigid Word."

Bemused glances were exchanged among three of the five. "Never heard of that one," Kit said.

"Possibly because there won't have *been* one until around 8:34 PM Eastern time this evening," Carl said. "But there's sure one *now*."

Everyone considered that for a moment, some of them checking their wizardry-synched watches or phones for the Julian-dated referent time to compare it to their own local time ticks. "She spoke a Master-word!" Nita said under her breath. "And not for another species. For her *own*."

Tom nodded, looking sober. "I don't need to tell anybody here how tightly managed the use of such mastery-and-control words is as a rule," he said. "Not least because their usage typically entails the payment of a tremendously high price... and using it on your own species is routinely strongly enjoined. But we're breaking new ground, here. Or rather, *she* is. For nonhuman species, new styles or roles of wizardry tend to arrive in forms that at first glance may not make much sense to us. Our job is to assist them without allowing our preconceptions to accidentally limit what unexpected shapes it wants to take."

"And this is unexpected, all right..." Kit said.

"Dr. Rodriguez's normal tendency toward understatement is in evidence," said Carl with a lopsided grin. "Always good to see." Kit rolled his eyes.

Carl glanced at his manual. "We're coming up on the hour, cousins. All your manuals or affiliated instrumentalities have their own specialty settings in terms of what phenomena they observe and record most preferentially. So if you'll hit your 'go' buttons, and lean back to observe... the show's about to begin."

Almost as if it had been waiting for his cue, the tree lit in a blaze of multicolored fire...

And within a matter of minutes, things got very interesting.

WHEN THE TREE had finally sailed out of sight with its escort, the five leaning against the Lego Store wall regarded one another with astonishment.

"Definitely," Lissa said, shaking her head, "not something you see every day..."

"So," Tom said. "Beyond that... discussion?"

"No question, she's a tremendous power," Nita said. She was glancing down at her own manual, paging through it. "She was administered a version of the Oath that was adjudged mindset-appropriate for her species. She accepted it. After a delay, she began to use wizardry for the first time. And when she was on the way down here in the last half hour and the Lone One challenged her, she *beat* It... and then continued right on with what she'd been planning: taking back her tree."

"So that's what happened," Carl said. "Next: who is she, besides an owl who's also a wizard?" He glanced at Kit. "What about it, Dr. Rodriguez? With all that power in play... is she the One for owls?"

Another eloquent eyeroll. "It's almost as if you keep forgetting my first name, Carl. Could it be some kind of *age* problem? I'd hate to get personal about it..."

"Ow! Somebody get me a cryo spell for that burn." And a laugh. "Kit. *What about it?*"

Kit considered. "The One for owls? ...I don't think so. From what I know about inhabitions and upper-level avatars, not to mention the One For Dogs, the power involved here doesn't feel to me as if it's on the same scale." He thought for a moment. "But something lower-level? Could be. And I *do* think she's the answer to some problem—a problem bigger than the one she was having. I think she's a conduit for power. *What* problem, and *what* power...?" He shrugged. "Probably it'll take a while for us to learn. It might be trying to stay covert; if it is, it'd be rude to out it before it gets its job done. But in the meantime—" He laughed. "I think that owl's someone it'd be *really* smart not to annoy."

"Agreed," Lissa said. "If anyone was considering some kind of intervention that would attempt to recover the Tree and put it back, I think that would be a big mistake. She felt *so* strongly that the tree was hers, that to get it back it looks like somehow she reached right down into the Speech's own language-generative routines and made it manifest a Master-Word that's never even existed before. If someone thwarted what she's just done—possibly as part of her Ordeal—she could well come back here and do it all over again, in a way that we couldn't cover or repair after the fact."

"I'd say there's an even better reason to let her keep that tree," Nita said.

Lissa regarded her with interest. "Oh?"

"Absolutely! Sure, she feels like the Tree's hers. But more to the point, the *Tree* feels the same way."

Tom's eyebrows went up at that. "Well, plants were one of your first specialty areas way back in the day, weren't they? Far be it from me to question your expertise on this."

Nita shrugged. "The sense I got was that before it was moved here, the Tree didn't really feel particularly owned by anybody. But it absolutely feels that way *now!* And when the owl turned up, that tree didn't feel like it was being stolen. It felt as if it was being *rescued.*"

Carl was nodding. "All right," he said. "We know the what. We know the who... or as much of it as we're likely to know in the short term. But the short term's the issue, right now. So, the third question: what's our move? How are we going to fix this?"

"Well," Kit said, "the simplest fix would be simply to patch the timeline. 'Make it didn't happen.'"

Tom gave him an incredulous look.

"What?" Kit said, and laughed. "I seem to remember how once upon a time we had about a thousand dinosaurs break through a malfunctioning worldgate into the middle of a Three Tenors concert in Central Park *and* one of them *ate Luciano Pavarotti,* and we patched *that—*"

"Within minutes of the event occurring," Carl said. *"And* without the event having been extensively covered on national and international news and social media." He shook his head. "Granting you that in the wake of a patch, even for *that* event, those would be minor issues. The kind of post-patch site scrub that Lissa here specializes in would remove the possibility of any echoes of the old timeline lingering. *However—"*

He started riffling through his manual. "There's a vital difference between that event and this one. There was *nothing* about the Central Park gating breakthrough that was either desirable or important to keep. But *this* time, our tree-napping event here—if we can really call it that when the Tree *wanted* to be -napped—has brought with it something else unexpected."

He riffled through his own manual and held it open to one spread of pages that obligingly reproduced, in the air in the midst of them, a line graph with a startling exponential spike at its downtime end. "This evening's proceedings have come associated with a *really* unexpected influx of positive energy that I don't think this region, or indeed this planet, can afford to lose at the moment. Look at the timing there!"

He pointed at the highest spike on the curve. "That's when our cousin the owl was in the midst of her Ordeal. With what seems relatively little fuss, she defeated the Lone Power in a way that involved thousands of others of her kind—all of whom seem to have become adjunct gateways for this power to make its way from its source and into our world." He shook his head and shut his manual. "Leaving aside a profound respect for a brand new cousin who came right out of the gate as a *serious* badass... I'd be very, *very* unwilling to tamper with that result." He looked meaningfully at Nita.

She said nothing for a moment, and then glanced up. "There was something unusual about how she framed her own challenge," Nita said. "'*I'm here to put things right.*'"

"An awfully broad invocation," Kit said. "A whole lot of good could travel down that road... if we don't accidentally block it."

"If we're going to patch this timeline and rewrite this particular piece of history so that it doesn't cause endless trouble in all the local cultures," said Lissa, "we'll need to be very precise about the moments where the patch begins and ends. *But they can't interfere with the owl.* They can't interfere with what she does. She has to take the Tree, and keep it. And people here need to have *no idea* that happened."

"That's my thought," Carl said. "And it's a hell of an ask. *How do we do that?*"

They were all quiet for a moment, staring at the empty space and the production people and tech people flocking around it. "I want to run that through again," Nita said after a moment, opening her manual.

Lissa came to lean over her shoulder. "What?" she said, concerned. "Did we miss something?"

Nita looked uneasy. "I don't know," she said. "It's as if there's something... I don't know. Something missing..."

"Take a moment to think about it," Tom said. "Take a breath and let it come to you."

Nita turned over a page or two in her manual, and another page or two, stepping away from the others and toward 49th Street. Kit and Lissa glanced at each other as they leaned against the window. Lissa was watching Nita, but Kit's attention was mostly on the spot where the Tree had been.

"It was a nicer one this year than usual," he said. "Weird that all this wound up happening around it..."

"'Nicer than usual?'" Lissa said. "Have you come down to see it before?"

Kit shrugged. "A few times. Mostly I've just watched it on TV... you know how busy it's been. Once or twice I came down here with 'Mela, before things got so hectic a few years back." And then he laughed. "One time she said, 'You know who ought to see this? We should get him down here and he'd just go green with jealousy. Except he's green already, so how would anybody even tell?—'"

And very loudly Nita said *"Oh my God!"*

Everyone whirled to look at her, even some of the people who hadn't noticed her before. The nonwizards immediately forgot to pay any further attention, of course, but Kit and Lissa and Carl and Tom all stared. *"Neets?"* Kit said.

"What?" Lissa said.

"Filif!!" Nita said: and vanished.

8

JD 2459186.63056 (2 DECEMBER 2020, 22:08 EST)

S o it was that the intervention team wound up adding to their number an expert of their acquaintance who could easily have been mistaken for the Universe's long-purposed answer for this very problem. That the expert happened to look like a mobile Christmas tree carrying his own small, red, occasionally intensely-bright lights around with him was (in later discussions) taken by the team as a sign that the Powers that Be aren't above the occasional very broad joke. And if the hi-vis vest with which Nita equipped him on his arrival struck an interestingly dissonant note, that was more or less par for the course.

He—at least it was "he" at the moment, or close enough to that concept—had quite a long name which most of his wizardly cousins tended to shorten to Filif. He was a Demisiv—a communal-arborid member of the dominant species native to the planet of the same name, the seventh world out from the star called 16 Aurigae. As a wizard, one of his specialties was working with the exquisitely tailorable semblance-management systems called *mochteroofs*. It took no more than a few minutes for Filif to arrive on site after receiving the request for a consult, the 48th-50th Street subway station's worldgate being brought back online just long enough to fetch him in.

"Sweet Powers, the way time flies!" he said to the gathered wizards when he'd had a few moments to greet everybody, and had turned his attention to where the tree had been. "Hadn't realized it was *that* time of year again here! Usually Carmela mentions. Hadn't heard anything about it from her, though…"

"She's offplanet," Kit said, sounding resigned. "More cocoa business. Oh, and there was something about getting one of her cargo ships' engines refitted." He glanced at Nita. "Dairine was in on it too… Some computer thing. Don't ask me…" He waved a hand and shook his head in the bemused manner of younger brothers everywhere when their older sisters were being discussed.

"All right," Filif said. "Replay the event for me, would you? Let's see how complicated this is going to be."

It took only a few moments to lay a wizardly event superstrate over the site that could be viewed by no one but them, and the event was duly replayed. Filif stood there admiring the recording both for the sake of the beauty of the Tree and for the unusual nature of what was happening. But even as he made vague frond-whispering noises of admiration, every berry was trained fixedly on what was happening.

When it was finished he shook all his branches out and thought for a moment. "So tell me if I've got this right," Filif said. "You need an exact duplicate of the Tree that was here, and all the electrical installations and connections that were on it. You need me to copy all of these from the data in the recording, pretty much atom for atom— but substituting nonliving surrogate tissue for the Tree—with an eye to swapping it in at the same time our new cousin and her people arrive—"

"Nearly," Tom said. "More accurately, it needs to be swapped in ten seconds or so before the lighting. But it needs to arrive perfectly in sync with it, molecule for molecule, and it needs to overlay the original perfectly for just so long as it takes the owls to grab hold of the living tree and take it away."

"I did something similar that time I came around for your holiday party, as I recall," Filif said to Kit. "Left the *mochteroof* in place and stepped out of it." He wiggled his (unseen) roots, and the cloud of cloaking field that hid them as usual shifted too. "It's no great mastery."

"Well, after that it gets a little more complex," said Carl. "We'll throw a stealth wizardry over the owls as they exit with the real tree, and cover their transit upstate to wherever the owl decides she wants the tree to go. The *mochteroof* that you construct will stay in place here until the time the people responsible for managing the Plaza take it apart and take it away to be disposed of."

"But we don't want to interfere with the owl, or her wizardry, in any way," Tom said. "In particular we don't want to take the chance of destabilizing it, or *her,* until we've had a chance for the situation to settle down and for someone expert in the avian mindset to have a chat with her. Too much rides on this."

Filif swayed backwards and forwards a little, gazing up at the presently-paused image of the Tree with all his forward berries, while he made a small wind-in-the-branches hissing sound very like what a plumber or mechanic produces before telling you that something's going to be difficult, or expensive, or both. "All right," he said. "It's all entirely doable. When do you want it?"

Carl raised his eyebrows. "Half an hour ago?"

Filif thought a moment, then shrugged some fronds. "Done," he said. "Check the backtime timeline; I'll have left you the *mochteroof* off to one side there, cloaked and rotated out of physical phase. We'll keep the dimensional rotation when we strike the cloak, so the *mochteroof* won't have any coexistence issues with the base installation."

Carl sighed. "Thanks, cousin."

Filif produced a you're-welcome rustle, while angling a fair number of berries in Carl's direction. "I'd have thought you'd have preferred to just patch this one, though."

"If we had no other choice, yes, we'd have gone into more aggressive patching options. But New York's fragile right now." Carl rubbed his face. "There are too many things we could accidentally affect here that could wind up costing lives... and there's been way too much of *that* around here lately, despite our best efforts. So this is better."

"Choice is always good," Filif said, and everyone smiled a bit at the feeling of what Demisivs used for a smile as it sizzled along their nerves.

"So," Tom said. "We'll sketch a timeline down to about the hundredth-of-a-second level, then refine it, find the spot where you'll drop the *mochteroof* into place and activate it; then construct the wizardry that'll stealth-cloak the owls past the local radars and follow them back up north. Can anybody think of anything else that needs doing?"

Heads were shaken. Kit, regarding the "paused" image of the Tree, said, "For such a big problem... it doesn't seem like we're doing enough, somehow. Seems almost too easy!"

Carl shrugged. "Not sure there's much we *need* to do here except make sure the owl's not interfered with as she leaves, and as she gets settled. The rest we'll manage later."

Tom nodded in agreement. "Sometimes it's just a matter of that old saying. 'To be the miracle, get out of its way...'"

"So let's get on with that." Carl said. "The Tree proper will need some help, of course. As a conifer, even after the treatment it's received since it's been cut down, there'll still be a lot of life left in it. We'll get it re-implanted and re-rooted pretty quickly." He smiled an innocent smile. "I seem to remember we've got someone on site who used to be good with trees..."

"*Used* to be!" Nita said, indignant. "I *beg* your pardon!"

Tom chuckled. "We don't often get much begging out of the Planetary's office, but hey, we'll take what we can get." He glanced at Kit. "Where's our new cousin now?"

Kit was leafing through his manual: he paused. "Looks like she and the Tree decided not to settle where it originally came from," he said. "Too much road noise. It seems she found a spot she liked better —not far from where they released her, near Saugerties."

"So we need to get the Tree re-implanted and its roots regrown ASAP," Carl said, "assuming it's someplace where it won't attract attention."

"And assuming it consents," Lissa said.

"That's a given," Carl said. "But first things first. We backtime to the predetermined time fix a few seconds before the first owls arrive, and install the *mochteroof.* Then we render the real tree and the incoming owls invisible by the least invasive method possible, let them pull the real Tree offsite—leaving the perfect replica behind—and shadow the Tree and the owl to their new relocated."

"We'll make the rerooting process as non-invasive as possible," Tom said, "and make sure owl and Tree are safe and well as they can be... then leave them to their own devices." He glanced over at Lissa. "We've brought you a long way for not much work, cousin! Won't be much scrubbing to do here."

"Are you kidding? I'd have come even if there weren't other reasons." Lissa smiled at him. "This'll be one for the Book! Glad I didn't miss it."

"Then thanks for being on call. We'll make it up to you some other time." Tom looked around. "Any suggestions, people? Anything we've left out? I'm listening."

Heads were shaken all around.

"Then the ball's in your court, Nita," Carl said. "Go or no go? With an event this major, we can't move without Irina's office's sanction. If you want to take this back for an upline consult, or if you feel we need to spend more time discussing this, it's fine. But every extra minute we spend risks this whole business embedding itself more deeply into the event substrate."

Nita stood there very straight with her hands behind her, looking down and the paving, and holding her manual fairly tightly.

"This is as much your evaluation as mine, isn't it?" Tom said to Nita, with just a slight smile. "But no pressure."

"You," Nita said, giving Tom what was plainly meant to be a cool, annoyed look. For some moments no one said anything, and what

thoughts might have passed from mind to mind among the assembled wizards went otherwise unexpressed.

Finally Nita sighed. "Yeah," she said. "I concur. On behalf of the Planetary Wizard for Earth, and in her place, I sanction it."

And she smiled. "Let's go."

9

JD 2459186.67882 (2 DECEMBER 2020, 23:17 EST)

And so it went—smoothly and without flaw, as might have been expected when so experienced a team of wizards, who mostly knew each other well, were intent on getting an intervention right on the first try. Once everything's planned out, once the master strategy's in place, once the spell diagrams are laid down and triple-checked... good wizardry (once the spells' execution is complete) can be boring. The only thing guaranteed never to be boring are the people or creatures you work with, and the feeling of satisfaction you get from talking the universe into giving them what they need.

The five humans and the Demisiv stood together against the Lego Store wall, a little ways down from where the same five humans (slightly differently temporally positioned) were already standing watching the lighting ceremony the first time, and together they all watched it happen again. They saw the very briefest blink as Filif's *mochteroof* snapped into position and exactly coincided with every blink and every motion of the real Tree. They saw through the invisibility that shrouded the incoming owls, and heard their wings through the sound-baffling wizardry that kept the whistle of the birds' wings from being heard by nonwizards in realtime. They heard the cry *I've come to take my tree back! I've come to put things right!...* and at that all of them shivered a little; for some words, and some acts of intention, have their own power that make wizardry more potent, rather than the other way around. And finally they saw the owl and her Tree sail up into the night, shining, and vanish northward into the dark.

After that there was little to do but go home and get some rest—because wizardries of such complexity, regardless of having become boring, also require payment in energy from the wizards enacting them, and tend to leave one completely wrung out.

"But at least we had a chance to touch base without manuals for a change," said Tom to two of the younger three, while Carl did one last walk around the Plaza to make sure all the parts of the wizardry that needed to be collapsed or decommissioned had done so correctly.

"Yeah. And speaking of which," Kit said,"you really need to come and visit. I'm *serious!*"

"All right, all right, we will! If we can just figure out where the Autonomous Collective is even located these days. It was Prague, last I heard..."

"Nope, Neets decided she didn't mind the commute back to Irina's so much after all. We found a place in the south of France: we'll be there until the weather warms up. Then maybe back over here for a while."

"I thought it was going to be England," Lissa said.

"Still under discussion," Kit said.

"Scotland," Nita said, coming around the corner from the near end of the Channel Gardens.

"I told you I didn't want a vote this time!" Kit said. "Gimme a break. We going back now?"

"Nope, nope. We'll see you back home. Come on, Liss, I promised I was going to show you the Saks windows before we go..."

The two of them waved at Tom and Kit and headed off down the Channel Gardens towards Fifth, hand in hand. "She got her second wind," Kit said, watching them go with a smile. "She always does that somehow..."

"We'll come visit," Tom said. "Message us when you've had a chance to recover from all this."

Another brief spate of hugging ensued. *"Dai stihó,* Mars Boy," Tom said. "Tell them we said good night."

Kit grinned, rolled his eyes again. "You're hopeless," he said, "but I will. *Dai,* Tom." And he dropped a transit circle around himself and, with it, vanished.

Tom smiled and went to help his partner finish beating the bounds.

As far as the so-called Real World was concerned, the lighting of the Christmas Tree in Rockefeller Plaza went off without a hitch, and was shortly swallowed up in a rush of (theoretically) more newsworthy events. But shortly after the ceremony was over, an odd sequence of events centered on the Plaza area began to spread out from it in slow ripples, as if a stone had been thrown into a pool.

The local crime rate dropped (though when this statistical artifact surfaced in spring of 2021, reports of it were immediately rejected because its source was the police). Additionally, mortality of all kinds (not merely COVID-related) in hospitals around the area dropped off significantly for a thirty-six to forty-eight hour period. This statistic, too, was closely scrutinized in January of 2021, but health experts could detect no possible reason for it.

The authorities therefore discounted it as something that hadn't actually happened. The algorithm that had been used to process that period's data was therefore flagged as possibly faulty and scheduled for reassessment, and the conclusions resulting from it were never made public. Some health professionals who suspected the "reverse spike" was connected to some weird sort of holiday-associated confirmation bias began considering what kind of papers might be written. And it would have been strange to see—for anyone who knew all these scientists and statisticians—how these papers were set aside and never written, or how those that were written failed of publication in a number of interesting and non-traumatic ways.

In a far larger context, general discussions of the ways 2021 began to differ from 2020—in terms of occasionally unexpectedly-positive results in unlikely circumstances—would go on in popular-culture and social media venues for some time, routinely drowned out by the alarums and excursions of the insistent Now. But wizards, who have access to manual-and-similar instrumentalities that can reveal the true causes of things, will simply describe such occurrences in the Speech as *huheilth'amehn*—"Owl moments"—and get back to their never-ending business of fixing the broken world.

10

JD 2459209.04168 (25 DECEMBER 2020, 1300 UTC)

Meanwhile, in real time (or *"more*-real time", as some would put it) a most unusual tree can now occasionally be found in a forest reserve in upstate New York, not far from Woodstock. Wizards know where it is, and a few local humans who are good neighbors to beasts and birds, and know how to keep their own counsel about the strange things they see among the trees in the dark of night.

If one looks downtime at the Tree and its inhabitants, they will for many years hence find a perfectly shaped Norway spruce, thick-boughed and heavy-fronded, looking for all the world as if it had never previously been chainsawed off hundred-year-old roots and denuded of half its lower boughs. In that tree lives an owl who, after her yearly migration, comes back to it every year to nest.

Mostly the owl seems just like all other saw-whet owls. And mostly she *is* just as she seems. But there are moments when she wakes in the dusk and looks out of the hole where she and several generations of chicks have lived while they fledged out, and the owl remembers how it was, on that one night of anger and glory, when she took back what was rightfully hers.

On such evenings, casual travelers through those woods (some of them wizards taking time to look in on a cousin) have seen a peculiar thing: a tree made of light, a Tree with the remembered burning gleam of thousands of owls' eyes in it, shining with the preserved reality of fifty thousand less-unusual lights in every color that humans see.

By the time any non-wizardly observer comes within reach of this apparition, it has always faded into impossibility, and the woods around it are dark again. But wizards understand why things in those woods are always greener after such a moment... and why the Owl has been there so surprisingly long, and will continue to be so.

For power inevitably changes what it channels through. What suffers itself to conduct the light, soon enough becomes light itself. And in that quiet rural region of upstate New York, where all the owls (it's said) are wise, the battlecry of an ancient strength, new-fledged and new-inhabited, can yet be heard by those with ears to hear its greeting and defiance, deep-founded in the dawn of time:

I've come to put things right!

BY THE SAME AUTHOR

In the Young Wizards universe:
The main-sequence Young Wizards series:
So You Want to Be a Wizard • *Deep Wizardry*
High Wizardry • *A Wizard Abroad*
The Wizard's Dilemma • *A Wizard Alone*
Wizard's Holiday • *Wizards at War*
A Wizard of Mars • *Games Wizards Play*

the Feline Wizards sequence:
The Book of Night with Moon
To Visit The Queen
(UK title: *On Her Majesty's Wizardly Service*)
The Big Meow

Interstitial works in the YW universe:
Interim Errantry • *Interim Errantry 2: On Ordeal*

For adult readers:
the Middle Kingdoms novels
The Door into Fire • *The Door Into Shadow* • *The Door Into Sunset*

Interstitial works:
Tales of the Five #1: The Levin-Gad
Tales of the Five #2: The Landlady

Other standalone adult fantasy:
Raetian Tales: A Wind from the South
Stealing The Elf-King's Roses

Collected short fiction:
Uptown Local and Other Interventions
Midnight Snack and Other Fairy Tales

In the Star Trek (TM) universe:
The Wounded Sky • *My Enemy, My Ally*
Spock's World • *Doctor's Orders*
Dark Mirror • *Intellivore*
The "Rihannsu Quartet"
The Romulan Way • *Swordhunt*
Honor Blade
(omnibus edition: *Star Trek: The Bloodwing Voyages*)
The Empty Chair

For ebook editions of numerous books
not listed above,
please visit
https://Ebooks.Direct
or the Books page at the author's site:
DianeDuane.com

DIANE DUANE ON SOCIAL MEDIA

Twitter: @dduane
Tumblr: https://dduane.tumblr.com
Facebook: https://www.facebook.com/DianeDuaneWriter/

VERSION INFO

V1.01 (4 July 2017): Preorder edition for CrossingsCon attendees
v2.08 (27 July 2017):
Minor textual and formatting corrections
v3.01 (6 November 2019): Conversion to Vellum format
v4.01 (9 December 2021): addition of *Owl Be Home For Christmas*
v4.02 (30 December 2021): correction of print edition page numbering
issue

Made in the USA
Monee, IL
01 February 2022

90423600R00256